Bulletproof

Monica T. Rodriguez

DogStar Publishing
NEW YORK

Editor: Alida Winternheimer, Word Essential
Cover design: Tim Barber, Dissect Designs
Interior layout and design: BookDesignTemplates.com

DogStar Publishing
monicatrodriguez.com
monica@monicatrodriguez.com

First Edition: March 2020

Printed in the United States of America

*In memory of
Yadisa Disla, 1979-2012.
Your light still shines.*

1.

*The life of prey is one of vigilance, seeking safety in dark
corners, with sporadic panicked and perilous moves.
And life is short.*

Justine Bernard emerged from Vee's Diner into
the relative darkness of the Lower East Side of
Manhattan, stuffing her waitress apron into her
backpack. She tugged her black sweatshirt hood over
her head so watchful streetlamps and passing headlights would not turn her red hair into a beacon.

Wearing the darkness like a suit of armor, she darted
across Grand Street, dodging oncoming cars. Chilled
air stung her nose as she breathed the scents of exhaust
and more snow to come. Turning onto East Broadway,
the lights of One World Trade Center loomed in the
distance. The street was as dim as she could hope for,
dotted with bare trees webbed with white Christmas

lights and tenements bristling with decorated fire escapes.

At any rate, enough people scurried by for a sense of cover. As the wind picked up, she buttoned her secondhand peacoat and paced her steps with a family leaving a low-rise building with bagfuls of bright and shiny gifts. One child held a toy that squealed a Christmas jingle. Justine sped up. She'd rather abandon the anonymity of the group than be tormented by that forced cheer.

At Clinton Street, she crossed with a flock of chatty teenagers, turning her face away as they snapped pictures with their phones. These cameras in everyone's hands were a menace. As the teens strolled across the avenue, oblivious to traffic and to her, Justine felt decades older than them instead of only a handful of years.

Rather than turn left toward what she called home, she turned right toward Quinn's apartment near Houston Street. She hadn't taken this route in a while, so it should be safe. She checked behind her. No one closer than they should be, no one paying more attention than they should, no one she'd seen before. For now.

Still, she cut through the courtyard of a tall residential building into Seward Park, though the snowy path meant leaving footprints. She breathed in the hush of the park, its shrubs and benches dusted with snow. Streetlamps struggled to filter light through tree branches. Perhaps intimidating to others, to her the night was a comfort.

She tucked her hair into her hood as she cut toward Essex Street. A woman walked a dog along the path on her left that led to East Broadway. Two bundled figures huddled near a concrete bench. All any of them would see was her pale face. As long as nothing out of the ordinary happened, they wouldn't even remember that.

Quick footsteps pounded the walkway at the East Broadway entrance, followed by more steps and a shout. "Stop! You're under arrest!"

The woman and her dog and the other two in the park ran for the exits. Justine took cover beside a tree, snow crunching under her feet. To her rear, bushes and fencing blocked an easy exit. Damn it. A police chase counted as out of the ordinary.

She flattened herself against the tree's rough bark as a short, skinny man sprinted down the path. A taller man with brown tousled hair followed. She caught her breath. Detective Quinn Duncan was still working.

The first guy ran past Justine, reaching under his shirt. The semi-night revealed something darker in his hand. Only a short distance from her, he turned and aimed a gun at Quinn.

Her breath strangled in her throat. Time didn't slow. Their movements happened too fast for her to do anything but watch.

A spark of light. A firecracker snap. Justine flinched, her body frozen in place.

A grunt drew her gaze left. Quinn staggered but remained standing, clutching his arm and cursing.

Her throat closed. An image of her brother's body, bleeding in the grass by the river, flashed in her mind. She couldn't stand there while another person died. She couldn't let Quinn die, not when she could do something. Even though it could mean the end of her time in this city.

The shooter ducked behind a tree and adjusted his stance for another shot. Quinn took a tentative step, reaching for his weapon.

Now or never.

She tugged her hood lower over her face. Her heart racing, she jumped onto the pavement and faced the shooter. She planted her feet, resisting the urge to run.

The young man's eyes widened, and his arm jerked as the gun fired.

The explosion echoed in her ears, and her attention narrowed. There was no dog barking in the distance. No Quinn to protect. No man with a pistol.

There was only the bullet and her hands.

She pushed. The ability that radiated from her hands, or perhaps from her mind, created a force to meet the one that propelled the bullet toward her.

The bullet slowed to a stop an inch from her palms, dropped to the pavement with a faint clink, bounced once, twice, then rolled to a stop.

Justine's focus widened again, her breath coming in bursts. The shooter stood before her, gun drawn. His mouth hung open, a foot poised on its toes, ready for flight. But he was pinned by the sight of the bullet on the ground.

She clenched her teeth and muttered, "Time to go." Quinn might have questions for this guy, but he'd seen too much tonight.

The man didn't move. She closed in on him. "Now."

That broke the spell. He turned and ran without a word. By the time he got wherever he was going, he wouldn't believe he'd seen anything extraordinary.

With shaking fingers, she pocketed the bullet, still warm. Another to add to her collection.

Time for her to leave too. Maybe she should go home. Or she could rush to Quinn's place and wait on the steps, full of surprise when he arrived with an injury. No, she'd spent too much energy. Home it was.

Leaves crunched behind her. Her stomach twisted. Quinn was closer than she'd thought. She hunched into her jacket and hood, hoping to draw the shadows around her.

"What just happened?" Quinn said in a choked voice.

She kept walking. *You're alive. Enjoy it and leave it at that. Please.*

"I mean, what I saw, what I think I saw, that's not possible." He mumbled something. Clothing rustled. How badly was he wounded?

The silence stretched. She was a terrible, awful person to walk away like this. He might need help. But helping him was not a choice she could make right now. The consequences were too great for her.

"Do I know you?"

She ducked her head farther into her coat, her chest too tight to breathe. Once out of the park, among people, Quinn likely wouldn't cause a scene.

"Justine?"

Her heart was definitely going to do the *Alien* routine and burst out of her chest. She continued in silence. No looking back. She listened for footsteps, but she would never hear them over the pounding of her blood in her ears.

She let out a deep, shaky breath as she reached Essex. But it didn't matter. When Quinn had said her name, her steps had faltered. Quinn was a detective. That would tell him all he needed to know.

2.

Justine wiped down a table as an older couple left the diner. Nita, the waitress who shared the dinner shift with her, sat a small group of teens at the only window table. Justine moved to the next table in the row that ran to the back of the narrow dining area, parallel to the long black counter. She cleaned the tabletops and condiment jars again. She'd already filled all the bottles and shakers and napkin holders. She'd do them all over if—

"Excuse me—is our food ready yet?" A young woman with dark hair, sitting with a younger girl with glasses and hair dyed green, called out from the next table.

Justine's mind was blank. What the hell had they ordered?

"Wake up, chica!" Nita's face broke into a smile. "I'm so sorry, girls. There was a mix-up with the order," she said with a wink in Justine's direction. "They're cooking it up right now. It'll be out in a couple of minutes."

She herded Justine to the register behind the counter. "Thought they were talking to you. Turns out they were talking to the saltshaker." Nita tucked her order pad into her black apron and stuck her pen into her tight bun of straight dark hair. "Every ketchup bottle is full, and the chrome's so clean I need sunglasses for the glare. Give it a rest, okay?"

Without a word, Justine pulled tickets out of her pockets, not really caring if she found the order. She could never manage the sweet talk with customers. Nita turned on the charm like a switch. Justine could only bring out their inner cranky.

At the counter, one of the customers in navy blue uniforms raised her mug. Justine refilled the cup, her glance skittering across the stool where Quinn always sat. The clock on the wall said it was nearly ten. His usual coffee time had come and gone. Her fingers dug into the receipts she'd gathered.

If she hadn't been in the park last night, Quinn might have gotten more than a dinged arm. She hadn't always been fast enough, but this time she'd done it right, though it might cost her everything. She stomped out that thought. *Take the orders, serve the food, and clear the tables. Rinse and repeat.*

Nita laid a small hand on Justine's arm, her brown eyes full of concern. "Hey, something going on?"

Justine forced a smile. Only a few years older than her, Nita worried like a grandmother, though Justine had done nothing to earn her concern. "I'm only trying to keep busy." So close to the grill, the smells of grease and cooking meat overwhelmed the aroma of burnt coffee. Her stomach, already in knots, tightened further. She emptied the coffee carafe into the sink and started a fresh pot.

Nita unrolled a strand of silvery tinsel garland and started taping it to the customer side of the counter. "Dinner rush is over. I can take that table you have left, if you want to close out and take off."

Take off. She could do that. Leave town without a trace. Her mother had done it countless times, at the first hint someone had seen too much of what her unusual daughter could do, until Justine had figured out being special meant keeping secrets and keeping hidden. Staying where friends or strangers knew too much meant risking being taken away from her family to become a lab rat, used for whatever purpose scientists had in mind.

Now moving on was up to her. She had to decide whether to leave the place with the last memories of her brother, Devon. To abandon the few connections she'd made, people she'd allowed herself to call friends. To give up Quinn. Could she revert to who she'd been before she met him?

She pulled folded and crumpled bills from her apron pockets and brought her cash and receipts to the manager sitting in the back with a cup of tea and papers strewn around her. The older woman handed her a fat envelope in return. The cash payment was worth facing so many people each night. They were unlikely to remember her, but more important, neither would a computer.

"Next week's schedule will be up in the morning," the woman said.

Right. She might need to talk to Nita about that.

Justine clutched the envelope as she retrieved her belongings from the closet. She put on her coat and stuffed into her backpack the bag of food the cooks would otherwise have thrown out. As she gauged how far she might get with this paycheck, the front door opened to let in a blast of chilled air. And Quinn. She turned away as her own chill passed through her.

"Justine," Nita whispered. "Boy toy's here."

She kept her back to the door as she slipped her backpack over a shoulder. While her anxiety over his injuries eased, she dreaded facing the doubt she was sure to see in his eyes. He would ask for an explanation for last night, and she would refuse. She'd risk losing his trust, because she'd lose more of him if she answered.

Quinn stood at the door a moment, scanning the room before settling on his usual stool and unbuttoning his wool coat with one hand. The left sleeve of his coat hung empty at his side. His gaze followed Justine's approach, full of curiosity. "How are you?" He leaned forward with a smile dancing around his lips, his elbow on the counter.

Her legs refused to move to greet him. Heart aching, she struggled for a breath to force a word from her mouth. "Fine." As his smile faltered, she set aside her hesitation and leaned in to brush his lips with hers. They were cold. As she withdrew, his brown eyes sparkled as he tried to hold back a grin.

He always assumed her reluctance to kiss him in view of others was due to shyness. The truth was, under the bright lights of the diner, such display felt like revealing too much information. But if someone had gotten close enough to see a kiss, she had bigger problems.

"Any fresh coffee left?"

Her hand twitched. *Get a grip.* She cleared her throat. "Just made some. I know how you get without it." She drew a mug from the rack below the counter and filled it.

Quinn poured cream from a miniature carafe with his right hand, his brown hair falling into his eyes but not covering the tension in them. He looked like he did when he was in the middle of a case. When he had a mystery to solve. "Can we get a table?"

A breath escaped her. One moment at a time. "Let me clock out."

As she punched out, she considered the rear exit. So much to leave behind, more than she'd ever had. But walking away from her life here wouldn't put an end to Quinn's questions.

She was getting ahead of herself. She poured a cup of decaf and shuffled to the table he'd taken. She tried for a smile as she took a seat, but her face felt as if it would break. She averted her eyes from his arm and ignored the guilt that surfaced.

But if there was a chance she could stay, she had to know where he stood. "Something wrong with your arm?" Her words sounded breathless, as if she'd been running. She fought the urge to run, far, far away.

Quinn's eyes held hers. "My arm's all right. Got into a . . . situation last night."

Her stomach churned as she read the questions that all but flew from his lips. She had to give him a point for vagueness. She broke from his gaze and fidgeted with her cup, unable to drink though her mouth was a desert.

"Justine?"

"Huh? Sorry. I, um, I'm fine." She grabbed a napkin and twisted it tight.

His silent scrutiny clung to her like cobwebs. "Listen, if I don't make it here by the time you're off, don't walk home alone, okay? The side streets around here are dark but not empty."

She fiddled with a Band-Aid coming loose on her index finger, her chest relaxing a fraction. She could handle talking about safety. "I can take care of myself."

"I'm sure—you cut yourself?" He cradled her hand in his.

She flexed her finger. "A little bloodshed comes with the job, apparently." He raised his eyebrows, and she cringed. No more ad libbing.

"Look," Quinn said, "we found another body recently. Don't—"

"Where?"

He hesitated. "By the river. But that's not where the victim was killed."

Her heart fluttered. *You can't save everyone.*

"I'd feel better if you would take a cab."

He was only trying to protect her. It wasn't his fault he didn't know how unnecessary that was. She reached toward him, then paused when she saw his coat sleeve hanging empty. "You don't have to worry about me."

He let out a puff of breath and clutched his hair. "Well, I'm going to worry anyway. Any night someone could come up behind you with a gun." He shifted his gaze and sipped his coffee. Justine's heart thumped through the silence. "I don't want you to be the next body I find. Sorry if that's annoying."

Her shoulders sagged under the weight of his concern. "I really will be okay, Quinn. I do fine on my own. Please, I don't want . . . you shouldn't—"

He searched her face. "Is that it? You'd rather be on your own?"

She swallowed. What she wanted was not always what she needed. She laid a hand on his arm, then took his hand, still chilled, in both of hers. He grasped her fingers in a strong grip.

Devon would have been apoplectic over how close she'd grown to Quinn. Their connection had blossomed from a shared grief over lost mothers to reach past the walls she'd built around herself. But his worry had set her on alert. Most of those who had ever worried for her were gone. "I'm used to taking care of myself, that's all."

"And if that hasn't changed after six months, I guess it's not ever going to." He withdrew his hand to grip his mug as his face eased into a blank expression.

Her hands were cold without his. She grabbed the twisted napkin and started to protest, then stopped. Not correcting him might be kinder. No, not kinder. Easier. For her. His detective instincts would drive him to find answers unless she gave him a reason to file away his curiosity into the *Unsolved* bin.

"Look, at least until we find this guy, let me give you cab money, okay? Not that we have a suspect yet. Might have had one." He clamped his lips together as if to stop himself from talking, but it didn't work. "He kind of slipped away last night."

Justine tore the napkin to shreds. He had not set aside the events of last night. Ignoring that would not help her. "You ready to go?"

His eyes met hers. "You coming to my place?"

She managed to smile this time. "Sure." She'd endure his interrogation, though it would disassemble her life, if it would answer her only questions: What had he seen? And what was he going to do about it?

~ ~ ~

Quinn pulled out his keys as he reached the door to his Lower East Side apartment. Nails clicked on wood as he unlocked the three deadbolts. "It's me, Sully," he said as he opened the door and let Justine slip inside ahead of him. She scratched the German shepherd's ear while the dog licked her hand, his tail wagging furiously.

"I'm here, too, Sully." The dog greeted him as he dropped his keys into a bowl on the table by the door.

Justine crossed over to the tiny alcove that passed for a kitchen and put her food from the diner in the fridge. The dog followed the aroma, sniffing the bags, then her clothes as she returned to the small living room. The one-bedroom apartment was enough space for him, even with Justine here. He couldn't imagine what little box she lived in that she considered this place spacious.

Sully only abandoned Justine when Quinn picked up his leash. When Quinn returned from walking the dog, she was curled up on the couch, her coat draped over the arm and her knapsack on the floor. She had been quieter than usual on the walk home. He hadn't pushed her. Her silence had answered most of his questions.

He sat down with his good arm on her side and laid a blanket from the back of the couch over her. "Tired?"

Without opening her eyes, Justine shifted to lean on his shoulder, slipping her arms around him. "Yeah."

"You hungry?"

She shook her head. "Just tired."

He wrapped his arm and the blanket around her and rested his chin on her head. Her hair smelled like the diner, mostly meat with a hint of coffee. He didn't mind.

Once in a while, as they watched another movie he refused to believe she'd never seen, she would relax, her body easing back against him. Sometimes she'd fall asleep like that. Eventually he'd realized she held herself in a constant state of apprehension, as if waiting for something or someone to pop out from behind a corner. She held on to that apprehension now, alert despite her fatigue, his presence not enough to ease that anxiety. He would do almost anything to show her there was no bogeyman, that she could live without fear.

But maybe fear wasn't her problem. Justine's past and most of her present were a vague, fuzzy unknown—he wasn't even sure where she lived. He'd been hoping that wouldn't matter much longer and that she'd agree to stay with him. "Let's get you to bed then."

She nodded and let him pull her to her feet. In the bedroom, she found the T-shirt and pants he'd gotten her for when she slept there and put them on in silence.

Traveling miles to reach her across the room, he let go of his questions for the night, brushing the corner of her mouth with a kiss. "Into bed, sleepyhead."

He went into the bathroom, and when he came out, she had burrowed under the covers. He slid into bed next to her awkwardly, his injury aching with every movement now that he'd taken off the sling. He couldn't tell if Justine was still awake, but she molded her body to his, as if seeking refuge. He slipped his good arm around her, wishing he could keep her there and keep her safe. She insisted she could take care of herself. What if that wasn't bravado?

Quinn woke to a dark room. He stretched out to find the bed empty, the sheets cold. Almost seven, dawn hadn't yet cleared the rooftops, but it would soon.

He washed up and found Justine on the couch, eating cereal, with Sully on the couch next to her. Quinn followed the aroma of coffee to the kitchen and returned to the living room with two cups in his right hand, not trusting his left arm. "Thanks for making this." He squeezed a knee between her and Sully. The dog settled at her feet as Quinn sat and set her cup on the coffee table. "How'd you sleep?"

"Fine."

The single word expanded the gulf between them. He sipped his coffee, grabbed a remote from the coffee table, and turned on the lights of the small Christmas tree in a corner of the living room. "I know I nagged last night about how you get home."

Justine shrugged as she put the empty cereal bowl on the table and grabbed the mug. "I get that it makes you feel better to worry. Even if you don't have to."

"Doesn't it feel better to know someone's worrying about you?"

She looked at him as if he had asked about moving to the moon.

"Haven't you—" Whether or not she'd ever had anyone worry about her might explain a lot, but asking felt like barging into a room uninvited. All the missing pieces of her life had become stark black holes: what she wanted, what she needed, what she feared. And he never would know, if she didn't reveal her secrets. And she definitely had secrets.

He released his frustration with a breath. One day he would solve the mystery of her. If she gave him the chance. Now, he'd have to settle for solving the mystery of the other night. "Justine, I—"

She flinched, as if sensing a turn in his thoughts. Her face was remote in the glow of the living room lamp and the multicolored Christmas lights, her eyes too wide. She reminded him of a rabbit in an open field, ready to run for cover at the first whiff of a predator.

He looked into his mug, dread coming over him. "I'm sorry," he whispered. He ran a hand over his face. "I thought I could do this, just talk about whatever, but I can't."

She didn't even blink. She sat, rigid and silent, her hands tense around her cup.

"I just need to ... to clear the air, get my head on straight about"—he lowered his voice, unable to say the words any louder—"about what really happened the other night."

Her eyes shifted to something he couldn't see.

There was his first answer. His gut twisted, knowing this was tearing her up. Maybe tearing them up. He took a breath, then suddenly laughed. That drew her attention back to him. "I have no idea what to say." He reached out and pulled one hand from its death grip on her coffee mug. "In my work, witnesses can help or they can hinder. As my own witness, I am not helping me." He released her hand, as she seemed to pull into herself with his words. No, he would not let go so easily. He took her hand again and held it firmly. She stared at their hands as if they belonged to someone else.

"I don't know what I saw. Don't know what happened." He took another breath to try to loosen the tightness in his chest. "I'm pretty sure you saved my ass. I need to at least thank you for taking such a risk. I'm hoping that means you want me around a little longer. Unless you do that kind of thing all the time," he muttered. He cleared his throat, fidgeted with his cup, tried to laugh and failed. "I know asking for explanations is no way to show gratitude, but all I have is what my imagination is kicking around."

An ambulance siren rang out from a nearby street. A car alarm wailed.

"Justine, could y—"

"What's your imagination told you?"

Okay, so they were going the direct route. He released his grip on her to comb his hand through his hair. "My imagination. Right." He started to shrug, then grimaced as his arm reminded him not to do that. As he described his chase after the informant-turned-suspect, he rubbed his bicep. He was going to have to put that damn sling on again. "The park is dark, so smart move on his part, not a brilliant move on my part to follow. I catch up to him, he turns around, and I'm done. That's it—know what I mean?" He raised his hand in imitation of the gunman.

She sank farther into the cushions, galaxies away from him. Had he already lost her? He couldn't stop now. Whatever came of this, he needed to at least acknowledge what had happened.

As he related the events of the night, his spike of fear at the first gunshot, then the pain in his arm, came surging back. "The individual in front of me is shorter, so I can see over him—or her." With each word, he felt her slipping away. "I see—I *think* I see the person's hands stretched out as this guy takes another shot. It's too dark to be sure, but it's like they think they can stop the bullet in midair." He laughed. "Like when Neo stops the bullets. You know, the movie we watched last month?"

She stared ahead, her face impassive, her arms wrapped around herself.

His heart raced. "Crazy, I know. I mean, that's the movies, but this is real life. Things like that don't happen." He paused, giving her time, but he couldn't stay silent long. "I'm wrong, aren't I? There is an explanation. There has to be."

He got nothing for a full minute. His four years as a detective had taught him to look people in the eyes. Eyes always gave the game away. Trying to read her expression was like deciphering a crime scene with no evidence. That kind of obscurity took practice. A cold knot coalesced in his stomach.

Finally, she stirred but failed to meet his eyes. "Sounds like a great story to tell your partner. But you don't really think that's what happened, do you?"

His insides twisted as he was both relieved and disturbed by her brush-off. What answer had he wanted?

"Like you said, this isn't the movies. Besides, it was dark. Someone's shooting at you. How could you really see what was going on? That doesn't mean you're crazy. But you can piece together what's important for your report. Maybe the shot went wide. Maybe there was no second shot."

"There was ... you don't ... I saw ..." He paused, perplexed by his confusion. Could his memory of the night have been so scrambled? His question wasn't over the second shot though. And she hadn't considered the details of the third person credible enough to mention. "You do think I'm crazy."

"No, I don't." She reached out and entwined her fingers with his. "I think you're really lucky. And I'm glad, whatever happened." She sucked in a breath, as if the words took extra effort. "You need to get to work. I better get going." She grabbed her pack and her coat and walked to the door.

"Wait, Justine. Wait." He caught up to her at the door and laid a hand on her arm. Only then did she pause. "So you're right. I was lucky. Is it too much to ask that you stay?"

"I have to—"

"Don't leave, Justine." He swallowed, all his words stuck behind a boulder in his throat. The words he had managed seemed to grow and loom over them.

She opened the door.

"Justine, please, stay. I love you." She froze. He froze. He was sure even his watch didn't move. He hadn't meant to say that. Or maybe he had.

She turned to him in slow motion, as if fighting against a current, and the storm of emotions he found in her eyes took his breath away. "Don't." She walked out without looking back.

3.

In the pale-gray quiet of early morning, Justine let out a breath that fogged the crisp air as she neared a building on Henry Street adjacent to an empty lot. Plywood panels barred the doorways and blocked the view through windows. Graffiti had been the only recent effort at improvement of the crumbling facade. It was the perfect place.

She sniffled, the cold biting her nose. She'd crumbled as soon as she'd left Quinn's apartment. The naked expression of betrayal on his face had cut into her. Was the loss of his trust worth what was left?

She wiped her face and breathed in brisk air. In a moment when the sidewalk was clear of people scurrying from one source of warmth to another, she slipped through the empty lot's gate. Snow had begun to fall and made stark outlines of her footsteps as she trotted to the rear of the building.

Quinn's need for an explanation had hounded her steps through the near-empty streets. But his final words haunted her. Did his love make it more urgent that she leave or less so? She could accept for herself the heartbreak of relinquishing the comfort and safety of Quinn's affection. But she was adding lies and betrayal to his grief.

Shielded by a rare cluster of trees, Justine crept down the icy cement steps to the rear entrance. Loosening the knot on the improvised lock, she stepped into the building's basement. Though there was no heat, the air was not frigid. Water dripped from a hole in the ceiling, along a pipe and into a bucket rimmed in ice. Finally her eyes took in enough light to see the riot of colorful graffiti that masked the chipped and moldy concrete walls.

She navigated through the maze of territories, defined by cast-off furniture or items taken from construction sites, and past a low wall. She ducked through red-and-yellow curtains, disturbing the chimes that acted as her alarm system, and entered the corner space she'd claimed a year ago. After draping the walls in bright batiks and adding the bells, she'd given the small hideaway the feel of a snug nest.

Dropping her backpack, she groped to her right, where a padlocked steel locker kept out animals and humans. She unlocked it and pulled out a battery-operated lamp, switched it on, and set it on a pile of sci-fi paperbacks next to her mattress.

She missed the three locks on Quinn's door. And the four walls. And the heat. And Quinn. Here among the squatters, wrapped in her layers of blankets and a sleeping bag, her anonymity was guaranteed. But she slept easier in Quinn's bed than her own.

The couple in the adjacent space turned on their propane heater, so she unbuttoned her coat. Kicking aside a few used water bottles and crumbled balls of receipts, she stowed most of her food in the locker and rummaged through the container until she found a small cardboard box. Inside, cylindrical bits of lead rolled around. She dropped in the bullet from two nights ago.

Setting that aside, she took out a dog-eared photo of a whole and happy family. She smoothed it out and propped it up against the lamp. She didn't remember being held in her mother's arms for the photo or grabbing her brother's hair. She had plenty of memories of her mother and brother though. She kept the picture for the image of her father, smiling, an arm around her mom. It was a clearer picture of her father than her few and faded memories could provide.

The curtains parted as her rustling drew an animal to her. She crouched beside her mattress and held out her hand. The stray tabby that had adopted her trilled and rubbed up against her knee.

"Hey, Cheetah." She scratched behind the cat's ear, then scooted onto the makeshift bed. "Catch anything good last night?"

The cat climbed onto the bed and sniffed at her clothes and hair, cataloging every scent. "That's Sully you smell. He'd come in handy around here. Don't be jealous. You're a superb mouser." She drew him close as she stretched out on the blankets, his warmth and purring spreading through her chest. He began nibbling on her ear, then tried to climb over her arm into the bag beside her. "You're hungry. Got it."

She fed the tabby and herself from a chicken sandwich while a baby cried then giggled in the nearby space. As she removed a bottle of water from her backpack, she opened it wider. "Not much of a go-bag. Food for maybe a day and a half. Then what?" She wasn't sure she was ready to answer that. The cat climbed halfway into the bag to investigate. The feeling of being followed yesterday had not been paranoia. She had to be ready.

But she was not ready for this. She left behind the family and their giggling toddler next door to wander through the drafty basement. Some people still slept on whatever they used for a bed, covered in layers of sweaters and blankets, bundles of plastic bags beside them. Cheetah poked his nose into piles of discarded food containers while Justine hunted through clusters of debris.

It came down to Quinn and whether he'd bought her lies. And if he confronted her again, she didn't think she could keep her deception going.

She picked over beer bottles, a dirty sneaker, and plastic of all kinds, and pulled a few items from the pile. "Come on, Cheetah. Let's play." The cat snatched up half a hamburger bun as Justine carried her finds back to her nest. She sat on the bed and laid a curved section of rusty metal, perhaps some sort of fender, on the floor, then laid a strip of wood molding, once painted brown, into the fender.

Cheetah left his bread to sniff the scraps from end to end. She held out her palm as usual. "I don't know what I'm doing, so no judging, okay?"

Months ago she had been practicing pushing some heavy machinery. The hunk of metal never budged, but a nearby twig and some dried leaves had begun to smolder. She hadn't been able to re-create that ignition until recently, when she'd visualized the flames while trying to figure out how she'd done it.

As a child, Devon had helped her figure out how her ability worked. She'd had to work out how to control an imaginary muscle she shouldn't have had, without knowing what part of her body controlled it. Picturing a toy or a pebble moving away from her had seemed to help almost as much as extending her hand. So she imagined the molding turning black, smoke wafting up, then flames licking at one end.

Nothing happened.

She sharpened her mental picture of the burning wood. She put out both hands, as if sending heat into the slat. All that happened was her hands felt warmer. She put them down and tried again. "That twig didn't burst into flame by itself. So what did I do then that I'm not doing now?"

What she wasn't doing now was living with the caution and wariness that had long served her, that she'd learned after a childhood of carelessness that had prompted many moves to new little towns. When she and Devon had moved here from Albany, New York City had been a revelation of sound and light and smell. This city became the place where she could get lost among people instead of hiding from them.

After she'd somewhat recovered from the shock of her brother's death and returned to ground level from the tunnels, she soon forgot the nomadic ways of her childhood. But it turned out, her mom had had the right idea. A weariness settled into her limbs. Should she be this tired at twenty-four?

The cat crouched next to the fender cradling the wood. He sniffed, reached out with a paw, then recoiled and stood. He swatted at the piece of metal but again pulled his paw away.

"Leave it." She reached out to straighten the fender. She yanked back her own hand. The metal had burned her finger. "Should have thought of that. It's easier to heat metal than to burn wood." She tossed aside the molding—fire wasn't the best idea in here anyway—and concentrated her effort on the fender. It warmed until it glowed a faint red.

Then flame burst from the center of the rounded metal. She flinched and leaned back. When the fire remained in the center of the fender, she relaxed a bit. Debris stuck to the inside of the fender had ignited. She blew on it—and scattered the flaming bits across the floor. One landed on the discarded wood. Another landed on a wad of receipts that had fallen from her pocket. "Shit. Cheetah—" She pushed the cat back, scrambled up, and stomped on the embers.

"That's it for playtime." She scattered the ashes with her foot to be sure they'd gone out. "Today's lesson: fire spreads quickly. Okay, I'm tired. I guess if I'm ever stranded in the woods, I can try to start a fire. Or at least warm up my hands. Super useful."

She lay down again, and Cheetah scrambled onto her, laying a soft, cold paw on her face. She rubbed under his chin, and Cheetah nudged her fingers with his nose. She offered him another bit of chicken. He swallowed it in one bite and licked her fingers. "Enjoy the free food. You may have to learn to fend for yourself again. I'll see if I can do something about that."

Quinn would know her denial had been a lie, and he might not forgive her. That would break her heart. But what he now knew and what he did with that information could destroy her life.

She'd stayed in one place long enough to grow attached, long enough to be recognized in the dark. If she disappeared now, the few friends she'd made would never know what happened to her. A part of her crushed into something small and cold.

She got up, and the cat curled up in the warmth she left behind. The envelope of cash she'd gotten earlier was a weight in her coat pocket. She took out the envelope among a flurry of receipts. Gathering the receipts, she tucked them into her pocket to throw away later, then opened the metal locker. She paused and put the cash back in her pocket. She felt better keeping it with her. Rooting around the bags of warm-weather clothing beside the locker, she checked the pockets until her fingers hit a familiar square of card stock.

She used to carry the business card with her everywhere. Now it had been lost in a pants pocket. The card was soft from age and handling, the edges roughened, a corner bent. A Philadelphia phone number, with the name *Artie*, was written in her mother's handwriting on one side, given to her to use in case of an emergency, if her mom wasn't there to help her. This time she'd be going on the move on her own.

~ ~ ~

"You gave up too fast." Dr. Lawrence Hollister, founder and CEO of NextLevel Industries, shifted the tablet he had set up on the beat-up metal table to better record the work-out session. He confirmed a second device was syncing with the transmitter, recording data from leads attached to his subject.

Eddie Doyle shook his head, panting beside a treadmill set up before tall windows overlooking Lower Manhattan. "No, I didn't, Doc. Seriously. I'm doing better on the strength stuff. Look how much weight I added again today." He stretched his left arm against a bar of the treadmill. His right arm was thin and ended above the elbow. "But I've gotten a little faster only because I'm working out. Nothing magic about it."

"This isn't magic, Eddie." Hollister pursed his lips as he paced along the row of weight machines in the small makeshift gym. The top-of-the-line equipment gleamed against the scuffed walls and cracked linoleum floors of the former classroom. "This is science. Science is not about knowing the answers but finding them. We learn from the results, whether they are positive or negative." His father's words were little comfort when Hollister's trials failed. He tugged on a shirtsleeve.

Eddie's cheeks were bright pink, but his breathing was steady.

"Get on again. I want you to try a sprint. Give it everything you've got."

Eddie ran a towel over his face and sandy crew cut. "As long as our deal is on, I'm your guinea pig." He climbed back on the treadmill, eyes on the view of high-rise projects and the Brooklyn Bridge beyond.

Hollister increased the speed. "I keep my promises, Eddie. I will deliver you a new prosthetic limb with the most advanced functionality NextLevel Industries has achieved. And we are far ahead of the competition." He turned the speed up to ten miles an hour.

Eddie's eyes widened. He pumped his legs harder, his breath coming in short gasps. Hollister felt a small burst of hope.

But Eddie slipped backward as his speed failed to keep up, until he reached the end of the treadmill. He jumped off. "Sorry, Doc." He bent over to catch his breath.

Hollister jabbed his finger at his data tablet as he entered his notes. He paused, clenching his fist. Speed, strength, and agility had many genetic components. The genome he had targeted likely controlled only one of those components. He knew better than to pin too much on this one experiment. Besides, Eddie's increased neuromuscular strength was a positive result. He wouldn't have to start over yet again with a new subject.

"So I'm going to be able to move my fingers, right?" Eddie continued. "Not just flop them around. Flexing, picking up things, right?"

"Your new limb will be beyond anything the Veterans Administration has to offer, though they owe you far more than they owe me. Our neural interface technology is ahead of the entire industry. You will be the first to use the prototype once the software passes all tests." If his development teams didn't finish soon, they would risk losing their contract with the Defense Advanced Research Projects Agency.

Eddie laughed and stretched his legs. "Maybe I'll become a fucking piano player."

"As a trained soldier, the advanced prosthesis and interface, combined with this experimental therapy, will put you in an elite class. You will have more important duties than playing an instrument. Remember, we have a higher goal." Hollister resumed his pacing, his long legs quickly reaching the opposite wall still painted a hideous pastel green.

When his father created the Genetic Alteration for Military Advantage Program decades ago, he and his geneticists made little effort to predict the outcomes. He'd been proud of his best scientist, Jack Benoit, whose genomic alteration process made the greatest strides. After so much trial and error building upon his work, Hollister was close to surpassing Jack's achievements. When that happened, he would not waste the opportunity the man had squandered. That mistake had benefited no one, especially Lizzie.

"C'mon, Doc." Eddie pulled the electrodes and transmitters off his chest and leg and laid them on the table. "All work and no play, you know. That never ends well." He retrieved his gym bag from the closet in the corner and removed a simple prosthetic limb, sliding the rigid silicon and steel onto his flesh and bone. "Once I lost this, thought I was done. Army had no use for me anymore."

"The military needs you now more than ever. They simply don't know it yet."

"Thanks, Doc. I'm really—"

A third tablet that lay on the side of the table dinged a notification and sent adrenaline through Hollister's body. He set aside the device with his notes, clenched and unclenched his hand, and picked up the one on the table. He let out a slow breath. His video database searches had gotten hits before. He tapped the notification to bring up a list of matches to his parameters for scanning video feeds. His finger hovered over an icon.

"Hey, Doc." The tension drained out of Hollister as Demetri Kalakos waved at him. "You need a break from time on the screen?"

As usual the young software developer wore the cheeky grin Hollister yearned to surgically remove. He would be tempted to use him as a subject if he hadn't been one of his best programmers. "I believe you mean screen time, Kalakos." He snapped shut the cover of the tablet and laid it on the table, his fingers lingering on the device, then held out his hand. "Your report?"

"Before you say anything," Kalakos said, handing over his update on the progress of the hardware development team, "we've worked most of the night on it."

"On what?" Hollister scanned the report. "Another bug?"

Kalakos rolled his eyes. "Didn't I just say? We're working it out." Kalakos glanced at Eddie standing by the treadmill and drinking from a water bottle. The Greek man's dark eyes sparkled behind glasses. "Hey, Eddie, whenever you feel like doing that again, I'm up for sparring. Let's see if Doc's magic potion is working."

"Wait till I get my new arm. Then we'll spar for real."

"You are getting one of those? Good. It's a deal."

"Kalakos, get back to work. I want to know how this bug is doing by the end of the day."

Kalakos rolled his eyes and faked a jab at Eddie, laughing as he left.

"I've uploaded instructions for the coming week," Hollister said to Eddie. "You'll find them on your tablet."

"Do you only hire assholes?" Eddie asked.

Hollister continued to enter his notes. "I hired him for his technical skills, not his personality."

"Yeah, it's been great getting pounded by a computer nerd."

"That computer nerd is working on the software that will enable your prosthesis to receive commands from the implant."

Eddie returned to the window, looking south toward the bridge. "Can't wait till I can knock him flat. But I'm not moving any faster. Not in time to block most of his shots. My reaction time isn't going to improve either, is it?"

"Our agreement was that you submit to this protocol in exchange for the prosthesis. I made no promises as to what areas would respond to the therapy."

The man lingered at the window, focused on the view of the city through the tinted windows that gave the midmorning the dull gray cast of twilight. "I get it. And I understand that this virus is making me stronger—"

Hollister stepped up next to Eddie. "Remember, the virus is only a vehicle."

"Right, right. But it definitely can't make me sick, right? You're not going to tell me that now I can't get the implant because of the virus."

"The virus is transporting new genetic material that gives you the capacity to develop more strength. There is no infection involved. It's a complex process, Eddie, but you don't need to understand it. You need to trust me."

"I do trust you, Doc. You didn't just tell me I would change though. I would become amazing, you said. Was that true?"

"It is and you will. Give me time, and I'll make you into something beyond your imagination." He laid a hand on the man's shoulder. "With your new prosthetic arm and augmented strength, sparring with Kalakos will be child's play."

Eddie grinned, and Hollister led him to the table where he'd placed a tall, thin silver cylinder. "One last test."

"This one's definitely not working," Eddie said, taking a seat. "I've been waving my hand in front of this weight for weeks. Nada. Maybe I need an extra dose?"

"Patience, Eddie." He needed Eddie to be patient, since he could rarely find patience himself. He'd watched that video footage of the boy's murder too many times. His sister hadn't managed to save him, but she'd saved herself. His plan was possible. He only had to find the switch, the gene Jack had managed to turn on. But while Jack had disregarded his greatest finding in a pathetic moment of sentimentality, Hollister would not.

"Okay. Same deal then?" On Hollister's signal, Eddie extended his left arm toward the beaker, palm facing out.

Hollister hardly took a breath. His clenched teeth were giving him a headache.

Eddie snapped his hand forward an inch or two without touching the beaker.

Nothing happened.

Hollister's pulse raced. "Remember, use your mind as well as your arm."

Eddie frowned and jerked his hand forward again. The beaker remained where it was. Eddie sat back. "Looks like nothing."

Hollister's shoulders relaxed. "We'll try again later in the week."

"We done then? I'm wiped." Eddie had been tired after last week's session as well. "Doc, I was wondering. Maybe could I get out for a short trip? I'm not talking a road trip or anything. Just walking the streets, maybe get a slice at the corner pizzeria. The Christmas lights are out in full force, and I love all that stuff." He shrugged. "Just a walk around the block, you know?"

"Perhaps I can arrange something. Now, head to the lab for the blood draw, then eat something and rest up. Follow the instructions I laid out for you. We will add more tests to the routine in a couple of days."

As Eddie walked out, Hollister picked up the tablet with his search results. The hits were on a feed from a Lower East Side building's security camera. He'd picked the right area when he relocated his lab. His finger paused over the screen. He touched an icon.

A silhouette of a person, pale face, dressed in black. The image revealed nothing helpful. Another dead end.

He dropped into his chair. With most of his excitement drained from him, he opened the next result. A woman. That much was clear. Dressed in black, all the way to the hood over her hair. Again, the pale face, not much clearer than the first result. But enough to see a resemblance to the woman in the screenshot he had started this hunt with. *Is that you, Lizzie?*

4.

Justine left her shift that night before Quinn could arrive. Now she stood in the rushing wind of the departing F train at the East Broadway station, its roar fading into the dark subway tunnel. The few commuters waiting this late at night ignored her as she walked to the end of the platform. A short, narrow metal ladder marked with warning signs led from the platform edge to the murky level of the tracks and the maze of tunnels beyond.

She'd used that ladder once. When Devon had been killed, she'd taken the nuclear option and fled into that darkness to live among others with nowhere else to go. If she went back there, no one would ever find her, not even Quinn.

She turned away. She was here to check on Buggy. Homeless long before Justine had befriended him, the man usually spent the coldest hours of the night under a collection of old, stained blankets and belongings in the train stations. Tonight, after checking the Delancey Street station, there was no sign of him here at East Broadway. But December was not the time for staying on the slice of sidewalk he'd claimed under the Manhattan Bridge. If he was there, she'd have to convince him to get inside somewhere. She'd better try before she told him what she was considering.

She emerged next to Seward Park. Averting her eyes from the park, she headed down Rutgers Street toward the East River, where the Manhattan Bridge was an endpoint of light. It was snowing again, and flakes stuck to bare tree branches and chilled her cheeks. Shop owners rolled down steel doors over signs written in Chinese characters. Larger apartment buildings offered temporary patches of darkness. As she neared the river, the wind picked up, and she buttoned her coat.

She turned on South Street, the service road in the shadow of the elevated FDR Drive. Concrete barriers and chain link covered with tarp fenced off the sections beneath the FDR, under eternal construction.

As the bridge loomed ahead, glass crashed inside a construction area, followed by a shout barely audible over the rumbling of cars passing above. She picked up her pace to get past the fight. She'd had her ration of trouble for the week.

Another voice yelled back. Her pace slowed, but she pushed ahead. She couldn't save everybody, right? Amid sounds of a scuffle, she hurried past an open gate. Since any empty horizontal area in Manhattan was deemed a parking lot, cars haphazardly filled the space.

"Come on, ya fuckers, you afraid to take on an old man?"

Justine's feet stopped without asking permission. *What are you doing, Buggy?*

Inside the makeshift parking lot, reflected light from the bridge and the streetlights on the FDR illuminated a discarded sofa, a stack of bulging black garbage bags, and orange traffic cones among the cars. In a clear area, two young men, one tall and wearing a baseball cap, the other in a knit cap, flanked a shorter man dressed in enough layers to form a blurry outline.

She took a step into the lot. They didn't notice her, and she ducked behind the pile of smelly garbage.

Something long and thin dangled from the hand of the one in the wool cap, maybe a scrap of wood from the broken chair crumpled against the fence. "We know you have more. Hand it over."

The homeless man chuckled, a raspy sound.

Great move, Buggy. They love being taunted. Make my job harder. The angle was wrong. She risked moving out from behind the garbage bags so her line of sight to them was clear.

The baseball-cap guy shoved Buggy to the ground. His friend snickered as he waved the rod in Buggy's direction. It shone under the streetlamp. Metal, then, not wood.

Enough debating. She brought up her hand, braced her feet, then paused. This morning that metal fender had gotten hot to the touch. Time to see what good that could do. She focused on the rod and tried to heat it up.

The young man swung down to smash Buggy's leg. Buggy cried out. His attacker drew back for another blow, no apparent discomfort, his grip firm.

Too far away maybe. But she was wasting time. She shoved her hands out in front of her, as she'd done thousands of times before, and pushed.

The rod jerked in the young man's hand, loosening his grip. As he frowned at his weapon, she sent out a harder push. The metal flew from his hand, clattering on the pavement until it hit a car tire with a satisfying thud.

The man's mouth dropped open as the metal bar disappeared into the shadows. He followed the trajectory in the other direction, toward where Justine had been, then glanced at his partner, then Buggy. "What'd you just do?"

Justine crouched lower behind the bags, gravel crunching beneath her feet.

"Wouldn't you like to know?" her friend said, faking a lunge toward them. They flinched. One glanced at the pipe, the other toward a gate on the river side of the lot. The man in the wool cap started searching for his weapon.

"Are you sure that's what you want to do, boy?" Buggy said.

"Shut up and quit your tricks, old man."

Justine sighed. A slow learner. Her hands itched to shove him into the concrete column behind him. See how many swings of the pipe he'd get after that. She took a deep breath. That was not what this was for. She pushed the rod again, and it slid under a car.

That did it. The young men looked at each other, then back at Buggy. The tall one shook his head and backed away. The other edged around Buggy, and they trotted off, arguing over who to blame.

Buggy picked himself up, a frown wrinkling his long bearded face weathered by the hostile climate of the street. A little wobbly on his feet, he nodded as Justine approached. "A little dramatic for you, girlie."

"Hello to you too, Buggy."

He took a step and grimaced. "Doing your best to find trouble tonight?"

She tensed on hearing the blurred edges of his words. "Doing my best to see you stay in one piece. If muggings are what you're doing for fun these days, let me know."

His half smile faded, and he pointed behind her. "What if that one was working?"

She followed his gesture. A surveillance camera hung from a pier behind them, no lights announcing its observation. A brief chill went through her. How did she miss that? She turned back to him. "How's the leg?"

"Bruises heal."

The tang of whiskey tickled her nose and sprouted a new bud of anxiety. "Your lip is cut."

He touched his finger to his mouth and flicked out his tongue. "Thought I tasted blood." He caught her look. "I'm fine, girlie." He walked past her in a loping step.

As they walked down the middle of South Street, Justine offered him the bulging bag of food. "You lasted a long stretch this time."

He gave the bag a sniff and rummaged inside. "Mmm, chicken, and"—he sniffed again—"roast beef. Much appreciated." He took a bite of a sandwich. "Seen the cop lately?" he said around his food.

Her stomach knotted up. "Is that enough food?"

He kept his gaze on her. "We could go like this all night, huh?" He let out a long breath. "'Kay, I'll start. It's plenty of food, thank you. Not real hungry right now, but I will be." He paused. "Now, it's your turn. That's how this thing works."

She sighed. "You talking about Quinn?"

"Nah, the commissioner. Of course I'm talking about Quinn." He slipped a bottle out of his coat and took a sip. "Was a time you would never talk to the law. Now you spend all this time with this one. Not just serving him coffee either."

This was not going well. "Want to tell me what knocked you off this time?"

He took a minute to answer. "What else? Marilyn."

"She's in New York?"

"Not anymore. Just found me, somehow. Even brought Derek." He paused, and his voice roughened. "He's ten now. Old enough to know his dad is worthless."

The words she had not been ready to say died on her lips as they turned at Pike Street. Across the street, two men walked a tiny dog past bulldozers and other equipment stored under the bridge. Nothing else moved.

Buggy followed her glance. "Got a feeling about something?"

She shrugged. "That all you're wearing?" His old torn jacket was no winter coat, but it had a hood he could pull over his lank light-brown hair. Two, maybe three T-shirts underneath a flannel shirt clothed his thin frame. Not enough to fend off the cold all night. "Promise me you'll go indoors later."

His gray eyes stayed on her. "So what happened? You two have a fight?" he said, undistracted. "Or did you finally slip? If you've been half as reckless as you were tonight, you'd be—" His eyebrows rose. "You did slip." His tone implied he was foretelling the apocalypse. "Was bound to happen."

She crossed and uncrossed her arms. But she couldn't lie to Buggy any more than she'd been able to lie to her brother. "He really wants a normal explanation." Her voice dropped to a whisper. "I tried pushing him in that direction. Not sure he bought it." They crossed to the narrow median to avoid the sidewalk enclosed in scaffolding. She checked behind her again.

Suddenly alert, Buggy did the same, his eyes scanning the street. He gripped her arm. "Why are you still here, then?"

"Who else is going to check on you? What would you have done if I hadn't come by tonight?"

"Who cares? You need to stay safe—"

She let out a breath of exasperation. "That's why I'm here. Somebody has to care about what happens to you."

He wiped a hand over his face. "This is no joke. Cops have computers, you know, and they're all connected. A search is easy."

Her heart did a little flip, and her jaw flexed. "If he does a search for Justine Bernard, he'll get nothing."

"And when he finds a goose egg? You think he's just going to let that go? He's a *detective.* Once he catches a scent"—he crunched his fingers into claws and bared his teeth, growling his words—"it's terrier time. They don't let go."

"Don't get your panties in a twist. Quinn won't run a background check on me." They turned on Cherry Street. Up ahead, the road passed under the massive bridge support that provided Buggy with some shelter.

He laughed. "Because he's such a sweet guy?"

"Because he"—she swallowed—"trusts me." She spit out the words, angry she couldn't muster the conviction to back them. Yesterday, maybe. Today?

"Trust? Are you *trying* to end up a lab rat?" He stopped in the middle of the street to face her. "Maybe you think when they catch you, it'll be a blood-bank kind of thing. Come and go as you like—just give us a pint once in a while, pretty please?" He shook his head. "You'd be like a giant jigsaw puzzle to any scientist who got their hands on you. Once they solve your puzzle, they'll box you up and put you on a little shelf, or maybe a little cage, until they think of more questions." He leaned in. "And if the government's got the key, ain't no escaping."

"You think I don't know that?" she snapped and walked past him. Her breath came in quick bursts as her insides rose and dove on the hills of a roller coaster. That would not be her future. She'd promised Devon as he lay dying by the river. Her mother had given up everything to make sure that wasn't her future. Her father had given his life so she would have a future.

He caught up quickly. "A cop knows too much about you, girlie. Time to go, ain't it?"

Anger and fear made a nasty soup in her stomach. Buggy knew which buttons to press. Worse, he was right. She should have been stronger. "He's—I can talk to him. Or not talk. He doesn't mind."

His silence was sharp as the cold. "So you thought you could trust him."

She had. Now she was trusting him to not ask questions or look for answers. To not give away her secrets. "So I leave, and what'll you do? Drown in your bottle?"

"I'll climb out of this hole when I'm ready." He slowed as they reached the bridge where the structure buffered some of the wind from the river. A recess under the support created the protected area he'd claimed. "I won't lie. I'd rather you stayed. You've been a comfort these past years, helped me keep the bottle closed. But we both knew one day too many people would *know*."

"My father thought leaving him behind was the best thing too." Instead of going underground with his family like he should have. "And he paid for it." Now Buggy would pay for her choices, while she'd lose the closest thing she had left to family. "I could try going back to the tunnels."

"Tunnels are no place for you."

"If I abandon you now, they'll find you by the river covered in snow."

"Leaving ain't the same as abandoning. Sometimes it's just what you got to do."

"It will feel like abandonment," she said, her voice rising and echoing in the archway overhead. "Trust me. Doesn't matter the reason. When someone's not there, they're just gone."

He let a moment of silence pass. "Your daddy issues are going to be the death of you."

She shoved down the sludge of emotion he'd dredged up. His concern was like a warm yet itchy blanket. She wanted to cast it off but wasn't ready to step out into the cold.

Her words were almost too quiet to carry on the wind. "When I'd been sure I was alone in the world, you were one person who knew my face and my name." Her throat tightened, as if reluctant to let the words go. "I'm here because you kept me from losing myself. I'll be here as long as you need me, Buggy."

His eyes softened and his shoulders slumped. His raspy voice lost its edge, and he sounded far more than his fifty years. "If you stay, I'm thankful. Scared for you, too, but thankful all the same."

Air turned to broken glass as she breathed, so she shut her mouth and nodded.

"If you do leave, find a way to get a message to me. So I know you're okay?" He leaned toward her. "Whatever happens, no experiments."

"I will not be an experiment," she whispered.

Justine left Buggy to his whiskey and headed home, her mind churning like the river at the waterfront in a storm. Unsure what was next, she felt a wave of vertigo, the ground beneath her unstable. She pulled back her hood, letting the crisp air wash over her.

Her earlier unease lingered, so she passed Clinton and cut through the housing project at Montgomery Street. Broad paths crossed through the complex. She sped up, longing for the seclusion of home, a comfort that looked thin and transient.

She passed a couple of chatting men huddled around a cluster of metal benches too cold to sit on, across from an apartment building. Another man huddled in his hoodie crossed the wide sidewalk as she continued toward Madison Street.

He stopped in front of her.

His hood and cap shadowed his face. Was it paranoia telling her there was something familiar about him? Maybe the chill running down her spine was caused by the gun in his hand.

5.

"Good evening."

Justine stepped back. The conversation across the wide sidewalk faded as the men walked away. To her right, a small, dark courtyard with entrances to the apartment building was a tease. "What do you want?"

A smirk peeked out from beneath the baseball cap. "Confirmation." He spoke with an accent kind of like Dracula. He turned toward the building. To keep her distance, Justine pivoted and took a step into the small square. Her body went on high alert. This guy had cornered her in one move. She resisted the urge to shove a hand into her coat pocket, where her pay sat. Let him try to take it from her.

He lowered his hood. "I want to be sure I was not hallucinating."

Her sharp intake of breath burned her nose with cold. The man who'd shot Quinn. He had been following her.

"See, you know what I am talking about. That should be enough, but"—he lifted a shoulder, a slow smile curling his lip—"I want a little more. I want to see you do it." He gestured with the gun. "I will only shoot once. You only have to stop it. Don't bother to run. I will shoot either way." He lowered his voice. "I know you can stop the bullet in the air like you did the night before yesterday."

"What if—what if you're wrong? Maybe you were hallucinating. Then you'd—"

"Oh, I thought I was. For a few hours, I did. Except I wasn't high. So I came up with the way to know for sure. Right now you should be confused. Instead, you are scared. But not scared of me. I see it in the eyes. I am right. Get ready now."

This could not be happening. What would he get out of forcing her to use her ability? She backed up. The entrance behind her might be locked, but she could force a door open. Buy a little time. And prove him right. "What do you really want?"

"Please," he said, "this does not have to be difficult. It is a simple thing. I know I am right."

The only thing that would prove this guy wrong was getting shot. Float and you're a witch. Die and you're innocent. Those had never been good options. "If you're so convinced you're right, why bother?"

"Call it being thorough." He stepped closer.

She tried to match his steps and bumped into the brick wall of the building.

Where Quinn had chosen denial, this man had chosen to believe. That made him far more dangerous. None of her choices were good ones, but she'd rather not face the bullet. Heating up the metal didn't work with the man who'd attacked Buggy. Yanking the pistol from his hand would be harder than pushing. As tired as she was, she likely couldn't manage to push him down.

She focused on the gun without putting her hand out. She didn't have to give the whole game away.

He aimed his weapon at her chest.

Her heart raced, and she tried to control her breathing as she pushed harder. She was rewarded with a wobble. She might not be able to give him his damn confirmation. But she'd also get shot.

He grinned as he secured his grip on the pistol. "Ready?"

Well, fuck it, then. *You want proof, you got it.* She snapped her arm forward, while giving the gun a stiff mental shove.

It jumped from the man's hand, arcing behind him, and bounced off the pavement, sliding under a bush.

The guy's smile shifted into an O as he watched his weapon sail through the air. When he turned back to her, the smile was back.

She wanted to shove him into something solid. Instead, she shivered. "Bastard."

"Yes. Yes, I am. Thank you. Not what I was hoping, but this will do." He slipped his hood over his head.

"You can't prove any of this." Her eyes darted to the walls behind her. No cameras she could see.

He bent down to look for his weapon. "I should have recorded it though. Too bad." He found the gun and slipped it into his waistband.

"That's it? That's all you wanted?"

He shrugged. "We will see, won't we?" With a wink, he trotted toward the street.

She gaped at his back as he left, taking her anonymity with him. For years only Buggy had seen that. Now, three people had. After he disappeared around a corner, she retraced her steps. She would take the long way home.

And start planning her next move.

~ ~ ~

A stuffed manila envelope landed on Quinn's desk at the Seventh Precinct station with a slap. Officer Maxwell Finn dropped his long, lean body into the chair at his own desk, unzipping his parka. With short-cropped hair, dark skin, and a ready smile, Max had been easier to work with than Quinn's previous partners. "Next time I'll do the paperwork. You go to the morgue."

Quinn snorted. "Promise?" He leaned back in relief from the keyboard he'd been pounding one handed. He had tossed the annoying sling onto the pile of file folders on his desk, though his left arm now burned with pain. "I'll take a trip to the morgue if you'll write up my reports." With his mind already preoccupied, the usual hum of phone calls and clicking keyboards had distracted him today rather than receding into the background. Replaying his last moments with Justine had been too easy. He'd wanted her to stay, and instead he'd said the one thing sure to scare her off. After that last word she'd said, she felt miles away. All he wanted was a second chance.

He shut down those thoughts and pulled the report toward him. "Do we have cause of death?"

"Skull was caved in, pretty close to this high-tech implant he had."

"In his head?" Quinn asked as he sifted through the pages.

"That would be where the skull is located."

"How's the arm, Duncan?" Detective Rodriguez asked as he passed their cubicle, juggling a handful of files with his coffee.

"It's fine. Feels great, thanks," Quinn called out. Ignoring Max's cheeky grin, he returned to the report. "Medical examiner states he'd been 'worked on.'"

"Liar." With a grin, Max reached out toward Quinn's left bicep.

Quinn jerked away, then flinched and grabbed his arm with a hiss. He set his jaw and tamped down his temper. *Focus on the work.* He scanned the report summary. "Unusual results from the bloodwork. Unknown technology in the brain? Surgically and expertly implanted, she says. The tech is more advanced than she thought science was capable of."

"Sounds like med speak for 'I don't know what the hell this is,'" Max said.

"The implant was adjacent to the injury, but undamaged. Think the attacker was after the tech, trying to remove it?"

"Or trying to hide the fact that it was there. Same reason to take the prosthesis."

"That would have been a nice and easy ID too."

"I sent the report to IT anyway," Max said. "Maybe Gabby can get something traceable out of all this. Tell us why he had that in his head."

Quinn closed the folder. "Why would you let someone put something like that in your head?" He shook off the thought. "Without a witness who saw anything worthwhile, IT might be our only shot."

Max nodded at Quinn's screen. "Still working on your statement?"

Quinn gritted his teeth. "Yes, still working on it." He had too many blanks he couldn't fill. Even if Justine had answered his questions, none of those answers would help him. "Things are a bit fuzzy. But I've got nothing but time." He rubbed his arm. "I'm already over this modified-duty crap."

"Somebody's got cabin fever."

"I just want to get back to work." *And figure out how I'm still alive.*

"Anything on the ballistics?"

Quinn shifted in his seat. "Came up empty."

"And only one bullet?"

"Maybe the other went wide ... I don't know. I was a bit busy with bleeding at the time." If Justine was right about the second bullet—no, he was not losing his mind. Someone had stepped between him and that bullet, retrieved it, then sent off the shooter. Whose side were they on?

That was a bad question to not have the answer to. He threw the report onto his desk.

Max eyed him. "I know you want to find the guy who put you behind the desk. You've got to let that go and let the guys on the case do their job. Focus on our case."

He let out a breath and tried to banish all thoughts but those before him. "We can work both, I think. My shooter may be of interest to the case."

"You *think* he's of interest? So that's not an evidence-based claim you're making."

He glanced sidelong at Max. "Scumbag knew about the case, details not released to the public, like his prosthesis."

"You think he's keeping tabs on it? Or actually involved?"

Quinn shrugged, then bit down to keep from wincing. "Not sure. Said he had information." If Justine wasn't the third person, he could have told Max everything. But it was too late for that. He was stuck dealing with this on his own.

"So this guy asks for a meeting, then shoots you instead? I'm glad he's such a bad shot, but why?"

Quinn ran his hand through his hair. "Seemed like he was actually fishing for info. Look, I bet he's guilty of something. We'll find out if this murder is one of them."

Max leaned back. "I have to say it. You would have had a witness if I'd been there." Max raised an eyebrow.

Anger surprised Quinn as it kicked up from a simmer to a full flame. He struggled to turn it down. "Yes, all right, I screwed up. I should have brought you along to meet the informant. Happy?"

He would have had a witness, and Max could have set him straight on when he'd crossed from reality into fantasy. Now, all he had were hallucinations and denials. He stood and snatched his coat from the back of his chair. "I need some air." He strode down the hallway, panting as he reached the lobby.

Quinn slipped one arm into his coat as he nearly ran out the front door. He trotted down the steps and along the row of cars parked facing the building. Not until he reached his Jeep did he notice there was someone inside.

6.

Even as Quinn's hand went to his gun of its own accord, he recognized the passenger leaning against the car door window. He ground his teeth and yanked open the driver's-side door. "What are you doing here, Cayden?"

His younger brother's body jerked. "Nice to see you, too, Q." The leather of his jacket creaked as he ran his hand through thick dark-blond hair well on its way to shoulder length.

"Well?"

Cayden rubbed his thighs, laughing a little, and looked out the window as if there was more to see than traffic. "Just wanted to talk. That a crime now?"

Quinn straightened and bit down on his words, then dropped into the driver's seat and slammed the door. His frustration still simmered in his gut. Now his brother was going to throw his own ingredients into Quinn's stew.

He raised his arm to lean against the doorframe and flinched with a sharp breath. He massaged the muscle around his wound. He should have grabbed his sling.

"What's wrong with your arm?"

Quinn stared ahead. A pair of uniforms passed through a pool of light on the sidewalk as they escorted a man in cuffs to the front entrance of the precinct. "It's nothing. Just a scratch."

"Just a scratch? Were you in a fight?" Cayden's eyes narrowed, then widened. "Did you get shot?"

Quinn heaved a breath as his patience vanished like water on a hot pan. "Damn it, will you be quiet?"

"You weren't even going to tell me?"

"No need to make a big deal about it. Like you're doing now." Silence, finally. Quinn breathed slowly. "Should be asking you what's going on."

"Nothing." Cayden rubbed his hands together. He wasn't wearing gloves. "Something's gotta happen for us to—"

"The last time you paid me a visit, you needed money. Same as always." He dug into his pocket for his keys. Cay was going nowhere soon. He couldn't freeze him out while he was here.

As soon as Quinn turned on the car and cranked up the heat, his brother held his hands up to the vent, though it only offered cold air. "This is your problem. I come here so maybe we can talk like actual brothers. You ask why I'm here like I gotta have an ulterior motive to see you."

"With the people you hang around, you should worry more about yourself than me." Quinn bit his lip. That came out harsher than he'd meant it. Business as usual. A fine sibling relationship built on mistrust and resentment.

Cayden looked out the window again. He looked younger than his twenty-five years in the light from the streetlamp. "How's police work these days? Still catching the bad guys?"

Quinn wasn't getting any peace in here. He shut off the car and got out, gulping the brisk air as he leaned against the Jeep's hood. He'd been banging his head against walls all day. He was either losing his mind or losing Justine. Or both.

The other car door slammed. "I didn't come here to fight, you know." His brother took up a spot against the other end of the hood. "I didn't even come to ask for money. I just wanted to, you know, see how you're doing. Which seems to be the only way I'd find out you were shot."

"There's nothing to talk about. It's not serious."

"Getting shot isn't serious? Dude, how often do you get shot?"

"Never. Not really. Only minor stuff like this. It's a graze, that's all."

Cayden eyed Quinn's arm and shook his head, turning to face the street while two police officers walked into the station. "You know, one day you're going to need to ask me for help. You'll wish you hadn't been so uptight."

Quinn sighed. "Look, you caught me at a bad time, okay?" Farther down the sidewalk, two young men skirted around a woman and her dog, the streetlight brightening their animated faces as they talked. He couldn't remember the last time he and his brother had

had such a cheerful conversation. Definitely before their mom had died.

"Should I just assume it's always a bad time and never talk to you?"

Quinn clutched at his hair. No matter how they started, Cay would eventually say something stupid that would set him off, and they'd end up here. He rolled his right shoulder. "There's a lot going on right now. I'm on modified duty, so I'm stuck behind a desk most of the time."

"Modified duty? What'd you do?"

Quinn threw him a scowl. "I got shot."

"Seems weird to punish you for that."

"It's not supposed to be a punishment. Feels like it though. I'm stuck typing while they investigate the shooting."

"I heard there was a weird murder somewhere around here. That yours?" Cayden tucked his hands under his arms.

"Where did you hear that?"

"I don't know. The news probably. They didn't say much. But I know this is your territory."

That was ridiculously fast for a leak. "It's not really weird as a case. Just murder." Maybe the press had gotten the autopsy report.

"People like to talk murder. Especially the weird ones. So until you're healed up, that case goes nowhere? That how it works?"

"Not exactly." Cayden hadn't looked this interested in what he'd had to say in years. Figured that murder would catch his attention. "Max, my partner, is doing the legwork, while I get to make calls and do paper-work."

"I guess that's why they give you partners, so the case isn't held up while you're sidelined."

"It's still my job. What good am I hitting keys and filling out forms?" That shut Cayden up. And maybe he should shut up too.

"You'll get him, Q. You just need a dose of patience."

Hearing the phrase their mother had used so often was like a gut punch. The silence grew thick. Quinn finally spoke for the sake of making noise. "It's hard to be patient when someone else could die. Besides, the guy who shot me—never mind. I can't go into it."

"The guy who shot you is involved with that murder?"

"It's only a hunch. Let's forget about my case, okay?"

Cayden let a quiet moment pass. "Maybe this one's more dangerous than you think. Staying off the streets a couple days might be a good idea."

"You need to tell me where you heard about this case."

His brother threw his hands in the air. "Thought I heard it on the news. Why's it matter?"

"Because I only got my hands on the autopsy report tonight. If it's already on the news, then someone somewhere talked to a reporter. If you didn't hear it on the news, I need to know who's talking to you."

"I don't remember."

"Think, Cay. This is important. You should not know about that case. No one should. If you're so interested, help me out and think about who you've talked to in the last couple of days."

Cayden kicked at the curb, his feet crunching on gray snow. "I was just asking because, you know, it's your job. I don't—"

"You don't get it. If you didn't get that information from someone else, it's going to look like you're the connection."

Cayden looked up at him, eyes wide, shoulders drawn up. "You really think I'd be involved with a murder?"

The question threw ice on Quinn's frustration, and he paused to choose his words. "No, Cay. But these are the kind of questions that come up when you associate with people involved in questionable business." He raked his hand through his hair. "Who are you working for these days? They're paying you well enough for the new leather."

"My work pays well. I have skills, man."

"Skills that only get you hired by shady businesses. If they were legit, why would they need a hacker?"

"Dude, take a pill. You always got to go for the jugular. Ease up."

"Ease up? You'd like that—"

He faced Quinn. "Maybe Mom would?"

Quinn stilled as the question smothered his outrage. "Leave her out—"

"She wouldn't want us always at each other's throats like this. Tell me I'm wrong. Say she wouldn't care."

Quinn pushed off the car, and Cayden backed up, as if he could see Quinn's anger spark back to life. Quinn paced, breathing deeply to keep from flying off in a frenzy. He tried to put some words together, but he wasn't sure what he was trying to say.

Only a few years older than his brother, he'd stepped into the empty spot their father had left years ago. Yet he still couldn't admit to Cay that he was right. He could tell the truth though. "She would hate it." He couldn't help continuing in a quiet voice, "And what do you think she'd say about what you do?"

His brother flinched and twisted away.

"Exactly. So don't use her like that."

Cayden's voice was tight. "I'm paying my debts. I don't have the luxury of worrying about who's writing the checks."

"Hacking for sketchy companies is how you're going to solve your problems?"

"It's a lot less likely to get me arrested than my other options."

A chill went through Quinn as his brother's words blew away his denial. "That depends on what they're involved in, Cayden. Who do you owe? And how much?"

"That's not important."

"How else can I help you? Tell me, Cay."

"I don't need your help!"

Quinn flexed his hands, itching to knock sense into his brother. "Maybe not today, but some day you will. You get into trouble. I get you out. That's how it is. If you'd tell me what's going on, maybe we could get ahead of things, and you won't find yourself in these situations."

"Well, I am in the situation. And I'm handling it." Cayden let out a long breath. "I can't make this kind of cash anywhere else. Not without doing something with a way higher mortality rate. As soon as I'm paid off, I'm out of there."

"How did you get in so deep?"

"It was the horses, man. You could win such big money. I won big money. Then I got cocky, lost big, tried to make it back, usual story. Should have known better." He kicked some gravel. "I haven't been to the horses in nearly a year. Nine and a half months. That's the truth. So don't start."

Quinn closed his eyes. Various oaths passed through his mind, but he held his tongue. "That's something. If you kept getting yourself in deeper, you'd never break even. Thing is, you associate with people like this, when shit hits the fan, you get splattered. The boss will be smelling of roses, while you'll smell like crap." He continued his pacing, trying to think and calm down. He needed some way to nudge his brother and give him a sense of purpose. That was what he always came back to when talking failed. "Maybe you could do me a favor."

"You need help with your case?"

He rolled his eyes. "No, I do not need help with my case. This is personal." Even as he spoke, he wanted to take the words back, but he plowed ahead. "You still over on East Broadway?" Cayden nodded. "There's someone I'd like you to look out for."

"Look out for, not for a case? What, you want me to stalk someone for you?"

Quinn covered his eyes with his hand. "Sure, I'm asking you to stalk someone. Can you be serious for a moment? I'm worried about Justine. She walks that way late at night."

"You still hanging out with her? How's that going?"

He gazed down the street. "Not actually sure right now." At Cayden's look, he added, "She's a hard nut to crack, okay?"

"So you want me to stalk her."

Quinn pressed his lips into a line and spoke through his teeth. "I do not want you to stalk her. I just want to make sure she doesn't run into trouble while walking home."

"She one of those, you know, trouble finds her?"

Quinn's eyebrows shot up. "Could be. But until we catch this guy, I don't want her finding him first, you know?"

"Have you tried, you know, talking to her? Or do you need help with that too?"

"I do not need you to help me talk to women."

Cay tried to hold back a laugh, but he didn't try hard enough. "But she's not talking to you, is she?"

"I told her to be careful." He shook his head. "Stubborn woman said she could take care of herself."

"Always had a way with the ladies, dude. Sounds like you pissed her off. If she says she can take care of herself, maybe she can. And you did what you could. What more do you want?"

"I want her not dead. I want her safe. And …" He turned away. If she hadn't saved his life, then why did he feel like he still needed to repay her?

"Boy, you did piss her off, didn't you?"

"I did not piss her off. I might have said the wrong thing."

Now Cayden started laughing.

"Very mature. I know, it's hilarious. Saving someone's life isn't a bad thing, you know? Actually, I never said it was her."

"Wait, what? Who saved whose life? You're not making sense, man."

Dread came over him, because he couldn't stop his next words from leaving his mouth. "I don't know what happened, Cay. It's driving me crazy."

His brother had the decency to not laugh. "What do you think happened, Q? Does this have to do with you getting shot?"

Quinn shrugged, then grabbed his bicep and winced. "No." He sighed. "Maybe. It was dark. She's right. I really can't say for sure what happened." Wow, he sounded even more insane saying it out loud.

"But?"

"But … I think she saved my life." He did. Despite what she'd said, he knew he was not wrong.

"Wait, you *think* she saved your life? How can you not be sure? Not that it's bad for a relationship, but— Hey, she didn't get shot, did she? Never mind, stupid question. So what'd she do?"

Quinn waited for the questions to end. This was biting him in the ass already.

"What, is that confidential? Is she part of your case now?"

He rubbed his chin with the back of his hand. Dragging her into police business was definitely not the way to get on her good side. "I really don't know, Cay. It was surreal. Really. I can't say what happened, because I don't know."

"So maybe she saved your life, maybe not. I'd drop it if she doesn't want to talk about it." Cayden shrugged. "And maybe drop the stalking. Why don't you try talking to her again?"

"I'm not ask—" He ground his teeth, making his headache throb. "Make sure she gets home safely. That's all I'm asking. Can you do that?"

"Okay, okay, I'll watch out for her. Make sure she doesn't get into trouble." His lip quirked, but he managed to hold back the smirk. "You really got to learn how to talk to girls, dude."

"I need to learn how to talk? You're still calling them girls. I hope the ones you talk to are old enough to be considered women."

"Oh, don't start, please. Aren't you lectured out by now? I said I'd do it. Leave it there. When does she get off work? You know where she lives? I need something to go on."

Now it did sound like stalking. "She lives somewhere near the diner on Grand. Not sure exactly where. Usually works till tenish. I try to meet her when I get off work, but a lot of nights I can't get there in time. And she walks down to the river, from what I've gathered."

"The river? At night? She really is looking for trouble. How long you want this going on?" A car with tinted windows crawled past them, though there was no traffic. Cayden turned to face the building.

"Until this case is solved, I guess." Quinn had not thought this through. "You're not stalking her. And if I can, I'll try to talk some sense into her, get her to take a cab or something."

"Okay, dude, I gotta get going. We done?"

Quinn nodded. "Cay." He paused until his brother looked his way. "Be careful."

"You're the one who just got shot. Watch your back better."

7.

As Quinn entered the diner, he tried to set aside the conversation with his brother. But that only left more room for anxiety over Justine.

Max sighed as he stepped inside, loosened his scarf, and claimed a stool at the counter. Quinn took the stool beside him, brushing snow off his coat and tugging off his one glove with his teeth.

Nita stood talking with someone at a table, but Justine was nowhere in sight. Since she refused to use a phone, Quinn had to hope she was working to try to talk to her. Talking with Cayden about what had happened the other night hadn't made anything clearer except how she'd downplayed and brushed off his concerns. The lack of trust that had shown stung. But it had also proved he'd touched on something important, something she wanted to keep hidden. How bad could the truth be?

Max unbuttoned his coat and opened up the day's newspaper as Nita poured their coffees. "Oh, goody, a storm's coming. Looks like we'll get our white Christmas."

"Still means I have to drive through it. I'll pass."

"Tell that to Mother Nature. You do anything special for the holiday?"

Quinn sipped his coffee. "It's just me and my brother, so it's a quiet day."

"As long as you're with family. Remember, you're always welcome at our place. Family's not only about blood, you know?"

"You got that right. Thanks for the offer, but I'm good. My brother and I will probably not even argue. We'll play some video games, then go out to dinner."

"And he'll beat you badly at those video games. Am I right?" Max asked.

"You are. He always kicks my ass."

"Girl, what have you gotten yourself into?" Nita said as she returned from the back with a box. Justine followed, still in her coat, carrying another. Nita stashed the coffee and tea from the boxes on a low shelf. "I told you. I can't take the cat."

Justine stood beside the cook at the grill, watching the man flip burgers. "You'll find someone to take him before your landlord even notices."

"If he finds out, I'll be on the street in seconds. I can't lose that apartment. It's rent controlled."

Justine's voice dropped. "Cheetah's quiet."

Quinn leaned forward. "Who's Cheetah?"

Justine turned to him with eyes wide as a deer's facing an oncoming car. She opened her mouth but didn't speak, instead grabbing the coffee carafe and filling a mug. Then she stood there, holding the cup as if it contained the last caffeine on earth, casting furtive looks at the door. "Cheetah's kind of my cat."

"You have a cat?" Not what he'd planned to say, but she was talking to him.

"You need a cat sitter?" Max said with a wide grin. "Here's your man." He clapped his hand on Quinn's shoulder. Quinn bit down as the impact jerked his other shoulder and arm.

"He was a stray," she said. "I kind of took him in. But I've got it covered."

"Doesn't exactly sound like it," Max said. "Duncan was just telling me he needs a friend for his dog." His grin grew wider as Quinn muttered and threw him an evil look. But he continued. "How's the mutt with cats?"

Justine seemed to force the words out. "Nita will come around. She'll take the cat."

Quinn kept his eyes on Justine as Max went on, but she found plenty of other places to look than him.

"Not if she has a rent-controlled apartment. Give the critter to Duncan. His building allows pets. How long do you need?"

Justine's eyes widened impossibly. "Never mind. I'll figure it out."

He was missing something. He looked her over. No bruises, no new scratches on her hands. Most of her hair was caught in a ponytail. Her clothes hung loose on her, but that wasn't new. Neither was the darting of her eyes. But the fear—that was new.

Quinn said in a measured tone, "You being careful out there, Justine?" He was glad he'd asked Cayden to keep an eye on her.

She swallowed. "Of course." He began to say more, but she turned to grab the coffeepot, eyes on his cup as she refilled it. "You can't bring a cat home. What would Sully do?" She tucked a stray curl behind her ear as she scanned the dinner crowd.

"Sully's dealt with cats and survived." He paused as her words sank in. "You never mentioned leaving town. Where are you going?"

As she returned the carafe to the machine, Justine's hand twitched, causing the glass pot to wobble on the hot plate. She grabbed one hand with the other. "This isn't such a good idea."

"It is a good idea, even if Max came up with it." Max had pulled off what Quinn hadn't managed to, with only a few words. "Bring the cat by tonight."

She looked out the front window and sipped her coffee, one arm wrapped around her waist. "I don't know."

"It's not that big a decision."

"Okay, okay." She passed Nita a dish from the pickup counter by the grill. "Give me a couple hours. I'll be there some time after ten."

"How long are you going to be away?" Quinn asked before he could think about the answer he might get.

"Hm?" She flinched, and forks and knives clattered on the prep area below. She gathered them up, glancing at Quinn and Max, then the door again.

"Justine, what's going on?"

She finally met his eyes. Her silence seemed to reach out to him, then her eyes slid away.

"Can I get a menu?" Max asked. "Need some soup or something to warm me from the inside out." He rubbed his hands together.

Justine handed him a laminated card, her hand trembling. She took an empty dish Nita passed over the counter.

"Top off the coffee at the window table for me, would you, hon?" Nita said. "Sorry. Don't mean to put you to work."

Justine filled two mugs without a word. She replaced the carafe, but she missed the hot plate. The coffeepot wobbled again and teetered on the edge.

Before Quinn could warn her, Justine turned back to the machine. The carafe slid back into its place on the hot plate before she could do any more than raise a hand. But the pot kept going, sliding over the other side of the machine and falling onto the counter. The heavy glass bounced then cracked, leaking the last of the coffee onto the countertop and the floor.

Quinn blinked.

Nita rushed over, set down a dirty dish, and grabbed a roll of paper towels. As the coffee dripped onto the floor, Justine stood frozen in place, her fist hovering over the counter, her knuckles white.

It'd been like a video playing in reverse. The glass carafe had begun to slide off the edge of the machine. Then it had reversed direction and slid onto the hot plate. But it'd had too much momentum. As if someone had pushed it a bit too hard. Except no one had touched it.

Justine's hand drifted to her side as Nita wiped the floor. She turned to Quinn, devastation in her eyes.

He could only stare back at her.

Nita glanced up at her and stood. "Are you okay?" She laid a hand on Justine's arm.

But Justine pulled away, skirted around her and the spill, and rushed out the front door.

When Quinn could no longer see her, he turned back at Nita. The woman shook her head and finished cleaning up. "What did you say to her?"

"Nothing. I offered to watch her cat." Then he'd asked where she was going and for how long. She hadn't answered.

But she had answered his questions about what had happened three nights ago. With an impossible answer. Which meant she'd lied, or at best, evaded his questions last night. "Max—"

"Yeah?" He looked up from his paper after a sip from his mug.

Did you see that coffeepot move by itself? Right. "Never mind." Maybe he should have taken a few days off. Maybe he should go after her.

"Duncan, just talk to her. Ask her what's on her mind."

Quinn set down his cup. He would see her in a couple of hours. Then they'd talk. But *what* wasn't the question anymore. It was *how*.

~ ~ ~

The cold lights of the Lower Manhattan skyline, dimmed by the glare of the Brooklyn Bridge, challenged Hollister through the tinted office window. He'd gambled on moving here five years ago from Washington, DC, dropping a mountain of cash to get this vacant school building from the city. All based on a blurry piece of footage.

"Two days ago your prosthesis software team was working out a bug." Hollister turned to the three who had joined him. He took a seat at the end of the dull and dented conference table that just fit within the small meeting room with the faded paint job. "Today you're finding new bugs while you fix the old ones." Hollister leaned back, his gaze locked on Kalakos, the lead for his prosthesis software team.

Kalakos slouched in his chair in his sweatshirt and ripped jeans, flipping a pen between his fingers. "I need more people if I am to work faster."

"You'll work with what you have. Stop wasting time."

The younger man pulled off his glasses to rub his eyes and yawned. "You think sleep is a waste of time," he snapped, his accent softening his consonants. "I'm not going to kill myself for this job."

Valentine Moretti, Hollister's chief of operations, leaned forward, her dark hair brushing her shoulders. Her white blouse looked crisp even after a twelve-hour day. "Do not cause us to miss our deadline," she said to Kalakos in a quiet, steady voice.

Even Hollister bristled at times over Val's obsession with deadlines. But she kept his company running, sometimes despite him.

"You're messing with the schedule, Kos. If the prototype isn't ready on time, DARPA will cancel our contract and hand it over to MedTech."

"Relax, Val," Kalakos said with a grin. "Take a pill or two. You're too uptight." He straightened, losing the smile. "DARPA gave us this contract because the code I wrote for NextLevel is better than MedTech's code. They are not going to give up that. They will wait a little longer. I need more time to work out this bug."

"Without DARPA's money," Hollister said, "this entire project goes nowhere, and I have no need for you. Make the deadline."

Kalakos released a slow sigh, his eyes on nothing in particular. "Whatever you say, Doc."

"And your latest subject?" Val asked Hollister.

"We've made considerable progress. It looks promising."

"Do you still intend to fit him with the prototype?"

"All indications show he's a good fit. He is becoming restless though. All the more reason to push for our deadline."

"Let him get out, take a walk," Kalakos said. "If he starts to get a little nutty, he will try to sneak out."

"This is not elementary school. There will be no excursions. I'm not risking my work on the streets of Manhattan. If he tries to leave"—Hollister tilted his head a fraction—"he'll only try once."

Val turned a page in her planner. "The Biomedicine Convention is due to publish their updated guidelines for genetic modification of humans. I would advise you to complete your work before they do."

"I'm not concerned about the convention's guidelines."

"Their ruling could spell the end of your work."

"DARPA is only marginally aware of my genetics work. The department concerned with the prosthetic system prototype doesn't communicate with any team I have worked with in the past. We will not be shut down."

She pursed her lips. "I hope you're right. I've got enough to worry about trying to deliver the prototype on time." She glared at Kalakos. "The good news is, I've come up with a strategy to get us over this bump."

"Let's hear it."

She glanced to her right. "I want to go over some details with Cayden first."

Cayden Duncan, lead for the team developing the neural implant software, looked up from his laptop in apparent surprise.

Kalakos sat up. "You're not handing over my code to this—"

"Cayden, is your team still on schedule?" Hollister asked.

The young man's eyes lingered on Kalakos before meeting Hollister's. "Yes, it is."

"He won't be touching your code, Kos," Val continued with a minute eye roll. "No need for a tantrum. I'll be using his expertise to gain us some leverage."

"Talk to me as soon as you work those details out," Hollister said. "Kalakos, worry about fixing the mess you left behind. You still have eyes on the detective?"

"My mess? I wasn't—"

"Yes, tell me what you weren't doing." Hollister crossed his arms. "Since what you did do was leave a bright, bloody trail for the police."

"Should have kept that guy in the lab if you thought the police could trace him back to us," Kalakos said with a scowl.

Hollister stiffened. "Perhaps you would prefer to be reassigned to a project a bit more experimental?"

Kalakos closed his eyes, then looked away. "I am watching him, Doc, him and his partner. They stopped at the morgue, talked to some people who don't know nothing. They've made no connection to us. They only have a body. None of the hardware you put in him—"

"You didn't get the neural implant."

Kalakos blew out a breath. "The investigation will go nowhere. And that is more than Cayden found out chatting with his brother."

"My brother doesn't talk to me about his cases. Nothing I can do about that."

Kalakos smirked. "I could do something."

"Continue talking with him," Hollister said to Cayden. "I need a sense of his progress."

Cayden hesitated. "He's not making progress. He's on desk duty or something. He got shot."

"Oops."

Cayden threw a murderous look at Kalakos. "What's that supposed to—If you had anything to do with my brother getting shot—"

"I only said 'oops.' Don't mean I shot the guy. Relax, man. You're too high strung." Kalakos sat back, eyes on Cayden, a wild cat watching its prey. Except no cat felt so much hatred for its food.

"Desk duty means he's still on the case, correct?" Hollister asked as he stood.

"Suppose so."

"Then nothing has changed. We have a deadline to meet. Get it done."

Val rose and gathered up her planner, notepad, and phone. "Cayden, let's talk before you leave for the night. Hollister, how is first thing in the morning?"

"Call me when you're finished with Cayden. Doesn't matter the time."

Kalakos shifted in his seat. "Doc, I need to talk to you when you have a spare minute."

"No such thing as a spare minute. What's wrong with right now?"

Kalakos watched Cayden pack up his laptop, eyes burning into Kalakos.

So he wanted privacy. "Do we need to go to my office?"

As Cayden left with Val, Kalakos said, "I only want to run this past you. I think you would want to hear it."

"I'd rather you were working."

"Doc, I saw something. Blew my mind. You will want to see this—I know it. If I can find her again, maybe you can."

"Her?"

"Yes. I saw this woman do something I would say was impossible before I worked here. Even better than what you did to Eddie. Trust me, Doc. You are going to want to check this out."

8.

Justine's hand paused midair before knocking on Quinn's apartment door. What was she doing? She hadn't even come up with a plan. She should go check on Buggy, see if he was somewhere warm. Maybe by tomorrow Quinn would have dropped his questions. She could meet him after her shift tomorrow and come back here with him as usual.

On the other hand, maybe Buggy was right. After six years in the same city, she'd gone soft and let herself imagine she might stay in one place this time. Her mother had never gone soft. She'd left her husband behind for her daughter's sake. Never again did her mother develop the ties that now caused Justine to hesitate. Moving on now meant leaving Buggy to struggle alone. Quinn would be left with only unanswered questions and betrayal.

Cheetah squirmed beneath her coat, and she tightened her grasp on him. She rapped on the door before she could change her mind.

Inside, a dog barked, then footsteps neared. Nails clicked on hardwood. The tabby popped his head up.

"Who is it?"

Deep breath. "It's me."

Locks clicked, a chain rattled, and Quinn opened the door. Wearing cotton gym pants and a long-sleeved T-shirt, he used his leg to block Sully from the doorway. "Hey." He paused. "Everything okay?"

"I brought Cheetah." Her hand shook as she held the cat more tightly in her coat, to keep him from jumping out.

"In your coat. Okay." He stepped aside, pushing the dog away from the door. As she entered the apartment, he brushed her lips with his, leaving her lips tingling.

The dog followed at her heels, tail wagging. "Sully." Quinn snapped his fingers, and the dog sat. "I guess let the cat poke around." He took a plate and fork from the coffee table to the kitchen. "You want something to drink? You hungry?"

"No, thanks. I'm fine."

Sully knew something was up and circled her, rising up on his hind legs to sniff at what she was hiding. Justine scratched his ear and pushed him down. Sliding her backpack—a fully equipped go-bag once again—from her shoulder, she let Cheetah take a look at his surroundings.

Quinn came over and peered down at the occupant of her coat. "Do you have a litter box or anything for him?"

"I feed him what I'm eating. Otherwise, he takes care of himself. He's a bit wild, but he's been coming to me for food since he was a kitten. I'm afraid he won't make it on the street long."

He started to say something, then seemed to rethink it. "I'll figure it out."

Instead of leaning into him, she moved to the couch, sinking into the soft cushions. Cheetah climbed from her lap to the coffee table. Sully came forward a step at a time. The cat eyed him, tail flicking.

Quinn sat next to her. He started to put his arm around her, and flinched. His wound hadn't healed. The wound she could have prevented if she'd acted sooner.

"So where are you going?"

She covered her eyes with a hand. The part of her that wanted to bury her head in Quinn's chest was winning the war within her.

His voice was a whisper. "Justine, what's going on?"

She managed the words on the second try. "I'm trying to make sure Cheetah is in a safe place."

"Don't you need a safe place?"

She picked cat hair from her coat. "Yes."

Quinn's body stiffened. He leaned away, his eyes boring into her.

She struggled for a breath to speak. "How's Sully with cats?"

"They'll be fine," he said in a hard voice. Neither animal looked like he agreed with him.

She scooped the cat into her arms and held on as he tried to scramble away. She nuzzled him as he settled for sniffing her hair.

"Talk to me, Justine. No need to make a mystery out of it. What could be so bad you don't want me to know?"

Aching with answers she longed to give, Justine buried her face in Cheetah's side. When she got her breath, she held him out to Quinn. "He's harmless. I promise."

Cheetah leaned forward, nose quivering. Quinn rubbed behind his ear, his eyes on Justine as the cat climbed onto his lap and sniffed his shirt, which had apparently been washed in tuna. Quinn gasped when the tabby kneaded his lap, claws catching on his jeans.

The ache inside her eased a fraction. "He likes you." She tried to laugh, but it tasted as bitter as medicine, and she choked instead. She stroked Cheetah's head. He licked her hand, and she almost took him back.

Quinn let out a heavy sigh, then set the cat on the floor. "Forget the cat. You're trying to act like nothing's happening while you get ready to leave town without a word of explanation. And here I'd begun to think you trusted me."

Her throat constricted further. "There's no mystery, Quinn. Nothing to find out."

"Will you be back before Christmas?"

"Christmas?" She'd forgotten. She couldn't wait till January, when she'd be free from Christmas cheer for another year.

"Yeah, it's only a couple of weeks away. I was hoping you might spend it with me."

"I don't do Christmas."

"That wasn't my—" He straightened. His next words were quiet. "Are you coming back at all?"

"I'm not going anywhere, Quinn." It was true, for the moment.

"Fine. Then take off your coat. Have something to eat."

"I . . . I have to get home. Have to work early tomorrow."

"So go to work straight from here. You've done that before."

The silence stretched, her limbs thrumming with tension like electric wires.

Quinn reached out and cupped her chin in his palm, turning her face to his. She swallowed. "Stay, Justine. Maybe in the morning it won't seem as if the world were ending."

She shut her eyes. She would never win this battle while looking into his. But it was also true that leaving tomorrow wouldn't change anything. Perhaps she'd allow herself this illusion one more time.

Quinn touched his forehead to hers. "Whatever's going on, I can help you, if you let me." He brushed her lips with his. They felt hot enough to burn her. Then he pulled back to search her eyes for the answers she couldn't provide.

He kissed her again, and this time she couldn't pull away. The scent of his shampoo mingled with the taste of cherry lip balm. Suddenly she needed air, and he was the only source. Her body clung to his.

This was why Buggy had wanted her to stay away from Quinn. This was why her mom had avoided people in every town they'd moved to. Their nomadic life, meant to hide Justine from prying eyes, had left her feeling like an outsider watching the world go by. Quinn had managed to draw her in, so for the first time, she felt she belonged here. He truly saw her, so she was no longer a wraith haunting the edges of life.

Who would she be without him?

He drew her up and walked her to his bedroom. He climbed into bed beside her and pulled her to him. "It's just me and you, no one else to worry about. Nothing to be afraid of. You're right where you belong."

With those words, Justine surrendered the battle. She let her worries fade into the background, wrapped herself around Quinn's body, and drowned herself in his scent, his skin, his warmth, drawing from them the semblance of security and belonging she craved.

It was dark when Justine awoke. The room was cold, but under the covers, Quinn's body was warm next to hers. A weight leaned against her back, and as she shifted, Cheetah's head popped up. He stretched, then climbed over her to nestle between them.

Quinn jerked away. "What—oh, right." He eased back onto the bed.

Justine pulled the cat to her and drew up close to Quinn.

Quinn gathered her in his arms, quiet in the dark. "You don't have to go through with this."

Breathing was like trying to inhale through quicksand.

"Am I going to see you again?"

That was a question she couldn't bear to answer, even if she knew. Under the blanket, she covered her mouth to suppress a gasp.

If she told him everything, he wouldn't believe most of it anyway. She could stop hiding, stop lying, maybe stop running. "I—" She searched for the words and came up empty. He'd think she was a freak. Or a liar. He might want to find who was after her. He might make her leave.

And telling him wouldn't alter the fact that Quinn was safer the farther she was from him, whether he liked it or not. And whether she liked it or not. She curled up against the warmth of his body. She should have known better than to get used to this.

Quinn untangled himself from her and went into the bathroom. As the shower ran, she burrowed under the blankets. It would be easy to stay here, safe and hidden.

Except she was no longer hidden. She wasn't safe. And neither were those around her. The guy with the gun might show up at the diner and aim his bullets at Nita. Or find Justine as she walked with Buggy. Perhaps she'd already shown him where Quinn lived.

Cheetah stretched and nuzzled her chin, and she broke. Gasping, she pressed her face into the pillow to silence a sob. She breathed deeply to calm herself. Her mother had managed to leave her life behind over and over, and so would Justine.

Quinn emerged from the bathroom and dressed by the light seeping in through the curtains. He slammed a drawer closed, yanked another open. After pulling on a pair of pants and a shirt, he turned to her. "When are you leaving? Never mind." He paused. "Did you ever trust me?" Without waiting for answers, Quinn left the room.

Justine's stomach churned. Whether she explained or remained silent, she'd lose.

When he returned to the bedroom, Quinn had his coat on. He sat on the bed, his back to her. Then he rummaged in his night table and drew something from the top drawer. "Here, in case you need it."

She picked up a set of keys on a small ring he'd laid on the bed. "What are these to?"

"To my place. You can use them if you ever feel in danger. Or"—he paused—"if you decide you need somewhere to call home."

She looked down at the four keys, glinting in the morning twilight, so she wouldn't have to meet his eyes.

"It's not an engagement ring, Justine. I just want to make sure you always have a place to go, somewhere you can feel safe."

A safe place. If only it was as easy as a new set of keys. "You're trusting me with your—"

"With my home, yes."

She felt the pressure of his gaze.

"Is there a reason I shouldn't?"

Her mouth was too dry to form words, to tell him all those reasons, so she fiddled with the keys instead.

Quinn reached out and squeezed her hand. He started to say something, then decided against it and walked out.

After the door shut and his steps had faded, Justine rose and dressed. She gave Cheetah one last scratch behind the ears and said goodbye to Sully. She grabbed her bag and looked around at the small apartment where she'd come to feel at home. "I'm sorry," she said and walked out, leaving pieces of her behind.

9.

Hollister stepped out of his company's building by the riverfront, buttoned his long wool coat, and slipped on his gloves. The snow was falling more heavily this morning, and the temperature had dropped. "Did you hear anything useful from their conversation? Names perhaps?" he said, his breath fogging the air, as Kalakos joined him on the sidewalk.

"Not really." Kalakos led the way across the street, dodging a woman in a parka, and they turned onto Cherry Street.

"Either you did or you didn't. Which is it?" Kalakos had told him next to nothing regarding this woman or the man he'd seen walking with her. But it had been enough that he couldn't ignore the wild claim, no matter how untrustworthy the source. That this cretin might have stumbled upon Lizzie after Hollister's years of searching was a bitter thought. But searching surveillance footage for a sighting of her was a game of chance he was tired of playing.

"They used, like, nicknames or something. I think she called him Bugsy or something."

Useless. If this turned out to be nothing, he would return to the lab and review Eddie's performance data, after burying Kalakos in a dumpster.

Hollister kept to the street, where the snow was not sticking, though his boots provided enough protection for a blizzard. As they neared the ramp to the Manhattan Bridge, the road cut a narrow path through the massive support structure.

Kalakos skidded to a stop about half a block from the bridge and gestured with his chin where the road beneath the support remained in shadow. "I think the guy has a spot under that bridge. See all those piles? Those are people. It doesn't look like too many are there now. Maybe went to a shelter."

"Or they got a job."

Kalakos grunted. "That's not an easy thing these days. In my country, could have been me on the street." He stomped his feet. "Okay, I'm fucking freezing. This is your best bet to find her."

"I'm not interested in a bum on the street. Where did you see her?"

"I told you, down the street." Kalakos rubbed his bare hands together, then stuck them in his coat. "They walked up to here, he stopped, and she kept going."

"And that's when you thought you should stop following her?"

"No, but I lost her after a few blocks. She doesn't walk in straight lines. That's all I got, Doc. I have to check on the detective, then I can head back to the dungeon to work on that bug you want magically fixed yesterday. I guess I sleep when I'm dead."

"You'll fix it. Because you don't want me to hand your precious code and your team to Cayden."

Kalakos's eyes hardened, and he headed up a side street, muttering a stream of Greek that needed no translation.

Wan winter dawn peeked over the skyline across the East River and set aglow the intricate brickwork of the arch ahead. Parked cars narrowed the road farther and shielded those sheltering within. On one side, a recess in the wall held a collection of belongings, graffiti creeping up the wall like strange urban blooms.

Then a pile of clothes separated from the wall, and a figure draped in a shabby coat and a faded blue cap scuffled through the passage toward the cross street. He matched Kalakos's generic description enough, so Hollister trailed this so-called Bugsy as he started up Pike Street, away from the river.

After passing bus stops and empty school playgrounds, Hollister's quarry turned at East Broadway toward the park. With more pedestrians on their way to work or school, he could follow the man more closely. The bare trees of Seward Park soon appeared. Green balls marked a subway entrance where commuters streamed into the stairway. But the vagrant turned onto Essex and continued past the park and basketball courts. Hollister couldn't trail this man through the city, but he had to eliminate the possibility he would lead him to Lizzie before leaving him to his wanderings.

The buzz of traffic increased as they approached the bustling intersection of Delancey and Essex. Bugsy headed for the subway entrance at the corner and made his way down the stairs, step by step. While he rested at the bottom, Hollister descended the slushy stairs, his chin tucked into his coat so his blond hair shielded his eyes.

As he drew near, he reached out for the man's shoulder. He'd have to question him carefully. He could not waste such a strong lead because of impatience.

At that moment, the homeless man surged ahead. Perhaps he'd sensed Hollister's approach. Bugsy wove through the crowd and jumped the turnstile with perfect timing and none of the fragility he'd shown on the stairs.

Hollister trailed him, struggling to keep sight of him in the crowd. He paused to swipe his MetroCard, then entered the large tiled waiting area.

But the man a few feet ahead of him had a different color hat. Hollister scanned the crowd as his blood pounded in his ears. Commuters swarmed the large waiting area, most much taller than his target. Even with his height, Hollister saw no sign of the man or his blue cap. His lead had slipped away.

10.

Hollister was tired of dead ends, wasting time on searches with no results. He'd lost his lead and his morning. He wanted to punch something, but instead he took a breath and then another, watching the waiting area empty of commuters into a newly arrived train.

In the center of the now empty platform, another set of stairs led to a lower level. He had to check before giving up entirely. With one more glance among the few remaining passengers, he descended to the lower level.

The large waiting area on this level held a few people, but the long arms of the platform were empty. At one end, something dark moved beyond the last garbage can.

As much as Hollister needed out of this hole in the ground, he needed a link to Lizzie more. He took a few steps into the narrow section as another train rumbled in its approach. The trash can offered a small bit of cover to a man sitting among plastic bags and blankets. He wrapped one around him as he settled onto his makeshift bed. It could be any homeless man. Perhaps he knew of or had seen Bugsy. And perhaps he was Bugsy.

Hollister stepped closer. The man was bearded and wore the same cap and coat as the man he'd followed. Adrenaline shot through him. Not time to give up yet.

The disheveled man rifled through one of his bags until he found what he was looking for and took a healthy swig from a paper bag. He paused when Hollister's shadow fell over him, and the man tucked away his bottle, eyes on Hollister.

Hollister caught his breath as a new thought occurred to him. If the man needed such an isolated spot, perhaps he was an addict. And if this bum was indeed a friend of Lizzie, might she be using the same drugs? For the first time in years, he felt a distance between them. After so long, he had no idea what kind of woman she'd become. And yet her face in the footage, her expression as she sprawled across her brother in protection, hands outstretched—he knew that look. That was who he was searching for.

Hollister crouched before the man. "What would she want with you?" he muttered, irked he couldn't answer that question. "You're a drunk sleeping in a train station."

The man sat still, looking to the side and then past Hollister. "You talking to me?" he whispered, his words slurring together. His rank breath nearly made Hollister's eyes water. "Or somebody else here?"

"I'm looking for someone."

He squinted at Hollister. "Real or one only you can see?"

"I'm told she hangs out with you for some reason."

The man muttered while rummaging again. Then he looked up and scowled. "You still here? Don't know anybody. Can't help you, blondie. Now fuck off."

"Does she get drugs from you?" Hollister asked, though he didn't want to hear the answer. He might have to be forceful in separating Lizzie from this man's bad influence. "She must get something from you."

"You a cop or something?"

He raised an eyebrow. "She's better off with me than the cops."

This Bugsy paused for a fraction of a second, and his expression lost all curiosity. "She. She. You keep talking about her. Don't know any *her*. Got no friends." He went back to his bottle.

"You've got one friend." This Bugsy wasn't hard to read. "I'm a relative. Her only one. I can help her."

"Don't need nothing or nobody. Can't see straight. But I can see lie and truth. I see the truth won't help you, 'cause that was some bullshit there."

Hollister smiled, rewarded for his patience with this man's ramblings. "How would you know I'm lying, unless you're lying?" *And why would you try to hide a friend unless she had something to hide?*

"You like to hear yourself talk, dontcha? Talk, talk, talk." Bugsy cocked his head, like a dog listening to a sound only he could hear. "You got lies written all over your face."

"And the truth is written all over yours."

The homeless man's head tilted back a fraction, then his shoulders slumped. He took another drink, and when he looked at Hollister again, he seemed to have aged ten years. "She's got no family. No relatives. No friends. Sure as hell don't need nothing from you." His frown deepened. "But she's not alone. Even she don't know that."

Lizzie's mother and brother were gone, if his investigations were accurate. This might really be her. He bit his lip. He could almost reach out and touch her. It had been so long, since that Christmas party, since he'd seen her with his own eyes. Did this homeless piece of shit think he could stand in his way now? "I need to know where she lives."

He put his flask away, muttering, "Told her to stay away from that cop." He shook his head. "Now get gone. Got some sleeping to do." He settled back on his blanket.

"I get it." He pulled bills from his pocket. "Fifty dollars to change your mind?" He got silence as an answer. "Just think how much booze fifty dollars can buy."

The man's gaze bored into Hollister. "Promised, keep her safe. Can't go back on a promise. You should know that. I know that. May be broke, but I still got my principles."

This man had nothing but a blanket and a bottle of booze to his name, yet in the face of cash, he spoke of principles? No wonder he lived in a hole. Hollister put away his money. "This woman is more important than your principles."

"Dontcha mean she's more important than *your* principles?" He closed his eyes, muttering, "What you know about promises? Ever keep one?"

Hollister's breath came faster as he tried to remain calm. Enough of this. He yanked the man upright by his coat and shoved him against the wall. The sound reverberated through the platform, but the babble of commuters and the clamor of a train arriving on another track was louder. "Tell me where she is, you filthy shit," he said through clenched teeth. "You have no idea what you're ruining."

The man regarded Hollister with his sharp gaze. "What about the life you're ruining?"

He grabbed the drunk by the shoulders and slammed him against the wall again.

The man's head smacked the tile, then bobbed forward. He went limp, forcing Hollister to hold him up. Except his eyes. The man's eyes held his and did not let go.

Hollister tightened his grasp on the homeless man. "Your silence is useless. I'll find her as soon as she pays you a visit."

"She don't find me, you're outta luck."

"I don't need you here when she comes looking for you." In fact this man could only be a hindrance.

The homeless man regarded Hollister with an intensity that left him feeling naked. "She'll never show."

"The moment you warn her is the moment you give her away." Even so, he could not risk him warning her.

The man scowled, but doubt overshadowed his defiance. He knew Hollister was right. "She lays eyes on you, she'll know who you are."

"And I'll know who she is. You see, I don't need you at all."

He settled back against the wall. "So I'm dead either way."

"Who said anything about violence?"

He laughed hoarsely. "My head, asshole." He struggled in Hollister's grip with impressive strength and shoved him back. Hollister let him. He wasn't going anywhere. To his surprise, the man scrambled up to standing, though he swayed considerably. "You'll never take her."

While the next train roared into the station, Hollister shoved him back into the wall, holding him with one hand. "I will. That's a promise I will keep." His phone buzzed, but he ignored it.

The man grappled with Hollister's arm, giving him a poisonous look. "Over my dead body."

Hollister shrugged with one shoulder. "If you insist." He needed to ensure this man's silence. Aware of the potential audience behind him, he eased his hold on the man's shoulders, letting him slip back to his makeshift bed. But instead of releasing him, Hollister slid his hands around his neck.

The man had the audacity to laugh.

Hollister's gloved fingers searched for his pulse. As the train roared into the station in a rush of heat and wind, he clamped down on his neck.

The man's eyes widened, and he grabbed Hollister's wrists. His body twitched, then relaxed as he lost consciousness.

He held the position for a minute more, with an eye on the boarding commuters. As the train left, he covered the man's body and rose. He straightened his clothing and moved to the empty waiting area. His phone rang again. He checked the screen. Kalakos. "This had better be important." He started up the stairs.

"Pretty sure this qualifies. I froze my ass off, but you just got real lucky."

"You're following the detective?"

"Better."

"So you're not going to waste my time?"

"We can take care of two birds with one rock. Get him and get her."

"Your English needs more work, Kalakos. What's your point?"

"Where are you now?"

"I'm leaving the Delancey station. Where are you?"

"The subway? Do you know where the detective lives?"

"I'm waiting."

"Okay, okay. So I went to the detective's place, like I said. He's on Stanton. And guess who left his apartment right after he left?"

Hollister paused at the top of the stairs. "Stanton is near the Delancey station, isn't it?"

"Two blocks from there. So listen, it's the girl, okay? The girl that did the crazy shit? I just showed you where I saw her friend."

"The same woman you told me about last night was at the detective's apartment? Cayden's brother's apartment?"

"Yeah, must be dating."

His mind raced. "Does Cayden know this woman?"

"Don't know, but I wouldn't bring him into this. He'll tell his brother, then she'll know."

He searched the sidewalk, where streams of people headed toward the subway. "You have eyes on her right now? Where's the detective?"

Hollister could hear Kalakos smiling. "He left. Then she left." He paused. "Know what? If you left the station, you should turn around. I think she's headed to the subway."

11.

Justine slipped into the cluster of people entering the stairs to the Delancey Street station, then checked behind her. A few extra turns after leaving Quinn's apartment hadn't rid her of that nagging sense of being observed.

The warmth of Quinn's body beside hers lingered, like the scent of smoke after a fire. She could still taste his lip balm. Sharper still was the bitterness of his disappointment. He'd taken her silence for a lack of trust. And maybe he was not wrong.

Enough of this waffling shit. She was going back to her old ways.

Reaching the platform, she maneuvered through the crowd clogging the waiting area. She should have waited till after rush hour. But Buggy had been in bad shape last she'd seen him. She hoped he'd stayed inside today, since it was snowing again.

He wanted her to stay, no matter how much he said she should go. But if he knew about the other night and the man apparently following her, he'd put her on a train himself. Maybe the news would go down better if she had food for him. Buggy's face always lit up when she arrived with a bag in hand—a food present, he called it.

The platform emptied after passengers boarded a northbound train. The back of her neck itched, and she paused. A woman and her child arrived and took a seat at one of the wooden benches. No one else waited or watched.

Justine walked into one side of the long, narrow boarding area where Buggy would often find a secluded spot to rest far from people. She reached the pile of blankets and bags under which her friend slept and crouched down, sliding off her backpack. The air was staler here, with the acrid tinge of alcohol. "Buggy?"

No answer. He'd probably been sucking on his bottle. She poked the mound of blankets. "Buggy, rise and shine. It's me."

Nothing. She nudged him harder. "Buggy, come on. Clock's ticking." Her stomach started gymnastics. She pulled the blankets away, her heart pounding as he remained still, his face relaxed and pale.

Too pale. Her breath caught. No, no, no. She forced herself to reach out and touch his cheek.

It was cold.

Panting, clinging to denial, she pulled his jacket from his neck. Cold. No pulse.

Shit. Shit, shit, shit. This was impossible. She dug under the blanket, found his hand, and squeezed hard, desperate for some sign she'd made a mistake. She had to be wrong. *Buggy, you can't leave me.*

She wasn't wrong. Tears burned her eyes. She should have taken him to a hospital when she saw he was drunk. Or the shelter. She shouldn't have left him alone.

Instead, he'd died alone. She sat next to him and laid a hand on his head. He looked at ease. She adjusted his clothes, then leaned closer. His neck was red and swollen. She pushed back the collar of the jacket and found purplish smudges ringing his neck. A breath escaped her. Had his muggers found him again? There was little he had of value to anyone else. An icy finger ran along her spine. Had the man with the gun figured out they were friends? Buggy would never talk. But if he wasn't clear headed, he could have let something slip.

Whoever had killed Buggy had left him for her to find. They knew she'd look for him here.

She wiped her face with a shaking hand and scanned the platform. The waiting area was already crowded again. No one looked her way. With a caress over his bearded, weathered face, she covered Buggy with the blanket. Having to leave him here deepened her grief. But he would say the same thing her brother had said as he lay in a pool of blood. *Run. Don't look back.*

She stood, slung her knapsack over her shoulders, and turned from Buggy's body. She hadn't been there to protect him, like she hadn't protected—she crushed down the thought. She needed to be gone before the transit officers discovered him. Then she would find whoever had done this.

Slow down. Too many things had happened in the last few days. Too many for coincidence. Perhaps the guy who'd pursued her after shooting Quinn had not tracked her down by accident. And maybe he wasn't alone. Even vengeance was not worth ending up in a lab.

She had everything she needed in her bag. Time to move. She could get on the next train, get off randomly. That would give her time to make a plan.

One thing she knew: whatever game this murderer was playing, he was going to lose.

As she walked to the stairs, the hand in her pocket found, among receipts and loose change, the keys Quinn had given her, of no use to her now. She'd already cost one friend his life. She had to do this on her own.

She weaved among the commuters, most of them with their eyes on their phones and ears filled with music. The rumble of an approaching train grew louder. She stepped toward the edge of the platform. Light filled the tunnel. Maybe she'd take this train to Penn Station.

More people filled the waiting area. She took a breath to calm herself.

A tall blond man in a long coat stepped to the platform edge as the train arrived with a roar and a rush of hot air. Then he turned around and locked eyes with her.

Her blood chilled. She hadn't seen this man before. But he clearly recognized her. Eyes rabid with excitement, his steps quickened toward her.

Her throat closed. Her legs, so used to running, were now stuck in place.

He stopped a few feet from her and smiled. "Hello, Lizzie."

12.

"I'm not Lizzie." Her mind screamed, Run. The train dinged a warning that the doors were closing. All she needed was for this man to go on his way, sure he'd been mistaken.

But instead he smiled, and a shiver went through her down to her bones. "You were once, though, weren't you?"

Before she could think of all the reasons not to, Justine ran to the end of the platform, away from Buggy, away from this man who knew her by a name she hadn't used in twenty years. She hopped down the stairs as the train swept by, and she plunged into the dark dank of the tunnel.

Her heart pounding, she moved as quickly as she dared between crumbling concrete on her right and metal rails on her left, a collection of plastic and Styrofoam strewn down the middle. Her first few steps were lit by the station, but all too soon she lost that light. She continued blind, trailing a hand along the gritty wall.

The clang of heavy footsteps on metal echoed behind her. He had followed her. Now her only option was to move forward faster than he did. She'd negotiated these tunnels before and she could do it again. Only four blocks to the East Broadway station.

He knew her name. Her real name. What else did he know? She pushed away the questions that only fueled her panic.

Warm, moist drafts came out of nowhere, assaulting her with putrid odors. When her eyes had finally adjusted, the tunnel ahead was less familiar than she expected. Her hand tracked through some unidentified moisture dripping down the wall. She jerked her hand away, but she needed the wall to guide her steps.

Light burst into the cavern. Behind her, a shallow circle of illumination bobbed. She kept her eyes ahead to avoid ruining her night vision and continued groping forward.

As she put distance between them, the darkness deepened, and her progress slowed. She stumbled on something at her feet but fought to regain her footing before she fell. She slowed her steps further, despite her urge to run, feeling with her toes for obstacles and protrusions from the wall. She did not want to find out up close what she was walking over. The occasional squeaks of rats was already too much information.

Justine's heart leapt into her throat when she wobbled and lost her balance as the wall beside her disappeared. She caught herself in a doorway missing its door. That way likely led deep into the underground. She backed away. Get to the next station, then figure out what to do. Especially if Buggy—

Her grief washed over her. A sob escaped her, and she clamped her mouth shut. She could mourn Buggy later. The bouncing flashlight was close enough to illuminate her path again.

On and on she went, groping and shuffling, tripping and scrambling for footing. Her fingers stung from skimming over the rough concrete. Her toes ached from bumping into rubble. The thick air made every panting breath an effort. The bag on her back grew heavy.

After an eternity, a pinprick of light appeared. She aimed her steps toward that glow like a swimmer at sea. The light soon brightened her path enough that she could speed up.

The ground vibrated, followed by dull, distant thunder. This part she remembered. The rumble grew, then died away as the train stopped at Delancey. As the train continued on its route, the roar of the engine started up again, louder than ever. Justine flattened herself into a niche, held her breath, and closed her eyes. A whistle blew as the cars rushed past her. Dust and debris bit into her face. Her hood flew off and her hair beat her cheeks. The metal wheels shrieked as the cars hit the curve, then the brakes added to the cacophony as the train neared East Broadway.

Finally, the wind and clamor died down. Her skin felt grimy. Grit coated her lips. Behind her, somehow her pursuer had gained on her. He was now close enough for her to see his face above his light, smudged with dirt but just as eager as when he first saw her.

Justine turned, searching for a clear path, her eyes on the platform ahead. But she stumbled again on an outcropping of concrete.

She gasped as a hand grabbed her arm and pulled her up before she landed on the ground. The man didn't release her once she'd regained her balance.

"Careful, don't hurt yourself." He looked her over. "Look at you. All grown up now."

13.

The man looked her over in the meager light from the station ahead. He held on to her arm with a grip of steel, blond hair disheveled as he loomed over her. His long, dark wool coat was dusty, the edge lined with dirt.

His grin turned Justine's stomach and took her panic up a notch. Blood pounded in her ears as she struggled to breathe. The station wasn't far, but it might as well have been in Canada.

"I've been searching for you for so long," he said breathlessly. "We have so much to talk about."

She tugged her arm, trying to wrench herself from his grasp. "What do you want?"

His smile faltered. "That's a question with a long answer. Let's get out of this sewer, and we can discuss it."

"You followed me through these tunnels for a discussion?" She pulled again, but his hand didn't budge. "Like to see what you consider talking."

The tracks beside them vibrated with the approach of another train. One of those rails was electrified.

Her arm was not stronger than his, but her ability was stronger than her muscles.

He turned her toward the platform, where its light no longer spoke of safety.

She turned into his grip to face him and drew back her arm.

He shoved her forward. "That way."

If this man was the one trailing her all these years, getting rid of him could mean freedom. And if he had killed Buggy, it was the least he deserved.

She lowered her hand. There had to be another way.

He prodded her on, and she let him.

The path widened as they neared the station. A few people waited beyond the stairs for the next train. No one noticed as they climbed onto the platform.

The man who'd hunted for her for any number of years drew her toward him. His eyes lit up. "Finally, we come face to face."

She cocked her head. "That's your conversation opener?" she said over the screech of an oncoming train.

"Your family no doubt told you how unique you are. But do you understand your importance?" He vibrated with energy, undeterred by her questions or by the muck he'd just crawled through.

Unique. Special. Gifted. She'd heard it all her life. How her father would want her to put her ability to good use. And how it needed to be kept hidden from a world that would only want to use her for it. "What's your point? I want nothing you have to offer."

"I'm not selling you anything. I only want to show you what you're capable of."

He was definitely selling something. She would not waste all her years of caution, of secrecy and isolation for someone else's vision of how she should live.

As the wind of the arriving train rushed around her, Justine dropped to her knees, letting herself fall freely. The man's body jerked, forced to follow her sudden movement. She tucked her knees in and rolled over her backpack away from him, pulling him with her. As he fell across her, she threw him to the ground with her feet, breaking his grip on her. She rose to her feet on her momentum.

He rolled to stand in one motion, surprise on his face, and stepped between Justine and the exit. "This doesn't have to go this way, Lizzie."

"Stop calling me that." Behind him, the platform was empty.

He reached out for her. She sidestepped him, but his arms were longer. He grabbed her with both hands.

She dropped her weight again, this time straight back. But he was ready for the move and pulled her back, keeping her upright. She twisted to try to get out of his grasp.

"Your father would want you to live up to your potential."

His words froze her in place. When she spoke, her voice was a raspy growl. "The people my father worked for killed him. Were you one of them? Maybe you killed Buggy too. You think I want anything to do with you?"

But she had done what he wanted. She had stopped struggling. He wrapped his arms around her, immobilizing her. Her face crushed against his chest and the wild beating of his heart. "Don't you want to know all you can achieve?" he whispered into her ear.

To her right, a staircase led out. Another train rumbled in the distance. The few passengers who could see them around the stairs ignored the two in what looked like an embrace.

Then he shifted a hand to grasp her head, releasing his other arm. He tried to lead her by the hair, and she resisted. He tugged harder, and she yanked her head back. A sharp burning pain seared into her scalp as she broke free and stepped away.

He grinned like she'd given up.

Anger and pain filled her limbs with fire. Instead of running from him, she moved toward him. "You don't know my full potential." She thrust her palms forward.

The man's eyes widened as he fell back two, then three long strides, flailing as he neared the edge of the platform. There was nothing beyond but the tracks and an oncoming train car.

A waiting passenger gasped as the man disappeared below the platform with an echoing metallic thud.

Justine stared at the empty space where the man had been. Then she ran.

14.

Justine tugged her hood lower on her face as she rested her head against the New Jersey Transit train window, the cold glass soothing on her skin. Trees dressed with snow and tightly packed homes passed in a blur as the car rocked gently, wheels clanking rhythmically on the rails, on its way to Philadelphia. Away from New York and everything she had except what she carried.

She checked the tissue she'd pressed to the tender spot on her scalp to stop the bleeding. Bright red. So much blood. He must have gotten skin along with her hair.

If he'd gotten the strands out by the root, he had her DNA.

Her scalp tingled while nausea rose up in her throat. He had grinned when he'd gotten the clump of hair. Was that what he'd been after all this time? Or was the DNA a consolation prize? Maybe he'd stop pursuing her now that he had it. If he hadn't been run over by a train.

A cold trickle rolled along her scalp. She put more pressure on the wound. From his expression when she'd hit him, she'd shown him what he'd been looking for, perhaps since she was four years old. He'd never leave her alone now.

He had known her father. And he knew what mentioning him would do to her. Worse, he knew the name she had not used since her mom had packed up her brother and her and left town in a panic twenty years ago. An unfamiliar ache came over her. A longing for a home and a father she didn't remember.

When her mom had received her dad's warning call—the one she learned years later meant someone at the lab where her dad worked had learned about Justine—her mom had followed the plan they'd made. She'd moved them from safe house to safe house, picking up new identification on the way. Her dad would meet them when the danger had passed. Except he never did.

She had to go back to that plan. She had to disappear. And there was one person who could make that happen.

She unzipped her knapsack. A few days' worth of clothes, a handful of protein bars and water, her family photo, and the envelope with her last paycheck. She slipped the wad of cash into her inside coat pocket. Buggy wouldn't like her carrying around so much cash.

Her grief for Buggy surged again, catching her by surprise. She turned to the window, blind to the scenery, and struggled to stuff down her sorrow with a dose of anger. If this second stalker had killed Buggy—she sucked in a breath. Maybe she'd already killed him. When she'd pushed him, she hadn't expected him to move much at all, much less across the platform. But the tracks were only a few feet deep there. Not a fatal drop. He likely even had help from commuters who'd seen him fall.

The train to Philadelphia's 30th Street Station slowed as it approached Trenton, cutting through more woods and snowy fields than suburban neighborhoods. She remained alert for a tall blond man while she switched trains.

She took an aisle seat, ready to run for the exit, as the car filled with passengers. Two young women passed, talking rapidly in another language. A man rolled a suitcase through the aisle. A guy about her age dropped into the seat across the aisle. Vague familiarity niggled at her, and she moved to the window seat.

He leaned over and offered a crooked smile. "Hey."

Justine froze, pulling her bag closer.

"I'm Cayden, Quinn's brother."

She covered her face with a hand. This was wrong six ways to Sunday.

Cayden raised his voice over the noise of new passengers dragging luggage and slamming doors. "I'm not trying to be weird. Actually, thought it'd be weirder if I didn't say hi."

The exits were still open. But if she got off here, she'd have to wait for the next train. She swallowed. "Did Quinn send you after me?"

His leather jacket creaked against vinyl as he shifted toward her. "No, I—"

"So you happened to get on the same train to Philly as I did?"

"Nah, I just, you know." He threw up his hands. "Okay, he's worried about you, damn it. You walk the streets at night like you own the place."

"So he did send you."

That crooked smile again. "And what if he did?"

"Here's a shocker: I can take care of myself."

"You sound like my brother." Cayden leaned closer, elbows on knees, blocking the aisle. His dark-blond hair hung in his face. "Thinks he can handle everything on his own. One day something'll come along that he can't. I keep telling him, everybody needs somebody at some point."

"Am I supposed to need you right now?"

"People worrying about you is so irritating?"

"Now you sound like your brother."

"Don't tell him that. Look, it's just, he'd be upset if anything happened to you."

"What makes you think something's going to happen to me?"

He shuffled his feet, ran his hand through his hair. Like Quinn did when he was flustered. He seemed to share a stubborn gene with his brother too. Perhaps not much else though. Cayden was shorter than Quinn, hair and eyes lighter. Even the leather jacket was something Quinn never wore.

He looked around the car. "I don't know if you noticed," he said, "but there was someone following you. I wanted to make sure you were okay."

The man had survived then. Justine suppressed a shiver. She hadn't wanted to kill him, but she would have been satisfied with some major injuries to slow him down. "Did he get on this train?"

"No, he lost you before that. At the subway, I think."

"You mean he started in the subway."

"No, he started back by my brother's place. You had just left, I think."

Unease crawled through her, like she was looking at a picture too close to see the whole image. "So you've been following me because someone else was following me?"

Cayden shifted aside to let a woman pass. "I'd say I was tracking the guy following you."

"What did he look like?"

He shrugged, then moved to her side of the aisle, leaving one seat open between them. "On the short side, kind of thin, wears glasses, and a black-and-white cap. Some Greek soccer—rather, football team."

She hadn't lost her first stalker. "He was the only one you saw?"

"Um, he was the only one following you."

"You're as bad at lying as your brother is."

"He lied to you?"

She'd lied to him, and he hadn't bought it either. "Who else did you see following me?" A scratchy voice announced the train would leave soon.

"Nobody." He shrugged. His eyes searched for something else to look at. "Just some sort of ruckus on the platform at East Broadway. Then you were sailing up the stairs like the devil was after you."

A nest of butterflies hatched in her stomach. She hadn't noticed him among the passengers on the platform. But she'd been a bit distracted. "So the one tracking me from Quinn's place, you followed him to the station?"

"Yeah, but he never went into the subway. Was there somebody else on your tail?"

Whatever he'd seen, it was too much. She got up and squeezed past him.

"Where are you going?"

"You did what you came to do. You can go back to New York now."

"Are you sure no one's tracking you now?"

She caught her breath and glanced around the car, then stepped up to him. "What else did you see?"

His gaze slid away from her. "I told you, not much. Something had just happened. People were helping this guy who fell onto the tracks."

He wasn't telling her everything, but she didn't have time for lies. She headed for the door, stepping into an unoccupied row to let a passenger by.

Cayden blocked her way out of the row. "Quinn wants you to come back. He can help you."

"He can't help me. And neither can you."

"I can make sure you're not followed, that you're left alone."

"Or slow me down. How do I know anything you say is true?"

He opened his mouth, then shut it and shrugged a shoulder. "I guess you'll have to trust me?"

She rolled her eyes. "Let me pass."

The warning sound rang out, and the doors slammed shut. He gave her his half smile as the train lurched into motion. "I guess you're stuck with me."

She dropped onto her seat. "And so are you. So drop the grin and describe to me every moment of what you saw in the subway. Start at Quinn's house."

~ ~ ~

Philadelphia's train station was spacious and high ceilinged but not actually that large. Classical columns stood at attention at both ends of the main concourse, connected by an ornate coffered ceiling and tall windows. It felt empty with much fewer people hurrying toward their gates than passed through either Penn Station or Grand Central in New York.

It had been years since Justine had traveled to anywhere new where she knew nothing about her surroundings. She didn't even know where the cameras were. She tucked her hair into her hood. The gray midday light barely penetrated the tall smoked windows, leaving the waiting area in twilight. Maps and ticket-dispensing machines dotted the edges of the space. A small bank of pay phones lined a nearby wall. Dreadful Christmas music played over a speaker.

She had a call to make, but she had one more thing to handle first. "You can leave now."

Cayden paused beside her, hands in the pockets of his jeans. He'd refused to leave her side even after they'd arrived in Philadelphia. "And then what? You know anyone in this city?"

"I have someone to call. Your babysitting duties are over. Tell Quinn I'm fine."

His expression was unreadable. "I get it. You needed to get away. But you left town alone instead of turning to friends or family."

She turned away. "I have no family."

"Well then, your friends are your family, right? That's who you go to for help when . . . when you make mistakes you can't undo by yourself."

She glanced at him from the corner of her eye. "Is that Quinn's job, fixing your mistakes?"

He started to protest, then thought better of it. "I'm just saying, I could help make sure you get wherever you're going safely. And if there is trouble, you're not alone."

"You've given me no reason to trust you."

Cayden opened his mouth, then closed it.

"Exactly. We're done. Goodbye." Only yesterday Buggy had told her she was trusting too easily. Her throat tightened.

He rubbed at his stubbly jaw. "Whoever you're running from, you think they won't find you here? Let me help—"

"And help me get caught? No thanks. Adios."

He looked like he wanted to strangle her, but he'd get over it. "Fine. Do what you got to do," he said through gritted teeth. "Just one thing." He dug into his backpack. "Take this phone."

"No way. Those things can be tracked. You probably already gave my location away."

He wiped his hand over his face. He looked tired. "No, I haven't. I've disabled all that. For real. No one can track you with this. It's, like, an alternate phone I carry, if I need to, um—"

"You carry an alternate, uncrackable phone? That doesn't sound shady."

He rolled his eyes. "You do what you gotta do. I do what I gotta do." He tapped the screen, then typed with his thumbs. "If you want to feel better, shut it off. But you can contact me if you need to. If you feel like you're being followed. For anything, anytime."

"And you can call me."

He rolled his eyes. "Yes, I can call you and see if you're all right. I know. I'm a terrible person."

"Who else might call me?"

"No one. No one has that number except Quinn." He put his hands up as she tried to speak. "But he doesn't know you have it," he said slowly, as if explaining to a three-year-old. "So he's not going to call you on it. There won't be any calls from him. He hardly ever calls me." He grabbed her hand and placed the phone in it, closing her fingers around it, then closing his fingers around hers. "Please. Just in case."

She drew her hand from his and peered at the block of metal and plastic in her palm. It would be convenient. If he was telling the truth. "How do I know it can't be tracked?"

"I hacked it, okay? Don't worry about how."

"So how do I use it?"

Cayden looked at her like she'd said she had six toes on each foot. "Jesus, you're serious. It's not all that complicated. You've used a cordless landline?"

"Sure."

"Numbers are stored in the contacts. I just added my number. Quinn's home and cell are in there already. Look for the phone icon." Her expression must have told him how much his words meant to her. With a sigh, he took the phone and showed her the steps as he explained. "You'll figure it out."

"I guess so." Just holding the thing made her nervous. On the other hand, she'd avoided technology, kept entirely off the grid, and still she'd been found. Perhaps there now were ways to track her she was unaware of, that required more than avoiding security cameras and cell phones. "I have to go. And so do you."

Shaking his head with a dramatic sigh, he strolled off to the trains.

After making sure he didn't double back, Justine shut off the phone as Cayden had shown her, shoved it into her backpack, and headed for the phones she trusted.

She dug through her coat pockets until she found the card with the Philly number. Devon had called this Artie to update their IDs with current pictures once they decided to stay in New York City. Before that, her mom had contacted him after the September 11 attacks to build a stronger history into the fake identities he'd made for them when they'd first disappeared. Justine had never spoken to this person much less seen him face to face. Would he know who she was?

She took a seat on a bench in possibly one of the last public phones in existence and fished change out of a pocket. She stared at the card. If this didn't work, she didn't have a backup plan.

Dial and stop thinking. The line rang. First hurdle overcome.

It kept ringing. She got up and paced the one step the space allowed.

"Yes."

Second hurdle. She opened her mouth, but nothing came out.

"Speak up or I hang up."

"No, wait. I need to speak with Artie."

"What's the word?"

"Word? I haven't spoken to—"

"No password, no Artie."

"He didn't ask for a password six years ago."

"Lots changed in six years, darling. No word, no call. Gotta come in person."

"But—"

"No calls."

She started to say she didn't know where he was, but it didn't matter. A dial tone buzzed.

Justine slammed the phone down on the receiver. Then she picked it up and slammed it again. And again. Some guy who never met her had taken away her best chance at freedom. She held in the scream building inside her.

She plopped down on the tiny bench in the tiny booth and clutched at her hair, then flinched as her scalp wound pulled. What next? This was the plan, her only plan.

Her knee hit something soft. A frayed book dangled from a cord attached to the wall, half the pages missing. A phone book. Even rarer than a phone booth. She paged through it. Columns of businesses with their numbers, and blocks of ads in larger print.

A number caught her eye. But it wasn't an exact match. Only the first three digits were the same. A few pages later, those first three digits appeared in more ads. Different businesses. But two were on the same street. Another street repeated. More on the first street. She needed a map.

She ripped out the page and went to the middle of the concourse. Between two rows of benches like pews in a church stood a kiosk with a map of the station and one of Philadelphia. A red dot pinpointed the building's location. She searched in circles around the dot. After a few minutes, she found the street most of the businesses had listed as their address. And nearby was the other one that had repeated. She checked the page of ads and found another one with the matching first three digits. That street was in the same neighborhood.

Justine had a place to go.

15.

Quinn rummaged in the cupboards of his miniature kitchen for a snack bar. He hadn't been able to eat before Max had called him. A body had been found in the Delancey subway station. Maybe he should skip eating until he was done looking at dead bodies.

Sully jumped off the sofa and trotted to the door, tail wagging. "Now? You had your chance earlier—" As the German shepherd sniffed at the bottom, there was a knock, and he gave Quinn a doggy grin. Someone he knew. "Good boy, Sully. Earning your keep."

Quinn checked the peephole, and a chill went through him. He undid the chain and locks and opened the door. "What are you do—what happened?"

His brother's body was drawn taut, and there were lines between his brows Quinn rarely saw. "Hey. Got a minute?"

"I'm headed into work. Walk with me and tell me on the way?"

Cayden nodded, no smart answer, no swagger.

That was as much of a distress signal as he ever got from his brother. He left the door open as he got his coat. "I always tell you to call me before things get out of hand, Cay."

"I haven't done—" Cayden did a double take as Justine's cat came out of hiding. "When'd you get a cat? Sully approve?"

Quinn grabbed his keys and wallet. "Okay," he said in the doorway. "Sully, Cheetah, don't kill each other. Let's go, Cay." As he locked up, he added, "Sully's learning the new order of things. But it's not my cat." He started down the stairs. "It's Justine's."

"Justine dropped off her cat? When?"

"Last night."

As they exited the brownstone, Cayden muttered, "How did she know?"

"Know what?" Quinn's anxiety spiked.

"That she was going to have to leave."

He turned down Stanton, hunching into the wind. "She knew," he said, failing to keep the anger out of his voice. "Wouldn't say a word about it, but I could see it all over her face."

"She didn't plan this morning, I'm telling you."

"What are you getting at?"

Cayden sighed. "She kind of got into it with somebody in the subway this morning. Over at East Broadway."

"What do you mean, 'got into it'?"

They skirted around a woman carrying groceries, silent for half a block. "Justine pushed somebody onto the tracks."

"What? Cay, Justine would not push anyone onto the tracks. Quit messing around."

"Dude, I wish I was."

Quinn stopped, his jaw clenched. The snow was falling more heavily, and a few flakes caught in Cayden's hair. "Then you didn't see things right. She wouldn't do that." He stopped at the corner. "I'm going to hop into the deli and order a sandwich. Want anything?"

Cayden shook his head and followed in silence until Quinn had ordered, then continued in a low voice, "Technically, you're right. She didn't push him." He paused as a couple passed them in the narrow aisle. "But he still went flying off the platform."

Quinn glared at his brother while waiting for his sandwich, and continued glaring as he paid. Once out of the deli, he slipped his dinner into a pocket and rounded on him. "What the hell are you talking about?"

"You ever seen her do some weird shit?"

He ignored the quiver in his stomach and started down the street until there was no one close enough to overhear them. "Weird how?"

"Like that," he said, pointing at him. "Whatever made you make that face, that's what I mean. Did she—wait. You said she saved your life. Did she, like, push someone out of the way, even though she was too far?"

His brother's arm stretched out in front of him much the way Justine's had that night in the park. He swallowed. "Not exactly," he said as he waited for traffic to pass at the corner.

"Yeah, okay, whatever. Look, let's not waste time. How long have you guys been together?"

"Almost six months." He thought he'd figured her out, gotten through that wall she'd put up. Now he wasn't sure of anything.

"So you never noticed something, you know, different about her?" Quinn crossed the street in silence. "I'll take that as a yes," Cayden continued. "Thing is, somebody else has too. This person in the subway, whatever he wants with her, she wasn't having any of it. She pushed him to get away from him."

Somebody coming after Justine explained a lot, but not enough. "And how did you happen to see all this?" Cayden didn't offer an answer. "I don't have all day, Cay."

His brother sighed. "I was on my way here earlier today. I saw Justine leave your place, and somebody was following her."

"He followed her from my place?"

"Actually, this was another guy."

He stopped in the middle of the sidewalk. "You're saying two men are following her?" He wiped his face with a gloved hand. He felt like he was running through sand to keep up with her. Or maybe that was Justine slipping away from him. "What haven't you told me?"

Cayden checked behind him. "I'm telling you what I can."

"What you can?" He stepped closer to him. "Tell me everything."

Cayden took a step back. "Dude, look, I'm trying to help. Why're you getting bent out of shape?"

He closed his eyes, took a breath, and eased back a step. "Listen, Justine's in trouble. I want to help her. But acting on incomplete information leads to mistakes."

His brother stuck his hands in his pockets. "Look up Demetri Kalakos." His eyes tracked passing cars as he described the man. "You should find plenty."

"And who is this?"

"He was following Justine from your place."

"The one she allegedly pushed?"

Cayden heaved a sigh and ran his hand through his hair. Quinn forced himself to keep quiet. "No, that was . . . his name is . . ." He paused. "Lawrence Hollister." He released a breath as if relieved to get the name off his lips. "He's the owner of NextLevel Industries. Not sure what you'll find on him."

"NextLevel Industries? What kind of company is that?"

"Biotech, mostly software."

A chill ran down Quinn's spine. He took hold of Cayden's arm. "Cay, how do you know so much about this?"

Cayden inspected his feet. "I work with them. Dr. Hollister's my boss. I work with Kalakos."

Quinn leaned over him. "You work with people going after Justine? And you're just mentioning this now?" He seized his brother's coat collar and shoved him into the brick wall behind him. "I kept telling you, one day you're going to find yourself in too deep. All this time, you were already knee deep in shit. What kind of place is this? Who are they? And what do you do for them?"

"Hold up, hold up, will you—" He squirmed out of Quinn's grip. "Chill, Q. Were you not listening? I said I'll tell you what I can. The rest—" He shook his head. "That's all I can say, man."

"The hell that's—"

"I've heard it all already, okay? I'm swimming in shit. Got it. But that doesn't mean I'm involved."

Quinn took a breath. When he was sure he could speak in a normal tone, he asked, "Do you know why this doctor is after her?"

"I just told you I'm not involved. That means I don't know." Cayden lowered his voice. "You asked me to look out for her. When I saw Kos following her, I wanted to be sure she was okay."

He looked his brother over. He seemed to be telling the truth. At least, most of it. "So this Dr. Hollister is the owner of this company? Like a venture capital type?"

"Don't think so. Mainly, he's a scientist. Directs our projects, but has some other projects we don't work on."

"And the other one?"

"Kos? He's a coder, works on the software side of things. And other stuff."

Quinn had some research to do then.

"Q, be careful where you poke around. Seems like Hollister's got connections to the Defense Department or something."

The flutter in his stomach returned. He ran a hand through his hair, already wet with snow. "This was all this morning? You couldn't have told me earlier?"

"I just got back."

"From?"

Cayden scanned the street and the sidewalk, anywhere but Quinn. "After all that went down, she bolted. Hopped on a train to Penn Station, took another to Philly."

"Philly? As in Philadelphia? Why didn't you call me?"

He threw up his hands. "No time. I felt like—whatever. I tried to get her to come back, let me help, something. But in the stubborn department, she puts us both to shame. She wanted no help and basically sent me home."

"So she's in Philly?" At least he knew where she was.

"Last I saw her. No clue what her plan was."

"And you just left her there?"

"What the hell was I supposed to do? Drag her back to New York?"

His full day was now overflowing. "Did she give you any way to get in contact with her?"

"I gave her my phone. It's—never mind. I told her no one would call her on it, so she probably won't answer, if she even kept it on."

"I'm surprised she took it. She refuses to carry a phone. I mean, I know they're tracking our every move—heard it all. She takes paranoid to another level, so I guess it shouldn't surprise me." He shook his head. "So since this morning, you been to Philly and back?"

"And going in to work now."

"Is that phone the number I have?"

Cayden nodded.

"I'll try calling, in case she left it on. Don't know how late I'll be working, but call me later. There's got to be something we can do."

Cayden looked surprised. Perhaps asking for his help had been a good idea after all. "Dude, maybe waiting till tonight isn't a great idea. I mean, she could be who knows where by then. Just saying."

"You're right. But I've got a crime scene to get to. I can't take a drive to Philly."

His brother watched traffic pass, then turned to him. "I'll go."

Quinn paused at the corner before turning on Pitt Street. "I thought you were going to work."

"I should have tried harder to convince her to come back. I've got to check in at work, but if I can put off some things till tomorrow, I'll get back on the train. If I can find her, I'll convince her to come back with me."

Something eased in Quinn's chest. "Thanks, Cay. I don't care what you have to promise her. Bring her back. Please."

~ ~ ~

Quinn sipped his coffee as he and Max returned to the entrance to the Delancey subway station. The snow had let up but left a soupy slush on the stairs. Most pedestrians turned around when they saw the yellow crime scene tape, to find another way into the subway. A small group gathered to watch investigators come and go, as interested in them as in the situation below.

Cayden's news was still sinking in. Whatever Justine had done to save Quinn's life, people wanted a piece of her for it. He still had no way to help her. He hadn't heard anything from Cayden, and his calls to the phone Justine now had went straight to voicemail.

He paused before heading down the steps, reluctant to mix his coffee with a crime scene. "I'll give you points for getting me out of the station, Max." He stretched out his left arm, the ache in his bicep more tolerable than the sling.

"You looked like you were gonna pop," Max said. "But there's not much to work with here. No witnesses. Preliminary COD may be strangulation, but the guy smelled like he was already pickled."

"If it's who I think it is, the man goes by the name Buggy. He's been on the street a long time. And I know someone who brings him food." No way could he bring Justine into this case.

Max shook his head. "Hard to believe no one noticed a dead body as they got on the train." Technicians emerged from the station, carrying their equipment. "Maybe you can track down that good Samaritan, see when they last saw him."

"Yeah, I'll try that." The guy hadn't been dead twelve hours. Justine had still been at his place. He hoped Cayden was correct that he'd seen Justine at East Broadway and not at Delancey. If she'd run because she'd seen the murderer or the victim, this was about to get messy. He needed to make sure Cayden hadn't left anything out of his story.

He checked the growing crowd milling around the entrance. A man in a hooded coat had not moved from the barrier that kept him from the scene.

"We might have something else to check out," Max said. "A victim from a case next door in the Ninth Precinct. Buddy of mine heard we had a victim with a missing prosthesis. He had a similar case a few months ago."

Quinn nodded, an eye on the man in the hood. "That's more than what we've got."

"These artificial limbs must do something special, the kind of thing someone wants nobody to know about."

"Maybe it's bionic," Quinn said, "like the six-million-dollar man." His partner gave him a blank look. "You know, that old show about the bionic man? Guy had implants made him super fast and strong? They have reruns on some channel at night."

"I'm afraid my TV time is determined by the three-year-old. She's the ruler of the house, that's for sure."

"Okay, no reruns for you." Quinn put a hand on Max's shoulder, looking into his coffee. "That guy to your left look familiar? Glasses, black coat with a hood."

Slowly, Max scanned the area. "Afraid not. Got a feeling?"

The man sensed their scrutiny and turned away. The familiarity nagged at Quinn, and he started after him, tossing his cup into a garbage can. Max followed as Quinn weaved through the onlookers.

Halfway down the block, the hooded man got into a car. Quinn called out the license plate numbers.

Max had his phone out at once and scribbled on the screen with his finger. "Got it." He repeated the numbers. "You've seen him before?"

"Could be." They returned to their car, and Quinn logged on to the laptop in the console. He brought up the National Crime Information Center database and soon had a mug shot on the screen. "Will you look at that."

"Someone you know?"

"It was dark that night, but I think this is the asshole who shot me."

"The guy who shot you is tailing you now?"

"Looks like it." The face was somewhat familiar, but the name was even more so. "His name is Demetri Kalakos." The coder who worked with Cayden. His brother had forgotten to tell him something after all.

16.

Justine gathered up the remains of her meager meal and left the burger place that made her miss the diner. The temperature had dropped with sunset, and now the wind was picking up. Tugging her hood lower and tightening her scarf, she set out into the bewildering unknown territory of Philadelphia.

After reviewing maps of the city at a library, she had briefly tried a search of records. She'd even called the Department of Motor Vehicles and asked for Artie, since her mom had referred to him as the DMV. After that came up empty, she headed west, trudging through the snow until she was too hungry and cold. Now she resumed her walk down Lancaster Avenue, a wide street where businesses alternated with clusters of three-story homes.

When the business district changed over to mostly residential, she turned southish until she hit Fifty-Second Street, bright with lights from furniture stores, restaurants, nail salons, and barbers. She weaved around people leaving shops or boarding buses until she found those first three digits on a store's awning announcing the business's phone number. After another block, she found that set of numbers a few more times. She was in the right neighborhood.

After another frigid half hour weaving between side streets and Fifty-Second, she stopped at a two-story corner building. Only the neon beer signs in the windows covered in grating announced it as a bar. A blue sign for a pay phone stuck out from the facade. She hadn't seen one of those since she left the train station. She ducked inside.

The small interior was dark. Though it was early in the evening, a good number of people sat at the few square tables in groups of two or three. On the right a man clung to a pale beer at the bar, which stretched the width of the room. Directly across the entrance, a black pay phone hung from the wall.

Justine went straight to the phone. To her surprise, she heard a dial tone. She stuffed a few coins in the slot and punched in the number. It rang a half dozen times before she hung up and tried again. Nothing.

Her fingers were numb. Her nose started to run. She didn't have time to waste, but the warmth of the place was irresistible. She took a seat on a barstool, rubbing her hands together.

The bartender, an older African American woman, lumbered over at once. "Something to drink?" she asked without looking up as she wiped the counter.

She had to pay the price of admission. "Any coffee?" How much could coffee be?

The bartender gave her a glance. "I can make some." After putting up a pot to brew, she refilled a drink for a man at the end of the bar.

Justine loosened her scarf. She'd thought she was getting closer. But she was still looking for someone with only a first name. She needed to narrow her search.

The bartender set a steaming mug on a napkin in front of her with a small carton of milk. She slid over a container of sugar. "Anything else?"

Justine shook her head and put a precious dollar on the counter, hoping it was enough. The mug was almost too hot to touch, and her chilled fingers savored the heat. The napkin had the business's name and phone number printed on it. And there it was: the same first three digits. This had to be the right area.

"Are you sure, hon?" She paused her cleaning to eye Justine.

She swallowed. "Know anyone named Artie?"

"Artie who? He live around here?"

"I think so."

"You think so?" Her eyebrow went up. "No last name or nothing? You better ask Pokey." She twitched her chin toward the man at the end of the bar. "He knows everybody."

The guy she'd referred to had spent more of his time at that stool than not. His large hands clutched his glass, his eyes on the TV behind the bar. His skin was dark, his hair a mixture of black, gray, and white.

She stared into her coffee. Asking anyone for help felt like failure. And there wasn't much she could say without singling herself out.

"Hey, hon, you look like you need a friend."

Justine's skin crawled as she looked up to find a bearded man with a wool cap and cigarette breath standing too close to her. His face was blotchy, his cheeks red with veins. She edged away. "I don't need anything. Goodbye."

"Hey, no need to be nasty. Just trying to help you out. I could buy you something better 'n coffee. Better 'n sitting here all alone."

"Or you can go away."

Instead, the man moved closer. "You could try being a little nicer, missy."

She resisted leaning back further. "Why would I do that?"

"'Cause if you don't, I might get mad." He laid his hand on her arm. "You wouldn't want to do that, now."

"I might just do that," she said with a smile. "Because then I get to get mad. Like I will if you don't get your hand off me." She leaned into his grizzled face and noxious breath. "And you will not like that."

He gave a short chuckle. "You're trying to be big and bad, but you're just a little thing." He squeezed her arm.

"And yet I could toss you across this room without lifting a finger." If she wanted to attract attention. Or she could try her new thing. She tried not to smile too much.

The man sputtered and laughed, then he shook her. "That was rude."

She pulled back, but he tightened his fingers around her arm until it was painful through her coat. She would have loved to give the creep a good slap. But that would get her nowhere. She kept her hand raised as he held on to her, concentrating on heat and fire, on pushing forward without pushing him.

He pulled her toward him. "You need to learn to be nice." He frowned, but his hold on her didn't loosen. He leaned back until his arm was stretched out straight. He tugged her arm. "What are you doing?"

"I'm just standing here." She sharpened her focus, and her palm began to sweat.

He eyed her hand, his fingers tightening their grip. Finally, he flinched and let go of her to move away. He touched his chin. "What are you, a witch or something?"

She rolled her eyes. "Right. I'm a witch. I forgot to say." She relaxed her arm, resisting the urge to shake out her hand.

He glanced at the bartender and other patrons behind him, then with his eyes on Justine, returned muttering to his table and his laughing buddies.

While that was satisfying, she was wasting time. She grabbed her coffee and moved to the stool next to the man called Pokey. "The bartender says you know everyone, so I should talk to you. I'm looking for a guy named Artie. Lives around here somewhere."

After a few seconds, Pokey turned to Justine, looked her up and down, and turned back to the TV. After another minute, he answered without turning from the TV. "You just walking around asking random people if they know a guy named Artie?" He chuckled. "Might as well go down the street calling out his name. What's he look like? Got a last name?"

She fiddled with her mug. "I haven't seen him in a while, so I can't really say. I spoke to him on the phone. He hung up before telling me where he lived."

Pokey scratched his patchy beard, took a sip of his beer, and laughed some more. "If he forgot to give you his address, I don't think he really wants to see you ."

This was going nowhere. "He's the only one who can help me."

Pokey eyed her for a long moment. "Doesn't mean he wants to help you. What sort of business he into?"

That was more information than she wanted to part with. But she'd run into walls everywhere else. "He's ... he's like a DMV." This felt like peeling off clothes in front of a stranger.

"A DMV?"

"He's somebody you go to when—when you need to start over." Her heart skipped a beat. That was uncomfortably close to the truth. She sipped her coffee.

"Now we're getting somewhere. That's someone you might walk through snow and cold to find. Might know somebody in that line of work. Not sure he goes by Artie. But maybe he can help you."

"Where?"

"I'm getting to that, young lady. Hold your horses."

Justine shut her mouth and willed herself to be patient.

"This guy, maybe look for him on Clement. You know that street?"

"No."

"That's right. You're not from around here, are you? Okay, let me show you." He grabbed a napkin, pulled one of several pens sticking out of his shirt pocket, and drew a rough map of the surrounding streets. He added a couple of names and circled a spot in a corner of the napkin. "Once you find Clement, you can start asking around. Someone should know something."

Her heart raced. "Thanks." Getting directions from a stranger, in a strange city. Apparently, there were worse things.

He nodded solemnly. "Be careful out there. It's not real easy on these streets. Watch your back."

"I will. Thank you." If she got this right, she wouldn't need anyone's help again.

~ ~ ~

Outside the bar, Justine breathed deeply, the air crisp and fresh after taking in the fog of cigarette breath and stale beer. She smoothed out the napkin, its aid more than she'd hoped for when she'd gone into the bar. Following the sketched map, she turned onto a narrow side street lined with three-story homes, pale-yellow windows lined with white or colored twinkling lights. Trees stood stark in their coats of snow on tiny patches of grass that passed for yards, one with a squishy, leaning snowman. A woman brushed snow off an older-model car. A couple laden with grocery bags climbed the steps to their house.

She turned where the napkin drawing seemed to say go left. A larger apartment building replaced smaller homes. Across the street, shouting and banging echoed from behind a building. Justine's shoulders tensed as she tried to ignore the sounds of struggle. She could not come to anyone's rescue tonight.

Despite the activity, the streets seemed deathly quiet without the hum of traffic. In New York, the shadows had been more comforting than the light of homes or businesses. Here, neither light nor dark held safety or solace.

Pokey's map wasn't entirely accurate, but she managed to find Clement Street. Some of the streetlights were out. It started snowing again, but a small group of young men remained on the steps of a narrow three-story building, bundled in layers of jackets and sweatshirts. They quieted their chatter as Justine passed.

She kept her head down, sharply aware she was a stranger to the neighborhood. These kids probably saw a lot from their perch and knew all the familiar faces.

She stopped in the middle of the sidewalk and returned to the group. They were younger than she'd thought, teenagers. "Hey, any of you know Artie?"

They turned to her as one, then threw their questions at her all at once.

"Who are you?"

"Where you from?"

"Yeah, not from around here."

"Nope," Justine answered, "not from anywhere near here. I was told Artie lived somewhere nearby."

"You just get straight to the point, don't you? How about a hello, how ya doing?"

"What you need him for, babe? You got me."

"I can give you whatever you need."

She rolled her eyes. "Is that a no then?"

"Maybe, maybe not. What do we get for it?"

She sighed, her breath fogging the air. "So what about anyone who goes by DMV or acts like one?"

They broke into laughter, smacking each other and shaking their heads. Except one boy seated on the top step. He leaned forward, eyeing her. "Things are serious if you need a guy like that." He might have been older than his friends. It was hard to tell under the streetlight.

"Pretty serious, yeah. You know where I can find him?"

"Not really. Heard of him. That's it."

Behind the building, someone shouted.

"Am I in the right area?" she asked.

He shrugged. More yelling from the back.

"What's he look like?"

The boy shrugged again while the others continued their joking. "If it's who I think it is, he's kind of a big guy, not someone you're gonna mess with, know what I mean?"

"How about some details? So I'm sure we're talking about the same person."

"Well, he's got kinda rocker hair, you know, long, in a ponytail and shit. He's sorta light skinned, know what I mean? Like, he's probably Latino or something. Can't really tell."

"That sounds like him." She hoped. She'd never seen Artie. But maybe she'd just gotten a description.

The shouting grew louder, then quick, light footsteps sounded up the narrow path between buildings. A kid of about twelve or thirteen darted onto the sidewalk. A cluster of teenagers ran after him. The fastest of them tackled the kid halfway down the block. He cried out in a high-pitched yell. The pack descended on the kid, kicking and punching, slipping on wet grass and snow.

"Hey, you gotta mind your own business around here," the kid said to Justine. "Better for your own health. Some things you can't do nothing about."

She tore her eyes from the fight. This was no time to worry about anyone else. But he was just a kid. Outnumbered and outsized, he had no chance.

If she didn't get to Artie, she'd have no chance. "So where'd you see this guy who might be Artie?"

The boy waved his hand. "On the street."

A tall kid in a wool cap left the brawl to pull something from the trunk of a car. He slapped an aluminum baseball bat against his palm.

Her mom had often reminded her of her father's hopes that she would put her ability to good use. Yet when her brother had needed her, when Buggy had been in trouble, she'd failed to protect them.

She took a step toward the fight.

"You're just bringing yourself trouble."

No shit, Sherlock. How'd you think I got here?

It was dark, but not dark enough. She moved into the street and crouched alongside an old sedan covered in snow. The guys on the steps couldn't see her, but behind her, five or six people watched from a front yard across the street. She drew her hood lower and tucked in her hair.

The teenagers yelled about stealing and teaching a lesson. The boy raised an arm in defense. He tried to throw a few punches back or squirm out of the way, but he only made things worse.

The tall teen in the wool cap swung the bat high and brought it down fast. The boy cried out, and the guy hit him again. They were going to put him in the hospital or worse.

Justine stretched out her arm, then paused. The bat was aluminum. She was closer than she had been the other night. She brought up her hand and visualized the bat glowing red with heat, hoping this bully would burn his hand.

The attacker stepped away, tossing his weapon from hand to hand. She took advantage of the moment and thrust her arm forward on his next toss with a mental shove. It jerked back as if pulled on a string, bouncing on the sidewalk with a clang.

Silence fell over the group, until one of them laughed.

The puzzled look from the one handing out the beating was worth this detour. That never got old.

His buddy elbowed him. "What the hell, Masher?"

Another guy snickered. "Yeah, you dropped something."

Masher swiped the bat from the ground. "I didn't drop it."

While all eyes were on Masher, the boy inched away and started to stand, holding his side, his jacket muddy and wet. Justine scurried around the vehicle, closer to him.

"Hey, punk, where you think you're going?"

Two boys took hold of the kid's arms to halt his escape. Masher looked up, and his eyes fell on Justine. "What are you looking at?" The group followed his gaze.

Their leader approached her, tapping his weapon against his leg. "You need to get going, girl."

She rose from her crouch and stepped back onto the sidewalk. She clamped her mouth shut to keep from saying something stupid, but then said, "I think he's learned his lesson." Apparently her mouth had stopped taking orders from her brain.

Masher shrieked with laughter, then grew serious. "I take care of my business. You mind yours."

A kid whistled. "Bring her over here. We'll take good care of her."

She kept her eyes on Masher and off the weapon. His frown turned into a scowl when she didn't look away.

She was being reckless. She had no idea what street she could run down and get lost in. She wasn't aware of when the next cop would drive by or even if the area was patrolled. They were on a sidewalk with plenty of witnesses. This wasn't what she was here for.

But if she walked away now, the boy might not. Another body lying on the ground she could have saved.

She backed up until she bumped into the car. Her retreat satisfied Masher. He nodded, pointed his weapon at her as a final word, and turned back to his crew. "Now where were we?" His friends looked among themselves, then the bat, then closed in.

She ducked behind the car. There was no yelling this time. They did their work quietly. As did Justine.

When the bat flew out of his hands again, Masher walked over to the piece of aluminum in the snow and shoved it with his toe, while the rest speculated. He looked up and down the street, then came around the car and yanked Justine up by the arm. "What did you do?"

She tugged at his iron grip. "What do you think I did from here?"

He held her a moment longer, then shoved her away. A few more gawkers gathered on steps a few houses down, and a couple of people had come into the street. A girl held a phone in front of her, recording the fight. Justine slid between cars, turning her face from the camera. She was exposed but should be nearly invisible in her dark clothing.

The others cackled. "Masher's scared of a piece of aluminum. Thinks it's gonna smack him back." One kid dared another to pick up the bat.

"Hey, leave that thing, will ya? That shit's possessed."

Masher grabbed the bat from the one who'd picked it up. He sauntered over and got in the face of the guy who taunted him. "Maybe it's gonna smack you instead."

As everyone tensed, light flooded the sidewalk. White from headlights. Blue and red from the top of the police car.

The crowd vanished.

Justine's heart leapt into her throat, and she broke into a run. Her feet felt as if they were sinking into mud. She switched directions to follow one of the boys. They would know the best way out. She ran between two buildings and skidded as she crashed into a gate.

As she stuck a shoe in a chain link of the fence, the passage brightened. "Turn around slowly. Hands out at your sides."

Not an option. She put another toe between links, grasped the fencing with shaking hands, and started to climb.

Footsteps crunched on gritty snow. The cop raised his voice. "Stop where you are! Turn around. Drop any weapons you have."

She swung a leg over the gate as one cop grasped her shoulder. Struggling to breathe, she strained against his grip and tried to swing her other leg over, while keeping her face turned from the officers. The second cop grabbed her calf.

After all her father had given up to make sure she lived free, she could not screw up. A police station would be a fast track to a lab.

She tugged at her leg, leaning toward the freedom side of the gate. She gulped for air but felt like she was suffocating.

"Calm yourself. You're not going anywhere. Climb down and put your hands where we can see them."

Desperate, she twisted toward them and thrust out a hand with a mental push. The officer holding her leg leaned back. He frowned, then pressed forward. She sagged. She was too tired.

Her heart hammered and she tried to breathe. She kicked, and her foot hit something soft.

One of the officers grunted. The cop holding her shoulders tightened his grip. "Now you're coming down to the station. Come on. Don't make this harder than it has to be."

She clutched the fence as the cop pulled her back to his side. She didn't have the leverage or the strength to escape his grip, even if she threw her full weight over the fence.

She panted as she lost her grip on the fence. This could not happen.

The policeman pulled her off the fence and drew one of her arms behind her, then the other. Something hard wrapped around her wrists, cutting into the skin.

This was happening.

17.

Hollister buttoned up his wool coat as he shifted deeper into the doorway of the apartment building on Grand Street, still aching from the astonishing demonstration he'd gotten that morning. His right hand returned to his pocket to clutch the tube containing the precious scrap he'd come away with. The hostility she had shown still shocked him. That shock had allowed her to slip through his fingers.

He had spent years searching databases, using facial recognition, following a trail he hoped would lead to Lizzie. Yet in a matter of weeks, after he'd tasked Kalakos with monitoring an investigation into a body that should have never been found, the man had discovered her working as a waitress. *A waitress.*

Hollister kept his focus across the street, where Kalakos sat at the counter of an inconsequential diner with a cup of coffee. Each time the waitress passed, he said something, but received little more than a frown in response.

When the waitress grabbed a plastic bag bulging with containers and headed out the door, Kalakos slapped some money on the counter and followed her out. He reached the sidewalk as the woman shut the wrought iron gate to a courtyard beside the building, and he trailed her inside.

Hollister crossed the street between passing cars and slipped through the entrance. The younger man had made the right decision in calling him after discovering Lizzie's place of work. But he still might make mistakes that could cost Hollister this lead.

In the soft glow of tree trunks wrapped in white lights, Kalakos called out to the waitress.

She squinted. "Who—Did you not hear me? I'm not telling you jack. You're lying, anyway." She turned and continued toward the entrance to the next building.

Hollister scowled and stepped closer as Kalakos let the young woman walk away from him. Finally, Kalakos pulled her around by the arm.

"What is wrong with you?" the woman said. "You ask me about someone without even a name? You're probably the one she was all worked up about."

"I don't think so. But I need to find her."

"Can't help you. Bye." She pulled on her arm to leave.

"Nita, Nita. You work with her. You are her friend. You have an idea where she goes when she leaves, maybe where she lives."

Nita pulled away, the first whispers of fear crossing her face. "I don't, okay? She doesn't tell me much. I don't even know if she thinks of me as a friend. She doesn't seem to have any."

Kalakos's mouth screwed up into a snarl. "Don't lie to me." His arm shot out and struck her across the face.

Nita's head snapped around. Her bag fell to the ground and split open. She stumbled back, wide eyed, a hand cradling her cheek. "What the fuck?" Her voice rose a notch as she glowered at him. "You want me to make shit up? I can't tell you what I don't know. Look, she's just a girl like me, waiting tables. What the hell do you want with her?"

"She's not just a girl. Trust me. She's got people looking for her. Don't tell me you don't know." His hand came up again, but her reflexes were on alert, and he only caught the side of her head. She pushed him, but he grabbed her wrist and the collar of her coat. She tried to peel his fingers open, but he held on. Panic bloomed in her eyes.

Hollister sighed as he approached the two. "Kalakos, it appears you need some lessons on information gathering."

Kalakos frowned at Hollister but didn't let go of her. "I told you I can handle this."

"You're not going to frighten the answers out of this woman." Nita's face was red, and she kicked at his legs as she struggled in his grip.

"You have a better way to get this bitch to talk?"

Hollister took measured steps toward the waitress and kept his voice calm. "I am searching for the woman who works with you. Anything you can tell me will help, even if it doesn't seem important."

She tugged at Kalakos's grasp on her coat until he released her with a huff. With shaking hands, she straightened her clothes and pushed strands of hair off her face. "I don't know anything." Panting, she bent down to pick up her package. A container of food had spilled onto the ground.

"Has she ever said anything that concerned you?"

The woman moved closer to him, but her eyes remained on Kalakos.

Hollister added, "She may be in trouble. You can help her by helping me."

She held the bag in front of her, eying each of them. "Okay, look, she was here last night, and she was real spooked." Her voice trembled. "I was sure she was taking off. But she didn't say where she was going or for how long."

"What did she say, exactly?" Hollister said.

Pulling her jacket closed, she looked past Hollister then behind her. They were alone in the courtyard. "She was trying to get me to take her cat. I couldn't, but a customer said he would."

"Who was the customer?"

"A friend, a regular. A cop, by the way." She glared at Kalakos.

He pointed a finger in her face. "You say she has no friends. Now she has one? You're still lying."

"He's as close to a friend as she's got, okay? Otherwise, she keeps to herself mostly."

"And maybe," Kalakos said, "they're more than friends?"

"Might this friend know her whereabouts tonight?" Hollister took another step toward her, forcing her to look up into his face. "It is vital that I find her."

Nita swallowed and edge back. "I have no idea. You'll have to ask him."

"And where might I find him?"

"He's a cop." She emphasized the last word like it mattered. "So go ask some cops. What more do you want from me?"

Kalakos patted her cheek. She flinched. "Thank you, honey. You've been very helpful."

Hollister nodded to Kalakos.

He nodded in return. "Will do." And Kalakos headed to the street.

Hollister turned to Nita. "You have been helpful. Lizzie needs guidance and assistance, and I can provide them for her."

"Wait, who's Lizzie?"

Hollister straightened. Behind him, Kalakos stopped at the gate.

"He asked about a red-haired woman. The other waitress has strawberry-blond hair, but that was close, so I thought that was who he meant. But her name's Justine. She's not who you're looking for." Her shoulders relaxed.

Excellent.

"So she's the wrong person, right?"

Hollister smiled. "Thank you for that. Don't look so worried. I only want to help her."

"But that's not the same person."

"My colleague was right about one thing. She's not just a girl."

~ ~ ~

Justine paced inside the tiny rectangular holding cell, too panicked to sit on the wooden bench. The scuffed white walls seemed to close in, threatening suffocation. Despite her earlier exhaustion, her limbs felt alight with fire. But too many obstacles stood between her and the outside to try anything.

A uniformed officer unlocked the door, followed by another. They'd taken the plastic ties off her wrists, taken her fingerprints, her picture, and her ID. And they'd taken her anonymity with them.

"Is this your only ID?" the first officer asked. She held a printed page in her hand.

Justine almost couldn't hear the woman over the pounding of her heart. Her mouth hung open, and she managed a nod.

"There's no current information connected with this identification. And it has an Albany address. You said you live in New York City."

Her mind had apparently taken off without the rest of her. Again, she nodded.

"So do you have an ID with a New York address, perhaps?" the officer said, her hand on her hip.

"No," she croaked. Her throat was almost too tight to speak. "That's my only ID."

"Fine. A record was created attaching this ID to your mug shot and prints. How about a local address?"

She swallowed and took a breath to keep her voice from shaking. "I'm visiting."

"You have a contact here?"

Anything she told them would be attached to her name in the system. And she had little to give the officer that would satisfy her.

"It's not a trick question. Who are you meeting while you're in Philadelphia?"

"Is that really something you need to know?"

The cop looked too tired to be annoyed. "You've been arrested. I need to know everything."

"I wasn't part of the fight. Just at the wrong place at the wrong time." She put her hands in her now empty pockets.

The woman was unfazed. "How long will you be in town?"

"Didn't really plan that far ahead."

"Listen, cooperation is your fastest ticket out of here."

She closed her eyes. She needed that fast ticket before some man in black showed up to make her disappear. "His name is Artie."

The woman wrote on the paper. "Artie what?" She tried to answer, but her mouth simply gaped like a fish gasping for air. "You don't know your friend's last name?"

Justine started to tell her it was complicated, but that wasn't true. "He's a family friend. I don't have anyone else to go to."

The officer sighed and rubbed her eyes. "Without any more information, you'll be charged a fine and released."

"I don't have much money."

"It'll be a couple hundred dollars. Can your friend help you with that?"

Justine went back to pacing. Two hundred bucks. She wouldn't get anything from Artie if she had no money. But she wouldn't find him if she was stuck in a cell.

"If you can't swing the fine, then we'll give you a date to appear in court. But you've got to identify someone in the area you can stay with until your appearance date. Those are your choices."

The second officer's radio squelched. He answered and gestured to the first. She nodded and they left, shutting the metal door with a bang.

Justine sat on the bench, barely aware of the whir of a distant printer or the aroma of stale coffee. She shivered at the clang of a metal gate somewhere nearby.

Maybe she'd had overreacted. She didn't know what the man in the subway wanted from her, except that he thought she could do more with her life. Would it be so terrible to find out what he had in mind? She could stop running, stop hiding. On the other hand, if he was part of the government, she could end up a prisoner for the remainder of her life.

Finally, the officer returned with a clipboard in hand. "You're a lucky gal. Your friend showed up, vouching that you'll be in the neighborhood for the near future. And he had some cash. Follow me, and we'll return your belongings. Then you'll be free to go."

She fought to keep her face composed as she went through the short list of people who knew she was in this city. Had Cayden come back? Maybe he'd told Quinn. Or maybe Cayden's phone was trackable after all. Had the blond man tracked her down? Or had someone else? "What does he look like?"

"You don't know that either?"

"I didn't expect Artie to find me here."

"Apparently he knew where to look," the cop said with a raised eyebrow.

She led Justine out of holding to a room with a desk and computer. Someone appeared with her backpack, money and ID, the keys, and a wad of paper. Sheepishly, she shoved the wad of receipts into her pocket. She'd rather walk around with them than let the police comb through them for information. While another officer sat at the computer and typed, she checked the contents of the bag and counted the cash.

She pulled up her hood and buttoned her coat as he brought her to another room. In a row of chairs, a woman wearing a parka, hat, and scarf sipped from a Styrofoam cup, and a man in a sweater typed on a laptop. A large man in a puffy jacket and a wool hat sat with his head down.

All eyes turned to Justine as she entered. The woman went back to her drink at once. The man typing glanced up, then returned to his work. The man in the puffy coat stood, eyes widening. After the smallest hesitation, he flashed a wide smile. "There you are. Got yourself into trouble real quick, huh?" He nodded to the officer at her side. "Thank you, sir."

"This the person you're here to see?"

The broad-shouldered man roughly matched the boy's description, though he was older than she'd expected. Whether he was Artie or not, he was her way out of here. "Yes."

18.

Justine exited the police station into bitter cold. Someone had brushed the snow from the entrance and salted the sidewalk, but it had continued snowing, and a thin layer coated the ground. She stepped back to avoid a woman walking by, and the woman sidestepped her to avoid the collision. Justine frowned and tugged her hood lower.

She followed the man-who-was-probably-Artie down the well-lit street in silence. With each step away from the station, her shoulders loosened.

As they turned the corner, he stopped. "Pull down your hood."

A chill went through her, but she slid the hood off her head.

Artie stroked his chin as he looked her over. "I'll be damned. It is you."

His recognition was both comforting and disturbing. "You vouched for me without knowing who I was?"

"To find out who was looking for me? You bet. Did not expect to see your face in there." He started walking.

Justine didn't follow. "And who are you?" she called out.

His eyebrows rose up into his hat. "Who am I?" He chuckled. "I just got you out of the cop shop. I'll be asking the questions. Let's go."

"I'm not going anywhere with a stranger."

"You walked out of that station with a stranger. Now keep walking." He continued down the sidewalk.

She let him take a few steps before following. They were leaving a clear trail in the snow. "If you turn out to be a serial killer, I'll warn you, it won't turn out well for you." She met his gaze. "I can take care of myself."

He paused at the corner as she caught up, a frown denting his forehead. "I bet you can."

Around them, the streets were bright but empty. Tire tracks cut through the accumulation on the road. A couple of people walked into a store ahead, while someone crossed the street behind them.

"Name's Artie."

"And you recognize me? From where?" Her heart pounded. She wasn't sure what answer she wanted.

He nodded slowly. "It's been a long time, but I know more than enough. Like, I know," he said as he crossed the road, "that you should not be here. You and your brother got your creds for New York years ago. So what are you doing here, getting into fights and getting arrested?"

She trailed after Artie, her head swimming. He spoke like he knew her, knew Devon. Did he remember her mother? "I wasn't in the fight. Bad timing."

"That wouldn't have gotten you arrested."

She'd given away enough information. She continued in the direction they'd been traveling. The wind picked up and whistled around her ears. She pulled her hood back up.

Quick footsteps crunched in the snow behind her, and Artie grabbed her arm. "Look, I don't know why you're here or what you're after. This is not how I work. I conduct my business remotely, none of this face-to-face. Now the whole neighborhood knows we're connected. And you got me into a police station. That's two strikes already. I will ask the questions, and you will answer. Or you can go back to the police and see what they do with you." He continued walking.

Maybe pissing off the guy she needed help from wasn't the best approach. "I was trying to stop them from hurting a kid. They might have killed him. I couldn't—"

"That's not what brought you to Philly."

She was too tired for this. "You did make credentials for me and my brother. But I need new ones." Her throat constricted. "They found me, Artie." Saying it out loud threatened a fresh wave of panic. The cold stung her nose as she drew in a slow breath.

He came to a halt, glancing around. "Who, exactly? Where?"

She cleared her throat. "A man came after me in the subway. Back in New York."

"How are you so sure it was *them*?"

Her words came out in a whisper. "He knew who my father was."

He froze, then stomped down the sidewalk. "And you thought coming to Philly was the solution?"

Justine traced his tracks with her wet sneakers. Her toes were going numb. "You have a Philly number."

"That's it? You followed a phone number?"

"I didn't have time to weigh my options," she said, her voice hard. "I had to leave, and this was the best I could come up with."

They walked several blocks in silence, the snow providing a faint glow of reflected light. They turned several times, winding through the neighborhood.

"Did they put you in the system?" Artie sounded calmer now.

She nodded. She should have headed north, tried it on her own.

"That complicates things. All around. With your fingerprints attached to this name"—he shook his head—"much more complicated."

"All I need is an ID with a name that won't attract attention. I'll only travel by train, only until I get to …" She shrugged. "The next place."

As they rounded another corner, he checked his surroundings, glancing at her with a heavy breath. After scanning the street again, he cut down a path between buildings and walked down the alley that divided the block, until they reached the back door to a four-story brick building with more plywood and graffiti than brick on its wall. The door squealed as he pulled it open. The foyer was dim, with a hint of a stairwell leading up into further darkness. The air was musty and as cold as outside.

A light flicked on, and a woman with gray hair appeared to one side, sitting on something large and soft, a camp lamp beside her. She wore many layers of sweaters and a long colorful skirt, black boots peeking out from underneath. Her hand rested on the head of a large dog seated next to her. The woman remained seated, but the dog rose, licking its lips.

"You're up late, Gracie." He stood before her. The dog's tail wagged as he put a hand out for him to sniff.

The woman leaned forward, lines creasing at her eyes as she squinted. "Evening, Artie. She with you?"

He nodded.

"She okay?"

He paused. "Best to check."

She snapped her fingers, and the animal approached Justine, sniffing her, checking her maybe for drugs or maybe for bugs. She kept still as he passed his wet nose over her, then returned to the woman's side. "Okay, you're good to go."

He proceeded up rickety wooden stairs to the second floor. She followed, her eyes eventually adjusting to the dark. At the top of the staircase, he reached up and pulled a string, and a bare bulb switched on overhead, hanging from an exposed cord that disappeared through the beams of the ceiling.

The hall smelled of dust and neglect. Unlike the raucous atmosphere where Justine had stayed in New York, only faint murmurs drifted through the thin walls. Some apartments were unlit and unfinished, but light seeped from beneath those with doors, creating privacy and a sense of space she hadn't had.

He stopped at a red door on the left and let her into a dark apartment without a word. Odors of propane and plastic filled the air. He locked the door behind him, turned on a gas lamp sitting on a wooden crate, then switched on a propane heater. The light revealed a small space with colorful bedsheets hung over walls. A stack of boxes stuffed with paper and plastic sat in one corner, a curtain across another. The floor creaked as she crossed to a lumpy, faded sofa and an armchair. Against the opposite wall, cans and boxes of food filled metal shelving. On a low table in front of the furniture sat a large, expensive-looking laptop.

Artie slipped between the couch and the table and turned on the computer. He removed his hat, revealing a round, stubbly face and dark hair tied back with an elastic band. He tapped the laptop keyboard, then rubbed his hands together.

She left her backpack by the chair, then toed off her wet sneakers and peeled off her socks, laying them out next to the heater. She stood as close as she could bear, reaching out for the warmth to defrost her fingers and toes.

"Have you talked to anyone aside from the cops? Anyone trailing you?" When she shook her head, he crossed his arms. "You talked plenty. What about those kids in the fight?"

"They didn't see much. It was dark."

"Not dark enough. And didn't your mother teach you not to take risks like that?" His voice dropped to a whisper. "Your mom not with you anymore? What about your brother?"

She gazed at the blue flames of the heater. "It's just me now." She frowned. "What did you mean, it wasn't dark enough?"

He leaned back from his computer. "You don't realize the half of it. You got found in New York, and your best idea was running over here, asking the whole neighborhood for me, and then getting yourself arrested." He opened his mouth, then shut it and shook his head. "That's not even the worst part."

"I kind of thought it was."

"That stunt you pulled out on the street?"

"You were there—"

"Just in time to see the cops roll in." He paused to scroll through a web page. "You know someone recorded you, right?"

"A few people had phones. I kept my back to them."

"That's what people do these days. They don't help. They pull out their phones and hit Record. Upload videos of them doing everything from taking a crap to eating dinner. They can't help themselves. This girl had eyes—and her camera—on you instead of the fight."

His words were like a bucket of ice water thrown on her. "I can't let her keep that. I have to find her."

"The best you can do is hope she doesn't upload it." He tapped keys. "But don't count on it. That video is way more exciting than either her crap or her dinner. The internet will have a party with that footage. It'll go viral in seconds."

"Viral?"

His mouth fell open a little. "Jesus, she really kept you away from the internet like I told her to. Everyone will see it. That's all that matters."

All of her nightmares were coming true at once. "I have to leave. Fast."

"Yes, you do."

She held her breath. "With a new ID."

He rubbed his face. "I should have taken your call. Sent you the ID. You sure you weren't followed?"

"If I had been, they had all day to take me."

"Well, you need to be gone before whoever that was in New York picks up your trail. I am not getting involved with them." His fingers flew over the keyboard. "My job is a lot harder these days. Takes time to create something reliable. More time than you have."

She bit her lip. "There's something else."

"No, there isn't. I don't do anything else."

"You don't have to do anything. I have questions. I don't use the internet. I avoid cameras. I do what my mom taught me to stay hidden. They shouldn't have found me."

"*Shouldn't* is a nice word. Doesn't mean much."

She started to protest.

"That's a longer discussion than either you or I have time for. I'll see what I can do with this. You have cash, right?"

She swallowed. "Yeah."

"That wasn't very convincing. Let's see it. And here you're asking for extras."

"I have money." She fumbled in her coat pocket. "Not sure if it's enough." She'd have to keep some of it for herself.

A longer silence passed. "New creds. That's all I do. But I don't work for free, hon."

A single rap at the door interrupted her answer. Then two more knocks. He got up and opened the door.

A short woman in a blue parka walked in carrying plastic bags. "I was waiting for you to get back. There's milk, so get that cold right away." An accent of some sort softened the edges of her words. "Rick promised me fresh fruit, and he came through. But you have to share that." She set the bags by the window, shaking snow out of her short salt-and-pepper hair. She turned to Artie but stopped when she saw Justine. "Oh, sorry. Client?"

"Sort of." He returned his attention to his laptop. A voice came from the speakers as he tapped and typed, then cut off.

"I'll give you all the money I have," Justine continued. "That's the best I can do. I've got to get out of here. But I won't get far with the ID I have."

"That's a fact." His gaze remained on the screen. "Any news today, Sonia?"

"I haven't been home all day," Sonia said, her eyes on Justine.

He stopped tapping as a newscaster's voice reported on a local political scandal.

Justine was not done. "You've helped me before, Artie. Has so much changed in six years?"

"The whole world changes every day, hon." Artie smacked the table, and she flinched. "Crap on a stick. She posted it. The girl posted it." He looked up at Justine. "Your problems just got bigger."

19.

As Quinn claimed his usual stool at the counter of Vee's Diner, Nita emerged from a door at the back and slipped a stack of bills into the cash-register drawer. Perfect timing. While he waited for results from the background check on Demetri Kalakos, he had a few questions for her.

She nodded as she swept past with plates of food. On her way back, she tossed a dish towel onto the countertop next to a plastic bag of melting ice, grabbed a coffee carafe, and filled a mug for Quinn. He pressed his fingers into the warmth of the cup.

Last night Nita's face had been unblemished and unmarked, her skin a smooth olive color, her hair tightly drawn into a bun. Now, her cheek was ruddy and blotchy, strands of hair hung around her face, and her eyes were bloodshot.

"How's work tonight?"

"Fine." She dumped the coffee filter and started a new pot.

"You got a minute? I have a couple of questions."

"Everybody's an interrogator tonight," she said with a huff. "I actually came here to work, you know?" She took a plate from the back counter. "I gotta serve this."

He sipped his hot coffee until she returned. "You really should put the ice on your cheek. It does no good on the counter."

"Like I have time for that." She dumped plates smeared with ketchup and remnants of hamburger buns into a plastic bin under the counter. "Don't worry about me. I can take care of myself." She upended the plastic bag into the sink. The ice clattered against the metal.

"Justine said the same thing when I offered to help her."

She sighed. "That girl would rather die than ask for help."

He swallowed the unease her words sparked in him. "Let's hope her choices don't come down to that. You know she left town, right?"

"Figured that. She was totally spooked yesterday. You took her cat, right?"

"Yeah, I've got him."

"Why'd you let her go?" she asked, hands on her hips. "Now she's who knows where, all kinds of people looking for her—" She threw her dish towel into the sink.

"What makes you think people are looking for her?" When Nita didn't answer, he continued, "The more info I have, the better chance I have of finding her."

She topped off his coffee. "Not if she doesn't want to be found."

"I'm not giving up that easily. So who's come in asking questions?"

"Mostly assholes."

"That doesn't really narrow things down."

"No, it doesn't. Because you're all assholes till you prove you're not."

"Are we talking cops here or men in general?" She gave him a smoldering look. "Okay, look, when she was here last, did she hint at why she was leaving? Did she say anything that didn't make sense?"

"She never actually said she was leaving. Just asked me to take her shifts. I figured out the rest." She picked up the towel she'd thrown. "She's not coming back, is she?"

"I'm not sure what she's planning. I'll do my best to convince her to come back. I'm going to make sure she's safe." His anger over her silence had been submerged by his anxiety. Cayden hadn't been able to leave work, and Quinn had begun to imagine he'd seen the last of her. "But first I have to find her. Has she ever talked about other places she lived in? Anyone she knows in another city?"

"I would think she'd tell you that kind of stuff. She doesn't talk to you either, does she?"

He hadn't pushed Justine, hoping she'd open up when she felt ready. When she trusted him more. He hadn't thought she had any real secrets. "Has she mentioned Philadelphia at all?"

"Is that where she went? You know what, don't tell me. Got a feeling that would be better for me."

Alarm bells went off for him. "Nita, if someone came looking for her, knowing who they were would really help."

She stopped wiping the counter and glanced at the door, biting her lip. "I think I've said enough tonight." She went back to cleaning up. The cook at the grill set another plate on the counter, and she brought it out to a table.

A new chill came over him. "Did he do that? Who-ever came in asking about Justine? Did he hurt you?"

She kept her head down as she washed her hands, then dried them with a towel. "I told you. I said enough."

"Keeping quiet doesn't help you or Justine. It just helps the asshole."

"And where will you be when they come back? You'll be here to arrest them?"

"Them, as in more than one?" Nita didn't answer. Whatever Justine had gotten herself into was bigger than he'd expected. His concern kicked into high gear. "Justine has a knack for making it hard for people to help her. If you give me some info about at least one of these guys, maybe we can do something. But we need to put a little effort into this. Maybe take some risks."

Her shoulders sagged. "There were two of them."

He waited, then prodded. "Describe the one who didn't hurt you. What did he want?"

Nita fiddled with a notepad. "Just wanted to know how to find her." She wrapped her arms around herself.

"If one of these guys did that to you, what do you think they'll do to Justine?"

Her laugh startled him. "I don't know about that. She may be a little thing, but I always got the feeling Justine could kick ass if she needed to."

"And yet she was scared enough to leave town. She thinks she can handle this on her own, but let's not wait till she figures out she needs a hand. Tell me about the guy who hit you."

Nita scowled. "He was annoying. He stopped me in the courtyard when I went to deliver an order." She took a deep breath and described how the man had tried to force answers out of her. "Then this other guy shows up, all stalkerish, out of the shadows. It's him you should worry about. He kept saying he wanted to help her. But he gave me the heebie-jeebies."

"What did he look like?"

She gave a general description of a tall blond man that meant nothing to him. "You get a name, where he's from? Anything out of the ordinary, like an accent?"

"The first one did." She gave a brief but generic description. Useless, except for the accent.

"Could he be Eastern European, maybe?" He groped in his coat pocket for his phone, tapped buttons on the screen. "Did he look anything like this?" He hoped he was wrong.

"That's him. If you catch him, put him in a dark cell and lose the key."

"You're certain this is the guy? Or does he just kind of look like this?"

"No way I'd forget that weaselly face. That's totally him."

He thanked her and buttoned up for the cold. "Do you want to file a police report?"

She snorted and rolled her eyes.

"You're right about one thing," he added. "It will be better if you don't know where she is. So I'm not going to update you until I can tell you she's safe." He paused. "Last question. Has Justine told you anything odd? I mean, about herself."

"She is odd. Don't need to be told anything to get that. I guess I don't really know her that well." Her voice dropped to a whisper. "Listen, I, uh, I told them she gave you her cat. And I told them your name. Sorry."

"Good to know. Did he say anything else?"

"He said I'd been helpful," she said in a small voice.

"He can't find Justine from what you told him. You didn't even point them in a direction. They'll have to work to find her, at least." He had work to do to make sure he found Justine first.

On his way back to his Jeep, he hit his partner's number. "Hey, Max, any word on the background check?"

"Demetri Kalakos knows his way around a computer. He's into software development and programming. Been in the US about a decade after immigrating from Greece."

"Any employment info?"

"Nothing on the record."

Quinn grunted. "We'll see what we can do with that in the morning. There's a chance this Kalakos is a busy guy."

~ ~ ~

"Not only is the video online," Artie said, turning his laptop around, "some local news channel picked it up. Now things are about to get interesting."

"News channel?" Justine pulled the computer to her. Sonia took a step closer, unzipping her coat.

A woman appeared on the screen, describing the video playing behind her. The view then switched to the background video. The recording was dark, but Justine could make out people on a sidewalk in front of a familiar row of buildings.

In the video, Justine had her back to the camera as she crouched behind the car. But it was clear enough that her arm thrust out at the same time the bat flew through the air, flying from the man's hand as if by its own power.

It was hard to breathe as she watched the recording play. Her image crept around the car, and her arm stretched out as the bat flew off again. Though her face was not visible, she felt stripped naked by the revelation.

Then the Justine in the video turned around. The camera zoomed in on her face, pale and bright against the darkness. She thought she'd lose what little she'd eaten.

The newscaster returned. "The woman in the foreground was arrested in connection with the altercation seen in this video. Although she was released, the police would like to question her further regarding her role in this incident."

She fell back in the chair. Artie took the laptop from her, his gaze like a scalpel. "The internet gets more interesting every day." He tapped the keyboard, and the newscaster stopped talking. "The video already has a few thousand views. And they added that you were arrested? It's only been a couple hours. Give it a few more, and it'll start getting real attention."

A few thousand views. She wasn't sure what that meant. "That was on the news?"

"Local channel, for now. Stations like to grab stuff off the net when they've got nothing else to talk about." He shook his head. "Don't know if new creds will be enough anymore."

"No one can say for sure what happened. The video's too dark." Her blood pounded in her ears.

"Your face is clear. People will decide what they think happened."

"They said the police want to talk to her," Sonia said with a frown.

Justine shivered. She'd always understood attention like this would be dangerous, but she'd never understood how terrifying it would be. She gripped the arms of the chair, fighting against the urge to run out the door. To run and run and never stop. And it wouldn't ever stop now. They knew her face. They knew where she was. She stood, her chest tight. "I need to get far away, fast."

Artie stood with her, laptop in hand. "You've got to leave *now*. Before someone tracks you to this building. Reporters are going to want a piece of this. They'll find out I sprung you, and they'll be looking for me too."

"You sprung her?" Sonia asked. "Now the cops know where to find us."

If she'd been in New York, Quinn would have talked to the police for her. Her heart ached to remember his goodbye. He had deserved better than her refusal. She'd been so stupid. Seemed to be the theme of the day. "For now, no one else knows I'm here," Justine said. "You can still create the new credentials."

He glanced at Sonia. "They only have my official address." He turned back to Justine. "You've found yourself a world of trouble. I want no part of that."

Her voice rose with her anxiety. "There's still time."

"You're not listening. Creating an identity so solid no one will blink? You've got to change your looks. I've got to connect that picture to new info." He shook his head. "That takes too much time. Once people figure out you're here, and they will, we're all fucked."

"I didn't traipse through snow across Philadelphia for kicks." Her fingers clenched into fists, trying to hold on to the escape route that was slipping through her fingers. "All I need is something with a name that won't raise alerts on the trains. Then I'm out of your hair. I'll give you all the cash I have."

"This isn't about the money."

"You're messing with a lot more lives than your own," Sonia said. "Everyone's got something they're not willing to give up."

"And what are you not willing to give up? This building?" Justine was yelling and couldn't stop, as the woman stood there stone faced. "So you'll find a new one. It's not like you'll end up a lab rat."

And then her hands pushed outward, heedless to what was in the way. Cans on the shelf rattled. A crate of books next to the sofa tipped over. Artie leaned back as if buffeted by strong winds.

But the small table before her received the brunt of her push. It slid across the floor, flipped up, and smacked into the wall with a crack. A corner dug into the wall, leaving a gash in the drywall. As the table landed on the floor, a leg snapped and the table tipped over.

Justine panted in the silence that followed.

Artie scowled, seeming to lean away from her. His gaze shifted between Justine and the table. Sonia stared at her with wide eyes and took a step back.

"If you work faster," she said quietly, her whole body trembling, "I'll be out of your life faster. Let me worry about them finding me."

"Artie?" The one word held all of Sonia's questions.

He drew his laptop to his chest. "If they find you, they've found me. You think I live like this for the hell of it? I'm not letting you ruin what I've got. You should've done things the way we've always done them."

Justine took a breath as if preparing to take a dive into the deep end of a pool. "Then will you do it for Claire? My mom always trusted you. She told me to come to you if she couldn't help me."

He froze, then his shoulders sagged. He set the computer on the couch, walked over to the table, and nudged the broken leg with his foot. In silence he grabbed a roll of duct tape from a shelf and taped the leg back in place. Justine felt Sonia's eyes drill into her, but she didn't dare meet them.

Artie righted the table and returned it to its place in front of the couch, dented corner and all. He straightened and eyed Justine. She faced him, shaking but calm. "What's done is done," he said. "We are not dragging out the past. We got enough problems in the here and now." He set his laptop on the table, making it wobble as he tapped the keyboard.

"… dark and unclear," the newscaster said as the video started again. "But I think we can agree—the young woman in the video seems to move in a way that's connected to what happens to the young man's bat. No wonder the police want to question her again." The woman turned to her partner at the news desk. "Perhaps this is a prank, but I don't know how you'd pull that off."

"Sure, it could be a prank," the second newscaster said. "But what if it's not? Maybe it's something else altogether." The man seemed to enjoy speculating. "Our viewers might remember our reporting on the latest in gene editing when we covered the upcoming Biomedicine Convention. It has gotten super easy with the development of CRISPR." He pronounced the word *crisper*, but didn't explain what it meant. "Considering our government has been using gene editing to enhance soldiers for years, who says they haven't succeeded? We don't know what's going on in some lab somewhere. Who says there aren't supersoldiers or other people among us who can do things normal humans can't?"

"If that were true," the first newscaster replied, "then the laws being debated to regulate human experimentation aren't theoretical."

"No, they're not. That's why we've scheduled a conversation with a genetic scientist later in the program. Tweet us your questions, and maybe we'll ask them live."

Justine closed her eyes.

Sonia's eyes darted between them. "Artie," she said, her voice full of warning, "is this—"

"She's Jack's daughter."

Justine sucked in a breath. She'd never been *Jack's daughter*. Since her mom had died, she hadn't been anyone's daughter. She clutched the chair as dizziness tilted the room. "You knew my dad?"

Sonia looked at her like she was seeing a ghost. "Why are you here? Why now? And who's with you?" She turned to Artie. "Should we be packing up?"

"I'm not going anywhere. She, on the other hand, is."

Justine went over to the boarded-up windows. A crack between a board and the wall revealed a view of the street. The snow was falling more heavily. No one walked or drove by. Christmas lights in the window across the street blinked like a strobe light.

There was more here, more to Artie and his connection to her family, than she understood. But she had no time to probe those secrets.

"Get a move on," Artie said. "When they catch your scent, I want you far from here."

"And what'll you do when they find this place?" Justine retrieved her socks and shoes from next to the propane heater. She slid on a sock, still wet, but at least it was warm. "You think you're going to point them in my direction and they'll just leave? You think they won't have questions for you?"

"Those questions will be easier to answer if you're not here."

"And when they find me?" she said quietly.

"That's for you to handle. You just showed how well you can take care of yourself."

Justine's chest heaved, and her hands itched to shove something again. "The first thing I'll handle is letting them know who you are. I'm sure they'll find your fake ID business interesting."

He shot up from the sofa. "You keep me out of this," he growled.

"I will. I won't say a word. All I need is an ID."

"You have no idea all I've done for your family."

"After all you've done, you feel fine throwing me out on the street to fend for myself. So I'm fending for myself."

"And where will that get you, giving me up? You'll still be caught."

"Not if you do this one thing. We'll both be free."

He seemed to deflate with the release of a long, slow breath. "Freedom is relative. But I've already lost too much. You got to go. Do what you got to do. I'll do what I got to do."

The propane heater hissed as they faced each other and their demands.

"Artie," Sonia broke in. Her expression told him something Justine could not read.

"Is this how you want to go down?" he said to Sonia. The woman looked away. "Make sure no one sees you leave. Keep that hair covered up." He gestured to the door.

Sonia stood between them, silent.

Justine searched his face for some hint he understood what it meant for her to walk out of here. She opened her mouth to argue one more time, then shut it. His eyes held no indecision.

Coming here for help was her mistake. She needed to rely on herself and no one else. Like she had for years. She grabbed her backpack and headed for the door.

"Where will you go?" Sonia asked.

She had no answer, so she gave none.

20.

Justine stepped outside as the door banged shut behind her. The rear of the building was dark and still. She followed the path of tamped-down snow to the street as more snow drifted to the ground. By the time she reached the slushy sidewalk, the cold had seeped through her still-damp sneakers.

So much time wasted, she wanted to scream. Her mouth was beyond dry. Her stomach had forgotten its hunger. She tucked her hair beneath her hood as a brisk breeze cut through her coat and sweatshirt. She shivered, hitched her backpack higher on her shoulder, and headed toward the lights of Fifty-Second Street.

The street was bright, though stores were closed, except for a few bars and fast-food places. A closed electronics store displayed tablets and phones in the window. The news played on every screen. She hunched into her coat and kept her head down as she hurried past.

She would have to buy an Amtrak train ticket and hope she wasn't asked for identification. Or she could slip onto an unwatched train car and see how far north she could get.

A woman walked toward Justine, her head down, hands in her pockets. Short dark hair fell onto a rounded face. She wore the same blue coat the woman in Artie's apartment had worn. Sonia.

Justine slowed her steps and stepped in the woman's path. As she dodged her, Justine moved in front of her again.

Sonia looked up and flinched as she recognized her. She brushed snow from her hair. "I'm sorry about all that."

"If you were, you could have said something back there to change Artie's mind."

"He's not wrong."

"What's he to you?" Justine moved away from a cluster of people at the entrance to a bar.

"That's none of your business."

"Okay. Let's talk about my business. Tell me what you know."

Sonia's lips clamped together. "About you? I don't know anything."

"So what I did in Artie's apartment, you see that kind of thing often? Because neither of you blinked."

"It certainly wasn't what I was expecting."

"And Artie was quick to change the subject from past to present. I thought he was trying to avoid talking about how he knew me. But you already know, don't you?"

"What's your point? I have things to do."

Justine clenched her teeth. "You know why Artie has done what he's done for me, why I need him now." She turned her back to the people leaving the bar.

Sonia's lips parted, but the words were some time in coming. "Artie needs anonymity to run his business, and now that video threatens all of it. Try to understand this from his point of view." She tried to step around her.

"No, no, no," Justine said as she blocked the woman. "You're not getting off the hook that easy."

"And what hook do you think you have us on?"

"You know what's at stake."

Sonia turned a searing eye on her. "I'm not sure *you* know what's at stake. Be careful what you ask for."

"I'm asking for one thing—"

"If he cuts corners, it might be worse than nothing and a waste of his time."

"He's got a day or so before reporters show up. I'm the one taking the risk."

Sonia turned to face the street. After a long span of silence, her next words were more gentle. "Claire and Jack, they were good people."

A pang throbbed through Justine's chest, laced with anger. She was tired of others knowing more about her family, her father, than she did.

"We each have to work with what we have, I suppose." Sonia turned to her. "I have information. You have ... skills. Let's trade."

~ ~ ~

Sonia led Justine back to where she and Artie lived. Inside the foyer, a lamp's light silhouetted the guard and her dog. This time, the animal briefly sniffed them before returning to his spot next to the woman.

She followed Sonia to the third floor, past plywood doors, until she opened a real door at the end of the hall. Inside, Sonia took off her gloves but kept her coat on. She lit a propane heater and turned on a battery-powered lamp on a wooden table beside a multicolored sofa. Her space was much like Artie's but closer to a finished apartment. Real walls with doors divided rooms. Patterned fabric hung over windows with no view but of plywood. Slices of ambient city light seeped through spaces between the wood and the wall.

"Are you hungry? How about some tea?" Sonia asked as she pulled mismatched mugs from shelving stocked with food and kitchen equipment.

"Tea is fine." Justine set her bag down by the couch as Sonia poured water from a plastic gallon jug into a metal kettle. "Thanks."

"Don't thank me yet," Sonia said as she placed the kettle on top of the heater. "You'll need to stay here. If Artie sees you, he'll blow a gasket."

"Where are you going?"

"I need to check on a few people in the building. Then I'll have a talk with Artie, see if I can sway him." She handed her a snack bar.

"Now? It's after midnight."

"People around here keep odd hours."

"We need to talk about this trade."

"We'll talk about that when I get back."

She tensed. "You're that certain I'll agree?"

"You need that ID, right?"

Sonia might be using all Justine had revealed for her own benefit. But she was right. Besides, Justine had given up many of her choices when she came back with her. "Tell him I'll color my hair."

"You could do that. Okay, I'll be gone for a while."

"Are you a landlord or something here?"

"People here look out for each other." She pointed to the kettle. "Eventually, the water will boil." Sonia grabbed some grocery bags and shut the door behind her.

Justine sank into the squishy cushions of the sofa. Exhaustion pulled on her, but she was too wary to sleep. Next to the sofa, magazines sat in a neat stack. She picked one up and leaned toward the camp lamp to read the cover. *Journal of Biotechnology.* A scientific journal. As she unwrapped and inhaled the snack bar, she flipped through the pages. Articles on gene sequencing, genetic engineering, DNA, CRISPR. Topics the news anchor had mentioned.

Beneath the covered windows, boxes sat against the wall. She carried the lamp over and found an array of dusty glass jars, a cracked beaker, a microscope, and other pieces of lab equipment. The collection felt vaguely familiar.

She pulled out a worn notebook with a heavy, dark cover. An eagle in the center of a circular embossed logo decorated the cover. Letters worn from use ran along the edge, but a layer of dust helped them stand out. *Department of Defense, United States of America.*

A chill passed over her. And yet an odd sort of warmth bubbled in her belly. Her father used to have odd equipment cluttering his office. Her recollection of that room was vague. Their dad had forbidden them inside unless he was home.

Notebook in hand, she returned to the couch and wrapped herself in the memory of her father, faint as it was, like an old blanket. She paged through the book, but most of the notes were written in another language. Those in English might as well have been. She fingered the impression of the logo on the front, then laid it on the floor.

The heater had yet to warm the apartment. She stuffed her hands into her coat pockets and found Cayden's cell phone. It was off, yet still felt dangerous in her hands. But if Cayden had told her the truth about the tracking, maybe she should take advantage of it.

She pressed all of the buttons until she managed to turn on the device, then searched the images on the screen for the one Cayden had showed her would make a call. The phone stared back at her.

She put it away and closed her eyes. The couch was soft, if a bit scratchy. Quinn's was more comfortable and smelled better. An ache swelled in her chest. Quinn would most likely be home sleeping. She hoped Sully was getting along with Cheetah.

Justine flinched as a door closed. She blinked and sat up, trying to banish the fog of sleep. Right. In a stranger's home. In a strange city. Couldn't have planned this better.

The apartment was warmer, and the kettle rumbled. Sonia removed her coat, disappeared through a door across the room, and returned wearing a thick sweater.

She gathered tea bags and the mugs and set them down on a beat-up trunk in front of the couch.

Justine tried to be patient but lost the battle. "Well?"

Sonia sat beside her with a sigh. "Artie's a work in progress."

"Did he say yes or no? It's not that complicated."

She threw a glance at her. "He's thinking about leaving altogether. Finding another city to set up in." Justine covered her eyes with a hand. "And yet he never said no." She shrugged. "I might be able to wear him down, but I'll let him cool off first." The water on the heater hissed and gurgled. Sonia retrieved the kettle and poured in silence.

Justine grabbed a steaming cup and savored the warmth sinking into her fingers. "How do you know him?"

The woman paused mid-sip. "We go way back." She leaned back into the cushions, staring at nothing.

Justine opened the journal. "Programmable genome editing tools and their regulation for efficient engineering. Targeted gene mutation. Cloning-free genome engineering." She closed the magazine. "You were a genetic scientist."

"I am a scientist." Sonia stood and paced beyond the lamplight. "I just don't have a lab right now."

Justine's stomach did a flip-flop. "Was Artie a scientist too?"

The older woman returned to the couch. "The past is not a kind place. I suggest you leave it where it is."

"The present isn't so great either." Justine wasn't sure what Sonia was demanding or expecting. There was something here she couldn't quite see.

"Why did you come here?" Sonia asked. "You could have gotten what you needed in New York."

"There isn't anyone else I can trust."

Sonia flinched and looked away.

"You study genetics, biotechnology. My father worked in genetics as part of some Defense Department program." Her heart beat faster as she picked up the notebook, angry she couldn't keep the trembling out of her voice. "Did you work with him at the DoD?"

Sonia slammed her mug on the trunk and resumed her pacing. "This was a mistake."

Questions flooded Justine's mind. She had set most of them aside long ago. A few had never left her. "Do you know how he died?"

Sonia paused. "Died?"

The confusion in Sonia's voice was a splash of ice water over her. "You—they killed him. That's what—" The floor seemed to tilt. "That's what my mom told me."

"I didn't know," Sonia said softly. "It's been twenty years since I've seen Jack." She went to the windows and peeked through a crack in the plywood.

Justine paced around the table. What Sonia had just revealed had Justine feeling like she'd been asking for food but hadn't realized she was dying of thirst until she'd been offered water.

She shook her head. She was off track. "You've conveniently avoided discussing what you're going to ask for this. So let's talk, because I want to renegotiate." That was going to be a trick, without knowing what was on the table. "Getting Artie to change his mind is still part of this. But I also want whatever information you have about my father." She had to force the next words from her mouth. "For all that, I do something for you."

With an inscrutable expression, Sonia again turned toward the windows, but this time she looked down at the boxes on the floor. She poked at one with a toe. Then she returned to the sofa, her expression softer. She sat, tucking a leg under her, and finished her tea. "How does it work, what you do?" she asked, fiddling with the cup.

Justine stiffened. But Sonia's eyes held only curiosity. Justine relaxed a fraction and picked up her mug without taking a seat. "I don't know."

"Haven't you wondered?"

"Of course I have," she shot back. "I've never found an answer. Trust me, I've looked. I found more explanations in science fiction than in any scientific text. I've got no answers for you."

"But you do." Sonia rose and walked past her and through a doorway beside the sofa. Pale light soon glowed from inside.

Justine followed but stopped at the threshold. "No, I told you. I don't."

A larger camp lamp sat on a high table in a room half as big as the one behind her. Cabinets and shelves lined the walls. Old equipment lay on every surface, some in pieces, others worn from use. Vials stood in stands. Another propane heater sat near the door, dark and cold. Justine took a step back, suddenly uncomfortable.

"There's always something more to give up." Sonia pulled equipment from a cabinet. "I want to take a blood sample."

Justine backed out of the room, ice running down her spine. "What do you need with my blood?"

"You may not understand how you do what you do. But your blood does. And I can read it."

"Read my blood?"

"Don't you want to know?"

"Why do *you* want to know?"

Sonia's answer was a while in coming. "It's all I have left."

It should have been an easy no. Yet Sonia promised answers to questions Justine had long stopped asking. "You're saying the reason for my ability is in my blood?" She should forget about this. Keep her blood inside her veins where it belonged. Keep focused on getting on the move.

"Not necessarily. But we could learn more by analyzing different parts of it. The DNA especially."

"And I get?"

"You find out how you work."

Sonia wanted that information too. She wanted it badly, Justine's gut told her. She swallowed. "And you'll tell me what you knew of my father?"

Sonia paused. "You may not like what you hear. And that will require more than a blood donation."

She took a breath. "I'm a big girl. I can handle it. But I'm not sure what I can do for you in return."

"To learn the secrets of your DNA? To learn about your father? How much do you want it?"

Sonia clearly knew the answer to that. "And the ID. That's part of the deal."

Sonia hesitated, then nodded.

"Okay," Justine said. "What have you got in mind?"

21.

Justine walked beside Sonia down a dark, narrow street lined with trees and long, low buildings. The empty streets made her feel safe, yet she wasn't alone. She wasn't sure how she felt about that.

After taking two buses in the quietest time of night, they'd reached the downtown university campus. Sonia had been tight lipped throughout the trip, telling her only enough for Justine to suspect she'd regret this arrangement. They now turned onto a wider street, bright despite the early morning hour.

She followed Sonia into the pedestrian-only part of campus. They skirted several small structures to approach a low brick building with few windows. Sonia led her around the side to a service entrance with a wide rolling steel door and an employee entrance. She swiped a plastic card through a card reader on the wall and opened the door when it clicked.

"Do you work—"

Sonia put a finger to her mouth and gestured into the building. Unable to change course, Justine stepped into a long hallway. Linoleum floors, scuffed beige walls, paper signs taped next to wooden doors. She hoped low budget meant low tech.

Hanging from the ceiling, a camera stared at her. So much for low tech. She swiveled away from the camera. "There's a—" She pointed over her shoulder, trying not to scream.

"Doesn't work. Stay quiet. Security roams the halls as part of their rounds. And there's always some technician staying late for a project."

Justine let out a breath and followed her through a labyrinth of passageways the woman seemed to know as well as the streets of Philadelphia. Despite her key card, they snuck around as if she did not belong there. Sonia paused to peek around a corner, then waved Justine back. They retraced their steps and took another passage. They doubled back again when Sonia discovered a new camera.

Finally, Sonia stopped before a door labeled Lab Unit 4. A square of glass revealed a dimly lit corridor and more linoleum. She tried the handle, then took something out of her bag and fiddled with the lock until it gave way.

Justine stared at the words on the door Sonia had gone through. No wonder her skin had been crawling since she entered the building. This was the last place in the world she should be.

Sonia was already farther down the hall. Behind her, the hall stretched away. She'd have to either find her way back on her own or stay with Sonia. If they could manage to not be discovered, she could get out without anyone trying to keep her there. She trailed after Sonia.

Keypads secured the rooms in this section. An open doorway on their right led to a large, dark space where counters and equipment made dull gray shapes. Sonia entered without turning on the lights, scanning the room with her flashlight. "No luck. I was hoping they'd left it in here and saved us the trouble."

She returned to the doorway, listened, then scurried to the next door. "The item I need is in there." She paused. "Can you open this?"

"You don't have the code?"

"Can you open it or not?"

"Considering what you're asking me to—"

"The time for questions was hours ago. Now you'll just get us caught. How will that work out for you?"

She began a new protest, but gave up. There was nothing to say. "What's in that room that you need?"

"The centrifuge. Equipment that will help me analyze your blood."

Justine eyed the keypad. "Is it alarmed?"

"Shouldn't be. But they've changed several things. Depends on how paranoid they've gotten."

Sonia had dangled an irresistible prize, and Justine hadn't even asked for proof she could deliver. She'd left New York to avoid being forced to engage in questionable activities. Was what she was doing now any better than what the man in the subway would have asked of her?

"Try to keep it quiet, all right?"

She glowered at the woman. "Keep an eye out for anyone coming. If an alarm sounds, I'm out of here."

Sonia moved so she had a view of the corridor on her left. She looked back at Justine, expectant, then returned to her watch.

The keypad mechanism used a button instead of a handle, likely with a bolt of some kind inside. If Justine directed force to the keypad, she might disable it but leave the bolt in place. She had to use the right amount of strength to break the bolt without slamming the door against the wall.

She ignored Sonia, ignored the security guards roaming the halls, and shut away her fear and anxiety. She extended her hand and jerked it forward, trying to not put all her strength into the push. The door shook in the jamb but didn't break free. Pushing harder only caused it to shake louder.

Sonia eyed her for a moment, then checked the corridor and nodded. "Hurry."

The bolt was going to need a lot more force. The door might not survive the process, unless she could weaken the lock. She smiled. Physics was her friend. She stretched out her arm, pushing without pushing. Maybe once Sonia explained how all this worked, she could use better words to describe it. After about twenty seconds, she touched the door. The keypad was warm. Just a bit more.

"Hurry up!" Sonia called out in a hoarse whisper.

She bit back her response, took half a step back, and shoved again. With only a fraction of resistance, the door broke free of the jamb, and she lunged for the door before it could hit the wall.

Sonia came to the doorway and stared at the mangled bolt and keypad as if they had come to life. Inside, she ran her light over counters full of equipment stacked on top of each other. "We've got the mother lode here. I should have given you a bag." Her light illuminated a small boxlike machine. She set her pack beside it.

Sonia's fingers moved nimbly from one piece to another, pressing buttons, unhooking latches, and removing sections until the machine was in pieces. She shoved the parts into her bag, then grabbed plastic packages of syringes. "Stuff these in your pockets. And these. Let's go." She zipped the pack closed.

Justine stuffed the packages and the smaller pieces of the machine into her coat pockets, each stolen item a weight she would carry beyond this night. At the room's entrance, she leaned out to listen. In the silence of the building, a lone footstep echoed off tiled walls. She shrunk back. "I heard something." More followed, drawing closer.

Security, Sonia mouthed.

Justine looked around as she fought panic. The room had no exit.

Sonia gestured, and they slipped behind the door, careful not to move it.

The squelch of a handheld radio and muffled speech grew closer. A guard on his rounds answered, "Got an open one here. Checking the hall. Unit four is unlocked too. That's three already. No students around, and nothing missing yet." The person on the other end of the radio spoke again. "I will check that out first."

Footsteps faded. Justine didn't dare breathe until all fell silent. Sonia inched to the doorway, and after a long look both ways, they ventured out.

They took a few more turns before the squawk of a radio alerted them. Justine pulled up short. Sonia checked another passageway and pointed in that direction. They continued in silence until they reached a wide intersection. Plenty of time for someone to see them as they passed.

Sonia checked the corridor, then waved Justine on. She held her breath and sprinted across, not daring to look, not wanting to know if she'd been seen. Another radio squelched. She flinched and flattened herself against the wall, sure the guard could hear her heartbeat.

"This hall is clear. Everything's locked." The security guard's steps faded as he moved on.

When it was quiet, Sonia crossed the intersection and kept going, leading Justine back the way they'd come. The lights were brighter here, the passageways narrower.

They were at the corner of the last corridor before the exit when a shout came from behind. Sonia froze, but Justine broke into a run.

"I've got two individuals heading south. Possibly two females heading to the south exit, by the service drive." The guard stayed on them, loud but slow. He picked up speed while calling an alert over his radio. The squeal of a stun gun powering up rang out.

The single door at the end of the hall seemed to stretch away from Justine, even as she sped up.

A guard left his post at the front entrance to join the chase. A member of ground security headed toward the service entrance.

Footsteps, radio static, voices grew louder. The building was awake. And they were coming for them.

Sonia caught up, the pack of booty thumping against her back in time with her steps. "The alarm will sound as soon as you hit the door. Just keep going. Don't stop no matter what you hear."

That was something Justine knew how to do. She hit the release bar at a run. The door swung open as a tinny alarm assaulted her ears. She ran out into the night with all her fears chasing behind her.

22.

Justine veered from the well-lit service drive and raced toward the cover of the trees ahead, hoping Sonia followed. A shout from behind spurred her legs faster, even as she peered behind her.

Two security guards bore down on Sonia, slowed by her backpack. Another approached from the side and cut off the woman's escape.

Justine stopped at the first tree. Calling out to Sonia was clearly a bad idea, as a fourth security guard came onto the scene, barking into a radio. Two of them got ahold of Sonia, and one pulled out something dark from his belt.

Justine gasped, then released her breath. Not a gun. A stun gun. The guard with the radio spotted her, pointed, then jogged toward her. "Stay where you are."

Sonia held her free arm up in surrender, her bag on the ground, her eyes wide and on Justine.

A guard came up from Justine's right and latched on to her arm. She flinched, adrenaline shooting through her, and she pulled away, but the man held on.

"Easy now," he said, pulling out his stun gun.

She rotated her arm, trying to knock the stun gun out of his hand. Twisting in his grip, she scanned for Sonia.

The two men still held the woman as she thrashed. "Just go!" she cried out.

She turned into the guard's hold on her. His fingers loosened. She twisted again and broke free. Then she ran like the devil was chasing her.

Blocks later, footsteps sounded fast and light behind her. Justine sped up, the crisp air stinging her nose as she panted.

"Keep going!"

Sonia was catching up, running surprisingly fast. She had lost her coat and the backpack. Justine turned a corner, keeping to the shadows. She picked up speed, glad for all the miles she'd run along the East River. She'd prepared for this moment for years.

After an unknown number of blocks, she slowed to a trot so Sonia could catch up. She pulled her hood up and tucked in her hair. Sonia soon came up beside her, and they caught their breath as they moved at an inconspicuous walk.

They shared Justine's coat, each wearing it for a few blocks, as the city woke. The sky faded to a paler gray, clouds thick with the promise of more snow. A store unlocked its doors. More cars filled the streets. Commuters and students appeared at bus stations.

A small group of young men walked in their direction, duffel bags and knapsacks hanging from their shoulders. Two of the teens looked at a phone as they walked. Another was reading his own device. He glanced up, went back to his screen, then looked up again, his gaze settling on Justine.

She tugged on her hood as the young man's eyes lingered on her. He looked back at his screen, tapped it, and held it up. "Guys, look. The girl from that crazy video. I told you that was around here." He followed Justine as she hurried past. "You're her, aren't you? How'd you do it? Was it a magic trick?" He was tall and gangly, dark skinned, with a mop of dark curls. He trotted beside her, the phone between them. "So what's your secret? Make this go viral."

His friends gathered around him as they trailed her. One of them laughed and asked, "Come on. Did you have someone working with you?"

Sonia tugged on her arm. "He's recording you," she whispered. "Let's go."

Justine glared at the camera. "Is his video on the internet yet?"

"I don't know."

"Hey, can you do your thing?" the guy with the phone asked. "Might as well. Everybody saw it already."

Sonia pulled her away again. Justine scowled and wrenched her arm from Sonia's grip. "This kid is not going to ruin my life for kicks."

The boy shifted to record his friend as they kept pace with her. "Hey, everybody, Trey here. Me and Ricardo are on Fifty-Second Street. We found the girl from the video, the one who pulled some trick to break up a fight—you know the one. Folks are getting stupid, saying she did magic or something. I think it's a setup. I'm trying to get her to tell us how she really did it." Ricardo laughed.

As Trey held his phone out in front of him, Justine wondered if she could heat up the phone enough to make it explode. She would enjoy that. Or maybe she could give it a yank and take it from him. Then stomp on it. Even better. She stretched out her hand, palm up, and drew it back. Nothing happened.

"She's doing it! How do you do it? Come on—people want to know," Ricardo said.

"Justine …"

Okay, no time for games. She shoved forward. The device jerked out of Trey's hand and flew into the window of a pizza shop behind him. The phone hit the glass with a hollow thunk. Cracks spidered through the pane. The phone landed on the sidewalk, bounced, and shattered on the next impact.

He stared at the pieces of plastic and metal on the ground, then at Justine as she stepped away. He scowled, his shoulders stiff with self-righteous anger. "My phone!" He ran up and blocked her path.

She craned her neck to look him in the eye. He was nearly a foot taller. "Do you need another demonstration?"

He hesitated, and some of his anger receded, his next words more subdued. "That cost a lot of money."

"You shoved a camera in my face like I'm an animal at the zoo."

He balled his fists. "I don't know what you are, but you're going to pay—"

Justine stepped close enough to feel the warmth of his coffee breath. "Next time, maybe it's not the phone I break."

This time, when Sonia drew her away, she let her.

But Trey was not done. He clamped a hand on her arm. "What about—"

Justine flinched, whirled on him, and thrust her hand forward.

He ducked, and the push caught his shoulder. He spun and slammed into the car parked behind him.

Everyone froze. Trey lifted himself from the car's hood. His friends took a step back. "What are you?"

Justine glanced around. A few people watched from across the street. A siren sounded in the distance.

"Come on, man," Ricardo said. "Let's get out of here."

"What are you?" Trey muttered again and ran off with his friends.

23.

onia and Justine slowed as they neared the apartment building after meandering for blocks. The
sun shone weakly through the thick clouds, and
the streets were busy with people heading to work.

"I don't think anyone has eyes on us," Justine said.
Now that they were almost home, her internal alarm
was insistent she get off the street.

"Seems that way," Sonia murmured. "Let's circle one
more time."

The urge to run inside settled as they walked on,
leaving her with Trey's parting words: *What are you?*

After a circuit around the block, they cut between
buildings and went inside. Justine pulled down her
hood and forced her shoulders to relax a fraction. The
door shut, and blackness enveloped them. Neither the
woman nor her dog was in sight. Justine's instincts
went into overdrive, and she stopped where she was
and reached out for Sonia.

Sonia moved forward, fumbling for her flashlight, but she'd left it with her coat on campus.

A scrape of a shoe on the cement drew their attention to the right. The hair on Justine's neck stood up. A shadow moved in and entwined with the outline of Sonia's form. A soft click echoed. Sonia let out a quiet gasp.

Justine backed up. "Sonia, what's happening? Who's there?"

"Let's get some light."

Justine gasped. She couldn't forget that voice. When he showed up, things always got worse. Her anger, frustration, and fear boiled over. "What are you doing here?"

"Oh, it's nice to be remembered. I suppose the accent makes it easier. I should work on that."

"Justine," Sonia said in a tight voice, "he has a gun to my head."

She took a step closer. She could see Sonia now, her head tilted back by the man's arm around her neck. "I never caught your name. Will asshole work okay?"

He chuckled. "Call me Kos. And turn on that lamp in the corner behind you."

"Where's the woman who watches the entrance? What did you do to her and her dog?"

"Relax. They are only taking a nap. Stop wasting time so we can finish our business here."

No one would likely pass through this entrance so early in the morning. They were on their own. Justine fumbled around the floor until she found the lamp. She felt for the switch and turned it on.

This guy Kos was only a few inches taller than Sonia, but he had a firm grip on her and the gun aimed at her temple. She held on to his arm, her eyes locked on Justine's.

A smirk crept across his face. "Think you can stop this bullet?"

Justine flexed her fingers, dying to send him into the next county. "You are like a bad infection. What do you want now?"

"So pleasant. You're making quite the name for yourself."

Damn news. "How did you find me?"

"Doc has eyes everywhere."

"Doc?"

"Lots of people interested in you now. Including my boss. He's interested in working with you."

"This has nothing to do with Sonia. Let her go. Work this out with me."

"She's not going to get hurt. As long as you come with me."

"Why the hell would I do that?" No one looking for her had good intentions, she was sure of that. But she couldn't leave Sonia with this nut. And shoving him into concrete would feel pretty good.

"I suggest you are careful about your next move. I can shoot her before you can pull any of your tricks."

That was true. What else could go wrong today? No, no, she didn't just say that. "Who do you work for?"

"His name is Dr. Hollister. Some sort of scientist. His company makes implants. But he also experiments with genes or something. Been searching for you forever, from the way he talks. He wants you to come back to New York and hear his offer. Could be a profitable arrangement."

She shivered. Of course this stalker would work for a geneticist. Like Sonia. Like her father. Was that how he'd found out about her? Sonia stood stiff in front of him, eyes wide, as Justine asked, "Does your boss work for the government?"

"Nah, has his own company. And he's ready to make you an offer."

"Doing what?"

"Come back with me and find out."

Justine crossed her arms. "You've been following me because your boss wants to hire me?"

"You're popular now. And valuable."

Something wasn't adding up. "You started following me before this video business."

And then Sonia fell off to the side, pulling him off balance. Kos's body jerked sideways. His gun hand shifted.

Justine shoved forward with her whole body.

Kos tumbled back. His weapon fell away and skidded on the concrete.

Sonia broke free, rolled away, and scrambled toward Justine.

Kos smashed into the banister of the staircase behind him, bounced off, and landed on the ground facedown.

The pistol hit the wall and slid in another direction. Sonia rose, panting, and retrieved it. Justine breathed a fraction easier.

Kos groaned and pushed himself up on one arm, then flipped onto his back with a gasp. He clenched his teeth and panted. "I can't . . . can't breathe."

"Pobrezinho," Sonia said, a hand on her hips. She held his gun in her other hand through her sweater. "Poor thing's crying because he got a little banged up."

He clutched his side. "Motherfucker." He paused to take a shallow breath. "What'd you do to me?"

Justine had pushed him with all the force she had. Might have been a bit of overkill.

Sonia shrugged a shoulder. "Maybe you have a broken rib. Don't move too much."

"And if it hurts to breathe, don't," Justine added.

On the ground, grimacing, he looked smaller, less threatening. But he was still a pain in the ass. She laid a foot on his chest.

The man cried out. He gripped her ankle, but the pain sapped his strength.

She eased up on the pressure enough to keep him quiet but still. "Why is a scientist who works with implants and genes interested in me?"

Kos made a chirping sound. No, the sound was coming from his pants. His phone. "You're going to want me to answer that."

"I'd rather smash it to bits. You probably gave away my location with that thing." She punctuated her statement with a kick at his hip.

He gasped then grinned. "You could take it out of my pants yourself."

She locked eyes with him in challenge and knelt beside him. His grin grew tentative as she slipped her hand into his pocket. She frowned and pulled out several wadded receipts. Tossing them aside, she pulled out more receipts with the still-ringing phone. She smoothed out a slip of paper. "Domino's Pizza? With great New York pizza all around you, you go to Domino's?" She shook her head.

Kos snatched the phone from her hand, glanced at the screen, and swiped, eyes on Justine. "Hey, Doc." He listened, then said, "Found her, no, no trouble at all." After a minute, his eyes widened. "Where is he now?" He grinned. "That might do it. I'll be in touch." He lay the phone on his chest and leered at Justine.

Nothing that made this man happy could be good.

"Well, well, well. You have an even better reason for coming with me. If you really care about him, that is."

"Can we skip the cryptic statements and get to the point?"

"You're no fun." He scowled briefly. "The detective."

She shivered. Something had been converging on her for days, and now drew closer. "Who?"

Kos's grin broadened. "Your detective. Duncan. He's with the doc. The man's comfortable for now. Doc's sure to find good use for him in his lab."

He hissed as Justine's foot pressed down more heavily. She eased up the pressure on his chest—she needed him talking. "What use could a detective be to your boss?"

"I told you, he does experiments, plays around with genes." He breathed. "Always needs new subjects."

"You mean he experiments on *people?*"

"And Duncan is next. Unless you come meet with the doc. Then he'll let him go."

This time, she meant to press harder. He squirmed. "You're a terrible liar."

"No lies," he panted. "He has Duncan. Thought it would get you back to New York."

"So you lay a trap, then tell me it's there?"

"It's a good trap," he said with a grin.

She pulled her foot back to kick him again, but Sonia yanked her away. "If he can't talk, you can't get answers."

Her fist clenched and crumbled something in her hand—a receipt. She shoved it in her pocket and blew out a breath. Her fury only told him he was right. They had set a good trap. She breathed for a moment to calm herself. "How did you find Detective Duncan?"

"We have our own business with him. It was just luck that you showed up."

"Quinn has no business with a company experimenting with genes. Try again."

"Call the doc back. He'll tell you himself."

"So he can lie to me too? Give me that." She reached for the phone, but the man stuck out an elbow in her direction. *Have it your way.* She held out her hand and focused on pulling the phone to her.

It took longer, but the phone jerked in Kos's hand. He pulled back on it, his eyes wide. "Shit, that too?" He tried to turn away, so she pushed down on his chest. He gasped again, and she gave the phone a firm pull. It jumped from his hands in a low arc, and she bent to catch it.

She nodded at Sonia and the gun, and the woman raised the weapon to cover Kos.

Justine withdrew her foot, dropped the phone to the ground, and stomped on it with her heel. "Hate. These. Things."

She stepped back, awash with relief. Sonia gestured for the phone. The screen was cracked, bits of the inner workings visible. Justine laid her foot back on Kos's chest as Sonia pocketed the gun. She fiddled with the phone until one side came off, pulled out something flat, and held it up. "All you had to do was take out the battery. Hope the stomping made you feel better."

"It absolutely did." She turned to Kos. "You were about to tell me why this Hollister is so intent on finding me. What does he have in mind?"

"What do I know? I'm only the messenger."

She kicked him in the side. He curled up, but she held him in place with her foot.

"Jesus Christ." He caught his breath. "I don't know all his plans. He wants to improve humans, make them better somehow. He's kind of obsessed, hardly sleeps. If he knows what you can do, maybe he wants to use your genes. If I don't come back with you, I guess he will make do with Duncan."

Justine pressed on his chest again, and the man cried out. "You will go back—alone," she said through her teeth. "Tell this Hollister to go fuck himself. I am. Not. For. Sale." She stepped back. "If I find out anything has happened to Detective Duncan—"

He raised a hand, the other wrapped around his torso, while muttering in another language. "Okay, okay, you crazy bitch. Ease up. I'll tell him you said no. But I can't say what he'll do to Duncan."

Her stomach turned at the thought. She kicked him again. He cried out and curled into a ball. Sonia grabbed her arm, but she yanked out of her grip and crouched over Kos. "For the sake of your health, you better be lying. Then I'll just kick your ass." She straightened. "This Hollister must be pretty stupid to risk kidnapping a cop."

"All for you," he wheezed.

"Why does he want me? Why not find someone else?"

"From what I've seen in the last couple of days, nothing he won't do to get you in his lab. Getting close to you in the subway made him even worse." Kos grinned. "Won't stop looking for you now."

24.

Hollister reviewed Eddie's stats as the young vet ran through his routine in the exercise room. His subject continued to grow stronger. But now that he'd merged material from Lizzie's DNA with Eddie's current therapy, he was eager to see more significant changes.

Somehow, Jack must have kept his colleagues at the GAMA program unaware of his daughter's capabilities. Otherwise, Hollister's father would have dedicated all of the team's resources to finding her.

With this video on the internet, everyone could learn what Lizzie was capable of, including anyone from the GAMA program. When they saw what she was capable of, far beyond what they'd hoped to accomplish, she would be in more danger than ever.

Hollister wasn't certain of the current status of the GAMA program, and he was less certain of Lizzie's capabilities. But he was sure he would find the switch. Once identified, he could turn on the genes that controlled those abilities and arm their soldiers with defense like none on earth. He only had to reach her before someone with dollar signs in their eyes tried to profit off her. She seemed wholly unaware of the potential she held in her hands. Jack's daughter deserved to know her worth, to know she was not cast aside and forgotten.

He checked the time. He should have heard from Kalakos by now. He pulled out his phone but stopped as Val entered the gym.

"Are you having trouble controlling your subject?" She handed him a small stun gun and leaned back against the table.

"I'm only investigating some options." He approached Eddie as he stepped out of a machine and used a bar to stretch his arm. His eyes shot up when the stun gun let out a sharp peal. "What the—"

Hollister touched him with the weapon, and the man's body spasmed. He caught Eddie as he slumped over, and eased him to the ground.

Eddie panted for a moment, then sat up and shook himself. "The fuck you do that for?" He eyed the weapon.

"Can you get up?"

After taking a second to glower, he rose, stretching his arm and flexing his hand. "Seriously, Doc, what the hell was that for?"

"I apologize, Eddie. I didn't think telling you ahead of time would help. Do you feel any pain?"

"No, thousands of watts of electricity shooting through my body feel great."

"Catch your breath and continue your workout. Tell me if you feel any different."

Eddie stared at him for a moment before returning to the exercise machines. Hollister returned to where Val waited.

"Trying out a new form of discipline?" she asked.

"As he has become stronger, I've realized I need a control mechanism that would not damage him permanently."

Eddie slipped his arm into the bicep machine he had last used.

"Weaknesses are as important to know as strengths," she said, nodding. "The stun gun was a good idea, and it appears to work the same on him."

As Eddie pulled, the weight lifted a fraction of an inch, then fell back down. He shot a look at Hollister. "What did you do to me?"

He frowned and returned to Eddie's side. "Try again." When he tried to lift the weights again and failed, Hollister's heart raced. "Reduce the weight gradually until you're able to lift it."

Instead, Eddie went back to his pre-enhancement weight. He was able to lift that and only a bit more.

Hollister shook off a chill. He might have negated months of work in seconds. "Try the other machines."

He paced as he followed the man's routine. "The electric pulse must have disrupted the enhanced genes. It should be temporary." Unless his alterations proved to be temporary. He began to sweat. "Try more weight every five minutes, until you can again lift what you could this morning."

"Fucking fantastic." He wiped his face with his towel. "Warn me next time you're gonna do that, will you?"

"Again, I apologize. I'm sure your strength will return. Be sure to let me know the exact time it does." Hollister returned to Val's side and dropped the stun gun into her hand.

"What if his strength doesn't return?"

His hands clenched, and he flexed his fingers, letting out a slow breath. "It will. In the meantime, I've learned something new about his enhancement. I will have to continue to test it."

"Meanwhile, the neural implant project has fallen behind."

"We will get it in on time."

"We've put our deadline at risk. Tinkering in your lab may—"

He rounded on her. "This is more important—" He stifled his rage and eased back from her half a step, then started again. "Transforming the way we wage war is world-changing work. Not tinkering."

She put a hand up. "Please spare me the grand pronouncements. For someone who can't walk, our software is world changing. It's a matter of perspective. I think you've lost yours."

"You're wrong."

"Kalakos lost days to that bug his team found before you noticed."

"And if you keep him on schedule, we will make the launch." He stretched his jaw to unclench it. "Is Cayden ready?"

"He'll go tonight. Once he finds the building plans, he'll know where to go."

"The hardware will be more valuable than the schematics."

"Those schematics will let us see what we're up against. And their code will show us where to adjust ours." She glanced at Eddie as he continued to struggle with the weights. "What's your plan for the detective? Dangling bait can be effective, but missing detectives are looked for."

"He won't be missing long enough."

"You're that sure? What if she doesn't respond?"

"The police have nothing to connect us to him. And he will be useful regardless of the outcome. He may even enable us to progress faster than I'd planned."

Val's frown eased into a smile, and she walked out. When she smiled, Hollister was always glad she was on his side.

He reached for the tablet to rewatch the video from Philadelphia.

~ ~ ~

After the women had secured Kos in the basement, with his strong disapproval, they returned to the apartment. Sonia turned on the heat and opened a box of cereal.

"Someone's going to hear him," Sonia said as they ate straight from the box.

"I plan to be long gone by then," Justine said, pacing. "Anyone asks, you don't know who he is or how he got here."

"I don't."

"I don't either, not really. There was a . . . an incident. Then he found me on the street and . . ." She paused.

Sharing this information felt easier than she'd expected. Before she could question that, she continued, "And demanded a demonstration. I had no idea he was working with *him*."

Sonia looked away. "Him being Hollister?"

Justine nodded.

"How do you know him?"

"If he's the guy who found me in the subway, he's tall and blond, with an obsessed look in his eyes." Justine shivered. This man had spun a far-reaching trap. She'd have to move fast but with caution.

"And this detective? Quinn Duncan? Is he a friend of yours?"

Justine's stomach twisted, and the cereal in her mouth turned to paste. She unloaded her pockets of the syringes and pieces of the machine they'd try to steal what felt like days ago.

"Okay, more than a friend." Sonia emptied her own pockets. "Damn rent-a-cops. Almost had that machine." Sonia examined a piece. "At least we got some important parts. I might be able to use them, with a little creativity."

"Can you still do the analysis?"

"Some of it. Let's draw some blood." Sonia retrieved a handful of supplies from her lab, ripped open a syringe packet, and gestured for Justine to sit beside her.

"How will you tell me what you find?"

"I'll give you a number to call. I should have some information in a few days or a week."

Who knew where she'd be in a week? She couldn't say where she'd be tomorrow.

"Call whenever you can," Sonia said.

Justine took off her coat and pulled up her sleeve.

Sonia wrapped her bicep with a piece of latex and swabbed the crook of her arm with alcohol. "Is there no way to safely meet with this Hollister? At least to find out if he has your friend?"

"I'd rather dive into a pool of sharks." She hardly felt it when Sonia inserted the syringe into her arm. Perhaps being a lab rat wouldn't be so bad. *Right.*

Sonia removed the latex band, and dark-red liquid appeared in the tube. "He'd have answers. Perhaps more answers than anyone else."

Her heart skipped. Maybe it was from watching the vial turn red with her blood. Or maybe it was the idea of finding answers. "Why would he know anything?"

Sonia hesitated. "He knows enough to pursue you this aggressively."

Justine struggled to breathe calmly. "What price would I end up paying for that information?"

"Right now, the price might be your friend."

"He was lying. Or very stupid."

"You're sure about that?" Sonia removed the syringe, capped the tube, and wrote on the label. She handed Justine a Band-Aid.

"I will be." Justine pulled out Cayden's phone, and a couple of stray receipts came with it. She shoved them back into her pocket.

"What are you doing with that?"

"It's not mine. It's Cayden's, Quinn's brother."

Sonia gathered up the plastic wrappings and put the vial in an insulated box. "This guy Kos might have tracked you through that."

"Cayden says he disabled all that."

"You trust him?"

Did she? "This Kos wouldn't have had to go through that trouble." With Sonia's help, she tried Quinn's number, but it rang until voicemail picked up. The other name in the contacts stared back at her. If she couldn't speak to Quinn, she could find out something from Cayden that would calm her unease. But there was no answer on that line either. She gripped the phone, wanting to hurl it across the room.

While Sonia carried her equipment into her lab, Justine tried the numbers again. Quinn's went to voicemail.

"Justine?"

"Yeah, it's me." To her surprise, she was glad to hear Cayden's voice.

"Didn't think I'd hear from you. You've been busy."

Justine sighed. Damn video.

"Are you still in Philly?" A dog barked. "Hey, Sully, buddy. Where's the big guy? Hey!" A door slammed. "Your cat is quick, but not quick enough."

"Are you at Quinn's apartment?"

"Yeah. I'm having trouble tracking him down. Was about to call you, see if he went to Philly after all."

"You told him where I was?" A cold knot formed in her stomach.

"Yes, I told him," he said with a huff. "Not that I needed to. He'd find out as soon as he got on the internet. Justine, he just wants you safe. If I hadn't worked most of last night, I would have gone to Philly to see if you'd come back with me. Or at least called repeatedly until you answered. Are you somewhere safe?"

"Somewhere."

"You haven't heard from him? When'd you last talk to him?"

If Quinn didn't trust his brother, should she? She didn't know, but his concern eased the knot inside her a fraction. "Yesterday morning. Feels like a week ago. Why are you looking for him? Isn't he working?"

"I needed to talk to him. He doesn't usually answer my calls, so I have to show up at his job. Instead, I got his partner, who told me he'd called in sick. Which, I guess seeing as he got shot, okay." He paused as things shuffled in the background. "This place is ridiculously neat. Bed's made. But no sign of him."

That was the wrong answer. "How about food for Sully and Cheetah? Did he leave any?"

"Must be some territorial issues. There's some water. One bowl is on the counter with a little food. The cat's, I'm guessing."

"So he was home earlier. You just can't find him now. He could be somewhere with no reception." Her chest tightened as she pushed the limits of credulity.

"His car is parked outside."

"Then he has to be close, if he went without his car. He walks to work sometimes."

"Except for the whole calling-in-sick thing. Look, there's something fishy about this. According to Max, get this, Quinn told him he was thinking of taking a few days to take me to a casino—me?" Cayden cleared his throat. "The last place Quinn would take me to is a casino. I . . . I need to stay away from casinos."

An icy chill washed over her. "So, what, you think that wasn't him?"

"No. I don't know. But it gets weirder. He said he was looking for a place to go nearby, maybe something in his backyard. What does that mean? There aren't any casinos nearby. Not good ones, anyway."

"Has he mentioned any plans like this before?"

"The only place he talked about going to was Philly. He was in the diner last night. I checked. So it's been about twelve hours since anyone's seen him."

"If he was calling to leave you a message, why didn't he just call you?"

Cayden let out a long breath. "I don't know. Look, none of this makes sense. I just . . . I don't like it."

"So you don't think he'll turn up." Justine swallowed as her hopes for Quinn's safety crumbled.

Cayden's voice hitched up a notch. "He's not a missing sock. He shouldn't be this hard to track down. His message means something. I'm just not sure what." After a silent moment, he said, "I was hoping he'd be with you, you know, helping you out."

"I don't need help." She shut her mouth and cut off her tirade.

"But I could use your help. Maybe Quinn needs your help."

Justine's heart stuttered. Cheap shot. "There's not much I can do from here."

"If you came back—"

"And do what? I—" There was so much to say. She let all those words go. "Call Max back. See what the police know or if they've heard from him again."

"Justine, listen, I know you feel safe going into hiding like this. But I think you'd be safer if you weren't alone."

"I'm fine on my own."

"But you could be better than fine. With people helping you out, you wouldn't have to do this all by yourself. Alone."

"Alone is how I do things."

25.

s Justine disconnected the call, she shut New York from her mind. Time to focus on what was before her. She stuck the phone in her pocket, and her fingers hit the cold metal of Quinn's keys. She pulled them out, but it hurt too much to see them, and she shoved them back into her pocket. Rummaging through her backpack, she found a granola bar and a half-full bottle of water. Her clothes were relatively clean. It would have to do.

Sonia stepped out of her lab after putting away the supplies and the blood sample. "So what's the verdict?"

Justine struggled to refill her water bottle from the gallon jug on the counter. Her hand wouldn't hold steady. "Time to go. Forget about the ID. Probably won't help me now. I'll try to call you for your results in a week or so, and we'll call it even."

"Are you sure Quinn's brother will be able to find him?"

She clasped her hands together to steady them. "The police will start looking for him soon. They'll find him."

"If Kos was telling the truth—"

"There's nothing I can do about that!" She heaved a breath, but she was still trembling. She wouldn't trust that man to deliver pizza. How could she know if he'd told her the truth? "I only have one move, one direction to go in."

Sonia hesitated, then nodded. "Give me twenty minutes to run to the drug store. I'll get you some hair color and a few things you can use so you look nothing like yourself."

Justine paused. She itched to get moving.

"Taking an hour now could save you more than time later." Now Sonia hesitated. "If Kos managed to get free—"

"He's in no shape to keep looking for me. He'll crawl back to New York."

Since she wasn't going anywhere just yet, she tried to give in to her exhaustion on the couch after Sonia left. But instead of sleep, the words *What are you* bounced around her head. Worse was that she had no answer.

So she paced from the boarded windows to the warmth of the heater. When that threatened her sanity, she wandered to the doorway of the makeshift lab. Vague familiarity drew her in, yet the more she saw, the more apprehensive she became.

She retained few clear memories of her father. One that had never faded was his directive: if she found herself surrounded by equipment like microscopes and centrifuges, or people in white coats, then she was either in a hospital or a lab, and she was to get out.

But this room was neither. Not really. She stepped forward and turned on the lamp on the high center table. The pieces of equipment she'd carried from the university lay in an orderly array. An ice chest sat on a cabinet in a corner.

Amid the stolen pieces sat a black-and-white marbled notebook. Curiosity overcame her unease, and she took a seat on a stool next to the table and opened the book. The first page read *Thoughts and Observations*, with the initials SDS below it. Small, neat handwriting covered the pages, some with diagrams or graphs. The first few were written in another language, then it switched to English. Pages and pages of notes.

Isolating gene sequences . . . clusters of repeated spacing in the genome . . . cells develop an immunity . . . These connections promised insights greater than we'd imagined.

She skimmed the pages.

. . . But was it worth Jack's life?

Justine flinched, then backed up to the top of the page.

I have so many questions Jack never answered. Yes, he described the protocol and the nature of the altered material he'd used. And yes, they were entirely illegal and unethical. But without taking that risk, we might have never made the connection, seen the potential in the enzyme. Geneticists would still be focused on fixing errors. The GAMA program might have never shifted focus to enhancement.

GAMA program. Had Sonia mentioned it? Someone had, but she couldn't remember who.

But was it worth Jack's life? What he did to his family? And my unasked and unanswered questions: What was the real reason for his family's disappearance? Did Jack's experiments affect his daughter?

She straightened. Her limbs went numb, and her breath came quickly as she scanned the page for her father's name.

If Jack hadn't been so impatient. And driven. His life might have gone differently. If he hadn't confided in me, trusted me with his secret, my life would have gone differently. I would have never had to leave.

I miss it. I miss the simple and complex process of analyzing a sample. I miss peering into a microscope and finding something unexpected. I miss learning something new every day, adding to the body of knowledge called science.

Her father had never felt so far away.

She turned the page and froze. Between the sheets laid a yellowed newspaper article, brittle with age. With a gentle tug, she pulled the clipping from the notebook. In a picture at the top, a small group of people in lab coats huddled around a man in a suit, with a younger man beside him in casual clothes. A caption read: *The Genetic Alteration for Military Advantage Program a decade ago, and some of the scientists who made many of the important initial advancements in our understanding of the human genome, left to right: Dr. Frank Hollister, founder of the GAMA Program; his son Lawrence, a doctoral student at the University of Maryland; Brazilian scientist Sonia da Silva; and American scientists Artie Johnson and Jack Benoit.*

Justine tried to breathe, but her chest was too tight. Her father looked shorter than she remembered. But otherwise her memory had held him true to life. She hadn't realized how young he'd been.

And there, next to the man referred to as Dr. Frank Hollister, was a younger version of the man who'd pursued her through the subway. Kos, who'd shot Quinn and stalked her, worked for the man pursuing her. He worked for this Dr. Hollister. And twenty years ago, this Dr. Hollister had worked with Sonia. And her father.

Sonia had said nothing when Kos had said the name. Had she recognized it? The web of connections surrounding her had been spun long before she'd sensed its presence.

As the story she'd cobbled together of how her father fit into her life fell to pieces, the front door opened and shut. She faced the doorway, questions for Sonia on her tongue.

Heavy footsteps crossed the front room. Someone set something heavy on the floor, and Artie appeared in the doorway. His eyes narrowed. "What are you doing here?"

She stood, clutching the notebook close. So many questions. Where to start? "What did my father do?"

He froze. "What's that you're reading?"

"What did he do that made Sonia and you leave your jobs?" She couldn't keep the tremor out of her voice.

Artie shut his mouth and stared stone faced.

So she was on the right track. "Were you and my dad friends?" she continued, her voice rising. "Were you someone he relied on, who left him when he needed you?"

He opened his mouth, then let out a guffaw, holding his ample waist as he laughed.

She crossed her arms around the book and tapped her foot, waiting for him to finish.

"You have no idea what you're talking about."

"So give me an idea."

He stopped laughing. "It's not my place to tell you what your parents chose not to."

The pang in her chest sharpened. "They're dead. They won't mind."

"Once you know, you can't unknow it," he said in a rough voice, eyes full of secrets long held. "The truth doesn't always set you free."

"It's better than lies."

He pressed his lips into a thin line. "Sonia know you're here?"

She nodded.

"What did she offer you?"

She looked past him, but the woman was nowhere in sight. "She's going to analyze my blood. Thinks it will explain things."

"Let me guess. She made it sound like she was doing you a favor."

She shifted, trying to keep any reaction off her face. "According to these notes, she blames my father for losing her career."

"Sonia needs to move on."

They faced each other in silence.

She might not get another chance. She took a deep breath. "It says in here, my father used some 'altered material.' What was he doing? Is that what got him killed?"

"Hold on, hold on. Slow down." He ran his hand over his face and muttered to himself. "He was alive when I left. So I don't know anything about him getting killed. You don't have the full picture either."

The door to the apartment slammed again. He went to the lab doorway as Sonia set down her bags. "Artie? What's going on?"

"I came up to talk to you about our next move. Found a surprise."

Sonia entered the room. Her gaze fell on the book in Justine's hands, and she froze. "That book is personal."

"It told me more about my father than you have."

Sonia dragged her eyes from the notebook to meet Justine's. "We need to do your hair so you can leave." She gestured for Justine to follow her and returned to the main room.

Justine brought the notebook and her questions with her and laid her coat on the couch. Sonia wrapped her shoulders in an old towel.

"I thought she left already," Artie said.

Ignoring his comment, Sonia placed a folded towel on the edge of the sink.

Clutching the notebook that held the picture of her father, Justine sat on a stool Sonia set in front of the sink. "Artie was about to tell me what my father did with something called 'altered material.'"

Sonia's hands paused as she ripped opened the packaging of the hair dye. "What did you tell her?"

"Nothing. Miss Magic Fingers here thinks she's figured everything out because she went snooping in your journal. Should lock up that room anyway. You never know who could walk through the door."

"Drop it, will you?" Sonia donned flimsy plastic gloves from the kit and opened a bottle of dye.

"Look," Artie said, hands on his hips, poking a finger in Justine's direction, "I don't talk about this. With anyone."

"Time to break the rule. I'm Jack's daughter. The one everyone seemed to wonder about. I don't care who decided who not to tell or what not to say. I'm making the decisions now. I want the truth about my father."

He stood with his hands on his hips, jaw set.

She closed her eyes as Sonia squirted hair color onto her head. "How much information do I have about you, Artie? How much would that info get me?"

"Word to the wise," Artie said, doling out each word, "don't get cornered. You could find somebody interested in locating me, sure. But that's not your get-out-of-jail-free card. They get you, they won't ever let you go."

"Not a get-out-of-jail-free card, but maybe an insurance card."

He threw his hands up and dropped onto the couch. "I have no happy endings for you, so spare me the dramatics. No closure. Just some bad decisions, too much ambition, and lots of questions with no answers."

"If I end up locked up in a lab somewhere, at least I'll understand how I got there."

"'Altered material,'" Sonia said, "refers to a genome that's been manipulated in some way. See, Artie? That wasn't so hard."

"Are you talking about DNA?" Justine asked as she glared at Artie.

"Yes, genomes are composed of DNA. Today, they can target abnormal genes, like bad code, and swap out some pieces for others or add better ones."

Artie crossed his arms and tucked in his chin, as if trying to hold in his secrets. "What Jack did ..." He shook his head. "Edited genetic material had not been administered to live humans at that point. We barely knew what we were working with. The freak-out going on now about genetic enhancement, germ line editing, CRISPR, some of the ideas that led to those discoveries, began with our work in the GAMA program."

She took a breath to slow the pounding of her heart. "Was some of that work part of whatever my father did with this altered material that you thought was so unethical?"

Sonia combed through Justine's hair with her fingers in silence, then came around to face her. "Your father went around regulations, bypassed protocol. He made *himself* the experiment, gave himself the altered material."

Justine stopped breathing. "Why would he do something so . . ."

"Risky? Reckless?" Artie asked.

"I can't tell you that," Sonia said. "I can tell you that when he told me what he'd done, he put me in a tough position. I had to keep quiet until he informed the director. Everything changed after that."

Justine tried to steady her voice. "My father was not a reckless man."

"How would—" Artie cut himself off. "Believe it or don't believe it. Won't change the past."

Her mother would have never agreed to anything like that. Had he kept it from her? As much as she tried to harden her voice, it wavered. "So if it's true, why didn't you stop him?"

Sonia gathered Justine's hair and pinned it on top of her head. "He knew I would try. So he didn't tell me until after it was done."

Justine swallowed, her thoughts swirling and her stomach churning. "Is that when you decided to leave? When he might have needed someone to have his back?" Truth and lies were becoming impossible to distinguish. The few people she could trust were the ones she'd left behind.

"She doesn't want to believe Jack did it to himself," Artie said, looking at Sonia, "on his own, no permission." His eyes returned to Justine. "You seem to think we left Jack in his time of need or something. We're not the bad guys in this story."

"It's easier to accuse the dead."

"I told you, you wouldn't like the answers." He turned to Sonia. "We need to get going. I might have enough time to erase our tracks."

Sonia cleared her throat. "Not as much time as you'd think."

"Did a reporter show up?"

"We had a visitor this morning." She peeled off the plastic gloves and wiped her hands with a towel, eyes on Artie, shoulders tense. "Sent by somebody named *Hollister*. Trying to get her to go back to New York."

"Hollister?" he said faintly. "Frank's got to be long dead—"

"Must be his son, Lawrence." Her eyes avoided meeting Justine's. "He did some work in the lab while he was getting his bioengineering degree."

Justine held her gaze on Sonia. She adjusted the towel around her, and when she thought she could speak without screaming, she said, "So when were you going to mention you worked with this guy who's running through train tunnels after me?"

"We didn't," Sonia said in a rush. "Not really." Justine waited. Sonia let out a breath. "He was just a kid back then, starting his grad work. We left before he graduated."

Justine opened the notebook and pulled out the crisp newspaper clipping. "This looks like more than *not really*. This"—she pointed to the youngest man in the picture—"this is the guy running after me through subway tunnels. You worked with him. You knew the name Hollister when Kos told us who he worked for. But you said nothing. Do you know this Kos guy?"

Sonia reached for the book, but Justine held it out of her grasp. Sonia scowled.

Artie frowned. "Why would Frank's son be looking for Jack's daughter?"

"Why wouldn't he?" Justine asked.

Sonia was quiet a moment. "Did he say anything to you when he found you in the subway?"

Butterflies flitted around her stomach. "He said my dad"—she cleared her throat—"my dad would want me to use my full potential." Those few words left her breathless.

"He's the one who found you in New York?" Artie and Sonia shared a look. "If that prick's son is after her, he must have gone into his father's line of work after all," Artie said.

"Why are you so surprised?" Justine asked.

"Frank created the GAMA program," Sonia said, "where we worked with Jack, but as far as I knew, his son wasn't planning on working with his dad."

The GAMA program. That was where her dad had worked. "So you're saying his son had no reason to search for me?"

Artie sighed. "Frank didn't know about you. No one knew about you. No one except Jack."

"And you. You said he told you, then the whole program—"

"Jack told me what he'd done to himself," Sonia added. "Nothing more."

"Justine, you"—Artie shifted—"you weren't supposed to happen. I mean, you should have been normal. But you were born after your dad's experiment on himself. Somehow he passed something on to you. I don't think even he expected that to happen. It's not how that's supposed to work."

She leaned against the sink, as if the weight of the words pushed her back. "The altered material ... he passed his altered genes on to me." She tried to pick out a thought from the jumble in her mind. "That's why he wanted my DNA."

"It's likely your DNA has mutations or alterations related to your abilities," Sonia said. "Did he say that's what he's after?"

Justine shook her head.

Sonia stepped closer, her eyes softening. "I have no doubt your parents wanted you to have as much of a normal life as possible. Forgive them if they kept too much from you."

Something squeezed, then stretched, deep inside her. An emptiness woke up, one she'd learned to ignore, and absorbed the space around it. Her voice came out small and quiet, like a child's. "Why couldn't my dad have lived that normal life with me?"

Artie's shoulders sagged. "That was never going to happen after what he did."

The expanded space inside her shrunk and hardened. She took a breath, and her voice regained its strength. "How did my father die?"

Sonia lifted her chin. "He was alive when we left. We have no idea what happened after. We cut off all communications and connections."

That was how they had kept themselves from the same fate as her father. And she'd done the same. She'd run, trying to cut herself off from everyone. Never telling Buggy everything. Never being fully honest with Quinn. She told herself she was protecting her friends, that Quinn's safety was worth his confusion and feelings of betrayal.

But like Sonia, Artie, and even her father, she'd been protecting herself. Her silence had been for her own safety. So Quinn wouldn't judge her and decide her world was too much for him. She didn't want him to send her away, so she'd gone away instead, when perhaps he needed her help more than ever.

"If Frank didn't know about me, how did his son find out?"

"You'd have to ask him that," Sonia said. "Lean back. Should be enough time."

She turned on the water, and Justine laid back against the sink. The icy water ran over her scalp and cleared her head.

This man coming after her would know the answers to the questions she'd stopped asking. If she agreed to talk to him, would he give her answers? Would he free Quinn? One thing Justine knew: she was done with being in the dark. She'd acted and reacted on misinformation her entire life.

Artie stood and breathed deeply, his voice calmer. "I suggest you pack up this place or leave your toys behind. See if Gracie will watch after those who need it. But make it quick. I'm not waiting around for Hollister junior to show up."

After he walked out, Sonia wrapped her head in a towel and let her stand. "I also got you some makeup to change your look. It might help." She eyed the notebook. "Have you heard anything from Cayden or Quinn?"

"No." She glared, wishing she could melt her face off. She could use the practice.

"You could—"

"I made some calls, okay?" Justine shifted. "He's not at work."

"Justine, what you do now can't be undone later. Regrets don't get easier to live with over time."

"You think I should go back to New York."

"What does Quinn mean to you? Consider what price he may pay for knowing you."

Justine gasped at the deep slice of her words. "I'm not sure what's really happened."

"So find out."

"You ran," she said, hating the tremor in her voice. "You left your life behind. Do you regret that?"

"Every day."

Shit. She pulled the towel from her hair and pulled her fingers through the wet strands. She pulled a damp lock toward her face. Medium brownish. Buggy would have been satisfied. "You think I should risk Hollister finding me because of your regrets."

"So you don't end up with the same."

She slammed the notebook onto the counter. "Did you choose between living free or being a prisoner?"

"No," Sonia said quietly. "My choices were much simpler. Leave my husband and my life behind, or stay and perhaps end up dead."

"There are things worse than death."

"Yes, there are. I know that now."

Justine dropped onto the stool and rested her head in her hand, letting the web close around her.

26.

Justine slipped through the back door of the diner and paused in the storage room to shake the snow off her coat, relishing the warmth of the room. After taking the next train out of Philly, she'd arrived that evening in a snowy New York. She'd avoided the subway and main streets all the way from Penn Station, and the cold had sunk deep into her.

The relief of familiar surroundings—the sizzle and smell of cooking meat, the clang of the plates as the dishwasher worked through his pile of dishes, even the strains of Christmas music playing over a speaker—took her by surprise. It was like Justine had walked into the house of an old friend. She stepped out of the storeroom and set her bag on the floor as Nita filled a bin with dirty dishes.

The waitress looked up and froze, then broke into a wide grin. "Jus … what are you …" Her dark hair was tied in its usual bun, but her face was ruddy, too red.

Nita glanced at the full bin in her arms. "Don't move." She swept past Justine and returned in moments empty handed, grabbing a rag and wiping her hands. "Didn't think I'd see you again." She brushed snow out of Justine's hair. "I like the brown. I guess the red was too noticeable, huh?"

Justine acknowledged the comment with a tilt of her head and gestured for Nita to step with her behind the wall by the closet. "What's been going on?"

Nita's left cheek was redder than the other, even a bit puffy. She rested her hands on her hips. "Your answer to that question is way more interesting than mine, I'm sure. This mean you're back?"

To her surprise, Justine almost said yes. "You don't look the same as when I left."

Nita covered her cheek with her hand and bit her lip, her eyes shifting away. "Everything changes. Don't worry about it."

She grabbed Nita's arm. "I'm done with leaving things alone."

Nita pulled out of her grip and tossed the rag on the counter. "I don't know what you've gotten yourself mixed up in, but two guys came around last night asking about you."

Cold washed over Justine. She surveyed the diner. A few customers ate and talked. No one looked her way. "What did they want?"

As Nita described her attackers, Justine's anger heated up. Perhaps marching straight into a well-laid trap was not the best strategy. Whoever was behind all of this knew how to get her where they wanted. She took a breath to try to stuff her fury down.

"Stop fussing. They left when they figured out they couldn't force me to tell them what I didn't know."

Justine clasped Nita's hands in her own. "They will not hurt you again."

"If they were why you left, why'd you come back?"

"I'm looking for Quinn. Have you seen him?"

"He was in last night. Asked lots of questions too. Everybody wants to know where you went off to."

"Yeah, popularity sucks, trust me." She hoped she gave Nita a smile, though it didn't feel right.

At the chime of the front door, Nita went out to face a new customer.

"I called this morning," the customer said, "about my brother, Quinn Duncan."

Justine's heart jumped.

"Could you find out if he's been in today?"

"Haven't seen him, and I've worked the whole day."

Justine pulled out the phone Cayden had given her. It had been on all this time. She pocketed it and came out from behind the wall. "So I guess you're here because you have good timing?" She aimed a level look at him.

His mouth dropped open. "Justine? You're ... not in Philly. What are you doing here? Why is your hair brown?"

She sighed. "Are you saying you weren't expecting me?"

"When we talked this morning, I thought you were pretty clear," he said with a shrug.

She walked up to him, inches from his face. "You said this phone was untraceable. Then you find me in the subway. You follow me to Philadelphia. Now you show up here as soon as I do. You have been tracking me."

Cayden scowled. "I gave you the phone after I found you. And I can explain the rest."

She crossed her arms. "So explain."

"I'm trying to find Quinn. Why are you here?"

"Same reason."

"So doesn't it make sense we end up in the same place?"

She scowled. "Have you looked for him at all?"

"I'm trying to. I've been at work all day and most of last night. Thought maybe he stopped in for coffee. Look, I don't have time for this. I want to check his apartment again before I get back to work."

"I'm going with you."

He threw his hands up. "Then let's go." He headed for the door.

She squeezed Nita's hand as she started to leave.

"Wait," Nita said. "What's this about him tracking you? Are you sure you should go with him? Do you trust him?"

"No, but he's the best I can do right now." She wanted to say more, but instead trotted out the door to catch up with Cayden. If he was keeping something from her, she'd get it out of him one way or another.

~ ~ ~

"I'm not blushing. My cheeks get red in the cold. Comes with being Irish," Cayden said, brushing snow off his coat as they climbed the stairs to Quinn's apartment. "Is it really important right now how red my cheeks are?"

Justine pulled out the keys Quinn had given her. She never thought she'd use them, much less like this. "It's important if it means you're hiding something from me."

"What? I'm not," he said, shoulders hunched.

As they entered the apartment, Sully came bounding out of the bedroom with a high-pitched whine and tail wagging. Cheetah followed the dog more sedately until he saw Justine. He broke into a trot and crashed into her calf, purring like a motor. She picked up the cat and held him close. For a moment, tension drained from her as she buried her face in his fur.

While Cayden took the dog for a much-needed walk, Justine curled up on the couch, where she had last spoken with Quinn. He'd left a mug with a reindeer on the coffee table this morning next to unopened mail. She pulled the blanket from the back of the couch, imagining it was Quinn's arms as she wrapped it around her, and cradled the empty mug in her hands.

Two days ago she'd had so much and known so little. To have Quinn back, she'd give up knowledge of her father's supposed role in her ability. Even if she gave up everything—and she would—what she would not give up was the conviction Quinn had given her that she belonged in the world and not as an oddity better off studied in a lab. And she would not give up Quinn.

The door slammed, and Cayden and Sully headed to the kitchen. After filling the animals' bowls with food, he peeked out. "You hungry? Want anything to drink?"

She shook her head. Cheetah jumped from her arms toward the kitchen.

After retrieving a laptop from the bedroom, Cayden settled beside Justine. He pulled equipment out of his backpack between glances at her. "The brown looks good on you."

She ran a hand over her hair. "What are you doing with all that?"

He connected a tablet to the computer. "I'm going to poke around his computer, check his calendar, notes, stuff like that."

"You have his password?"

"No." He typed for a few moments before shaking his head. "He's got to make a better one."

"Is this illegal?"

He closed his eyes and sighed.

She leaned closer. "Yes, I'm going to keep asking questions."

"The less you know, the better."

"Can you find his phone?"

"Not without doing a few things I don't have time for. I've got a . . . a big project at work I've got to get back to."

"At nine o'clock at night? Can't you talk to your boss?"

"Not an option." He tapped on the tablet, then typed on the laptop, lips pressed shut.

"What have you found?"

Cayden looked at her like she had asked him to jump out the window. "I'm good, but not that good. Give me a minute."

She gestured to the screen. "Explain what you're doing."

"I'm looking through the files he opened recently." He tapped the tablet. "Looks like he used this last night. I want to see if he was working on a case."

"So you think we can find him." Justine hadn't thought she'd held on to so little hope.

He frowned. "Of course we will. He's got to be somewhere."

"What if he hasn't called because"—she swallowed—"because he can't?"

He scrolled and typed. "First, I'm assuming he's alive, because—"

A flash of terror swept through her. "Of course he's *alive.*"

"There is no *of course*. He's in a dangerous line of work. We can't be sure of anything right now. So *assuming* he's alive, if he hasn't used his phone, yeah, it's a good bet he can't. But I think we'd hear from someone."

She looked away. "And you think whatever's happened to him has to do with his work."

Cayden squinted as he read a message. "It's a place to start. Looks like he was juggling a few cases." He opened several windows, then typed. "There we go. Yesterday's notes."

"What are you typing?" She pointed to the words *NextLevel Industries*. Below that, the notes continued. There was a New York address.

He checked his phone, then tapped out a message. "Um, that's just a company."

It was like he'd never tried to lie in his life. "What company?" She leaned in close to him.

He kept his eyes on the laptop screen. "It's the company I work for, okay? I told Quinn some things yesterday. I wanted to see if he'd looked into any of it."

"How does this help us find him?"

"It—" He let out a long breath. "Give me a minute." He tapped the keys, text scrolling up before she could read it. "He was working late last night. Seems like—crap."

"What did—"

"Hold on." He muttered as he typed.

She grabbed his arm. "Tell me what you found."

His phone buzzed. He checked the message. "Shit." He heaved a breath as he closed the laptop. "I've got to go."

"Wait, what? Just like that?"

"That was my manager. Can't say no. Not today." He stood, disconnected the devices, and packed up. "Look, I'll continue this as soon as I—"

Justine stepped in front of him, hands on her hips. "What was in those notes?"

He stiffened. "It might be nothing."

She held his gaze.

"Last night he was going after some leads." He swallowed. "And he discovered he was being followed."

"Followed? By who? How is that nothing?"

He ran a hand through his hair, then shoved his tablet into his knapsack and zipped it up. "I . . . I've got to go. I'm sorry."

She tried to stay calm. But she was tired of evasion. Of bad liars not even trying. She was tired of *No*. She ripped the backpack out of Cayden's hands and threw it across the room.

The shock on his face twisted into anger as the bag crashed against the wall and fell to the floor a couple feet from the Christmas tree. "What are you—"

"I'm not here to play around," she said through clenched teeth. "If you're not here to find Quinn, you're wasting my time." She lowered her voice. "Now, who was following him?"

He froze, eyes wide, then eased back a step, as if from a dangerous animal. He held up a hand. "Look, I'll tell you. Just don't jump to conclusions. It's not what it looks like."

She tapped a foot.

"He was investigating my boss—"

"You said that. You wanted him to investigate your company, NextLevel. Who's your boss?"

He grabbed his phone from the table and his coat, eyeing Justine, then the bag on the floor. She stepped toward him, and he backed up. "I'm going to tell you, damn it. Will you chill? You're freaking me out." His gaze lingering on his backpack, he said, "Not sure you know his name. I work for Dr. Lawrence Hollister."

She flinched. "Hollister?" All the warmth drained from her body. The threads of the web she'd walked into were far longer than she'd ever realized. "You've been lying to me this whole time." Her voice lost all its force. "You knew the man chasing me in the subway. I suppose you know this other guy, Kos?"

He rolled his eyes, then frowned. "Did he do something to you?"

"To me? I'm sure that's what he'll say happened." She crossed her arms again. "Tell me the truth. Are you tracking me or not?"

"Even if I had the time, that phone is not traceable."

"Then how did Kos find me in Philly?"

His eyebrows rose. "Kos found you in Philly?"

Justine put her hands on her hips.

"I swear on my mother's grave, I did not know about that. Look, I do want to look for Quinn. I just can't right now. I have . . . commitments."

"Commitments to the asshole chasing me down. What do you do for him?"

"Write software for medical tech."

"Software for what?"

"For implants and stuff that help people use artificial limbs. I'm not clear on all the details. I just do my job."

Maybe he was counting on her trusting him. And she did want to believe him. He was Quinn's brother. But if he hadn't told Kos, who had? Right, the internet. "Your boss is coming after me. After your brother starts investigating him, he disappears. You won't say who was following him, but it's not a huge leap to think Hollister might know where he is."

"Look, holding a cop, even just preventing him from leaving, that's serious. Hollister's ruthless, but he's not stupid."

"We'll see when I ask him myself."

"What? No, no, no. Hell, no. You can't go there." He skirted around her and collected his bag. "Listen to me," he said as he shuffled through the contents. "Don't go there. It's . . . it's not a good idea."

Was he trying to keep her away or tempt her into going there? She moved between him and the door. "Cayden, whose side are you on?"

He froze, his cheeks flushing red again. "You think I don't want my brother safe?"

"Maybe he's fine. Maybe your job was to get me where Hollister wants me."

Cayden's mouth opened and shut like a fish struggling for air. "I am not trying—" He took a breath. "Okay, look. Believe me, don't believe me—whatever. I know I can't make you do anything. But instead of going there, call them. Ask to speak to a woman named Val Moretti. Forget about Hollister."

"Why her?"

"Because she's more reasonable, and she'll answer your questions, if she can. Hollister's a little out there."

"They work together?"

"I report to her. She leaves the sciencey stuff to Hollister, but she really keeps the place going. If Quinn had called, say, to question someone, she'd know."

"So why haven't you talked to her?"

Cayden closed his eyes, breathing heavily, and ran a hand through his hair. "Why would I think NextLevel was involved? I just found out Quinn discovered he was being followed. Look, I've been working for like twenty-four hours straight. I didn't have time to waste asking my manager why—they do not—" He drew his hand over his face with a deep sigh. "I'll make some calls after I finish what I've got to do tonight. If he hasn't shown up by the morning, call Val if you want. Don't waste time going over there. It's a dead end. Trust me." He gestured to the door. "Can I leave? I've got to go now, unless I want to lose my job."

She tried to take a moment to enjoy thoughts of what she might do if he was lying. But the image of

Cayden slamming into the wall disturbed her instead. She stepped out of his way and followed him as he headed to the door without turning his back on her. "I don't need your help to find him. But don't stand in my way." She slammed the door in his face.

As his steps faded, she turned all the locks and the deadbolt. She hated that she was disappointed. She'd put too much hope and trust in him. She scooped up Cheetah and went to the window, peering out without moving the curtain to avoid illuminating her face by the blinking lights lining the window. Cayden trudged through the snow to cross the street, huddled against the cold.

She returned to the sofa. Cayden had left Quinn's computer on the coffee table. After a second of glaring at the machine, she lifted the top, and the screen lit up. The words *Log in* appeared on a blue background. She didn't know the password.

A rapping at the door made Justine jump while Sully barked. Cheetah's ears swiveled around, but he let the dog take care of security.

"Detective Duncan? It's Officer Ramos."

She froze, then took a breath. They were only here for Quinn. Not her. She released the cat and unlocked the door to find two men with badges hooked onto their belts. "Quinn's not here," she said, trying to keep her head down. The dog barked beside her, and she grabbed his collar. "Sully, quiet."

"Do you know where he is?"

"I figured he was at work. It's where he usually is if he's not home this late."

"I'm Officer Ramos. This is Officer Finn. And you are?"

Her throat shriveled, all moisture in her mouth evaporating.

"You're Justine, aren't you?" Officer Finn said.

She looked more closely at him. "Are you Max? Sorry. I didn't recognize you outside the diner."

"Duncan called in sick. I figured he finally decided to get some rest. But he's supposed to be at home," Max said.

"He called in sick?"

"That's right. Has he been home at all today?"

She tried to focus on Max's questions while her heart rate picked up speed. "No. I mean, I don't know. Does this mean you're looking for him?"

"If a fellow officer can't be located, we start looking immediately." He exchanged a look with Officer Ramos. "Let me ask you a few questions. It could help us to know where to start."

"Let me put the dog in the bedroom." She closed the bedroom door behind a barking Sully as the officers stepped inside. Cheetah watched her from the couch. *Lay low, Cheetah.*

"When did you last see him?" Max asked, still at the entrance, while his partner walked around the apartment.

"A couple of nights ago."

Max wrote in a notepad. "Have you talked to him at all since then?"

As she started to answer, Ramos called out, "Finn, can I get a moment?"

"Give me a minute, please." Max joined his partner by the couch, where he passed his phone to him. Max shot a look at Justine, then at the phone, and shook his head.

"What's your full name, miss?" Ramos asked.

There it was. That look of recognition. She'd expected it from Hollister in the subway. From the cops, not so much.

Until her face had been plastered all over the web. Until she'd been put into a database for all cops to see. She tried to control her breathing. Could they arrest her here if she was wanted in Philly?

"Justine, where were you last night?"

27.

Justine bolted down the stairs of the building at top speed. When the answer to the question was *I was on the run from a mad scientist who wants to experiment on me*, it was time for old tactics.

She'd left her bag in the apartment. Good thing she hadn't taken off her coat. Something hard banged against her hip. Cayden's phone in her pocket. All she had with her.

She burst out of the building as the officers scrambled after her. She clutched the railing and half stepped, half slid down the snow-covered front steps onto the sidewalk.

"Justine, wait! This doesn't help Quinn," Finn called out as he rushed out the front door.

She cut left. At the corner, she paused. Finn was navigating the stairs, and Ramos had caught up to him.

Finn was right. But she could not be taken into custody in New York. She turned onto Suffolk Street and sped down the middle of the street, where less snow had accumulated. Farther up the block on the right, a wrought iron gate blocked the entrance to a small garden. She'd staked out this shortcut for moments like this. She yanked on the gate just in case, but it was locked. With a glance at the officers jogging in her direction, she grabbed the icy bars of the fence and used the lock as a step to reach the top. She climbed over and jumped, landing hard in the snow.

Skidding along a walkway between trees and shrubs, she stumbled on a planter she'd forgotten split the path in two. She hopped over the next one and continued under an archway of dormant plants. At the rear, she scaled a chain-link fence, her frozen hands barely gripping the metal. Behind her, Ramos skidded to a stop at the garden entrance and, with a shout to Finn, started climbing. He couldn't have been an officer who favored donuts over fitness? As long as the snow revealed where she'd gone, her only hope was to outrun them.

On the other side, with buildings blocking ambient street light, the gloomy courtyard extended to her left. She ran around garbage bins and other obscure shapes as fast as she dared, until she crashed into another taller fence.

Bright lights glowed across an open expanse beyond the fence. Quick footsteps neared from behind. Forward was her only choice. She clambered up the chain link, her hands numb to the pinch of wires. She paused halfway up to catch her breath, the cold sharp in her lungs.

Behind her, a police radio squawked. "She's in the back of a building off Suffolk, heading toward Houston."

She pushed herself up the fence. While swinging over the top, she fumbled as she lost her grip, and panicked. The ground was so far away. Shoving her feet into the fencing and forcing her fingers to grasp the steel wires, she lowered herself until she could jump. Ramos stopped at the fence and barked into his radio.

She slipped and skidded across the large lot toward what should be Houston Street. Even this late at night, there would be enough people to obscure her, or at least distract the officers.

Over the last fence, she landed on shaky limbs and broke into a run.

Right into Finn's arms. She cried out and pulled away, but he held on.

"Easy, easy." Into his radio, he said, "I've got her on Houston," and it squelched in response.

Panic started her thrashing.

"Justine! I'm just trying to find Quinn. Don't you want to know if he's okay?"

She forced herself to calm down while continuing to tug at Finn's grip on her. "Then look for him. You're wasting time coming after me."

He tightened his hold on her. "Then why'd you run?"

She had no good answer.

"Why do the Philly police want to talk to you?"

Damn. "You need to look for Quinn. I can't find him. Neither can his brother. He could be in trouble."

"Then help me. Tell me what you know."

She twisted away until her arm jerked free and ran into the street. A blaring horn alerted her to the taxi barreling toward her. She darted to the median and trotted farther down until the traffic eased, while Finn was stuck behind the stream of cars.

Sprinting to the other side, she dodged a sedan, braced herself as an SUV screeched to a stop before her, and tumbled onto the sidewalk. At the corner, she cut down Avenue B. The snow on the sidewalk was well trampled, so her footprints wouldn't stand out. But she hadn't investigated any shortcuts in this area. She'd have to make it up as she went along.

Passing one side street, she turned left at East Third Street and found her answer in a shadowy cluster of trees between buildings. She tried to grip the fence, but she had no command of her hands and she slid to the ground. Only after pulling her coat sleeves over her hands could she scale the wrought iron bars. Panting heavily, each frigid breath like a knife in her chest, she scurried into the murky pathways of the garden among trees and benches, scuffing her footprints behind her. The night fell around her like a cloak.

She dropped behind a bench among bushes heavy with snow and sat back on her haunches, trying to slow her breathing as she waited to not be found. She shivered, and her toes lost feeling.

It seemed she'd spent her whole life hiding. There had to be a better way. Artie and Sonia had managed to live in hiding without cowering in shadows. She was clearly doing this wrong.

When she couldn't bear the cold any longer, she emerged from her hiding place and brushed snow off her coat. Step by cautious step, she approached the entrance and climbed out, her body aching. On the sidewalk, there was no sign of either officer. A couple of men scurried by, huddled in their coats. A group of women chatted loudly down the street. She returned to Avenue B and paused. To her right was Quinn's apartment, and beyond that the building where she had lived for a year. She didn't dare go back to either.

She headed down Avenue B, weaving among enough people that she didn't stand out. She tried to calm herself, but her body wasn't ready to relax. Sonia's couch hadn't exactly been easy on her back, but it might be far better than wherever she ended up sleeping tonight.

She'd come so close to a real lead. Quinn had been investigating Hollister's company. Cayden's company. The address below the name NextLevel in the notes must have been the location of the offices. She needed a map.

She made her way up Houston toward the Second Avenue subway station, on the other side of Roosevelt Park. Huge maps covered most of one wall of the station, and she traced the streets until she located the address on the west side of the Bowery.

It wasn't long before she reached Bond Street, in a neighborhood with glass storefronts and restaurants, likely with cameras at every entrance. The address was a glass door beside a restaurant leading to a second-floor office. Bits of letters and the outline of the rest remained on the glass. The word *Next* was clear, as was *Indust* below it. They'd removed the name when the company had left the space.

She leaned against the cold brick and slid to the ground. She'd run and walked and asked questions and demanded answers, but she was no closer than she had been when she'd arrived back in this city. She was out of solutions, out of ideas, or even a direction to turn.

She would not leave Quinn in the hands of a madman. She had to find a way to make sure he was safe while keeping herself out of those same hands.

The cold had seeped into her bones. She struggled to stand, brushing snow off her coat, and froze. To the left of the door, a camera stared at her, a small red light winking. An icy wave far colder than the night air passed over her. She'd likely passed many cameras on her way here. But only this camera mattered, if it was still monitored, if it was Hollister watching.

Her heart pounding in her chest, she started back the way she'd come. She'd have to see if the police were still at Quinn's apartment, and if not, she'd risk staying there. She had to get off the street.

A buzzing vibration in her pocket made her jump. Who would call her? She wanted to talk to Buggy. She wanted to talk to Quinn. Only Cayden had the number.

And one other person. She tried to steady her breath as she answered. "Sonia."

"What's wrong?" Sonia asked.

If only she had time to answer her. "What do you know about what Hollister was working on while he was in that program? Who does he work for now?"

"I thought you went back to New York to find Quinn."

"Working on it."

Sonia made a vague sound. "I couldn't say what he's working on now or for whom. I left soon after he started. But I'm calling because I have some results for you. Well, *some* would be generous. It's not much, but I thought you'd want to know."

"And?" She crossed the street to stand beneath a store's awning. She should be safe from cameras here.

"The results are interesting. At least to me. But it's not much yet."

"How about the highlights?" She scanned the street. There wasn't much of a chance the camera trained on the old entrance to NextLevel was still monitored and would lead someone here so quickly. But she was not one to gamble.

"It's hard to convey over the phone. Graphs and charts do it best. I can try to explain a few things so it can make some sense to you. And I'll try to write something up."

She ached to ask more questions, but she had other priorities at the moment. "Does the name NextLevel Industries mean anything to you?"

"Okay ... No, it doesn't."

"Yeah, I'm a little distracted right now. Could you find out what you can about it? And maybe an address?"

"Are you trying to find Lawrence or Quinn?" Sonia asked.

"Maybe both."

"So that jackass in my building was telling the truth?"

"Possibly."

"What about his brother?"

Justine paused. "I'm being more selective with who I ask for help."

Neither said anything for a long stretch. "You might as well learn how to use the internet, since you're all over it. Try a library—they'll help you. I can say, whatever Lawrence's doing, he'll need a lab. Equipment. More than what I have. That means space."

Justine wasn't sure what Sonia wanted, but she couldn't deny the woman had information she needed. And information she wanted. She took a deep breath. "What if you came to New York? You could show me your results." Silence. "I know you're taking off with Artie. This would only be a detour, for less than a day. And if you stick around, when I find Hollister, you can face the bastard yourself. Say what's on your mind."

Finally, Sonia answered. "That would be a bonus."

~ ~ ~

"Adjusting our timeline for another round of tests is more realistic," Hollister told Val as they took seats at the conference table. He set down a clear plastic box, but held onto a small vial containing the strands of hair he'd had the presence of mind to grab when Lizzie had slipped from his grasp. "The implant will be finalized in tandem with the electronics package."

Val set down her phone and notebook and went to the coffeemaker, stifling a yawn. "Kalakos has to incorporate whatever changes we decide to make. He's going to need more time."

Hollister slipped the vial into a pocket and steepled his fingers. He would have to address Kalakos's failures.

He had given the man a second chance, and he had come back from Philly empty handed. Val would not have returned without her.

"It's another moving part to track, one with a high level of risk." She had shed her business attire for jeans and a turtleneck soon after the end of business hours. A few hours after that, she'd started making coffee. "My suggestion would be to cut your losses. Don't use Kos though. That half-wit's mistakes always come back to haunt you."

"I have no intention of eliminating someone with so much potential." Without Lizzie—for now—he needed this backup option more than ever.

"Not unless she takes the bait," she said. "Keep in mind, DARPA's deadline is only three weeks away."

He gritted his teeth. "I will hire an additional coder or two. With your singular focus keeping us moving forward, Kalakos will maintain his pace, and we'll make the deadline." His phone buzzed, and he checked the message. "Cayden is back."

"Finally. It's two a.m."

Hollister rose to pace. He didn't mind the hour, but he would rather spend the time in his lab. Perhaps Val was somewhat correct regarding his focus.

Cayden entered the conference room, carrying his backpack on his shoulder and wearing dark clothes, a black baseball cap, and a deep frown.

"Any problems?" Hollister asked.

The younger man set his bag on the table, draped his coat, damp with snow, across the back of a chair, and dropped into the seat. "It was fine."

"Then what's wrong?" Val asked, sipping from her mug.

His frown turned into a scowl. "It's fucking two in the morning, that's what's wrong. Is committing felonies supposed to cheer me up?" His eyebrows rose as he noticed her mug. "Coffee."

With caffeine in hand, he drew several black cushioned cases out of his bag and laid them on the table before them.

Hollister grabbed the largest case, unzipped it, and slid out a clear plastic container a bit larger than a jewelry box. Inside, a neural implant, a piece of silicon mere millimeters on a side, rested on a cushion, gold hairlike electrodes dotting the edges. "Excellent." He set the box beside the case he'd brought containing NextLevel's version, and nodded. "We can use this."

"I would hope so," Val murmured as she pulled out her phone and photographed a second case with another chip inside.

"Any issues with disarming their security?" Hollister asked as he examined the implant from all angles.

"It was fairly straightforward," Cayden said, looking into his mug without drinking.

"Took you some time," Val said.

"Their system was pretty well set up."

Hollister moved on to the chip Val had photographed, a variation of the first. "You didn't trip any alarms? Fall into any traps?"

Cayden's glance at Hollister was brief. "Nope. By the time they figure out there was a breach, we'll have presented our prototype to DARPA. And MedTech still won't know who it was."

"Then don't look so morose," Val said as she wrote in her notepad. "Think of the healthy chunk of your debt this bonus will pay."

Cayden eyed her as he drank his coffee. "Fuck my debt. This is the last time I cross the line for you."

"Unless I pay you more," Hollister said, inspecting the chip while holding it with a tweezer.

Cayden took a sip of coffee. "So are we changing our design, working off of MedTech's version?"

Hollister returned the implants to their cases and rotated the view. They would learn from these, and their products would be better for it. "Val, find out who designs for MedTech."

"You want to hire them?" Val asked as she continued to take pictures.

"Perhaps." He turned back to Cayden. "You will modify your code based on the design of these prototypes. That will get us past the problems we're experiencing with our hardware." He turned to Val. "We will need to test the design. Now that we have an alternate subject, this shouldn't upset the schedule."

Val tilted her head in acknowledgment. "So we use Eddie for the existing prototype."

"This new arrangement will provide a more accurate and cleaner test."

"A new subject?" Cayden asked, shifting in his seat.

"Yes. An opportunity presented itself."

Cayden's eyes remained on the neural implants he'd taken from MedTech's vault. "So what happens to Eddie? Same as the last guy?"

"The last one was invalidated and so had to be discarded."

"Dis …" Cayden fussed with his coffee cup.

Hollister waited.

"So the new guy"—Cayden cleared his throat—"will stick around if he works out?"

"The well-being of the subject is not your concern. Now, I assume you were able to download the complete set of schematic files."

Cayden nodded, his eyes on his laptop screen.

"Send everything to me. But don't spend all night. I need you functional tomorrow."

Cayden chugged the rest of his coffee and stood.

"Nicely done," Val said.

"Yes, you did well."

"Hollister," Val said, "I suggest you reconsider how much Cayden can do for you. He's proven far more capable and careful than Kos."

The younger man froze amid collecting his things. Hollister forced himself to wait in silence. Val's ideas were usually worth the wait.

"We both know you need to focus on the development of these implants. You can't deny your efforts to bring in this young woman has been a distraction. Let Cayden take up the task of bringing her in. You'll be free to analyze the implants and oversee the redesign. We all win." She smiled.

"Uh, what girl?"

Hollister's lips quirked. Val was a genius. She deserved Cayden's bonus. He turned to the young man. "You did fail in redirecting your brother's investigation." Cayden opened his mouth, but Hollister cut him off. "We've taken care of that issue. Now—"

"You have?"

"Yes. Your bonus now has a few more requirements."

Cayden scowled. "I did what you asked."

Buying this man's debt was one of his best business moves. "And you will continue to do so. Your next task is to bring Lizzie in. You may know her as Justine." Adrenaline shot through Hollister as Cayden attempted with only moderate success to keep his reaction off his face. "I would be reluctant to hand this over to anyone, but you have proven yourself skilled and versatile. More importantly, she has a relationship with your brother. You likely know where she is right now." He stood. He'd wasted so much time. "If not, I'm sure you can find out with far less effort than I've already expended. Bring her here."

Cayden open and shut his mouth. "I know . . . I know the girl my brother's dating. But I don't know where she is. I don't even know where he is right now."

"I suggest you give up lying as a strategy, Cayden. It's not one of your strengths."

Cayden looked a bit green around the edges. "Look, my brother hasn't been seen in over a day. I need to talk to Kos. I don't have time for another hunt."

Hollister smiled. "No need to talk to Kalakos. Your brother is not missing."

Cayden's eyes went wide, and he swallowed.

"If the money doesn't provide enough of an incentive, I can supply another. I can make the well-being of the new subject your concern. In fact, his well-being will depend on your success."

28.

Justine squinted into the weak morning sun as she turned the corner of Essex at Rutgers Street. Last night she'd agreed to meet Sonia in Seward Park, but when she reached the place where her life had been upended, she'd opted to circle the block instead. She'd rather risk being caught on a surveillance camera than watch that movie replay in her head.

Lying awake last night in Quinn's bed, she'd promised she would do whatever she had to do to find him. Once he was safe, she could disappear and give the internet time to forget her. And with luck, Hollister would lose her trail. Maybe someday she could return.

She slowed as she neared the subway entrance south of the park. Down below, Buggy had died, alone. Would she die alone?

As Justine considered where she might wait out people's memories, Sonia emerged from the stairs. She took in the traffic and people and the park with its bare branches outlined in snow and nodded to Justine. "Snow always softened the edges of this city."

Justine nodded back at the woman who had known her father better than she did. Her shoulders relaxed a fraction. "It's good for leaving footprints too."

Sonia gestured to the park. "Let's find a spot to sit."

"We should keep moving."

"Not yet." Sonia tugged at a large tote she carried on her shoulder. "I need another sample."

"I thought you came here to share your analysis with me."

"I did. Since I didn't have all the equipment I needed, much of the specimen deteriorated before I could do anything with it. I'd like to try again."

Or she wanted something for the information she'd come to share. Her idea of an even trade. At least Justine knew where this sample would end up. "Let's go by the river. This is too visible."

"The riverfront is wide open. At least here we have the cover of trees. And a place where we can sit for a minute. This won't take long." Sonia headed into the park.

Echoes of a gunshot sliced through Justine's thoughts as she forced her feet to follow. Her pulse raced as she passed the spot where a mere week ago, she had almost lost Quinn. She'd been losing him since that night. But she would not leave him with Hollister, not when she couldn't be sure of the man's intentions.

The dormant fountain along the Essex side of the park sat in a long space ending in circular concrete benches covered in snow. Instead, they sat on the edge of metal benches closer to the fountain, cold and damp but clear of snow.

Justine tucked her backpack between her feet while Sonia unzipped an insulated case between them on the bench. "Take your arm out of your sleeve." She did as she was told, draping her coat over her bare arm.

When a couple approached, cutting through the park, Sonia paused her preparations. "Any news on Quinn?" As soon as the two had passed, she ripped open the packaging of the syringe and prepared Justine's arm for the blood draw.

"Maybe." Her heart beat an extra beat as Sonia plunged the needle into her arm. She kept an eye on their surroundings as the tube filled with dark blood.

A man walking his dog entered the park. Justine stiffened, trying not to dislodge the syringe. Sonia fussed with the opening of her coat, taking a peek at the syringe while blocking the equipment from view. "It's not that complicated. Either you know where he is or you don't."

Justine scowled. Once the dog finished his duty and man and dog left the park, she heaved a breath. Sonia removed the vial and sealed it, then removed the needle. As she stowed the tube in a padded pouch and packed the equipment, Justine put her arm back into her coat and stood, wiping melted snow off her jeans. "It's hard to tell who's giving me all the facts, some of the facts, or their version of the facts."

Sonia zippered her bag. "It probably was in Kos's interest to tell you they had Quinn."

"Or in Hollister's interest. Which doesn't mean it's true. All of them have been trying to get me within his reach. Maybe this is just another lure."

"*All* of them?"

Justine looked away, opened her mouth, then closed it.

"Where would Quinn be then, if not with Lawrence, or rather, Dr. Hollister?"

"They could have sent him on some wild-goose chase to keep him occupied. I know, I know," she said before Sonia could object. "Not likely. But I need to be sure, and that's impossible when I can't trust anyone."

"Regardless, you should focus on finding Quinn rather than Dr. Hollister."

"And if they're the same thing?"

Sonia seemed to sag, as if exhausted. After a moment, she walked over to the fountain, dusted with snow. "I met my husband in New York. We were at a conference."

Justine stepped up next to her, new questions popping up in her mind. But she returned to her old ones. "What was the GAMA program trying to accomplish when you were part of it?"

Sonia let out a drawn-out sigh and cleared her throat, her gaze shifting back to the fountain and back to the present. "DARPA is the research arm of the Defense Department. They're always looking for how to give soldiers physical advantages on the battlefield."

"Physical advantages?"

"Their goal is a soldier who doesn't need much sleep, heals quickly, and hits the target every time.

GAMA, as part of DARPA, was tasked with finding a genetic solution."

Justine swallowed. "What does that mean?"

"We were to identify dormant genes that could be turned on to enhance or amplify a characteristic."

"This was the work you and my father were doing? And maybe that Hollister is doing now?"

She waved a hand. "They've moved way beyond that now. I can barely keep up with the advances in the research."

All those journals. "You hope to go back to it, back to doing the kind of research that ended up with me." Justine held her breath as she waited for another drop of precious information.

"Artie says I live too much in the past. But I loved my job. I loved my husband. My life was good. The way Frank ran that program took away everything I had." Sonia shrugged a shoulder. "So, yes, if an opportunity appeared, I'd probably take it."

"Is that why you want samples of my blood?"

Sonia was silent a long time. "I'd like to solve the mystery of you, if I can," she said, retrieving her bag from the bench. "Dr. Hollister could still be with GAMA, or he could be on his own, working on something entirely different."

"So when he talked about my potential, he meant my potential as some sort of souped-up soldier?"

"I couldn't tell you." Sonia's eyes dropped to Justine's hands. "You pushed that kid in Philly into the car." Her tone was casual, as if musing on what she might have for dinner. "You broke Kos's ribs. If you hit the right spot, say, near the heart, it's possible you could kill someone."

Her fingers tingled under Sonia's scrutiny. Perhaps Hollister understood her ability better than she did.

"Did you find anything on NextLevel Industries?" Sonia asked.

"Hold up. You haven't given me your results."

"They're not all that conclusive. I mean, I didn't find out much you don't already know."

Justine bristled. "So what am I getting for that pint of blood I just handed over?"

Sonia raised an eyebrow. "It wasn't a pint. And you'll get more information. After I do more work." She pulled a sheet of paper full of bars and black lines from her bag. "This is your DNA profile."

Justine reached out but didn't take the paper. "And this tells me what?"

"There are definitely altered sequences within the DNA."

Altered. "That explains how I can do what I do?"

"Not yet. It points in a direction for further analysis." Justine took the sheet.

This might be what Hollister had been after. She hated to think what he would do with her DNA. But if that was all he wanted, he wouldn't still be pursuing her. "Thank you." She tucked the paper into her backpack and began walking toward the street. "I need to find his office."

Sonia stopped and grabbed her arm. "Did you hit your head or something?"

"It'll be easier to tell if he's lying in person. And"—she tugged her arm free—"he might need persuasion." She'd been prey long enough.

"Is that what you call what you did to Kos?" Sonia lowered her voice. "He won't be alone. And what happens when he calls the police?"

"If he has Quinn, he won't." But if her plan failed, Hollister would put her in a cage right next to his lab rats. She shoved down her nausea.

"How about this—you stay out of sight. I'll go talk to Lawrence. No way he remembers me from twenty years ago."

Sonia was right. And the cops wouldn't be so easy to slip past a second time. But too many had paid too much for knowing her. "I'm doing this myself."

Sonia looked at her, then away. "Did you decide to throw yourself in with him after all?"

Goose bumps rose up on her skin. If she went along with Hollister's plans, who—and what—would she become? Who would Quinn think she was? "I will not become an experiment because of someone's burning desire to remake humanity. No matter what I have to do."

"Once you're on his turf, it will be much harder to get out. Whether or not he has Quinn, you'll be where he wants you. The best strategy is to keep your distance." Sonia held up a finger. "If you won't do that, be sure—be very sure—of what you're willing to give up to make sure you do leave."

Justine swallowed. Hadn't she given up enough already?

Sonia let out a long breath. "So. You need his address. What happened with the library?"

"It wasn't open yet. We can get in now." She headed for the building at the east end of the park.

Inside the small library, Sonia found the computers at a table in a corner, and they settled in front of one.

"How does this work?" Justine asked, wary of getting too close.

Sonia gave her a look. "You've really never used the internet, have you?" She sighed and explained how their search was limited to what information had been put online.

Their search for the name NextLevel gave them a Washington, DC, address. Sonia widened their search to words resembling the company's or Hollister's name.

"That's it?" Justine asked after they spent an hour coming up with variations for their search.

"If you want to keep looking at random sites, be my guest."

Another dead end.

"Before I leave"—Sonia drew an envelope from her bag—"I wore Artie down last night. He didn't have a new picture of you, so he darkened your hair in the image he had. There's nothing backing up the name, so don't get stopped. Maybe this will help you to travel, by train at least, without being noticed."

Inside the envelope was a New York State ID card. The key to solving all her problems. All she had to do was turn her back on Quinn.

~ ~ ~

Sonia left the library, leaving Justine surprised by a pang of loneliness. A week ago she'd have welcomed the solitude. Even so, something had deterred her from mentioning the vacated office she'd found. She'd have to look for the information on her own. She set aside the envelope with the state ID card and pulled her chair closer to the desk.

A plump woman appeared at her left. "Do you need some help, hon?"

Justine flinched. "No, I'm ..." She sighed. She would have to get over this. "I'm trying to find someone."

The woman smiled behind her glasses as she pulled over a chair. "Okay, we can do that. Are they on Facebook?"

That sounded like something Justine should know about, but she could only give her a blank look.

With record levels of patience, the librarian led her on a hunt through a wilderness of pages and links, and the best they came up with was a post office box. At least that was in New York City.

Though the woman insisted she'd be wasting her time, Justine located the post office branch on a map and, after a long walk past the Brooklyn Bridge, found the building, only to learn the librarian had been correct. They would not tell her what she wanted to know.

She left the post office furious and frustrated and walked aimlessly within the zip code for hours while the snow had mercifully paused. She tried to keep to sidewalks covered with scaffolding to block view to any cameras and keep her face in the shadows.

The sun was tucked away behind steely clouds, and the wind sucked away any warmth. She pulled up her hood and tried to imagine a scenario where it wasn't terrible to work with Hollister, where Buggy's imagination was only the worst-case scenario.

In her pocket, among Quinn's keys, loose change, and receipts, her hand gripped the ID Sonia had given her. The identification was probably good enough to get on a train. She could leave everything behind and start over. She certainly couldn't use the keys. She might be warm in Quinn's apartment, but the cops could return at any time.

Passing a garbage can, she pulled out some of the crumbled receipts she'd taken from Kos's pockets in Philly and tossed them in. Wondering briefly if his ribs had healed, she pulled out the one for Domino's Pizza. She knew of one between the Manhattan and Brooklyn Bridges. She checked the address on the receipt. This was that one between the bridges.

Her heart skipped a beat, and she turned back to the garbage can, digging for the receipts she'd tossed. Thankfully, they were still on top and not too stained with anything mysterious. She flattened them out. Most of the receipt for the Chinese food restaurant had been printed in Chinese characters. But the information that stayed the same was in English, including the address. The next one was for a deli. Both were on Catherine Street, near the pizza place.

She marched back east of the Brooklyn Bridge. Her vague sense of that neighborhood led her to the wide intersection of Catherine and Madison cluttered with businesses. Down Catherine Street toward the river, the businesses changed to apartment buildings, schools, and a church.

She passed a large school faced in stone and brick, an expansive playground, and a smaller school, until the street ended at the FDR. The Brooklyn Bridge loomed large as she turned onto a narrow street. Most of the block was part of a large apartment complex.

Sonia had said Hollister would need space. Justine guessed he'd want privacy too. But few places in the vicinity matched that description. She turned again, away from the riverfront. The rear of the massive stone and brick school matched the front, wings jutting out, a parking garage entrance yawning dark at one end.

Rounding another corner, she soon reached Catherine Street again. As much as she'd been able to narrow down the location, she was still playing a guessing game.

Her pocket chirped. She shivered—she remembered shutting off the phone after talking to Sonia. She pulled it out as if it were toxic. Cayden's name was on the screen. She sucked in a breath of fury. "I shut this off," she spit out.

After a brief silence, Cayden said, "I need to talk to you."

"Why would I talk to you? You've lied to me about everything."

"Then why didn't you ditch the phone?"

"I'll do that right now."

"I know where Quinn is."

She paused. He was possibly her only connection to Quinn, and he knew it. "Tell me."

"He's where you thought he was. I didn't—"

"Is he okay?"

"I haven't seen him. But I . . . have confirmation that he has him."

"He, as in, your boss? Quinn is with Hollister? Where are you?"

Behind her, Cayden's voice answered. "Right here." He gave his usual half smile as he pocketed his phone. "Come with me. I'll explain on the way."

29.

Quinn marched down the wide hallway of what must have been an old school. The chipped and scuffed walls had faded from a light green to more gray. The linoleum no longer reflected the fluorescent light that buzzed above them. "Escorted" (he was sure that was what they'd call it) by two black-garbed and armed men with the word SECURITY on their backs, he counted the doors they passed. Each was shining steel, with a keypad and a swing handle.

He resisted rubbing his bicep, where some lab assistant had given him a second injection but refused to tell him any more than he was being made *better*. At least they'd switched arms when he pointed out his injury. He was having a hell of a week.

All he'd wanted to do was feel out the NextLevel management for when Max and he might formally question them. That would have also given him the chance to check out this Hollister character who'd scared Justine out of town. He'd also hoped to catch Demetri Kalakos off guard and confirm him as his shooter. What he'd found instead had been much bigger.

They'd been slick about it, he had to give them that. Against his instincts, he'd accepted security's requirement to hold his gun at the entrance. He'd thought he'd gotten on the right track when they brought him to the chief of operations, Val Moretti, since this Kalakos character reported to her. She'd answered his questions, but insisted they hold his phone to "protect the company's intellectual property." Then she'd left to find Dr. Hollister.

After an hour, he tried to leave, only to find the door locked. Eventually, someone had responded to his pounding and stuck him with something. He'd woken up in a small room on a bed. Banging on that door had produced no results, so he'd started yelling, insisting they let him call in sick. The right person must have heard that one, and they let him make the call from a burner phone.

That was yesterday. Maybe. When they gave him a second shot this morning despite his resistance, he realized he wasn't being sedated. Whatever they were doing to him, his call to the sick desk might not be enough, even if his message managed to reach Cayden.

One of the guards gestured to an open doorway. The other subtly corralled him in that direction.

With little choice, Quinn obeyed and found himself in a large room set up with various exercise equipment. Cabinets and a table occupied the left side of the room. Tall windows looked out from the second or third floor onto the high-rise buildings of Lower Manhattan, with the Brooklyn Bridge in the distance. Not far from home then.

"We'll come for you in two hours," a guard said before shutting the door.

By the windows, a solidly built man with a military bearing slowed from a fast run on a treadmill. He stepped off, wiping his face, neck, and close-cropped hair with a towel, panting softly. He wore a prosthesis in place of his lower right arm. "You part of the program?"

Quinn scowled. "What the hell is this place?"

The man laughed. "Oh, yeah, you're real new. It's all kind of confusing at first. But it's not bad, trust me. I've been here a couple months now. It's working out great."

"What is?"

"They changed my life, man. They're about to change yours." He extended his left hand. "I'm Ed Doyle. Call me Eddie."

Quinn released a breath. As much as he'd have liked to dig an immediate escape route, information would more likely be his way out. He awkwardly shook Eddie's left hand. "Quinn Duncan. Quinn is fine. And they haven't told me shit."

"Just you wait. I mean, if you're here for the same stuff I am. Let me show you. Be prepared—this might just blow your mind." He went over to an exercise machine for the upper arms. "I'm glad you're here, man. I don't mind all this. But it's kind of boring sometimes."

"There's no one else here?"

"You mean, as a subject? Not that I've seen."

Quinn bristled at the word *subject*. "Is this part of NextLevel Industries?"

"No idea." Eddie slid into the seat.

"Who's in charge here?"

"The doc. You must have talked to him." He grasped the machine's handle with his left hand and pulled. The weight he lifted was enormous, far out of proportion for his musculature. He pulled on the machine a few more times before getting up. Quinn was much taller than Eddie, but he didn't think he could pull that much weight, especially with one hand.

Eddie watched Quinn process what he'd done, with a grin that grew by the second. Soon he was laughing. "That's even more than I was doing a few days ago."

Quinn's unease spread through his limbs. "What did they do to you?"

"The doc's special therapy. I'm stronger than I ever could have been. That's probably what you're here for too. Since I turned out so well, he's got to want to expand the program. They give you anything yet?"

He eyed Eddie's gleeful grin, absently rubbing his upper arm and trying not to think about what might be running through his veins. Cold sweat cooled his brow. "They've given me injections twice now."

"Don't look so worried. That's the magic juice." He leaned closer. "Just don't say *magic* in front of the doc. He gets a little bent out of shape. He's really into the science behind it, trying to prove some theory, I think." He gestured to the machines against the wall. "You get your exercise routine yet? I'd get working. You never know when it'll kick in."

"How did you hear about this place?"

"Doc found me. I was fighting the VA for benefits, a better arm, and getting nowhere. And what was I supposed to do, a vet with one arm? Then Doc Hollister offered me a high-tech arm if I joined up with his work. Now they put me up, three squares a day. I'm getting an arm that I can move, fingers and all. It's a little risky—I'm an experiment, you know?—but they're taking care of me. I'm not just a number to them. I'm part of something important." He went over to a half-height cabinet, grabbed a silver cylinder from a counter, and set it down in front of him on the counter. "It gets even better. This you got to see to believe."

Quinn tried to keep up with Eddie's rapid rundown. "So have you left this place since you got here? Or do they not let you out?"

He shrugged. "I'd like to, but I've got no real need to. And I think they'd rather I stay. I'm going to be sporting some high-tech equipment. I got to be careful." Eddie set the cylinder on the table.

"What about your phone? They let you keep it?"

Eddie laughed. "You got a question for every answer, don't you?"

"I'm the new guy, remember?"

"Yeah, yeah. I didn't have a phone. Never mind that. Watch this," he said, his eyes and smile expectant. He stretched his arm out in front of him as he faced the cup, glanced at Quinn, then focused back on the cup. With brow furrowed, he thrust his arm out. The cup tilted away from him, then teetered back to its original position. He bit his lip and tried again, shifting his hand lower. This time the cup slid two inches away. Eddie never touched the cup.

Quinn froze, entranced by the distance between where the cup was and where it had been.

"That's the shit I'm talking about." Eddie grinned from ear to ear. "I'm gonna be a superhero."

Quinn shook his head. The recent events involving moving coffeepots and bullets stopping midair seemed part of another world he'd fallen into without warning. He did not know the rules of this world, nor even the physics. But he might know someone from here.

"Eddie is correct, mostly."

Quinn turned to find a tall blond man at the entrance to the gym.

"I wouldn't use the word *superhero*," the man continued as he approached with a handful of folders, "but you may be lucky enough to develop skills and abilities few on this planet have." He grinned. "Welcome to my lab, Detective Duncan."

Quinn tensed but set aside the question of how this man, dressed in the corporate uniform of a button-down shirt and dark pants, knew his name. "Your lab? Who the hell are you?"

"Try to withhold premature judgment. You may find yourself grateful instead of indignant."

"Grateful?" He snorted and stepped up to this man who might have been responsible for everything that had gone wrong in his life the last few days. He clenched his teeth over his next words. "You have balls, I'll give you that. You better hope NYPD's lawyers are having an off day. Otherwise, they will hand you your ass when they're done with you. Now who are you?"

The man glanced past him. "Eddie, why don't you take a break? You can come back if you like."

"I'm finished, Doc. I'm going to go take a shower."

"Good. We'll review your progress later."

Eddie walked out, nodding to Quinn and then to the guards on the other side of the door.

The blond man's eyes scanned him. Quinn felt like a piece of ham in a deli display case. "I am Dr. Lawrence Hollister. I run several projects out of this lab—"

"This isn't a lab. It's an old school."

He bobbed his head. "Large chunks of real estate are hard to come by in this city."

"This is just the kind of work the government would be happy to fund. I'd imagine you could put yourself up a bit better."

Dr. Hollister's smile tightened. "Government funding is hard to come by, particularly for innovative projects like this one."

"Innovative?" Quinn smirked. "The government funds innovative. Let me guess. The stuff you're doing here hasn't been approved for testing on humans." He crossed his arms. "And now you want to make me one of your guinea pigs. I pass, Doc."

"Detective, you have the privilege of participating in a project that will make the world a safer place. With your law enforcement background, you're ideally suited to help me rewrite the laws of warfare. Few people think this is possible." He gestured around him. "And yet I've already succeeded."

"That's great, Doc. What's that shit you injected me with?"

The doctor's grin barely wavered. "A similar treatment to what has given Eddie strength far beyond the average human, in addition to some unique skills. You now have this potential as well." He opened a folder and drew out a few sheets of paper and a small tablet.

"Unique skills?" Quinn's stomach quivered. "What have you done to me?"

"I've made you more than what you were. The word being used these days is *enhanced*."

"*Enhanced*? As in, enhanced human?" He thrust a finger at him. "That's the genetic stuff they're trying to regulate right now. No way. You can keep your hands off my genes. I want no part of your mad-scientist deal. Whatever you put in me, you're going to take it out."

Dr. Hollister gestured to the counter behind Quinn. "You saw what Eddie did."

Quinn stared at the cylinder, panting as thoughts whirled through his head.

"Imagine," the doctor continued, "moving objects using your mind, not your body. It will take some time to see results, of course. Your body has received new instructions, ones it wasn't designed for."

"What are these instructions made of?"

"Something I've been developing for a long time. Recently I obtained assistance that has made all the difference."

"I need more than *something* as an answer."

"In time I'll explain everything. For now I have your initial exercise routine."

"Exercise? You just injected me with some crap that's probably illegal. I will ask questions. I want answers."

The doctor stepped up to Quinn. "You seem to be under the impression you're in charge here," he said. "Allow me to correct your misunderstanding. I do not need you. You're a convenient opportunity to test the latest version of my therapy."

"Then why am I here?" Quinn asked, though he dreaded the answer.

"Because there is someone I do need. And she is apparently drawn to you, quite literally."

Quinn stifled a gasp.

Dr. Hollister smiled. "Now, you grasp the situation. You are merely a means to an end. There was also the issue of your problematic investigation.

"Keep in mind, I rejected my developer's proposal for a more irreversible solution, instead seeing an opportunity to test the latest version of my therapy. But if you refuse to cooperate, I can always resort to my developer's approach."

Quinn held the doctor's gaze and held his ground. "Is that developer you're talking about named Demetri Kalakos? He's more than a developer, isn't he? And he was watching my case, the victim with the prosthesis." He paused as more connections fell into place. "That guy was your test subject. And when he didn't work out, you had Kalakos deal with him."

He needed out of this place, and now. No one knew where he was. He wasn't sure how long he'd been here. His attempt at a message that would alert his brother didn't matter. NYPD would follow the trail here eventually, but eventually would be too late. They were already too late.

"I need to monitor you to determine how this enhancement will manifest in you. You have great potential, whether you see it or not."

A chill passed through Quinn. He had no weapon, no line of communication. Whatever threats he might make were empty, his demands meaningless. And whatever changes had been made to his genes, there was likely no turning back.

He was going to become like Eddie. Or perhaps, like Eddie, he was going to become like Justine. Maybe this was how she was able to move a coffeepot without touching it. And how she'd been able to save his life.

He looked down at his hands. When Max finally found him, would Quinn still be human? "Is this what you did to Justine?"

Dr. Hollister pressed his lips together. "I cannot claim to be the one who created Justine." He gestured to the machines across the room, then handed him the tablet and a typed list. "This is the exercise regimen you are to start with. Record your performance on the tablet so we can set a baseline and judge where the enhancements present themselves. That might be in any number of directions."

Quinn grabbed the tablet, wondering at the chances of finding a Wi-Fi connection. "You don't even know what this is going to do to me. Kind of random, isn't it?"

"Science is a process of discovery."

"You're messing around with things best left alone. If we were meant to move stuff with our mind, we would have evolved that way."

"Instead we evolved brains that could figure out how to imbue ourselves with such an ability. We are capable of far more than we normally accomplish. We hold ourselves back with objections to advances in genetic science based in a resistance to change. Meanwhile, those who despise us take publicly available technology and use it to change everyday objects into bombs and brainwash our own people into becoming our enemies. We need an advantage not available to the general population. This will be that advantage."

"You're making people into weapons."

"What do you think soldiers are?"

"Soldiers use weapons. They are not the weapons themselves."

"Naive and inaccurate. And irrelevant. Soldiers are already integrating with the tech they use. You will be the next step in a fuller integration."

Quinn struggled to maintain his composure as Dr. Hollister turned to the door.

"Eddie is eager for the implant I promised him. But I must do a trial run before he receives a perfected device that will interact with his new prosthesis."

Quinn cocked his head. "Implant?"

"A neural implant. It requires a bit of surgery. But your recovery should be brief."

30.

Yes, I lied. Sort of," Cayden said, eyes flickering from Justine's hair to her face. He was pale, and his clothes looked like he'd slept in them. His hair ruffled in a gust of wind. "I couldn't track your phone as it was. But I could turn it back on if I thought you needed help."

She scowled, balling her hands into fists. "Quinn is the one who needs to be tracked, not me."

He looked around and gestured to a side street entirely in shadow as night fell. "Turn here."

Surprised his paranoia matched hers, she followed him toward a gloomy recess for a side entrance to a church. Snow had begun falling again in thick flakes, making it even more unlikely she'd have a chance to slip into a building undetected. If she could find the one she wanted.

"So what have you done to help him?" he asked, hand on a hip.

She stiffened. "I could ask you the same thing." She locked eyes with his. "You here for Hollister?"

"He—" He took a breath and lowered his voice. "He doesn't know I'm here. For now. Look, can you listen to me for a minute?"

"But he asked you to find me?"

He ran a hand through his hair, reminding Justine so much of Quinn, she ached with the memory. As he let out a long breath, his expression held something she couldn't put her finger on, something Quinn lacked. No, she had that backward. He lacked something his brother had. "I'm on your side, Justine." The wind picked up and tugged at her hood.

His avoidance of her question kicked up her pulse. "You want the same thing I want. That doesn't mean I can trust you. Tell me where the company office is, if that's where he is."

Cayden looked down the street, as if he'd rather be anywhere else. "I promise you, it's more complicated than just where the office is."

His promises meant as much as the ID in her pocket. "Look at me and tell me this. Is this a lure to get me in front of Hollister?"

He leaned forward with a scowl, and his voice dropped. "My brother is the only real family I have left. I wouldn't be here if it wasn't for him. So whatever you think of me, maybe most of it's right, but don't ever act like I don't care."

She forced herself to not step farther into the dark entryway. "And yet you won't tell me where he is."

Cayden clutched at his hair. "You barge into that building, Justine, and you will never leave. Is that what you want?"

She shivered. "I am not leaving him there."

"I may be able to get you in there so you can walk out."

She grasped Cayden's arm, wishing her muscles had as much strength as her ability had. "All you have to do is tell me where this place is. I can handle the rest."

"In that place? I always feel like a minnow swimming with sharks. And you think you're just going to dive in? What's your plan? Trading yourself for Quinn?" he said as if hearing of a tragedy. "How will he feel about that?"

She couldn't say for sure Cayden wasn't one of those sharks. She kept her voice quiet so she wouldn't scream. "There will be no trades. I will not end my days as an experiment, and neither will Quinn. Whatever you do, make sure not to get in my way."

He met her eyes, his expression changing several times. For a second she thought she saw a gleam of hope, but the flicker dissipated. "This is not going to end the way you want."

She brushed off the chill his words brought on.

"Yes, I should have believed you last night. And they've kept me busy, perhaps not by coincidence." He seemed to deflate. "Now it's been a whole day. That's a day too long."

"What were you doing that you didn't notice your boss kidnapping your brother?"

He glared. "I don't know exactly what happened or when. I have very little information, in fact. He is alive. I'm pretty sure I can say that."

"Pretty sure?" she said too loudly.

"I know enough that we can operate under the assumption he's alive and with Dr. Hollister."

"There is no *we* here. And if you haven't seen him"—she swallowed, not wanting to consider the meaning of her next words—"you can't make that assumption."

He opened his mouth and then shut it. "I'm sure. I'm afraid you'll have to trust me on that." He gave a wobbly smile. "I know. I'm a liar working for the enemy." He dropped the smile. "But I want Quinn safe. That's the truth. I also want you safe, Justine. That's why, if you want to get out of there, you'll have to do this my way."

~ ~ ~

Justine trailed Cayden down a side street she'd already covered in her search. She'd had the right area after all. Cayden's head swiveled in every direction as they turned toward the river, rounding the corner of the massive school building. His wariness sent a shiver through her and reminded her she was going against the rules that had dictated her life.

He slowed as they approached the parking garage to the school building. "This way." With one more glance at the desolate street covered in a thin layer of snow, he turned into the murky entrance.

She balked. "Why do we have to go underground?"

He eyed the brick apartment building across the street, windows glowing with light as night fell. "Fewer eyes on us. Come on."

Wondering who he thought might be watching, Justine hitched up her bag on her shoulder as they skirted the long gate arm blocking the entrance and followed the narrow sidewalk down the ramp. Fluorescent lights took over as the fading sunlight disappeared. Graffiti and lime residue covered much of the concrete walls. She let him guide her across an expanse only half-full with cars and past a ramp to a dim lower level. Cayden's glanced darted from one corner to the next, and he crossed the aisles without warning. His meandering path seemed random until she saw a camera in a corner.

Finally, he paused at a door like the entrance to a vault. He looked into a small screen that lit up his eye, then hit a sequence of numbers on a keypad.

An eye scanner. She would have never gotten in this building without Cayden. "So where are we?" she asked as they entered a small alcove for an elevator and stairs.

He shoved his hands into his pockets and hunched his shoulders. "This is NextLevel Industries. The doc does his work here. We do mostly software development, some hardware, and there's other stuff I don't really know much about."

"All his work? Aren't these his offices?"

"He does all his work here."

A tremor passed through her body. She looked back through the small window in the door they'd come through. Had she made the biggest mistake of her life?

He heaved a breath. "Come on. We have to go up."

His hand shook as he hit the button for the elevator. For a half second, she considered that maybe she was making a mistake relying on Cayden. He'd shared scant information about his so-called plan. It was too late to turn back. She had no idea what was happening to

Quinn. She started toward the stairs. "This is faster, isn't it?"

He shrugged, and she gestured for him to go first. She wasn't going anywhere he hadn't gotten through already.

At the ground-floor landing, he paused before the door with a large number one on its face. "Let me ask you a question. Why'd you come back? To New York? You got as far as Philly. You could have kept going. I mean, that was your plan, right?"

Justine pulled up short. She'd rather not review all she'd lost to get here. She'd thought she could tear herself free. But the pieces she'd left behind turned out to be the ones she couldn't live without. "My plan seems to have been irrelevant."

Cayden waited for more, his brow dotted with sweat. He couldn't hold her gaze.

His nervousness didn't mean he'd been lying, but it didn't ease her suspicions. "I need to make sure your brother is safe."

"What if you—we can't find him?"

"If he's in this building, I'll find him."

"You think you can get him out?" His brows knitted in worry.

"I know I can."

His shoulders eased a bit. "So once he's out of here? Then what?" He waited wide eyed for her answer.

She would have laughed if she wasn't so wound up. "I don't know. I can't think that far ahead."

He looked down at his feet as he took that in. Taking a breath, as if he were diving into the deep end of a pool, he pushed open the door.

They came out into a wide entryway with several doors, all steel and locked with keypads. Three men and a woman stood in the center, built solidly and armed amply.

They turned to Justine and Cayden. The moment their eyes landed on her, their hands went to their belts. One said to Cayden, "Is this her?"

The hair on the back of Justine's neck stood up.

Cayden continued toward a door to their left, while one man set his bulk in her path. Without a look back, Cayden punched a number into a keypad and shoved open the door.

As the slam of steel on steel echoed, the man who'd spoken to Cayden asked Justine, "Are you Lizzie Benoit?"

31.

ayden, what are you doing? Cayden!"

The man blocking the door remained an unmoving obstacle, while the others spread out, moving with the steady, careful step of well-trained private security. She sucked in a breath as she backed up, feeling for the wall. When she hit the cold tile, she groped for the handle of the door she'd come through. She found only the buttons of a keypad. She glanced down. No handle.

Her heart beat wildly, and her throat contracted so that she had to force a breath. Cayden had brought her here with promises, then left her with these people, dressed in black and green with no badges, belts laden with equipment and weapons. They were more guards than security.

"There's no need for an escape route," said one man, an earpiece dangling from his ear. "Come with us. Dr. Hollister would like to speak with you."

"I'm here to see Detective Quinn Duncan."

"Dr. Hollister will answer your questions if he can. Please come with us."

This guard, calm and in control, with close-cropped hair and a jaw as sturdy as his arms, seemed to be in charge. Not insane. But he had to be if he thought she'd just hand herself over to his boss. Her problem was the door behind her was steel. She could only guess at its locking mechanism and certainly had no time to heat it up.

He closed the distance between them. "Listen, this is your best option right now. Security will hold on to your bag. We'll take the elevator to the third floor. You'll find answers there."

Her options were slim, that was true. She needed to find out if Quinn was in this building or if everything Cayden had told her had been lies. She dropped her hands to her sides in a show of acquiescence. "I keep my bag."

"Not an option." He held out his hand.

Anything of importance was in her pockets, but he didn't need to know that. She hesitated before giving up the backpack.

The man and woman behind him stepped toward the elevator on her right, while the fourth waited for her. She obeyed and entered the elevator car, sandwiched between the guards, fingers flexing, tamping down an urge to break free as they rose.

The doors opened with a ding onto a wide hallway, the walls and floor a faded green. Fluorescent lights gave everything a gray cast, one bulb humming in time with its blinking.

"Let's go." A guard tapped her back to urge her on. She stepped out with them, and they marched down the hall. Narrower corridors branched off on either side, labeled 3A, 3B, and so on, some dim and some brightly lit, each lined with steel doors locked with keypads.

Voices drifted to her as they passed the next wing, where an open door revealed a sliver of bright light and counters crowded with equipment. A microscope sat on a high center countertop.

Justine halted, causing the guards behind her to stop short. She ignored their reprimands, fixed on the narrow glimpse of the room. A man crossed in front of the door to take something from a shelf and disappeared again. He wore a white coat.

"I said, let's go," a guard said.

Ice cold washed over her. She turned to him slowly, holding her hands as still as she could make them. "What is that room?"

"Take your questions to the doc. Keep moving."

Her father's direction came back to her. This was indeed a lab. This was the time to do whatever necessary to get out.

So she did.

The guards had shifted their hands to their weapons, already on alert. She twisted left and blindly shoved away, propelling two men into the wall. The pair on her right moved in and grabbed her upper arms. She twisted back and forth but couldn't break free from their grasp. One snaked his arm around her waist, restraining her against his body. In front of her, the two on the floor were getting up. She dipped into a crouch, pulling on the guards' grip. But her weight wasn't enough to throw them off balance. They yanked her back up.

"Enough," the woman said through gritted teeth, shaking her.

She glared at her. Now would be a nice time for a fire. With no idea if it would work, she laid her hands on those holding her and tried to re-create the heat she'd somehow generated several times now. They still held on while the first two guards came at her again.

She focused on heat until the man holding her flinched and pulled away with a gasp, staring at his hand. The woman tightened her grip. With one arm free, Justine thrust her hand at her. The woman only swayed, but after a second shove, she fell back.

Without pausing, Justine turned and pushed at the pair about to grab her. They fell back only a few feet. But she was free.

She ran to the elevators, her limbs sluggish. The door to the right had a red exit sign above it. She slammed it open with her hands and raced into the stairwell. She took the stairs two at a time, gripping the railing to keep from tumbling down. At the next landing's door, she braced for delay, but there was only a handle on this side, and the door opened at once.

Quietly shutting the door, Justine faced a wide but dim hallway, until her first steps triggered the lights. The main hall was similar to above, but instead of open wings on each side, heavy doors shut off access to each branch. As steps pounded on the stairs, her breath ragged and her feet heavy as concrete, she yanked on every locked door.

A click drew her attention behind her: door 2A was ajar. No time for second-guessing. She ran in and pulled the door shut. A loud click—it was locked.

Her breathing was loud in the silence. The wing was lit only by the red exit signs above her head and at the other end of the hall. An opening on the right led into darkness. The wing was cluttered with boxes piled beside each door, some taped closed, others overflowing. She jumped at a loud click. On the left, a door labeled 2A2 drifted open. She held her breath, listened, then slipped inside.

Passing a jumble of shadows, she stumbled on shaky legs to a side of the room where tall closets lined the wall. She climbed into an empty cabinet and shut the door, her panting the only sound in the dark.

32.

Justine crouched in the safety of darkness as distant steps pounded, growing louder then fading as security descended the stairs. In the silence, some of the tension in her shoulders eased and a wave of exhaustion came over her. As her legs began to strain, she unfolded herself and inched out. The door squeaked, and she froze. But there was only silence.

She released her breath and stepped out. Perhaps once a classroom, the space was dark but not empty. Spindly legs jumbled together in the murk. Once her eyes adjusted, yellow muted streetlight reflected dully off metal tables and chairs piled in front of floor-to-ceiling windows, all wearing a thin veil of dust.

She squeezed between the equipment to get closer to the window. The glass was covered with a tinted material, but she could easily see people on the sidewalk below, passing like it was an ordinary evening, free to go where they wished. Christmas lights lined many of the apartment windows across the street. Quinn had mentioned something about Christmas. That seemed like a geologic age ago.

She was no higher than the second floor, maybe twenty feet off the ground. If she broke through, she might survive the drop, though she'd be in bad shape. The window opened with an old-style crank, but the handle was missing. She pushed up on the wooden frame. Nothing. The old wood had been painted as if one unit, sealing it shut. She picked at the lumpy paint job and found what appeared to be a metal line—she went still. A thin wire lined the sill and continued to the next. She might have already tripped a silent alarm.

She backed away from the window and the outside world and slipped through the furniture. A door slammed far away. She edged out of the classroom and negotiated around the stacks of boxes to cross into the dark, narrow corridor that led her to the next wing.

She took a deep breath and approached the door to the main hallway. She'd have to risk whatever was beyond it. Before she reached it, the door swung open.

She gasped. "Sonia." She relaxed a fraction at the sight of the woman, though she wasn't sure she should. "What are you doing here?"

Sonia opened the door wider. "Looking for you."

Justine backed farther into the wing. "How did you find this place? You know this is Hollister's lab, right?"

"After I left you, I tried another search and found the address we were looking for. I thought I'd feel them out. I met Val, who introduced me to Dr. Hollister."

"Why didn't you call me? We could have come to-gether." Steps pounded on the stairs. Justine braced herself again, but they continued up.

"I tried to get it into your head not to come near this place," Sonia said. "How did you end up here?"

"Cayden. He lied and told me he would help me get Quinn out. I'm doing it myself."

Sonia started to say something, then stopped.

"Have you seen Quinn or heard mention of him?"

"I've only talked to Dr. Hollister, and not for long."

Justine's legs trembled as she shuffled back. "What does he want? Did he send you to find me?"

"No." Sonia glanced into the main hall behind her, looking uncomfortable for the first time. "I heard your name mentioned by security. I thought it would be better if I found you first."

"Better how? Sonia, why are you here?"

Sonia eyed her. "Dr. Hollister is not the young grad student I met years ago. He's achieved some important milestones, some that I've been dreaming of for dec-ades. He is now considering bringing me on to his team. I think you ought to at least speak with him. You might be surprised."

Alarm bells went off in Justine's head. "So you got what you wanted."

The woman sighed. "I'm tired, Justine. I'm getting too old for living in half-finished buildings with rigged electricity, working cash-only jobs. I want to be part of scientific progress, not looking on as others do great things. Don't you want to be part of something?"

As much as she wanted to say yes, Justine's doubts gnawed at her. She had no interest in participating in any scientific anything. There had to be something, somewhere she belonged besides a lab.

"How long can you live in the shadows, Justine? Wouldn't it be nice to not have to constantly look over your shoulder? No more running. No more hungry nights."

"In exchange for what?"

Sonia shrugged. "Depends. Perhaps you should see what kind of deal you can work out with him."

"I don't need a deal. I need a way out."

"I thought you were here to find Quinn."

"I am." She let out a breath in frustration. "I need to do both."

Sonia took a step forward. "If you're going to get Quinn out, you're going to need to negotiate. You can't do that without knowing what the other side wants. What does Hollister want from you? Do you really know?"

The look in the man's eyes when he'd found her in the subway had told her all she needed to know. But she couldn't deny the truth in what Sonia was saying. "Negotiating will mean giving up something. I want no part of his grand plan. If I become a part of anything, it will be on my terms."

"Who says Dr. Hollister won't let you decide? Perhaps he's willing to work with you as a partner, and you can work on developing something new and exciting. All I'm saying is, you don't know until you ask."

Justine's shoulders sagged, the weight of her exhaustion as heavy as regret. To work with Hollister felt like giving up. Or worse. She might know where she stood with him. And he was likely the only way to free Quinn.

Could she forget about Buggy for the sake of Quinn? Could she pretend he wasn't the monster of her imagination?

Then something in Sonia's expression changed, and Justine's blood turned to ice. She was so tired, she hadn't seen what was right in front of her.

She turned on her heel and ran.

She darted left, retracing her steps through the connecting corridor. Sonia's steps echoed behind her. Back in Wing 2A, Justine turned right toward the exit at the far end. She raised her hands to shove at the door ahead of her.

The door swung open before she could push, and Justine ran into a tall woman, tangling with her as she grasped Justine's upper arms.

"Whoa, whoa, easy," the woman said. She wore a white blouse with dress pants and heels, dark hair loose and straight, falling to her chin. "Where's the fire?"

Justine pulled away, but the woman held her in a tight grip. She didn't look like a scientist, nor was she dressed like security, but she was not here to help Justine.

"I have to—" She panted, knowing that struggling in a trap only damaged the prey.

"You're her," the woman said with wide eyes. "I have so many questions."

"No, I—" She pulled back, trying to free one hand.

The woman released one of her arms and reached into a pocket. Justine twisted away, but suddenly pain lanced up her arm and she could barely stand. As her legs gave way, the woman caught her and eased her to the ground.

She lay unable to move, her body throbbing. Sonia joined them and nodded to the woman. The woman stood. "Welcome to NextLevel Industries, Justine."

~ ~ ~

Quinn paced the perimeter of his room again. No, not his room. His cell. He was definitely a prisoner.

This Dr. Hollister talked about having the privilege of participating in his project. Some class-A double-speak there. He was being enhanced against his will.

Had Justine gone through something like this? Hollister claimed not to have done anything to her—no, he'd said he hadn't *created* Justine.

Quinn ignored the quiver in his belly. Justine wasn't created in a lab. She was as human as he. That he knew in his bones.

But maybe she'd been enhanced. Had she been taken against her will, changed without permission, like he now was? That would explain so much.

He halted midstep. Of course. This guy, this so-called doctor, this was what had Justine so scared she'd fled the city. And Hollister knew she'd left. He thought she'd come back for him. The doc was going to be disappointed. He'd tried himself, and even he hadn't been able to convince her to stay in the same city as this man.

But Quinn would find her. When he got out of here, he would find her and make sure she knew she was not alone.

He had to get out first. All he had to work with was a bed, a couple of small metal tables, and an armchair in the corner. No windows. Even the walls were cold, impenetrable concrete. The door had no handle and seemed to open with a code from the other side. He'd seen a lot of doors with keypads. Were other people held behind those?

If the woman Tanya came back to give him another shot today, perhaps he could overpower her and get out. And step right into a guard's fist, more than likely.

He would not be this man's guinea pig. And he would not die here.

Someone knocked at the door. At least they gave him warning. He faced the door without responding. Anyone entering the room would do so uninvited.

That same woman entered carrying a hard-shell case. Her braided hair was pulled back in a ponytail, and she wore casual clothes without a white coat, so perhaps she was a lab technician. She set down her equipment on a table next to the armchair and put on a pair of rubber gloves. "How are you feeling?"

"Peachy. I love to spend my afternoons being held against my will."

"You'll be singing a different tune when you start seeing results." She gestured to the chair. "Please take a seat."

Quinn stayed where he stood. "Look, I'm done with this. I did not ask to be *enhanced* or to have my genes scrambled. No more."

She let out a deep sigh. "We've been through this. And the schedule is tight today, so come on." She patted the arm of the chair and began pulling equipment out of her case.

"Then take me off the schedule, because I'm not getting any more of that shit. You people don't even know what it's doing to me. All I get are maybes. Maybe I'll get stronger. Maybe I'll get faster. And maybe I'll grow a third arm."

She hung a stethoscope around her shoulders. "Oh dear. You might be faster or stronger. It's too late to complain. The changes have already begun. Stopping now would only leave the changes less fully developed."

"You mean I'll only be sort of a monster."

"As a detective, wouldn't having greater strength and speed help you do your job better?"

"Not interested. If you change my genes—"

She put a hand on a hip. "Do I have to bring in Pete again? He'll be a lot less patient than yesterday."

He stiffened. He didn't want to get strapped in again. If he was loose, he could act if an opportunity arose. He'd have to concede this battle to win the war. He relaxed his shoulders to appear cooperative and sat in the armchair.

The technician took his vitals, her motions mimicking those of caring for a patient.

"All of this you're doing, these are criminal and civil viola—What was that for?" he asked when she gave him a shot without a word of explanation.

"Antibiotics."

"Why would I need antibiotics? What I need is some food. They haven't brought me a thing since early this morning."

The technician straightened. "Has Dr. Hollister explained the procedure to you?"

A glacial chill passed through him. "Listen," he said, shaking her off as she tried to take his blood pressure. "I've been here not two days yet, and I've already had my DNA rearranged. No one is cracking open my skull or putting anything else into me."

The woman pulled out her phone. "Pete is kind of busy today. I don't think he'll appreciate having to deal with you too. Are you going to keep fighting me?"

Quinn forced himself to slow his breathing, but his heart hammered in his chest. If he continued his objections, he'd end up worse off than he was now.

He sighed and laid back, closing his eyes as the technician swabbed his arm and tied a tourniquet around his bicep. To distract himself as she stuck him with another needle and released the tourniquet, he mentally reviewed all the possible exits he'd seen since he'd awoken here. There had to be weaknesses or gaps in security somewhere.

The door beeped. He opened his eyes as the lab tech turned to the entrance and said, "That was locked."

"Yes, it was. Who do you think set the codes to lock it?" From behind the tech, a slim man appeared. His face, aside from a pair of glasses, matched the mugshot he'd found for Demetri Kalakos. The man smirked as he approached the chair.

The tech frowned. "This is a bad time, Kos. You can't be here now."

Quinn heard the accent Nita had described. This was the guy who'd shot him, then beat up Nita when looking for Justine.

Quinn sat up. "Yeah, you can't be in here. Because you're an asshole."

Kalakos laughed, then stopped with a grimace and wrapped an arm around his torso. He let out a slow breath, then glared at the tech. "I go where I please."

"I don't have time for your games," she said. "Come back later."

Kalakos stepped into her face. "Maybe it is time for games. Don't think you'll like mine."

She stood her ground in silence. He squeezed between her and the chair and turned to Quinn. "Hello, Detective. How's that therapy going? How do you like the idea of becoming some sort of mutant?" Kalakos grinned and tugged the vial filling with Quinn's blood.

"Don't touch that, Kos," the tech said with more force.

He grabbed her upper arm and shook her. "Did you not hear me?"

She pushed him away with an exasperated sound. She pulled out a phone. "He's right. You are an asshole." She tapped the screen.

Kalakos pulled into a back swing. Quinn reached out and yanked him off balance. "Leave her alone," Quinn said. "You're here to bother me, aren't you?"

"Stop trying to be a cop. Cops are always putting their nose in where it doesn't belong." Kalakos turned to him fully and looked him over. "I will let you in on a secret, Duncan. People think we have advanced, that we're civilized. But we're still wild, man. It's the wild west out there."

As he laughed again, Quinn wanted to stop his laughter with his fist.

"I'm just here to say my goodbyes, okay? Don't get too comfortable. Or maybe you should enjoy yourself. See if they can get you a beer."

"What are you babbling about?"

"Everybody uses everybody else and when they're finished—" He brushed his hands together. "So you always got to make sure you're needed."

"You're about as needed as an oozing sore."

He stepped close to Quinn and lowered his voice. "Doc Hollister thinks he needs you. Thing is, the doc doesn't always know what is best. I knew this plan, it was going to be more trouble, too much trouble. But"—he shrugged—"I do what he pays me to do."

"Newsflash: he'll only keep you until he finds someone who can do your job better than you."

Kalakos's eyes bulged, and his face grew red. Quinn began to stand, the syringe pinching in his arm, but Kalakos shoved him back into the chair. "You've caused me enough trouble. I should've taken care of you a long time ago." He wrapped his fingers around Quinn's neck and squeezed.

33.

Justine's legs were still wobbly as they rode the elevator to the third floor, and her hands and feet tingled from the stun gun. She flexed her fingers at her sides, trying to quiet the urge to shove everyone in the car into the East River. Lately, her choices had stunk like a restaurant sidewalk on garbage day in August. Despite insisting on doing this on her own, she'd never truly been alone until now. Her breath shuddered as she struggled against the strands of the web closing around her.

The woman who'd introduced herself as Val marched out of the elevator ahead of the guards. Sonia tried holding Justine's arm, but she shook her off.

Blinking under lights much brighter than on the second floor, Justine slowed as they entered the wide hallway. People scurried from one room to another, some in lab coats. Many paused to stare at their procession. A guard nudged her forward.

Sonia leaned in. "Don't do anything crazy, now," she said. "Let's just see what happens."

"I know what happens," she snapped in a harsh whisper. "Once I step foot into a lab, I never leave." She started to pant as the reins on her panic slipped from her grasp.

"You had no problems the other day—"

"I had plenty of problems the other day. But no one knew I was in that lab but a couple of guards."

"Whatever Hollister wants from you, use that to learn where Quinn is or what's happened to him." Sonia lowered her voice. "Use whatever you've got to get what you want."

"Is that what you did?"

That silenced the woman as a guard corralled them into Wing 3C on the left. A fluorescent light above flickered, and he keyed in a code to open one of the few wooden doors she'd seen. A second guard gestured for Val to enter. Sonia tugged Justine forward.

When she didn't move, the second guard grabbed her arm. She yanked away from him. "I know how to walk."

The man's face remained impassive. "Then walk."

There was no way but forward. With a shaky breath and her body trembling, she dragged her feet into a large office and came to a halt as she was pulled backward in time. The large desk in disarray. The shelves on either side filled with books and equipment at all angles. Even the standing lamps. Here they were on either side of the desk. In her father's office, a single lamp had stood to one side, and sheer curtains, instead of blinds, had covered the windows. There hadn't been a laptop on the desk, but otherwise, this room felt like her father's office. Vague memories of leafing through books or playing with a broken piece of equipment awakened an ache long dormant. The fuzzy memories of sitting in her father's lap as he showed her pictures from a textbook cut more deeply.

The man behind the desk jolted her back to the present. Lawrence Hollister stood with hands clasped behind him, blue eyes alert and eager, tension in his lips and jaw. His blond hair and his button-down shirt were neater than when she'd last seen him. Now he looked less mad and more scientist. But she knew better. She forced herself to breathe calmly and remained close to the door.

"Lizzie," Hollister said, stretching his arms out as if to hug her. "Or do you prefer Justine?"

She flinched at the use of her childhood name and glowered. "Don't talk to me like you know me. I don't know who you are. And you have no idea who I am." She hated the tremor in her voice.

As the silence stretched, he dropped his arms and his smile. "I'll do you the courtesy of addressing you by the name you currently use." He came around the desk. "I am Dr. Lawrence Hollister, owner and chief scientist here at NextLevel Industries. Now that we've met properly, we can have a conversation." He thanked the guards, and they left the room.

"I'd love to stay," Val said, "but I have a meeting with security." She leaned toward Justine, a smile playing on her lips. Justine's hand twitched. "I mean it when I say I'd love to stay. I'm still on the fence about whether I believe all the crap they say you can do. A live demo might convince me. And if it is true, then assuming a lab is where you came from, it's probably where you belong."

Justine stepped up to Val, craning her neck to look the woman in the face. "I'll give you a demo anytime. I can't tell you where you'll land, but I think it'll convince you."

Val grinned. "Of all the crazy projects this man has taken on, you are the most interesting."

When Val shut the door, Hollister said to Sonia, "Thank you, Dr. da Silva, for your help." To Justine, he said, "Don't hold Dr. da Silva's actions against her. She was working in your best interest, trust me."

Justine huffed. "You're the last person in the world I would trust. And Sonia doesn't know what my best interests are. You're oh for two."

Despite her words, he seemed to relax a bit. Arms crossed, he circled her, his gaze like a physical touch. He murmured, as if speaking to himself, "It's really you, isn't it? The same girl I saw twenty years ago. I doubt you remember. It was a Christmas party for the department my father headed at the DoD. You must have been no more than five years old."

She'd held on to few precious memories from before they moved that first time, when she was four. A Christmas party was not one of them.

Hollister continued to circle her as he spoke. "I was eighteen, so I went mainly for the free food. But I also wanted to meet Jack. Even when my father was aggravated by how he flouted protocol, I could tell he admired the man and his work. While I hovered nearby waiting for a chance to talk to him, you and your brother wandered away from your mother. The boy had quite a job keeping you away from the fragile Christmas decorations. And eventually he failed."

He grinned, reveling in his memory as he came full circle to stand before her. "Because you didn't have to touch the ornaments to move them."

The eagerness in his eyes intensified. "I thought I'd imagined it when an ornament began to swing. Then a glass ball jumped off its branch and rolled away. You stood a few feet from the Christmas tree, one little hand stretched out. Then you ran off to get it, your brother trailing. He found you clutching the ornament with such joy in your face, he let you have it."

The world tilted as Hollister described this memory she didn't share. She felt the sudden need for a bath.

Sonia let out a soft gasp. "Her ability manifested as a child?"

"I'm right here, you—" She pulled herself back and turned to Hollister. "You've been searching for me for twenty years based on what you remember from a party? What do you want from me now?"

"I had assumed you were the pinnacle of my father's accomplishments. But it turned out that my father and yours had much more mundane objectives. In fact, no one seemed aware that this milestone in genetic science had been reached. So I took up the question of your ability. For the next twenty years, I studied and discovered the potential within the human body. But then I saw the footage." He leaned back against the desk and clasped his hands. "The surveillance video of your attempt to protect your brother inspired me to reconsider my strategy."

She stiffened. The cold air of that night by the river as she lay over her brother's body swept over her, along with hot fury that this man shared that intimate memory with her.

"When you saved your own life with an act that defied explanation, everything changed. You had surpassed my father's goals and my own imagination." He paced in front of his desk. "So what do I want? I want to show you what I've learned, my efforts to discern how Jack accomplished"—he gestured to her—"how he accomplished you. But more than that, I want to show you what you can become."

"I don't need your help or anything from you." *Except for everything you know about my life.* What would she give up for that information?

~ ~ ~

Quinn struggled to breathe as Kalakos's fingers tightened around his throat, pushing him into the chair back. He needed air or he'd pass out. If that happened, he wasn't sure he'd ever wake up.

Tanya yelled at Kos to let go. Kalakos shoved her, and she stumbled back and fell to the ground, scattering her tray of supplies with a clatter.

Quinn took advantage of the moment and rolled out of the chair. Kalakos somehow kept his hold on his neck, and with both hands, pushed Quinn down as he forced his way to standing. As he rose, they staggered to the side, and Kalakos slammed Quinn into the wall. The impact would have stolen the breath from him if he'd had any.

He clawed at the fingers tightening around his neck. But the man's grip was too tight, and he couldn't get a finger around his hand. White sparks appeared at the edges of his vision. He needed to breathe.

Kalakos's face was red with fury. He pulled Quinn forward and shoved him against the wall again. Quinn's head snapped back, and he saw even more stars as his skull smacked into the very solid cement.

"Hey! Get off him," Tanya yelled. She was up again and tugged at Kalakos's arm.

Kalakos barely noticed. Quinn gasped, seeking any breath of air.

She grabbed her phone and texted someone, then pulled on Kalakos again. He shifted to try to elbow her. She dodged and punched his arm.

In his distraction, Kalakos's fingers slipped. Quinn got a hold of one finger, then two, and started prying them back. His hands were slick with sweat, and he almost lost his grip.

"Hollister's going to be pissed, Kos," Tanya said. "If you kill him, he'll kill you."

Quinn managed to get another finger between one of Kalakos's fingers and his neck. The pressure on his throat eased, and he gulped a deep breath of air. He looked down at Kos and grinned. "That's twice you tried to kill me," he said between pants. "Twice you failed."

Kalakos's scowl deepened. "And you've been a pain in my ass the whole time."

Quinn pushed forward, trying to use his greater height and weight to edge him back. One of Kos's feet slipped on the linoleum floor as he shifted his stance. He held on to Quinn's neck, but it was enough. Quinn grabbed Kalakos's arms and dropped to the ground. They rolled over each other, crashing into the bed, then reversed direction, each struggling for the upper hand.

The door beeped, and the guard Pete stopped short as he entered the room. "What the hell?"

"Help me break these two knuckleheads up," Tanya said.

Tanya held Quinn back while Pete pulled Kalakos away. The man tried to hold on to Quinn's neck, and Pete discouraged him with a punch.

Released from his would-be killer's grasp, Quinn climbed to his feet, his breath loud in the silence. He leaned against his knees for a moment, then stepped toward Kalakos.

Tanya held an arm out to block his path. "No, you are done. Both of you. Pete, get him out of here."

Pete held Kos back as he lunged for Quinn, yelling at him in another language, though his meaning was clear.

Quinn grabbed Tanya's arm, then reconsidered and backed down. This guy wasn't worth the effort.

Kalakos struggled in Pete's arms, murder in his eyes.

"Get out of here, Kos." Pete gestured to the door. "Do you know what the doc will do to you when he finds out about this?"

That seemed to register with Kalakos. He calmed and threw off Pete's hold of him. Grumbling, he stalked out of the room.

Pete turned to Tanya. "What the hell happened?"

"He tried to kill me," Quinn said, rubbing his neck. "It's not really complicated."

"How did he get in here?"

"He knew the code," Tanya said. "He sets them, so there's no way for him not to know."

"And there's no way for you to keep me in here safely. He'll come back." Quinn touched the back of his head and flinched. He had a nice knot already. His fingers came away sticky with blood.

"Not if he doesn't know what room you're in. Give me a minute. I'll find an empty room, and we'll move him." Pete left, talking into his radio.

Tanya surveyed the room. Her tray and supplies were strewn across the floor. The needle that she had inserted into his arm lay beside the chair, the tube still full of blood. "Look at you—you're a mess."

Quinn's arm and his shirt were smeared with blood. In the bend of his elbow, a welt oozed where the needle had been ripped out of his arm.

"Let's clean you up and gather this stuff together. Mind you, this doesn't change anything. We just have to start over. "

It changed a few things. A new room was a start. He would have to risk the first opportunity he found, perhaps while they moved him. He had to get out before they could do any cutting open of his skull. And he had to warn Justine. He didn't know if she'd return when she found out he was here. But he couldn't bear to think what might happen if she fell into the hands of these people. He might die. She would wish she had.

~ ~ ~

Hollister perched on the edge of his desk, hands clasped together. "It's understandable to think I have nothing to offer. I haven't yet proven myself to you. So let me ask you, what do you want?"

She opened her mouth, and he raised his hand. "Don't rush. It's an important question. What do you, Lizzie, now known as Justine, Jack Benoit's daughter, what are *you* looking to get out of life?" He leaned forward, eyes locked on hers like an eagle sighting prey.

Her stomach bottomed out at the reference to herself as a daughter. She hadn't been a daughter or a sister for what felt like a lifetime. After Devon's death, barely surviving in the tunnels under Manhattan, only Buggy's friendship had salvaged her sense of self. Later, Quinn had revived her sense of worth and had begun to draw her back into the world. But Hollister's memories of her family could fill the hole no one else had managed to fill.

The door buzzed. Hollister scowled and called out, "Yes?"

A tinny voice came from a speaker beside the door. "Sir, Eddie would like to speak to you."

"Not now, Eddie. Please come back—"

The speaker spit static for a moment, then quieted. "Doc," another voice said, "I just need a minute. I heard something"—more static interrupted him—"through the grapevine. I thought you could straighten me out."

His frown deepened. "Eddie, I'm afraid—" He glanced at Sonia. "Yes, why don't you come in. I have a favor to ask you." He lowered his voice. "Sonia, why don't you take this time to visit the labs? Eddie can show you the projects I'm working on and answer some of your questions."

Sonia crossed her arms, eyes sliding away from Justine. "Sure, I can do that."

The door opened with a buzz. A man dressed in the black and green of security stood beside a shorter, muscular man with a crew cut. His right arm hung at his side, a prosthetic hand peeking out of his long shirtsleeve.

Hollister turned first to the guard. "The speaker is still not fixed."

"Turned out to be a bigger job, sir. The whole building needs rewiring."

"I want the speaker fixed. Get it done." He then turned to Sonia. "Dr. da Silva, this is Eddie Doyle. He's working with me on several projects. Eddie, would you please show Dr. da Silva around the labs? Start with Wing A of this floor."

Sonia finally met Justine's gaze, her face blank. "You were right. I used what I had."

Justine's heart skipped a beat as she remembered something Sonia had had when she'd arrived. "What happened to your bag?"

"They took it at security," Sonia said, closing her eyes for a moment. "I asked for it back, but I haven't gotten it yet."

Sonia no longer had the vial of her blood.

"I really did want to help you. But you didn't want it."

Eddie stepped up next to Sonia, but his attention was on Justine. "You're her," he breathed. The recognition and reverence in his voice chilled her. "Sorry, Doc," he said, "I know you're busy, but this is her, isn't it?" He turned to Justine, eyes wide. "You're the first."

Her body went cold. The first of what? And how many were there?

Hollister pursed his lips. "Yes, Eddie, this is Justine Bernard."

"Without you I'd still be nobody." Even this man she'd just met seemed to know more about her than she did. He beamed at her, rubbing his crew cut head. "I have a lot to learn from you." He gathered himself. "I know, Doc. You've got things to talk about. I'll come back later. It's just, I heard talk about the new guy getting my implant."

Hollister's words were taut. "That's a test, Eddie. We're adjusting our design. Once we've made our changes, you will get the improved implant."

Eddie's shoulders relaxed. "Oh, okay. Thanks, Doc."

"I keep my promises, Eddie."

The young man nodded and turned to Sonia. "Nice to meet you, doctor. Would love to show you around. Lots of good stuff happening here."

Sonia followed the man out of the office without a backward glance.

The door shut with a click, and Justine was alone with Hollister. Anyone else nearby was not on her side. She turned back to him. "What have you done?"

"Eddie is my first success. Now I can try to discern Jack's method more precisely. Your help will be invaluable, of course."

His casual references to her father stung each time, but her thirst for information was greater. "He's the first of how many?"

"I'm still perfecting my process. But you seem to miss Eddie's point. When you are the first rather than the only, you are no longer alone."

And with that, he took from her both loneliness and pride. Instead of bearing responsibility for doing what no one else could, she was now the mold from which others were made. "Why?"

"Imagine an army of soldiers who can stop bullets before they reach their target." He approached her, his eyes gleaming with the promise of his vision. "We could end a battle without shedding blood. What better reason is there?"

Her stomach dropped to the floor. His words spoke of peace, but his plans were for war.

"Think also of the newly enhanced soldiers who will be in need of guidance only you can give." His voice and his eyes softened. "Give me the chance, Justine, and I will show you everything you can become."

"How long before you point me at whoever you've labeled your enemy? I will decide the best use of my ability."

She had more questions than answers now. And while Hollister could likely answer all of them, they were a distraction from what she'd come here for, from what was more important. "I want simple things. I want what's mine. Yesterday, a man calling himself Kos told me you had Detective Quinn Duncan. If this is true, he must be unharmed—I don't want to hear about any implants—and he must be released. I want to see him walk out the front door."

The light receded from Hollister's eyes, leaving a coldness she could feel from where she stood. "And what would I get in return?"

"You've already got my DNA from that chunk of my hair you took. I think that's more than enough."

"You can have anything, and that's what you ask for? No desire to better the world, to find a purpose, no grand plans for your life? You just met a young man more like you than anyone on the planet. Perhaps you need to think this over."

"You asked me what I wanted. I gave you my answer."

He cocked his head, quiet for a moment. A muscle in his jaw flexed. "I'm afraid those terms are unacceptable."

She swallowed. Negotiation meant giving something up. Her throat was so tight it hurt. "I'll give you whatever information I have that will help you with your work. But you must let Quinn Duncan go. Otherwise, I walk."

"Information? I know more about you than you do."

He just might. "And you have something of me you had no right to take." She tried to squelch the nausea rising in her stomach. "Fine. You can have a blood sample," she spit out. "I'm sure that's more useful to you than whatever you've got." If she could get Sonia's backpack, she could hand over the vial instead.

His eyes glittered, and he leaned forward. "You seem to be under the impression you have more leverage than you do."

No, she'd only hoped he'd been under that impression. Panic welled up in her throat again. "If you want me to work with you, then Quinn walks. Those are my terms."

"And what exactly are your plans for leaving this building?"

A silent breath escaped her. The silken strands of the web this man had woven had engulfed her before she'd felt the strength of their constraints. She'd promised her brother she would not become an experiment. But she *was* an experiment. And that was the only real bargaining chip she had. Quinn would hate what she was about to do. She forced the words from her mouth, her voice hoarse. "I'll say yes if you release him."

A moment of silence passed. "Yes to what?"

"I'll work with you." She tried to picture what sort of lab she'd be kept in. "However you want."

He leaned forward farther. "You're saying you would trade yourself for the detective?"

Her heart nearly jumped out of her chest. She nodded and held her breath.

"That's good to know."

She frowned. "Is it good enough? You get what you've always wanted. What more could you want?"

He smiled again. She tried not to squirm. "What I want is a successful test subject."

That was the wrong answer.

"I'm afraid I can't accept your terms. Detective Duncan is not on the table."

"You don't need him if you have me." She tried to breathe without panting. Her entire body shook. Her fingers balled into fists. If this man took everything from her, she wasn't sure she could hold herself back. "If he's been hurt, you are going to die with regrets."

Hollister approached, and she fought the urge to back up as he towered over her. "If you're going to make threats, be sure you are willing to follow through on them." Stone faced, he turned and stepped behind his desk. "I assure you, Duncan is in good health. Better, in fact, than when he arrived. He is responding well to the therapy. So, you see, I can't release him. I need to monitor his progress."

Her anger vanished in a cold wave. All this time fighting her way to Quinn, and she'd already failed. She hadn't saved him. Like she hadn't saved Buggy. She staggered back a step as the reproach of those she'd lost weighed on her.

Then that cold boiled over, and rage swept through her like fire. "You use whoever you can get your hands on. How many have you used and tossed aside because they didn't work out?"

"That is the price I must pay to change the course of human history."

"What about the price they pay?"

Hollister leaned over his desk. "There are things we need more than being right. This is for something bigger than me or you." He straightened. "Perhaps not you. You are why all of this is possible."

"I want no part of this. If you won't let Quinn go, I'll take him out of here myself." Justine shoved her hands forward, hoping to make a Hollister-shaped hole in the glass behind him.

Nothing happened.

34.

Justine gave up resisting the guard who led her from the office after Hollister stormed out with a phone to his ear. "What did you do to me?" she called out for the third time.

In his office, he'd looked back at her as stunned as she was when she'd pushed at him. He'd felt nothing. Her ability was gone.

As they turned from the main hall into the next wing, she turned her hands over before her. They looked the same as ever. But her only weapon had left her. Despite her coat, she felt naked.

Hollister continued his phone conversation. "Where is your stun gun?" His words were ice. "When was it last used?" After a longer silence, he spit out, "Never do that again." He put away the phone and punched in a code to a door with a large 3B1 on its face.

She shivered as they entered the bright cold room. An alcoholic tang stung her nose. Equipment of various sizes covered a long center worktable, where shelving running down the middle held jars and containers of all kinds. Larger machines along the walls hummed. A man and a woman operated instruments as small as what she and Sonia had stolen, while a younger man put a container into a machine as large as a refrigerator. The three lab techs looked up when they entered, eyed her, then returned to staring through microscopes or reading laptop screens. A camera covered in black plastic watched from high in a corner.

The guard closed the door behind her. The only other exit seemed to be an open doorway on the right.

Hollister finally turned to her, his face a mask and his movements choppy. "I apologize on behalf of my overzealous colleague. The good news is that your loss is temporary."

"The stun gun—that woman, Val—she, what, short-circuited me?" She flexed her fingers. "What's your definition of temporary?"

"That's accurate, in a sense. It won't happen again, I promise you." He approached her, and she stepped back. "You must understand, Justine, I have no intention of harming you."

She crossed her arms, trying to keep her breathing even. "You've got some way of showing it."

He softened his voice as he eyed her hands. "The power in your hands is what makes you so special. I would never take that away."

"Well, if you've figured out how to give this ability to someone else, then you don't need me."

"But I do. I can't do this without you."

"Then show me Quinn Duncan."

After a moment's hesitation, he turned to the man at the door. "Bring Duncan to the lab, please."

Surprised that had worked, she stayed near the door as Hollister walked around the room, describing the painstaking work of the lab technicians who analyzed and manipulated DNA with the latest technology. He then took her through the doorway to another section of the lab where larger equipment dominated the space. And with no doors but the one they came through. A small instrument sat unplugged on a counter. The refrigerator beside it was quiet, but two others across the room hummed quietly.

"NextLevel is advancing scientific knowledge in a way few are willing to try."

"Because they won't experiment on humans."

"Your father was one of those audacious enough to try."

"Don't use his sacrifice to pretty up the ugly truth of what happens here," she said, her voice tight.

He frowned, arms crossed, his gaze dropping to his feet. "I'm sorry you had to grow up without your father. Mine was a force in my life. I can't imagine what I'd be if he hadn't been there."

She wanted to punch him and his demonstration of sympathy right through a window. One question kept her contained. "Do you know how he died?"

He looked at her closely and was quiet for a long time. "No, I do not."

A guard appeared in the doorway. "Dr. Hollister, excuse me for the interruption."

"Where is the detective?"

From behind the guard, Kos strode up wearing an indignant frown, which deepened when he saw Justine, and a colorful bruise on his cheek.

She clenched her fists at her sides. "You again?"

He stopped a few feet from them, a hand drifting to his torso. "Doc, I wanted to tell you before the gossip started. They are lies. I saw Duncan for a couple of minutes, and he was alive and well when I left him."

Justine and Hollister spoke at once. "What did you do?"

Kos scowled. "Nothing, I just told you. People love to talk shit, don't care if it's true or not. I am telling you myself. None of it's true. I've been working all morning."

She turned to Hollister. "Take me to him. *Now.*"

"I will bring him here myself. Stay in—"

"I'm going—"

Hollister leaned in close. "If you want to see him at all, you will stay here," he said quietly. "I'll return shortly. Come with me, please," he said to the guard.

She fumed at her powerlessness. He'd said the one thing they both knew would guarantee her compliance.

As soon as he left the room, Kos began laughing to himself. She took a step toward him, and he stepped back. "If you touched him, I will slam you through a wall." She'd use her hands if she had to.

He glanced behind him. "These walls are old. Shouldn't hurt too much."

She closed the distance between them, and he stood his ground. "I'm getting out of this place," she said. "I suggest you stay out of my way."

"I can't let you do that. The doc will have my head."

"Sucks to be you." She stepped to the side, and he moved in front of her.

"Seriously, you're not going anywhere."

She grabbed his shirt and leaned in close. "One day I'm going to corner *you* in a dark alley. We'll see who walks away then. Right now, I'd move if I were you." He was lucky she couldn't follow through on her threat.

He shoved her against a cabinet, and she struggled to match his strength. "So come on. Toss me into a wall."

"You're making pissing me off your specialty." She pushed him with all the strength her arms could muster. She might have no leverage with Hollister, but she'd be damned if Kos would hold her back.

He bumped into the cabinet behind him, and she started for the door. He grabbed her arm and yanked her back. "Not such a tough girl now, huh? Stay put." He pointed a finger in her face.

She rounded on him with her fist. But he saw it coming and caught her wrist, pressing her back. The countertop dug into her back, and he leaned over her, grinning. She tried to move a knee, and he pressed himself against her leg. She stomped her foot, but he slipped his foot out of range.

Immobilized and without a weapon, she tried to keep her breathing in check and to not panic. Then she went limp. With her entire weight in his hands, he lost his hold on her, and she slipped down, her spine pressing into the counter as she slid.

She kicked at his leg but only grazed his shin as he hopped out of the way. "Bitch, I am tired of you," he growled and said something in another language that needed no translation. Reaching behind him, he pulled out a gun and aimed at her with shaking hands. She backed up until she hit a counter. "You are so lucky the boss likes you so much," he said, panting. Then he smirked. "Then again, you are bulletproof, aren't you?"

Her heart in her throat, she sidestepped his pistol. She had no idea what he'd do if he knew she couldn't stop the shot. "Too bad the boss doesn't feel the same about you," she said, forcing bravado into her words. "You're definitely not his favorite."

But she had miscalculated his recklessness. Kos's face grew red, and his grip tightened on the gun. She gasped and threw her hands up, twisting to duck away as a flare of fire emitted from the muzzle. A loud roar assaulted her ears. Out of habit, she shoved her hands forward to push at the bullet.

But Justine's ability hadn't returned. As she ducked, her left hand exploded in pain. She lost her balance and fell against the counter, sliding to the floor as she clutched her hand with the other. Her ears rang, and she watched Kos mutter something, tuck away his gun, and run from the room.

35.

Justine crushed her hand in the other till the pain ebbed from blinding to merely on fire. She struggled to get to her feet and failed. A lab tech from the next room ran to her as Kos fled, his eyes wild. Justine gritted her teeth as the woman slid her arm under her and pulled her up. The tech said something, but Justine couldn't hear through the ringing in her ears. She wanted to run after Kos, but her legs could barely get her to a stool.

Sitting somewhat steadily, she held her hand to her chest while the tech searched the cabinets and returned with several white towels. The woman spoke to one of the other techs who had come to the doorway. Justine heard nothing but ringing. She held her breath as the tech pressed a towel to the wound, then a second one once the first was soaked through. Blood covered the woman's clothes and her own, the floor, and cabinets. *There's your DNA sample.*

"That's enough," Justine said when the tech had secured a new towel. The two other techs returned and started cleaning up. "I'll keep the pressure on." She tapped her foot on the floor to try to control her shaking.

The woman shook her head with a surprised look on her face. "... bleeding." Her words sounded as if they were coming through a long tube.

"I'll never find him if I wait." She was going to put holes in that man. Then throw him against the wall. Maybe she'd try her heat trick on him, see what that was really good for.

"And do what? You'll ... trailing blood. Going after ... help." The woman laid a hand on her shoulder, leaning close. "You need to take a few minutes."

She closed her eyes. She was here for Quinn. Finding Kos could wait. Once the urge to shove and to break waned, she opened her eyes.

The woman unwrapped the blood-soaked cloth and dropped it into a nearby sink. The edges of the wound were ragged and purple. Dark blood seeped from the hole in her flesh in time with the throbbing that intensified with every movement. The tech began wrapping her hand with a new towel, applying pressure to both sides. Justine pressed her mouth shut to keep from screaming.

"Did I hear gunfire?" Eddie Doyle appeared in the doorway, his words sounding far away. He rushed to her. "Justine, what the hell happened?" He took in her bloody coat and the towel, then turned to the tech. "Just the hand was hit?"

The woman nodded. "I'm trying to slow down the bleeding. But I don't really know what I'm doing, so I can't tell you much else."

"Let me take a look," Eddie said. The tech tossed her once-white coat in the trash and went to the sink.

Justine bit her lip as he laid her arm on the counter. Taking care not to touch the injury, he unwrapped the makeshift bandage. Every nudge brought a spark of pain. "Who did this?" He turned her hand over. The palm looked somewhat better. Both sides were puffy and starting to swell.

She sucked in a breath. "His name is Kos, but I call him asshole."

His nostrils flared. He leaned close. "Your ears ringing?"

She nodded.

"It'll wear off." He shook his head. "I'll break that guy in half."

"You'll have more pieces to work with after I finish with him," she muttered.

His face relaxed a bit, and he gave a half smile. "Maybe we can work together on that."

The tech brought over a first-aid kit and water.

"Can you open the bottle for her? Thanks." Eddie rummaged through the supplies, pulling out what he needed. After laying a cloth over his prosthetic arm, he draped her arm over his. "This won't feel good," he said as he opened a bottle of alcohol with his teeth.

She squeezed her eyes shut and held her breath.

"Do you know where the doc is?" he asked.

She hissed as he lit her hand on fire. She opened her eyes to check for actual flames. Red-tinged alcohol dripped from her fingers.

"Listen to my words. Don't look at your hand." After making her drink some water and take a painkiller, he described every step as he opened packages of gauze and tape.

"You've done this before."

"Military training is thorough. A little bit of everything." He looked more closely at the injury, then opened up the antiseptic. "Good thing it hit your hand. That probably redirected the bullet away from your body. You could have some fractured bones, but a doctor can tell you that. You may eventually get back full use of the hand—if you get to a doctor, and soon."

"No doctors."

"You've been shot—"

"Just make it so I can move."

He paused his work to give her a silent *Really?* with a tilt of his head. "I can make it so you don't die. No promises beyond that."

"Perfect," she muttered. She bit her lip and tried to focus on the sharp throbbing that shot up her arm rather than the more painful truth: she was down to one hand.

"So any idea where he is? Hollister, I mean."

She sighed. He meant well in trying to distract her. "He went to get someone."

He tightly wrapped the wound in gauze.

"Do you know someone named Quinn Duncan? Have you seen anyone new here?"

"Quinn? Sure, I met him a few hours ago."

He'd been alive when she arrived. "I need to see him. I think Kos hurt him."

He snipped the gauze from the roll and secured the end. "The guy's a bit wild, but I don't really think he'd do anything to the people here. Doc keeps him around, so he must be good for something."

"He shot me. You don't know what he'll do to any of you."

"Can't argue with that. Now if you're looking to see Quinn, the doc would know where he is. We should—"

"I don't want to find Hollister. I want to find Quinn."

He paused and looked her over. "What've you got in mind?"

She straightened. "He's not here by choice. Neither am I. In fact, I bet neither are you."

"Of course I am. The doc changed my life. Made me a new man."

"Eddie, he's experimenting on you. He's not even sure what it'll do to you."

"But it worked. Let me tape this up and I'll show you." He washed his hand and returned the supplies to the kit. Eager as a puppy, he grabbed a glass beaker from a shelf. He glanced around, but the techs had retreated to the other room. He then stretched out his arm much as she did when using her ability. Holding his breath, he stared in concentration at the jar, then jerked his hand forward. The beaker slipped forward a centimeter or two. Though a meager demonstration, it was more than she was capable of at the moment.

He looked at her, eyes shining. "It was even easier to move it this time." He laughed and patted his chest. "Doc gave me superpowers."

She stared at the glass, then at Eddie. The pain left her for a precious moment. Eddie had her ability. He was like her. What other things could he do? Could he use heat like she was learning to? Would he develop other abilities she didn't have?

She reined in her jumble of thoughts. "Eddie, I know this is exciting for you. You feel like you can do anything. But you're still a lab rat. There's nothing super about that. When he's finished with you, or if you don't change the way he wants, he'll have no use for you. What do you think happened to the ones he tried this on before you, the ones who didn't work out?"

His smile faded. "No one was here when I got here."

"And if you don't go along with his plans, you won't be here either." She grabbed his sleeve. "You don't have to stay. You could help me, and we could all get out. No more tests. You could be free."

He looked at her like she had proposed he go to Mars. "Why would I want that? Go back to being a use-less, one-armed vet? He's not going to throw me away, because it worked." He paused. "He made me like you. I thought you'd like that."

His words stole the breath from her. It was true—the world felt less lonely already. But at the same time, she'd had so little to claim as hers. "Has he told you his plan once you learn how to use this?"

"I'm getting a new high-tech arm. I'll be able to move the fingers and everything. And I'm already stronger. I'll worry about plans later."

"Is that what the implant is for?"

"Yeah, they have to stick a doodad in my head. Then I can move my hand just by thinking. And you want me to leave? Come on—what's the downside to this?"

"What's the point of this ability if someone else has control over your life?"

"You don't get it. He's giving me my life back, only better."

She laughed without humor. "Hollister is definitely not interested in improving my life."

"So your life was great before? Didn't want to change a thing, right?"

Justine mustered the energy to glare at him.

He nodded at her non-answer. "Maybe you should think this through more before rejecting the whole idea."

"I came here for Quinn. He never asked for this. If Hollister won't let him go, I will get him free." She tried to stand and failed.

"Easy." He steadied her on the stool. "You've lost a lot of blood."

Her left hand and most of her arm pulsed with pain. Her fingers felt too hot. She moved her index finger a fraction, and electric pain lanced up her arm. She gasped and held her breath until it passed.

He winced. "It's going to hurt for a while."

"Feels like my arm got ripped off."

"Here, let's do this." He got a roll of gauze from the first-aid kit, quickly made a sling, and eased her arm into it.

The pressure on the injury eased at once. "That feels a lot better. Thanks." She tried standing again. He reached out to steady her. She hesitated, but she could find no deceit in his face, and she leaned on his arm. She was a bit wobbly, but she was on her feet.

"You want to make sure Quinn is okay. I get it. So stick around and you can do that. Adjust your priorities."

She had one working hand, no ability, no defense. She could barely stand. And she had yet to locate Quinn. What she had to do was adjust her strategy.

"I know you're not happy about all this, but we can work together. It won't be so bad, I'm telling you."

She hated to disappoint him. "I can't force you to do anything. All I'm asking is that you tell me where Quinn is."

His gaze sharpened. "Look, he's already gotten some of the magic juice. He might as well get the rest. I just don't want him getting the implant that was meant for me."

"It's not magic. He's messing around with your genes. And there's no reason he'd put an implant in Quinn when you're getting the arm."

"That's why I thought it was a rumor. He promised me this arm, and I'm getting it."

"If he wants you to have it. If he changes his mind, you can't do a thing about it. If the experiment does something weird to you, if the surgery goes badly, there's nothing you can do. You have no way of knowing how any of this will affect you."

"You turned out fine. Why are you so worried about me?"

She swallowed. How could she begin to explain when there was so much she didn't know? "Quinn is not getting an implant. I can promise you that." She turned to leave, hoping her legs would work.

He grasped her shoulders, gently but enough to hold her in place. "Justine, you can't."

She stepped back, but he held on. "Eddie—"

"You're in no shape to be running around yet. Why don't you rest for a few minutes?"

"I'm letting you do things your way. Let me do this my way." She started to pull from his grip. But her legs were still shaking, and she felt every movement of her hand.

"How about this: You stay here. I'll go check on Quinn myself, and I'll come back and give you an update. I can tell him you're here if you want."

Justine dropped onto the stool. Sitting definitely felt better. She wasn't sure what was keeping her upright. "Fine. Check on him. But don't tell him anything. I'm not here."

36.

After Eddie left, Justine shuffled to the larger, brighter lab where the technicians had gone back to work. In the corner, the camera kept watch. Had Hollister seen all that had happened? Where was Quinn?

She was steadier on her feet already, though every step jolted her hand. She would sit only long enough to figure out how to get out. Hollister had taken enough from her. She would not give him another hair on her head or drop of her blood.

As she settled on a stool, a static pop and fizzle from the central workbench startled her, and she wobbled on her seat.

"Not that one." The woman who'd helped Justine earlier leaned over and yanked out the plug to a piece of equipment. "Anthony, pay attention. You're working with flammables."

"Sorry. I forgot which one it was in this room."

"Any outlet but this one." The tall young tech moved his machine to a counter against the wall.

The woman glanced at Justine, eyeing her sling. "How are you doing?"

"I'll survive. Thanks for your help."

The woman nodded and returned to her laptop in the corner of the room.

Sparks had left black smudges around the outlet built into the countertop. She welcomed the threat of flames to this prison and would gladly fan them with her own heat.

Hollister had insisted the stun gun's short circuit was temporary. She'd taken him at his word because the alternative was unthinkable. That he understood her ability better than she did was aggravating. Was she passing up a chance to learn more from the one person who could teach her?

Her free hand flexed. She had taught herself to use her ability, with Devon's help. Whatever she might gain from working with Hollister, she would lose much more. And Quinn had already lost too much. All because this man had the audacity to think he could reshape humanity.

She had no idea how many others there had been, but there would be more after she left. His infernal research would continue.

An electric thought jolted her. Sonia had told her to use whatever she had. Right now what she had was an abundance of science.

She could do more than escape this place. She could prevent this place from becoming someone else's nightmare. She slipped off the stool. Once she was sure of her footing, she walked over to Anthony, the camera's eye drilling into her back. She put on what she hoped was a welcoming smile.

He paused his work over a set of samples in a tray. "How are you doing?"

"Good enough. I don't want to bother you. Hollister explained some of the work you guys are doing, but not everything. What are you working on?"

"Are you sure you want to be walking around? Looks like you should be seeing a doctor."

"For right now I'm fine. I thought this might distract me."

"I get it, sure. Um, my job is just to separate out cells they've targeted so they can work on extraction."

"What are they going to extract?"

"DNA. We're trying to zero in on specific traits. It takes a lot of trial and error."

"Where do you get the DNA from?"

"We buy samples in bulk. Companies sell them in the form we need. Very little prep."

Creepy. She nodded, hoping she looked interested. "Is this the machine you use to do that? The one that got you in trouble?"

"It was the outlet, not the equipment. Seems every room in this place has electrical problems. The wiring wasn't built for the kind of loads we put on it."

"Would that have fried the machine? You've got some expensive equipment here."

"Yup. But it's worse than that. We've got a lot of acetone and other liquids that do not mix well with fire. Even a spark could—" He let out a breath and shook his head. "It was a really stupid mistake." The shelf above the worktable with the defective outlet held containers filled with clear liquids. Some of them had a flame on the label.

Flame was what she needed.

"So if you'd turned the machine on, would we all be in bits scattered over Manhattan?"

He chuckled. "Not so much bits as ashes. We're really careful, mostly. There's a cabinet over there to suck up flammable vapors. If they would fix the wiring, we wouldn't have that problem. But that costs money."

"Is there some sort of alert or automatic shutoff if there are leaking vapors or smoke?"

"There's no kill switch, if that's what you mean. Use the flammables in the hood, vent the vapors out, and working equipment isn't going to spark. It's just that outlet."

"So it's okay to sit here with all this stuff?"

"Oh, sure. You're fine."

Justine moved to the center worktable, reading labels and instructions until Anthony appeared engrossed in his work again. She walked around until the shelves blocked the camera's line of sight to her, then took a bottle off the shelf. She set it down quietly where no one could see it beside a boxy instrument. Struggling with one hand, she soon got the cap unscrewed and set the cover aside.

She continued her stroll around the counter. It had been well over an hour since she'd been tased. It was time to find out if she still had any ability.

She found a spot that might be out of the camera's range. First ensuring everyone was engrossed in their work, she then stepped back, extended her arm, and gave the boxy gadget a shove. It didn't budge. She swallowed. Perhaps it was too heavy. Her heartbeat racing, she tried again with a plastic tray beside the machine. It rattled and shifted a fraction of distance. A ridiculous amount of relief shot through her. It had moved. Her ability would come back. She only needed to wait.

But she didn't have the time. With every hour, Quinn was in more danger. She didn't know what they were doing to him or what plans they had for him. Ability or no ability, she had to act now.

The acetone had been open for over five minutes. It would have to be enough.

She returned to where she'd begun her circuit. Stomping out the protesting voice in her head, she unplugged the nearest machine and plugged it into the faulty outlet.

The two older techs worked at the other end of the room, one scrolling through his laptop, the other making notes in her notepad. Anthony was at his centrifuge. Did they know what purpose their work would be put to? Even if they did, she couldn't put them in danger.

She jumped when someone turned on a large and noisy piece of equipment. *Thank you.* Her left hand throbbed in time with the pounding of her heart as she poured the liquid over the countertop. The acrid vapors tickled her nose.

She set down the bottle. No one had noticed yet. She opened her mouth, then paused. How did you announce you were about to burn down a room? She waited until the machine quieted. "I hate to interrupt everyone's work." She paused until they turned to her. "Actually, I do want to interrupt—"

"What—"

"I smell acetone."

"Did you plug that in there?"

Justine rested her hand on the switch. "Yes. You smell acetone, and it's all over this table. I plugged this contraption into the faulty plug. So it would be bad if we were all here when I turned this on, wouldn't it?"

"Are you crazy? You're going to start a fire."

"I just told to you how dangerous that is," Anthony told her.

"Yes. Thank you for being so helpful. I don't want to hurt any of you, so I suggest you leave." No one budged. "I mean now. I'm going to turn this on, and who knows when it'll spark."

"You're ruining thousands of dollars of equipment and research."

"I'm not known for my patience. So I would leave *now*." What did she have to tell these people? "Maybe you need more incentive. Here. I'll pour more of this around." She opened up the bottle again and poured it on another counter, wondering if she were making the fire bigger. The techs cried out for her to stop. One inched toward the door. "When I turn on this switch, I think you'd be happier if you were far away." She touched the switch.

Now they all moved, horror hanging their mouths open. Anthony looked offended.

Once she was alone, Justine took a deep breath and switched on the machine. She didn't die in an immediate fireball, so she backed away from the volatile materials. A spark jumped from the outlet. She made a dash for the door. As she reached the hall, a loud *foomp* warned her. She braced herself and ran faster.

37.

As a roar spread through the room she'd set alight, Justine ran for the end of the hall and slammed into the stairwell door with the right side of her body. She gripped the railing and pounded down the stairs. Her left hand screamed at the jostling of every step. By the time she reached the second floor, someone had pulled the fire alarm.

The second-floor storage level was dark and cool. The lights flickered on, and the screech of the alarm continued to stab her ears. The entrance to every wing was shut except for 2B, the one in which Sonia had appeared only hours ago.

People shouted on the third floor, and footsteps pounded as they ran for the stairwell. Her heart in her throat, she ran into 2B and shut the door. It clicked, and she was locked in. She fell against the door, gulping air. Her left fingers felt like balloons stretched beyond their limit. The sling only helped to restrain her arm while she moved.

What had she done? To destroy Hollister's work, she'd risked killing herself and many others.

And she'd do it again.

The dark-red glow of the exit signs outlined the boxes crowding the corridor. She checked the corners of the ceiling. Nestled in one was the black cover of a camera. There was nowhere to hide.

The door from the stairwell to the main hall crashed open. Two men called out to each other over the alarm as they searched each wing of the floor. Distant pounding assured her people were leaving the building. Something crashed upstairs as glass reacted to the heat of the fire.

Short on options, she ran through the connecting hall to Wing A and into the room she'd hidden in earlier. Leaving the door ajar, she started to slide down the wall but stopped. She checked the corners of the ceiling, but didn't see a camera. They couldn't see her in here. But she couldn't stay. She had to get to Quinn before they figured out where she was headed.

As she started to leave, a beep and a squelch nearly made her jump out of her skin. In the wall beside the door was a speaker like the one in Hollister's office.

"Justine." Cayden. His voice was breathy and quiet, as if he were whispering.

She sucked in a breath and leaned closer to the speaker. "You son of a bitch. What more do you want from me?"

In the main hallway, the guards called out their search progress.

"I'm sorry—"

"You lead me into a trap, then apologize? Is this another trap?"

"There's no time for this." Static crackled over the speaker.

"Why should I listen—"

"The guard will check your wing next."

So he was watching on the cameras. "Fine. I'm out of here." She headed out the door.

"I know where Quinn is."

She stopped breathing entirely.

"I need you—you have to save Quinn," he said. "Please. Call m—" There was a surge of static, then silence.

The traitorous bastard wanted to help her now? Perhaps she was a means to an end, to save his brother. She could use him to that end as well. Cayden would know this building better than she did.

Blood seeped through the bandage, her coat, and her shirt. She adjusted the sling to try to ease the throbbing, but it did nothing to help.

The guards shouted to each other, then one headed for the stairs.

She ran from the room and its illusion of safety and plunged into the darkness of the connecting passage. As she reached Wing B, she almost crashed into piles of equipment. She ducked behind them as the lock on the door to Wing A buzzed. Crouched in the red-glowing dark, her breathing was as loud as the footsteps of the guard searching the wing. Cayden's warning had saved her.

If ever Justine needed help, it was now. She'd been offered help many times in the last week. If she'd accepted even a little of it, she might not be in this mess. She took Cayden's cell phone out of her pocket and held it in her bloody hand. She laid it on her knee and swiped the screen, streaking blood across the glass. Her finger shook as it hovered over the phone icon. Through the smear of blood, she tapped the icon, then Cayden's number. She listened to the line ring while her hand throbbed.

Of all the bad options before her, not doing this alone seemed the least scary.

~ ~ ~

"You're in the wrong wing," Cayden said in a rush.

"Wait, where are you?" Justine glanced up into the camera. "Can you see me?"

A brief pause. "I'm in security. Listen—"

"Is everyone out of the third floor? Was anyone hurt?"

More silence. "I don't think so. What were y—"

"Who else can see me?"

"No one knows where you are but me, for now. You—"

"Can you see Quinn?"

"Not directly. I've—"

Her heart leapt into her throat. "But you know where he is? Is he okay?" A door slammed.

He paused again. "I think he's okay for the moment. He's in room 2D4. You're in Wing 2B. Wing D is right across the main hall. You won't be exposed long. Try to avoid security." The phone rustled with movement, then he added, "I'll try to call when I find a way out. Good luck." The line clicked and went silent.

She looked at the screen. A message appeared: *Battery low.* Terrific. She pocketed the phone. Something crashed above. The fire was spreading. If it reached this floor, the whole building might go.

A chill passed over her despite the warming air. Her sling cut into her neck. Her entire body ached and trembled with exhaustion. She couldn't remember the last time she'd eaten. Her ability had barely returned. Yet she was surrounded by cardboard. Weighing potential destruction and potential harm, she turned from the door to the main hall. *In for a penny…*

With footsteps crashing around Wing A, she knelt in front of a box, extended her shaking hand, and pushed out heat toward the cardboard. Her hand grew warm, and after minutes that passed like hours, the paper in front of her palm darkened, then smoldered. She stared at her palm. It was smeared with blood and dirt. To be certain Hollister's work ended here, she had crossed the line she'd drawn for herself. She wiped her hand on her pants. Great, now her pants were bloody too.

As smoke wafted from the boxes and paper peeled away to ashes, she crept to the doorway of the corridor, then stopped short. It was locked. She didn't have time for detours. At the other end, a window offered no help.

The answer came with a buzz and a clear and quiet click. The door to the hall sprung open, then drifted back to the jamb. She grabbed the handle before the door could shut again. She looked up into the corner. A camera stared back at her.

She nodded and inched through the doorway. Echoes of the evacuation and the search for her bounced through the hall. While they searched the wings, she edged out into the wide space that seemed to stretch for miles. The wailing of the alarm was louder and the scent of smoke stronger. When no squad of guards came for her, she took a deep breath and ran across to the door labeled 2D.

The door buzzed and opened as she approached, and she threw herself inside. This wing was brightly lit, but like the others, equipment and boxes choked the corridor. To her right was a mirror of the dim connecting passageway between Wings A and B. On her left was 2D2, and on her right, next to the passage, was 2D3. The last door on the left was 2D4.

It was open.

Justine rushed to the doorway. Lights blinked on. The room was nearly empty. The door said 2D4, the room Cayden said his brother was being held in. It was the wrong room.

Her heart thudding, she reached into her pocket for the phone, then paused. Had Cayden given her the wrong room, or was this exactly where he meant for her to go? The other doors in this wing were shut with similar keypads. But the wing was silent aside from the fire alarm. She stepped into the room. A chair was pushed all the way into the corner. Plastic wrapping peeked out from under the chair. The table beside the bed was askew. Someone had used this room, and recently.

Voices drifted to her. Not far away. She stepped behind a collection of equipment in the hall. The squelch of radio static, then a woman's voice. "Head to the first floor." Coming from Wing E, at the end of the passage.

She inched through the dark narrow corridor and crouched beside a stack of boxes. The air here was warmer, and acrid smoke wafted near the ceiling. At the other end of the short hall, crashing and slamming of doors and equipment competed with the alarm.

A stocky guard stood in the doorway, her back to Justine. "Should I bring the guy in 2E4 down?" the woman said into her handheld radio. She nodded at the staticky response, then pocketed the radio. "Let's go. Everybody needs to get downstairs," she told the lab techs, waving them out.

They filed out with arms full of materials and proceeded to the rear exit that opened to a stairwell.

Justine slipped back into the connecting passage and took out the phone. "You gave me the wrong room number," she whispered as soon as Cayden answered.

"What? No, that's where they put him. 2D4."

"That room is empty. I need you to find him. And then unlock the door."

"I ... I can't. Are you—"

"You did it before. You can do it again. It's not like I can go knocking on each door to see who answers."

"Look, I had to leave security." A door slammed in the background. "So I can't—" Sounds of movement mixed with someone's voice, then Cayden spoke, his voice muffled. "Yeah, I'll be right there—" His voice became clear again. "I can't do any of that. Sorry. You have your own ways, don't you? Figure it out. But do it quick.

The fire just ate up the third floor and is starting on the second." He breathed heavily. "You don't do things half-way, do you? Just make your way, uh, down, uh, all the way, however you can." The line went quiet.

No help, but no hindrance from him either. She was back where she'd started. With even less time.

She crept back to Wing E and peered around a box. Maybe she could force this woman to tell her where Quinn was.

Someone pounded on a door on the left. "Hey! If there's a fire, you can't leave me in here."

She stifled a gasp. Quinn.

The guard led the last tech out. "Hold your horses," she called out to Quinn.

Was she really going to make it that easy for Justine? As soon as the keypad beeped and the guard opened the door, she stepped into the corridor.

The woman turned to her, a hand on the door handle. Sweat dotted her brow. "You have to get—" Her eyes fell on Justine's makeshift sling. "What the hell hap—"

Quinn stood in the doorway behind the guard. Adrenaline shot through Justine. "Thanks, I'll take it from here." She rushed forward.

"Justine!" Quinn looked at her as if he were seeing a ghost, then he frowned. "You're hurt."

She soaked in the sight of him. He was alive and safe, almost. A little disheveled, possibly bruised, but otherwise whole and well. Her relief overwhelmed her, and her voice shook when she spoke. "You okay?"

He grabbed the doorjamb. "It's not safe for you to be here."

The guard stepped in front of him with a hand in Justine's face. "This is lovely, but you need to get yourself out. I'll deal with him."

"I'm getting you out of here," she said around the woman.

The guard pulled out a stun gun, pointing it first at Quinn, then Justine. They both backed up. "Has no one noticed that the building is on fire? Now, I'm bringing him to the first floor. You can come too. I've got no problem with that."

"Let him leave with me," Justine said, "and we'll be out of your way."

While the guard was focused on her, Quinn rushed at the woman. She spun back, planted her feet, and struck out at him with the stun gun. Justine yanked on her arm, jostling the hand holding the weapon. Quinn dodged it and only received a glancing zap on the wrist. With a grunt, he staggered back, shaking his arm.

Justine dragged the guard toward her again. The woman fell back, but not before grabbing the door handle. Quinn caught the door as it swung shut, but he could not hold on. The keypad mechanism whirred and clicked as it locked.

Justine threw her right shoulder against the steel, though the pain on her left side made it a feeble effort. Of course it couldn't be easy. And she had wasted precious minutes.

Quinn banged on the other side of the door.

"Stand back, Quinn!" she said. Shouting came from somewhere above, and she wondered if her second fire had caught or gone out.

The guard reached out for her. "Look—"

Without any thought, Justine turned to her and pushed out while trying to figure out how to open the door.

And the woman stumbled back.

Only a little, but it was more than she could do a couple of hours ago. She pushed at her again with more force. The woman pitched into a stack of equipment behind her. The boxes and materials tumbled onto her, and she cried out as she fell to the ground. Justine went over to the remaining boxes and toppled them onto her. The guard grunted and quieted.

In desperation, Justine tried the door handle, but got what she expected. The door was like nearly all those here, wider and thicker than usual, and had been installed into the old sickly green walls. Except—she knocked on the wall. Not concrete. Sounded like wood and plaster. She smiled. She could manage wood and plaster.

She shoved aside the pile of heavy boxes beside the door, feeling the passage of each second. With a deep breath, she raised her right hand, drew back her arm, then drove it forward with her whole body and mind.

A few pieces of plasterboard chipped off.

She needed to put more into her push. Except she didn't think she had anything left.

"Justine? Are you still there?"

"I'm here, Quinn. Stay away from the wall." She was certain he was running his hands through his hair and pacing. He was almost close enough to touch.

The boxes she'd shoved aside were overflowing with equipment. Beside one box lay a small piece of machinery heavy enough to do some damage as a projectile. With the right timing, she might pull this off.

The guard groaned and moved beneath the equipment, while the ceiling boomed with the collapse of something upstairs.

Hefting the instrument to steady her hand and judge its weight, she then tossed it into the air. As the machinery fell, she threw force toward it with as much strength as she could muster.

The black piece of plastic and metal flew into the wall with a loud crash, bits of plaster and plastic spewing in all directions. For a half second, it sat lodged in the mangled wall before falling to the floor.

The wood studs, lath, and drywall on the other side were visible but unbroken. She almost screamed in frustration. With a growl, she sent another push. The plaster of the interior wall shuddered and cracked.

"It's working, whatever you're doing," Quinn said. "Wait." Something inside scraped, then the crack lengthened as the drywall shook with a pounding from the other side. "Back up, okay?"

Justine stepped away as a metal table leg punched through the drywall. Quinn pulled the leg down through the plaster. Then he broke off plasterboard and wooden lathing with his hands. She rushed in to do the same on her side.

The guard muttered as she pushed through the pile of equipment on top of her.

As plaster dust drifted in the air, his face appeared in the hole. He half smiled. "I thought you went to Philly."

Her grip tightened on a piece of drywall. "I did."

He met her eyes. "But you came back."

She kept her gaze on the hole they were making as the last few days crashed over her. "Did you think I wouldn't come for you?" she whispered.

The sound of ripping plasterboard mixed with the peal of the fire alarm and the grumbling of the guard, but his silence was louder. "I don't know," he said finally.

A new pain bloomed in her chest. She'd earned that.

After a few moments, he said, "This nut Hollister seems to think you're going to work with him." He broke off more drywall. "Are you?"

She paused after breaking off a piece of lath. She'd kept so much from him that he didn't know the answer to that.

"What the hell have you done now?" the guard yelled as she stepped over the spilled contents of the boxes around her.

Justine pushed out toward her. The guard fell back a few steps but stayed on her feet, looking at her chest, then at Justine in shock.

Quinn eyed her for a moment. "What did you do?"

"I'm keeping her out of our way. Keep pulling."

The guard took a wary step toward her. "You must be one of the doc's pet projects."

Quinn's gaze lingered on Justine, but he continued to break away the plaster, then started kicking at it. Soon he got a leg through and began shoving a shoulder through the lathing.

"This is crazy," the guard muttered. She latched on to Justine's wrist. "You can't come in here and break down a wall and take a subject out."

Justine met her eyes. "Watch me," she said quietly, yanking her arm from the woman's grip. She stepped between the guard and Quinn as he forced his way through the wall.

"You are not the one in charge here," the guard said and grabbed Justine's shoulders.

Her left arm flared with pain that shot into her hand. She stifled a cry and twisted away.

As Quinn set foot into the corridor and began wresting himself from the opening, the guard reached for him with her stun gun. "You are not going anywhere."

Justine tugged at her arm, then pushed out before her. The woman smashed into the opposite wall and staggered before falling onto one knee.

Behind her, Quinn brushed plaster dust from his hair and shirt. He looked at Justine as if seeing her for the first time.

She swallowed. From the yelling and shouting, the sparks she'd left behind had caught and spread. And sirens now added to the cacophony. But she would finish what she'd started. "Watch her. I need a minute."

"We don't have a minute."

Justine pushed through the opening they'd made. At least he'd had a bed. And the sheets should work. She held her hand over the bedsheets and sent out heat. Her brow broke out in a sweat, and her fingers throbbed. Maybe it would be easier if she sat down.

But if she stopped moving now, she'd never move again. She stood over the bed and soon smelled the faint scent of singed fibers. Smoke rose from the sheets, and then an ember appeared, eating through the fabric. That would have to be enough.

She emerged from the room, covered with plaster dust. He glanced past her and frowned, then turned to her with wide eyes.

Justine reached out for his hand. "Time to go."

38.

Justine ran for the door to the main hall. Quinn called out from the other end of the corridor. He peeked through the doorway. "Stairs are clear."

She rushed to his side, and they ran into the stairwell. Her legs buckled, and she stumbled and clutched the railing. Her vision blurred.

Quinn wrapped an arm around her. "Easy. Breathe. I've got you."

"Basement," she said. With his support, she plodded down the stairs beside him. Haze lingered in the air. Sirens grew louder as fire engines neared.

"Why the base—"

"Cayden." She focused on breathing, slowly, evenly. She could not pass out now.

"Where is he? We could use his help."

"Don't know." She allowed herself to lean on him as they rounded the landing. "Probably too many people on first—"

They froze as two guards entered the stairwell from the first floor.

"Everyone is gathering in the lobby on first," one of the men said, "while they work on containing the fire on third. There's no evacuation." A thick moment of silence followed as the man's eyes fell to her bloody sling.

Justine took a step, then another.

The guards straightened, their hands drifting toward their weapons. "No one leaves without being cleared by the boss."

"Look, I'm NYPD. I am not here voluntarily. You're better off staying out of this. In fact, I'd leave if I were you. This won't end well."

"You have ID?" the guard asked, his eyes on Justine.

"They took everything from me."

"Then our instructions stand." To Justine, he said, "You're the one Dr. Hollister wants."

"Where is he?" she asked.

"Don't know."

"Well, we're leaving." She descended two more steps with an eye on their hands. Sure enough, one drew his pistol, the other his stun gun. While she felt spent, her last shove at the guard upstairs had been stronger. Time for a test.

She pushed at the gun. The weapon jerked in the man's hand. With another push, it hit the wall behind him, then bounced down the steps.

While both guards were distracted, she pushed the stun gun out of the other man's hand. It bounced into the corner. As he reached for it, she shoved the stun gun again, and the plastic casing shattered against the wall. He twisted away, shielding his face.

Quinn stepped in and gave him a push of his own with his fist, and the man's head bounced off the concrete wall. Quinn grabbed his head and smacked it into the concrete again, and the man slid to the floor in a daze.

The first guard had retrieved his gun down the next flight of stairs. As he started back up, Justine pushed at him as she descended the steps. He tumbled to the landing but scrambled up at once. Before he could draw his pistol, she kicked him in the face. He caught her foot, and she fell back into Quinn's arms. As he held her, she kicked the man in the side. She pushed at him again, and his head smacked against the wall. He wobbled and tipped over.

She panted, holding on to the railing to steady herself. Her racing heart made her hand pulse harder in the sling, and blood seeped from the wound down her chest. She took a few wobbly steps, then with Quinn's support hobbled toward the basement.

"You really did that."

She nodded. If they got out of this, they had a long conversation coming.

He looked behind them as one of the guards moved on the landing above. "Sounds like he might have needed a harder hit." His face was devoid of expression.

"Any harder and I could have killed him."

"And?" He paused in the middle of the stairs.

Her breath caught in her throat. "You think I'd kill him just because he was in my way?"

His eyes met hers with a challenge. "Seems like you could have."

"So could you when you're carrying your gun."

He cocked his head, then nodded.

"I choose how I use this ability," she continued. "Not Hollister. Not a guard. Not anyone but me. Ever."

Quinn's brow eased and his body relaxed. He wrapped an arm lightly around her shoulder. She wrapped her one good one around him, clutching his shirt with all the strength she had left, easing into the warmth of his body. She'd be content to let the whole building burn around them.

"Let's go," he whispered.

She stepped away. "Is that blood?" She tugged at his shirt.

"Yeah, it looks worse than it was."

Right now she had to take him at his word. She nodded, and they resumed their trek.

As they reached the basement level, Justine leaned her forehead against the door to the parking garage to catch her breath. The metal was cool, so close to outside. She and Quinn were nearly free. Her entire left side ached and burned, and blood now soaked the sleeve of her coat. Her legs felt like jello.

Quinn squeezed her shoulder. "We're almost out. Hang on."

She sucked in a breath. She could do this. "I don't know if I can walk to your place."

Quinn opened the door. A gust of icy air blew into the stairwell. "You need a hospital, Justine, not my apartment."

"No hospitals. Please." Quinn glared but gave up the argument for the moment.

The parking garage was cool and lit by garish halogen lights. Sirens grew louder as the fire department approached.

Passing through the lower level, they rounded the concrete pylon on the ramp leading to ground level. Justine froze, and Quinn stiffened beside her.

Cayden stood among boxes stacked beside the open trunk of a car.

Hollister stood next to him. On their approach, he snatched Cayden and brought a knife to his throat. "Looks like we have another chance to negotiate."

39.

"Cay, what are you doing?" Quinn said. He started forward, but Justine held him back.

Cayden clutched Hollister's arm, stretching his head back while trying to keep an eye on the blade at his throat. "Sorry, Q. I tried. But I screwed up. Again."

Under the halogen lights, Hollister and Cayden stood beside the car surrounded by boxes overflowing with papers and equipment. Justine guessed they were about fifty feet farther up the garage ramp, with at least another fifty to the exit. They might be within reach of a push, if she could manage it. But that knife was too close to Cayden's neck.

"Hollister, you think all of this is a game." Quinn's voice rose in timber and volume. "You play around with people like they're rats. Change their lives whether they want it or not."

While Quinn berated him, Hollister's eyes were on Justine and her wounded hand. He clenched his jaw, and the knife trembled in his grip. Cayden leaned back farther. "I apologize, Justine, for Kalakos's behavior. The man has no self-control. He will be dealt with."

"If your other hired maniac hadn't tased me," she said, "I would have been able to defend myself."

Hollister's expression hardened.

Sirens grew louder, then cut off as the fire trucks arrived. Police wouldn't be far behind. She was better off leaving before they arrived with their questions, but the only exit was past this man.

A car door slammed, and Eddie stepped out from behind the sedan. He slowed as he approached the confrontation and took a stance by the car.

"Killing Cayden won't get you anything," Quinn insisted. "Let him go, and we can talk."

Justine took a step toward them as he talked.

"That's hardly a negotiation."

"Deal with it."

"Detective, you've been given a rare gift. Will you waste it?"

"I don't know what you've done to me. You don't even know. Now release Cayden."

Hollister tilted his head toward Cayden. "Your little brother, right?"

Quinn took a sharp breath.

"You've spent your life looking after him, making sure he doesn't get hurt. Getting him out of trouble."

"What do you think this will get you?" Quinn asked, breathing heavily. "Fire department's here. NYPD is on their way. You take me with you, and they will look for me till the end of time. What are you going to do, flee the country?" He paused, but Hollister was unmoved.

Justine took another step toward him.

"You're not in a good spot, Doc."

Hollister inched the blade closer to Cayden's skin. Cayden's eyes shifted between the blade and his brother. "Your brother is in a worse spot. You've put his security above yours for years. Now when it counts, you'll turn your back on him?"

Quinn heaved a breath, his nostrils flaring. "As long as you have that knife at my brother's throat, we have nothing to talk about."

Hollister pressed his lips together, clenching his hand around the knife handle. He turned to Justine, and she paused her advance. "For so many years I've longed to share my knowledge. You can accomplish more than you can imagine."

"Be all I can be, blah, blah, blah. Heard this before."

"You have the power to save countless lives," Hollister continued, his voice heated. "What do you say to those you are turning your back on?"

"I can think of better ways to offer me a job than shooting and tasing me."

His shoulders slumped for a fraction of a second. He shook his head. "Your father's biggest mistake was sending you away. If he hadn't, you'd know how wrong you are."

The mention of her father burned like a whip. She swallowed all she wanted to say in return, though her whole body shook with the effort.

"I can guide you as your father should have. I can—" He stopped, pressing his lips shut, as if to stop forbidden words from tumbling from his mouth. "I can usher you into this elite community, this family you have always belonged to."

The ache Sonia and Artie had awoken yesterday returned, and she clenched her fist in an effort to will the ache away. When that didn't work, she flexed the fingers of her left hand. Pain seared through her arm and body, but it cleared her head.

She needed to get creative to find a way around Hollister. The parking garage was like all others. They were surrounded by cars and walls, concrete and metal. The knife in Hollister's hand was steel.

She was likely too far, but she had to try. She turned her right palm forward and started pushing out heat toward the knife. "You have no right to talk about my father." She strolled toward him, her voice growing rougher as she spoke. "He sent me away so I would be safe from people like you. You and your *program* killed him. Your words mean nothing."

The hope and eagerness vanished from his expression, replaced by something dark.

"The truth is, you don't need Cayden," she said quietly with another step. If her efforts were working, the knife would be getting warm now.

"No, I don't need him." He tightened his hold on Cayden. "You'd rather let him die than work with me? If I were him, I'd be a bit disappointed."

"No," Quinn said and stalked up the ramp.

Hollister stepped back, pressing the blade to Cayden's throat.

Cayden sucked in a breath.

"Detective," Hollister said in warning.

Justine dropped her hand and ground her teeth.

Quinn stopped twenty feet from him. "If you kill him, you'll have nothing left to stop me with."

Hollister chuckled. "And what will you do? Murder me, right here with your fellow officers on the scene?"

"Don't tempt me," Quinn said, his hands shaking. He wouldn't stay still for long.

"Choose, Justine," Hollister said, his voice echoing off the concrete. "If you'd rather this young man live, come stand with Eddie. Stay and work with us." He glanced at Quinn. "You as well."

If she gave up here, gave in to Hollister, she wouldn't lose everything. She'd give up her hope of living a somewhat normal life with people she cared for. But she'd have the security of food and shelter. No more hiding in the shadows among feral cats. And Quinn and Cayden would be safe. "They both leave."

"No way," Quinn said.

Eddie stepped forward, wary eyes on her.

Hollister narrowed his eyes. "You'll stay if I allow Quinn and his brother to leave?"

"Yes." She swallowed hard.

"You know," Eddie said, "I thought you'd want to join this team, that you'd be happy to teach me. But you want to keep your secrets to yourself."

"The only secret is what this man has done to you. You don't know, and neither does he. But you don't have to stay. Is what you're getting worth your freedom?"

Eddie seemed to deflate. "You don't get it. It's not freedom I need. What good is freedom if I'm useless?"

"Your worth doesn't come from how many limbs you have, Eddie." She shook her head. Whatever she could teach him, he wasn't interested in learning. Justine might no longer be the only one with this ability, but she was still on her own.

Hollister's eyes remained on her. "Eddie, put the rest of the boxes in the trunk and get ready to leave."

She edged closer, coming up beside Quinn. "Release Cayden first."

Quinn held out his arm to block her. "Sorry, but she's not going anywhere. And you are letting Cayden go."

"Am I?" Hollister smiled. He pressed the knife to Cayden's throat again. Cayden hissed as the blade cut into his skin.

She grasped Quinn's arm. "He's your brother."

He squeezed her hand. "There's got to be another way."

There might be. And all she could lose was everything.

She brought her hand to his face, gritty with plaster dust, bits of drywall in his tangled hair, his eyes full of worry and fear. Fear for her as much as for his brother. Despite her lies and secrets, he hadn't written her off. They were the family she could have had. "Thank you." She stood on tiptoe and kissed him lightly on the lips. Would it be the last time?

She stepped back, soaked in the sight of him, then rushed at Hollister. She shoved her one working hand forward and sent out a stronger push of heat.

"Justine!" Quinn called.

Hollister frowned, looking from the knife to Justine. His eyes widened, then he grinned and tightened his grip as he retreated, taking Cayden with him.

Movement from her right distracted her as Quinn cried out, "On you're right!"

Eddie came at her from the side and wrapped her in an iron grip. She cried out as he crushed her injured hand. He released her but grabbed onto her uninjured hand. "You ungrateful bitch, you're ruining everything!" He shook her, and her whole body jerked, sending jolts of pain through her. As she panted to recover, he released her to pull a stun gun from his pocket.

Her body trembling she gritted her teeth and thrust her hand toward him, pushing with her entire body and mind.

He flew back as if hit by a truck. His body smacked into the concrete wall of the garage. He fell forward and lay still.

The stun gun in his hand was hit with her push as well, and it smashed into the car. The casing burst into pieces. Sparks flew out as the impact hit the battery.

The sparking battery fell to the ground. A bright burst seared her side, and Justine raised her arm to shield her face. A loud bang echoed through the garage. An arm wrapped around her, and Quinn pulled her away from the small fireball. Pieces of plastic, metal, and the battery flew in all directions.

Sparks landed on the boxes, and a few stuck to the cardboard. Hollister, crouched several feet away, scrambled to his equipment as smoke rose from the pile.

Eddie lay on the ground, unmoving. A red smear oozed down the cement.

Beyond the smoke and flames that were now spreading from the boxes to the trunk of the car, Cayden lay facedown. Blood stained the floor by his head.

40.

Justine pushed herself up. Her ears were ringing again. A singed scent lingered in the air. In the distance, shouts of emergency personnel grew louder.

Eddie lay where he'd fallen, utterly still. Hollister slapped at the flames destroying his work as they spread to the contents of the trunk. Quinn hurried to his brother's side. When Cayden groaned and tried to get up, a tsunami of relief washed over Justine. Quinn held Cayden down to keep him from moving too fast, then dragged him away from the burning boxes and propped him up against a concrete pillar. Blood soaked Cayden's neck and shirt.

The back of Eddie's head was bloody. He—

Quinn laid a hand on her arm and shook his head. He bent close to her ear. "Don't."

Fighting nausea, she tore her eyes from Eddie and crept to where Cayden sat. A shallow slice in his neck oozed blood. Quinn dabbed the wound with the edge of his shirt and applied pressure. "You didn't have a choice. But don't touch him." When the bleeding around Cayden's neck slowed, Quinn checked his scalp. "EMTs should find us in a minute. We'll get you checked out."

Cayden nodded and held his head.

Quinn jumped up, looking past Justine.

Behind her, Hollister aimed a gun at him, a case stuffed with papers in the other hand. Behind him, flames engulfed the car's trunk, consuming what he'd left behind.

"We are not done here." The gun in Hollister's hand shuddered. "You agreed to exchange yourself for the detective's brother. Were you negotiating in bad faith? Or did you think you could take everything from me? Eddie wanted to learn from you. He never wronged you. And you killed him. Did you think you would just walk away from that?"

"Hollister, give it up. You lost," Quinn said, stepping in front of Cayden. Shouts of police filtered into the garage.

Hollister stepped closer as Justine struggled to stand. "I know you would rather not have another conversation with the police, not after the one in Philadelphia. So we can leave right now, together. Or we can all stay and explain to the police how the fire started and how this man died."

"The police will be just as interested in you," Quinn said.

Hollister smiled. "You know all too well the doors your badge opens. I have my own connections, which open far more doors."

Between Hollister and the approaching police, there was no escape. The police would have questions about the fire, and they'd have more once they found the record of her arrest in Philadelphia.

Despite losing so much and making so many mistakes, at least she'd accomplished what she'd returned for and freed Quinn. And she'd destroyed Hollister's lab, though with even one backup of his research, he could pick up where he'd left off.

But she had killed Eddie. With her ability. Maybe a lab was where she belonged. "I'll go."

"No—" Quinn squeezed her hand.

"If she has to talk to the authorities," Hollister said, "it will not go smoothly, even with your badge."

"Quinn, I took a gamble, and Eddie lost his life because of it. Besides, Cayden needs you." She grasped Quinn's arm and tried to convey all she could not say to him, all she should have said.

"I also need you," Quinn said.

She pulled away. She would have to do this alone.

Behind them, the door to the stairwell slammed. Before Justine turned back to Hollister, he wrapped an arm around her shoulder. She gasped as he put painful pressure on her injury and forced her to move. "This way, slowly. Now faster. You've destroyed my car as well, so now you'll have to walk."

She glanced back at Quinn hovering over his brother, but she had to look away from his stricken expression. She allowed Hollister to lead her out of the garage.

~ ~ ~

On the dark sidewalk, snow was falling again. Hollister turned from the crowd that had gathered to watch the burning building. He held Justine tight. "Keep walking."

"I can't," she said as pain shot down her arm. She skidded on an icy patch of sidewalk covered in a new layer of snow.

"Yes, you can. If you don't walk now, the police will find us." He yanked her forward as they approached the corner, slipping his bag over a shoulder.

She stumbled across the street on legs that felt like rubber bands, trying to hold back her nausea. She shifted her injured hand, still in the sling, to relieve some of the pressure.

"Where are we going?" Her voice was hoarse and her tongue felt too big. She needed to go to the hospital. But hospitals had to report gunshot wounds. Hollister would want that even less than she did.

"Let me worry about that." He scanned ahead and behind them. The street was dark and empty, the few shops in this block shuttered for the night.

"Are you looking for a taxi?" She laughed despite how much it hurt.

"Why is that funny?"

"Because cabs don't come here, not at this time of night, you nitwit."

He stopped and grabbed her by the hair. "The lying is over," he said through gritted teeth.

"Besides, do you think a cab will take me looking like this? You better try the train."

He tightened his grip on her. "You have destroyed years of painstaking work. Do not test my patience."

"You're going to make me a lab rat. Who knows when I'll smell fresh air again. The least I can do is make you miserable with me."

He grasped her arms and slammed her against the bricks of the building. She struggled to breathe through the pain in her hand, in her arm—it was everywhere. Then he did it again. She pressed her body against the rough brick to hold herself up.

He stepped back, and the anger drained from him. He scanned the empty street. "I apologize. I did not want to hurt you. I—"

"You don't give a *fuck* about me. All you care about is this fucking mutation in my genes. Drop the concerned routine."

His eyes bored into hers. "I care more about you than your father ever did."

"My father," she said in a rough whisper, "never slammed me against a wall!"

"But he sent you away."

His words cut deeper than every injury she'd received that day. With monumental effort, she squashed her rage. "My father sent me away so I would be safe."

His silence was like a slap.

"Still won't find a cab," she said with some satisfaction. "There's a train station at the park, on East Broadway. Anything else is too far. I won't make it."

He leaned over her. "You understand we need to get away from the authorities."

She swallowed and nodded. "Turn left at the corner. Then turn right on East Broadway." He glared for a long minute, then pulled her up the street.

By the time they reached the station, she needed Hollister's support to stay upright. She was chilled. The bright lights stabbed at her eyes. The floor rumbled as a train passed through the station below. No sign of cops or security.

They pushed through the turnstiles and descended to a long, narrow, and empty platform with tracks on each side. The air was cold yet moist. Water dripped somewhere. Voices echoed above, then footsteps clattered on the escalator.

He held Justine with an arm over her shoulder as they waited toward one end of the platform, turning away from the newly arriving commuters and blocking the view of her bloody sling. She tucked her free hand in her coat pocket for warmth and tried not to lean on him for balance. Her fingers found Quinn's keys. She clutched them until they stuck into her palm, but the ache in her chest only grew tighter.

She wasn't sure what would happen to Quinn or his brother, but they would take care of each other. Cayden's deception in getting her into the lab still stung. But without him she would likely not have gotten into the building so quickly, nor would she ever have gotten out. And she wouldn't have found Quinn. She couldn't have done any of it on her own. But in this, she was alone.

Hollister eased his hold on her a fraction. "I am going to show you that you are more valuable than you imagine. The life you've led has been difficult and treacherous, but that is over. You will never be in danger. I will assure your safety and security. You deserve that and much more."

Rats were safe in their cages, depending on how you defined safe.

The small group of passengers rustling with shiny packages clustered around a nearby steel column, laughing and talking loudly. One of them wore a fuzzy red hat. Quinn had said something about spending Christmas with him. Her mom had never made much of the holiday. For some reason the whole season left her with a lingering pang in her chest.

The yawning blackness of the tunnel invited her. Buggy had said the underground was no place for her, but it might be better than a lab. Even if she didn't make it out, she would be free.

As long as Hollister held on to her, though, she was going nowhere. She did not have the strength to break away. Her fingers fiddled with the keys. She wouldn't ever again use them for what they were intended. But the jagged edges might still be of use. Already missing the security of Quinn's arms, she slipped her fingers between the keys, took a deep breath, and forced herself to relax.

"Genetic science is already advancing rapidly in research labs around the world. I must work quickly if I am to guide the progress in the right direction. It's what my father wanted when he started GAMA." He paused. "It's what Jack wanted."

"Leave my father out of this," she said with as much ice as she could muster. Her skin crawled where his arm lay over her shoulder. Her fingers tightened around the keys. Quinn had given them to her so she would have a safe place to go. Even when he knew she'd kept secrets from him. Perhaps if they could not bring her to safety, they could help her get away from danger.

As more passengers arrived, he pulled her closer. Now, the slightest movement pained her. Still, she needed to pull up her hood to hide her face. She stopped. Who was she protecting? There was a good chance some of these people had seen her face on the internet. Allowing them to see her would only expose Hollister.

"Jack would be disappointed in your lack of interest."

"You know nothing about my father." *Nothing to lose.* With the keys sticking out between each knuckle of her fist, she drew her right hand from her pocket and swung it into his face.

At the last moment, he dodged, but not before the keys raked across his face. Blood rose from three gashes along his right cheek.

She teetered back into a blue steel support column and leaned on it to catch her breath. The rumble of the next train began deep in the tunnel.

Hollister looked her over, his bag of salvaged research inches from the edge of the platform, a hand on his cheek, eyes bright with rage. "You're persistent. I'll give you that." He wiped his face with his coat sleeve and strolled over to her, eating up her lead in seconds. "You're much like your father in that respect."

She didn't know if he was lying, because she didn't know what her father had been like. She backed up a few more steps, leaning on the rim of a garbage can for balance before reaching the next column. She rested her forehead against the cool steel. At this rate, someone walking with a cane would beat her to the exit.

He shifted his stance to block her from view of the waiting commuters. "Jack should have thought more for your long-term safety and well-being."

Behind her, the escalator steps rose to the upper level with a soft rhythmic hum, toward the exit and fresh air and freedom. It was closer than the end of the platform where she could access the tunnel. If she could reach the escalator steps, she might get out. But she'd never outrun him.

"You were wrong when you said I know nothing of your father. I know more about him than you do. For example, he's always been part of GAMA."

Trying to block out his obvious manipulation, she shuffled to a wooden bench where passengers waited. Some glanced up as she leaned on the arm of the seat. "Are you going to tell me something I don't know?" she said, enjoying his discomfort in the attention she drew as she projected her voice.

Conversations around them lulled as theirs grew louder. He hesitated, then came closer. "I can do that," he whispered.

She gauged the distance to the escalator.

"Your father's alive, Justine."

She stiffened and her stomach lurched. "That's what you think will stop me?" He eyed the passengers as they stole glances at them. "What next? You're going to say you're my father?" She rolled her eyes. "I saw that movie. Didn't end well for Dad." Fighting vertigo, she wiped sweat from her lip.

More commuters watched, some discreetly, others openly. One of them giggled. The attention of strangers had always felt risky, but she welcomed their curiosity now.

The oncoming train's clatter grew louder. With an eye on their audience, he took a careful step toward her, keeping his voice subdued. "If you were my daughter, I would never have sent you away. I would have kept you close and raised you in your full potential." As close as he was, her legs were reluctant to move. "But your father made you leave. To be so-called safe. And then he continued his research. He's continued that work for twenty years."

Her body wanted to give out, but she refused. "Why would I believe a word out of your mouth?" she spit out. "You're a desperate crackpot trying to regain your past. And you're using my dead family as a weapon. You're disgusting." Her last words were hoarse with rage. She wanted to smash his face into a wall.

Someone in the group of shoppers said, "Is that blood? Maybe we should call 911."

Another called out, "Hey, do you need help?"

She wasn't sure how to answer to that. She squashed the urge to shield herself from their scrutiny and instead inched closer to them.

Hollister hesitated, his piercing gaze shifting between the shoppers and Justine. "I have lied to you. And I would say anything I thought would make a difference. This time that something is the truth. Your father is alive." He closed the last few feet between them. He lowered his voice to a whisper. "He still works in a classified top-secret lab of DARPA. I could bring you to him. I'm not sure how, or whether you or he would want that, but I would do that for you."

She wanted to vomit, but a worm of doubt crawled through her belly. She swayed on her feet, and her good hand felt clammy and warm.

One of the commuters probably had a camera recording them. Any of them might have seen the video from Philly. She wanted to hide her face, hide her ability, seeking safety in shadows and seclusion as she'd always done. And that was what Hollister wanted now.

He would not take her away to lead a life of seclusion and secrecy. She already had a life. It was here.

He took another step toward her. Close enough. She thrust off the bench toward him.

Hollister's coat flared with the arrival of the train as he reached out for her.

Gathering all the strength she could find within her, she planted her hand over his wounded cheek and pushed out heat.

He lurched back and cried out. With wide eyes, he touched his face and flinched. The outline of her hand was bright red over the dark gashes on his cheek.

He beamed. "You've exceeded my wildest hopes," he said above the roar of the train.

The passengers fell silent as the wind quieted and the train doors opened. They boarded, murmuring questions. She pushed off the bench and propelled herself into the car behind them.

His face red with fury and blood, Hollister hopped onto the train. He grabbed her arm as she reached for the vertical handrail. Pain flared through her body and lit a new fire. She grasped the pole as he pulled her back. The train dinged a warning that the doors would soon close. Commuters around her shrunk away, uncertain what to do.

She lost her hold on the pole. A few passengers leaned forward as if to grab her.

If she used her ability in front of them, there would be no hiding. And maybe it was time she lived without hiding. Without secrets.

She twisted toward him as he pulled her. Yanking her arm back, his hand still gripping her arm, she thrust out her one good arm with all she had left.

Hollister flew out of the car and bounced off the side of a steel column. He landed in a heap on the platform as the doors closed. As the train pulled away, the speaker squawked the next train stop amid a silent car, all eyes on Justine.

She collapsed against the pole. He'd probably survive the impact, but he would have trouble following her now.

Someone in a seat behind her started clapping. Someone else joined in. Soon, the entire car was applauding. Justine didn't know what to do with that, so she closed her eyes and held on to the railing to keep herself upright.

At the next stop, she shambled to the escalator and the exit, her whole body shaking with pain and exhaustion. But so much more hurt inside. Her father was alive. And Justine felt more alone than ever.

41.

J ustine opened her eyes to bright morning light. She was warm beneath blankets. Pillows propped her up so she could sleep without rolling onto her hand. Quinn's arm draped over her, holding on to her even in his sleep. Cheetah had wedged himself between them, and Sully snored somewhere.

Some hours before, Quinn had answered her call from a bar's pay phone—Cayden's phone was dead— and picked her up. She couldn't bear the hospital yet, so he'd brought her to his apartment. Cayden had lain on the couch where he'd collapsed after they'd gotten him first aid and explained what they could to the police. Quinn had done his best to redress her wounds while she'd tried not to fall asleep.

She'd slept like the dead, but she needed about a month more. Yet for the first time in a week—no, much longer—she felt safe.

Then she made the mistake of moving. She groaned as her whole body screamed in protest.

Quinn shifted beside her and leaned over. "Painkillers worn off?"

"Definitely." Her voice was hoarse with sleep and exhaustion.

"We should look at your hand again. And then I'm taking you to the hospital. You need stitches, at the least." Climbing over Sully, he headed to the bathroom and then handed Justine two pills and water from beside the bed.

Sitting up made her want to go back to sleep, but the chilly air cleared her head. She sat with her glass in her hand, looking at nothing. *My father's alive.* Cheetah climbed over her and off the bed, and she slipped back beneath the blankets.

Quinn let Cheetah, then Sully, out of the bedroom, climbed back into bed, and gingerly pulled her close. She draped herself over him. He pushed her hair out of her face and met her eyes. "Has it really only been a couple of days since I last saw you?"

"A year at least," she said. She scratched at his stubbly chin. "It was a couple of days too late. I didn't stop what they did to you." She leaned against his chest. "I'm so sorry."

"You got me out."

"He did to you what I've tried to avoid my whole life."

He was quiet a long moment. "So how did you get away from him?"

She sighed. That was probably the first in a long list of questions. She'd avoided saying anything last night by being barely conscious. "I managed."

"Justine—"

"I will tell you. I'll—" The words caught in her throat. Damn, this was hard. Her mouth didn't know how to talk about some things. She swallowed. "I'll tell you everything. You deserve that." As long as he never again looked at her the way he had last night while she'd been breaking him out.

"Is there a body?"

Her heart fluttered. *Killer.* "No—I don't think so." His sigh was salt in her many wounds. But they were past the time of avoiding the truth. "He was unconscious. At least, I think he was. I don't think he's dead."

He nodded and turned her face toward him. "You risked everything for me." He stroked her chin. "I won't forget that. But sharing your problems with me—I know it's hard—but it can also prevent bigger problems." He leaned over and kissed her softly, as if she might break.

She wrapped her good arm around his neck, holding him as tightly as she could. She would never let go, never again.

He ran his hands through her hair. "If I'm honest, I don't know what I would have thought if you'd told me about all this months ago."

The ache in her chest threatened to suffocate her, and she buried herself in his embrace. "What do you think now?" She could barely take a breath.

"At first I thought I didn't know who you were. But then you kept acting like the Justine I knew. You hadn't changed. Though some things made a lot more sense." He lay back. "I'm glad you destroyed his research, even though it will likely be considered arson." He stretched his arm out in front of him. "I don't feel any different."

She hoped that vial of her blood had been destroyed as well. "Your genes have been changed. We have no way of knowing what effect that will have on you."

He nodded and was quiet. "I could get used to having a personal superhero."

"I'm *not* a superhero. I'm …" *a killer.* She swallowed and said, "An experiment." She looked up at him. "And I'm never wearing tights."

He smiled, and she knew she would do anything for him. Even tights.

"Okay," he said, "not a superhero. Maybe a bullet-proof vest then? I could use one of those, custom made just for me."

She laughed and kissed him again.

The front door slammed. "Coffee's here," Cayden called out.

She pulled away and sighed. "I could really use some of that right now."

"Agreed. This morning, coffee wins." He helped her dress, and they moseyed to the living room.

In the corner, Cayden lay on the floor trying to distract Cheetah from low-hanging Christmas tree ornaments with his key ring. He stood as Justine approached the couch, and he pulled a cup from a paper bag on the coffee table. "How're you doing?" He handed her the cup without meeting her eyes.

"Alive." Every muscle in her body complained as she eased herself onto the couch.

Quinn offered Cayden a couple of pills in exchange for a cup. "How's the neck?"

"Intact." Cayden's hand drifted to his bandage.

They dove into breakfast in silence. Justine sat between them, clutching her coffee while keeping her injury elevated. Cheetah purred in her lap, and Quinn spread cream cheese on a bagel for her before preparing one for himself.

She couldn't decide how to ask, so she blurted it out. "What were you thinking, Cayden? You were supposed to get me to Hollister. Instead, you left me with those guards."

Cayden squirmed and his face reddened. He cleared his throat, his eyes on his buttered bagel. "Uh, yeah, sorry about that."

"You brought her to that place?" Quinn scowled around the bagel in his mouth.

"I had to," Cayden said, his back stiffening.

"Why, because your nutjob boss asked you to? Did you know what he wanted her for?"

"Yes. And I knew what he wanted you for, Q." That quieted Quinn. Cayden rubbed his thighs. "Hollister made it clear worse would happen to you if I didn't bring Justine in. Eyes were on me all the time. I had no way to help you. So"—he glanced at Justine—"I rolled the dice. Thought the odds were good you would want to get Quinn out more than the doc would want to keep you in."

"So you handed me over to him and hoped I could break out."

He kept his eyes on his food. "From what I'd seen, you could handle it." He played with the lid of his cup.

"And I watched from the cameras in security as long as I could. Didn't expect you to burn the place down though."

She took a sip of coffee. "It seemed like a reasonable solution at the time."

"A nutjob like that will have backups," Quinn said.

Cayden nodded. "Probably won't take him long to get back to work. Especially if he's still got people like Kalakos. Either of you see that guy on the way out?"

"Not after he shot me," she said. She wished she'd gotten a chance to express her feelings about that to him.

"He shot you?" Quinn said. He swore elaborately.

"Sorry I couldn't stop him," Cayden said. "He's … impulsive."

"Did you see a short dark-haired woman? Or a tall one?"

"Are you talking about Val? She was with a shorter woman up on the third floor. They came down to security, and I had to adjust my strategy."

"And after that?"

"No idea. When I left security, the doc found me and forced me to go with him."

Quinn hunted through the bags and cups on the coffee table until he found a remote. He pointed it at the base of the tree. There was a loud snap, and the remote crumbled into pieces.

Everyone flinched. "Q, what just happened?"

Quinn sat gaping at the pieces of plastic in his hand. "I just pressed the button. It always needs a bit of extra pressure. I guess I pressed too hard."

A moment of silence passed. "At least the lights went on," Cayden said.

A chill passed over Justine. "It worked," she said. "What he did to you, it worked."

"Just because he broke a remote? It's probably just cheap."

She couldn't decipher Quinn's expression as he dumped the pieces of plastic into one of the bags on the table. "Eddie claimed he'd gotten stronger," he said in a subdued voice. He leaned back. "When I go back to the department, they're going to want me to get a physical. What's a doctor going to find?"

"What if you don't get the physical? Would the department not take you back?" Cayden asked.

Quinn shrugged and rubbed his thighs. "Maybe. They also might not take me if a test comes back weird or something."

A minute passed before Cayden spoke up. "Any idea where he is now? Wondering if he might have someone looking for me already."

Quinn looked at Justine before answering. "You should probably stay out of sight for a while. Both of you," he said, putting a careful arm around her.

"You think he's around somewhere?" Cayden asked.

"Who knows. Justine got away. Was she supposed to put him in cuffs?"

"Oh."

"It's not her fault," Quinn said.

"I'm not saying that. It's just not great he's roaming free, that's all."

"Just ease up, okay?"

"I'm not—"

"Shut up," she said.

They shut their mouths and looked into their cups.

She leaned forward. "I'm not blaming myself or anyone. It's ... a lot happened. Hollister took me as far as the subway—"

"He took you to the subway?" Cayden asked.

"It's not like we were going to get a cab."

"Hasn't he ever heard of Uber?"

"Uber?"

"You never—" He closed his eyes.

"So you lost him in the subway?" Quinn asked.

"It took a few tries, but I got free from him." As soon as she said it, she knew it wasn't true. She'd never get him out of her head.

"What state was he in?" Cayden asked. "What?" he said, looking at Quinn. "I need to know, okay?"

She swallowed. She might as well get used to this talking thing. "I'm not sure. He was ... down when I last saw him."

"With any luck, he didn't get up again."

"Cayden—"

"Come on, Q. He got what he had coming to him."

"We don't know that," Justine said. "I did what I could, and it almost wasn't enough. Not after what he told me." They remained silent as she scratched Cheetah's chin. "I'm not convinced it's true. It contradicts everything I've been told. I have to find out more." She took deep breaths, looking for the right words. But the only way to say it was the simplest. "According to Hollister, my father is alive."

"Who told you he was dead?" Quinn said.

"My mom. From the beginning, she told me they'd killed him. That was why he never met up with us after we went underground."

Quinn opened and shut his mouth before asking, "And how would Hollister know otherwise?"

Might as well start at the beginning. But she couldn't do this sitting down. She stood, walking around the table as she spoke. Cheetah returned to harassing the Christmas tree. "My dad worked as a scientist in a program called GAMA, created by Hollister's father. It seems to be where Hollister got his ideas. He talked a lot about war and battle."

"I did hear the doc talk about supersoldiers," Cayden muttered.

A puzzle piece fell into place. "If he's trying to make supersoldiers, I guess my father was—or has been—working on something similar."

"And where is he now?" Quinn asked.

"That's what I need to find out. Somehow." Right now all she wanted was to go back to bed.

"Do you believe him?" Cayden asked.

"I don't trust him enough to take his word for it. But I can't not try to find out."

Quinn cleared his throat. "How old were you when all this happened?"

The day her mother had thrown them and a few belongings into the car and driven away from their home was as clear as the day it happened. "I was four when we first left, my mother, my brother, and me. We moved a lot and kept to ourselves to prevent anyone from discovering my ability because *They* would want to know. I never knew who They were, only that if They found out, They would take me away to figure out how I could do what I do."

Quinn leaned back, eyes wide. He cleared his throat after a minute. "I don't know where to start."

"Yeah, I know. But I don't actually have a lot of answers. Not nearly as much as other people do."

"You don't know if anything this guy has said is true."

"No, but it's not only him. In Philly I met a woman who also worked with my father. She said his work apparently caused my abilities." Thoughts of Sonia awakened her anger at the woman's betrayal. "If my dad's work is connected to my ability, he would have tried to keep me away from the rest of the staff. He must have decided he couldn't keep me secret any longer when he sent me into hiding." She swallowed the lump in her throat. "I've lived my life feeling indebted to a man I thought sacrificed himself for me. If he's alive—and working on the same project—my entire life is a question only he can answer."

"So what are you going to do?" Quinn asked.

"It doesn't look like Hollister's working with this GAMA program, but finding out what they're up to could prove helpful." She glanced at Cayden. "Not sure how much will be on the internet, since it's probably one of the more secretive programs of DARPA. And it's not like I'm going to walk in there, not if I ever want to leave. So Hollister's my only real lead. I'll look for him first. This time we'll talk on my terms. If I have to hunt every corner of the world, he will lead me to my father." She released a steady breath and met Cayden's and Quinn's eyes. "I'll need help. I have some hunting to do."

The prey would now become the hunter.

Thank you for reading!

If you'd like to know when
the sequel is available, go to
monicatrodriguez.com/sign-up

If you have a moment, please
support the author and leave a review
where you bought the book.
It can help new readers find the book.

ACKNOWLEDGMENTS

So many to thank, where do I start? I couldn't have finished this book without the support I found in many corners of my life.

Online there is a treasure trove of support if you know where to look. The writing community of the #5amWritersClub has been an oasis of positivity and encouragement on Twitter. I couldn't have gotten the words in without the persistence and perseverance of the folks who consistently showed up at that ungodly hour. Shout-out to National Novel Writing Month, aka NaNoWriMo, for providing the inspiration and support for my first novel and for an earlier version of Bulletproof.

The knowledgeable folks of the CrimeSceneWriters community (first on Yahoo, now at Groups.io) have answered innumerable questions on law enforcement and crime and no doubt helped bring innumerable books into the world. Now they can count mine among them! Thanks also to Lt. JoAnne Fratianni for the tour of the Clarkstown police station. More research help came from my dad, a retired NYPD detective, who fielded constant questions related to police work, even though he retired before DNA. My sister Veronica, an RN, answered all sorts of medical questions. I don't know what it must have been like to receive a text out of the blue asking for the best place to get shot.

My family and friends have been so patient during all these years I've spent in my cave pounding away at my computer. Some were brave enough to read early and not-so-early drafts. Thank you to Tara and Esther who made it through the whole thing. Special thanks to Aimee who lent her writerly eye to my words and pointed out many inconsistencies and plot holes. Can't wait to do the same to yours! Laura, I am so grateful for your constant support on every step on this journey.

Thanks to my editor, Alida Winternheimer of Word Essential. I've learned so much from you! Can't wait to do it all over again. And thanks to my proofreader, Dori Harrell of Breakout Editing. You greatly improved this book. My cover designer, Tim Barber, of Dissect Designs, has had the patience of a saint and talent to match.

I must add a thank you to Joanna Penn of The Creative Penn. An author, podcaster, and an inspiration to thousands of authors, I followed her career from nearly the beginning. Watching her succeed enabled me to believe I could do this too, with some perseverance and hard work. Thank you for setting the example for all of us!

ABOUT THE AUTHOR

Monica T. Rodriguez is the author of the technothriller *Bulletproof.* Her fascination with the eerie, odd, and supernatural began with the six-fingered hand of the Creature Feature movies crawling out of the ground and into her imagination. In addition to nightmares of bugs making words on her wall, those movies provided a lifetime's worth of fuel for stories that bend the laws of physics. Today her thrillers end up somewhere on the way to science fiction.

Monica prefers to read thrillers, science fiction, and fantasy that straddle the border between reality and the realm beyond that fascinates us all. Her current favorite series is The Dresden Files by Jim Butcher, and she's a particular fan of the audiobooks narrated by James Marsters. Other favorites include the Pendergast books by Douglas Preston and Lincoln Child, the Dave Robicheaux series by James Lee Burke, and yes, she's read and enjoyed the Game of Thrones series by George R.R. Martin.

Monica lives in the Hudson Valley region north of New York City, far enough to be considered upstate by city dwellers but close enough to be considered a city dweller by those upstate. There is always a crossword puzzle nearby for when her brain goes on strike or she can't sleep. For now it's safe to assume she's writing the sequel to Bulletproof. When she comes out of her cave, there are often sightings of her on Twitter @docmon67. Find out more on her website monicatrodriguez.com